Daughter of Satan

Daughter of
Satan

Jean Plaidy

COMPASS PRESS
* OXFORD * MELBOURNE *

First published in 1952 by Robert Hale Limited

Compass Press Large Print Book Series; an imprint of
ISIS Publishing Ltd, Great Britain, and Bolinda Press, Australia
Published in Large Print 2002 by ISIS Publishing Ltd,
7 Centremead, Osney Mead, Oxford OX2 0ES,
and Bolinda Publishing Pty Ltd,
17 Mohr Street, Tullamarine, Victoria 3043
by arrangement with Robert Hale Limited

British Library Cataloguing in Publication Data
Plaidy, Jean, 1906–
Daughter of Satan. – Large print ed.
1. Witches – Fiction
2. Persecution – Fiction
3. Great Britain – History – 1689–1714 – Fiction
4. Historical fiction
5. Large type books
I. Title
823.9'12 [F]

Australian Cataloguing in Publication Data
Plaidy, Jean
Daughter of Satan / Jean Plaidy.
1. Large type books.
2. Love stories
3. Historical fiction
I. Title
823.912

ISBN 0-7531-6667-4 (hb)   ISBN 0-7531-6668-2 (pb)
(ISIS Publishing Ltd)
ISBN 1-74030-765-8 (hb)
(Bolinda Publishing Pty Ltd)

Printed and bound by Antony Rowe, Chippenham

CHAPTER
ONE

Tamar was conceived one midsummer's night during the most glorious and triumphant year which England had, up to that time, known.

Her mother was a poor serving-maid, and when she was asked who had fathered the child, she would lower her eyes and do all she could to avoid giving the answer. If she were pressed, she would mutter something to the effect that it had been no fault of hers; the child had been forced on her in the darkness of night and she had not even seen its father's face. But she, the child's own mother, was one of those who believed Tamar's father to be none other than the Devil himself.

*   *   *

It was Whit-Sunday.

The sea sparkled and the sun beat down on the rocks so that it seemed as though they were streaked with amethyst and chrysoprase, rose quartz and jade; the gorse had never seemed so golden as it did that Maytime; even the clumps of sea-pinks — that most modest of flowers — appeared to jut out from the slated rock with a new-born defiance. The haunting fragrance of hawthorn blossom was in the air,

1

mingling with the scents of the sea and land; and the unparalleled charm of English springtime was doubly sweet that year.

On this Sunday morning, Richard Merriman had been unable to remain in his house at Pennicomquick; there was too much excitement in the air; and he, like many others, must go into Plymouth to attend the special church service. He left his horse to be watered and fed at an inn a stone's-throw from the Hoe, and he walked out to face the keen wind and look out across the Sound before making his way back to the town.

One look at him was enough to show him to be a most fastidious man. His breeches were made of velvet and he wore no garters to keep up his stockings, which might have suggested he was rather proud of his calves; the sleeves of his jerkin were open from shoulder to wrist to show the rich cloth of his doublet. He was pale of face, haughty and most elegant; he looked what he was — a mixture of savant and epicurean. His love of learning was not shared by his friend and neighbour, Sir Humphrey Cavill. Sir Humphrey was a man whom all men — and women — understood; a heavy drinker and fast liver, Sir Humphrey had sailed the Spanish Main with John Hawkins and Sir Francis Drake, and it was said that half the children between Stoke and Pennicomquick had the Cavill nose or those deep-set, striking blue eyes of Sir Humphrey's. Richard Merriman was more selective than his friend, who was merely his friend because he was his neighbour.

What a sight it was on that sunny morning! Richard stood on the Hoe, and looked at that array of colourful glory. *Ark*, *Revenge*, *Elizabeth Bonaventure* and *Mary Rose* — there they lay, pulling at their anchors as impatient, it seemed, as Sir Francis certainly was to break away and go out to meet the Spaniard; then *Victory* and *Nonpareil* — all flying the red cross on a white background, the flag of England. And there were many more — a fine fleet, but Richard knew that, on the way to meet them, was what some believed to be an even prouder and more magnificent armada of ships.

At any moment now the first of the Spaniards might appear on the horizon. At dusk that very night the beacons might suddenly begin to blaze along the coasts of Devon and Cornwall.

The bells were pealing as he left the Hoe and walked into the town. He went on to the Barbican and walked thoughtfully along the fishing quay. On such a day as this there was much for a man to think of. On these very cobbles, not so long ago, King Philip of Spain had walked, an honoured guest; for the greatest enemy of the reigning Queen had been the adored husband of Bloody Mary, her predecessor. Times changed and these days were pregnant with great happenings.

He went through the cobbled streets past groups of people who shouted and whispered, laughed and looked grave. From diamond-paned casements girls called to others who leaned towards them across the narrow streets, which were teeming with apprentices and merchants, fishermen and old sailors.

He reached the square, but there was no room inside the Church of St. Andrew on that Sunday morning, and it was necessary for him to take his stand with those outside.

The tension in the crowd was such as he had rarely witnessed. So, he thought, must the burgesses of this old and noble city have felt more than a hundred years before on that sunny Lammas Day when the corsairs of France had tried to subdue them. Excitement was stronger than apprehension, for excitement was what these people craved; here was the cradle of those adventurers who were determined to challenge and subdue the power of Spain.

Among them now, here outside the church, was many a man who had sailed with Drake and hoped to sail again. These men would flock to their ships when the hour for action came. They loathed the Spaniard as only those could who had come into contact with his fanatical cruelty. They knew that when the dignified galleons appeared on the horizon they would bring something besides men and ammunition — thumbscrews, the scourge, the rack and all the instruments of torture of the dreaded Inquisition. They would bring a fanaticism and an intolerance into a land which had had a taste of these things when the wife of the Spanish King had ruled them.

"Never again!" said the men of Devon; and men were saying this all over England. It should not

4

happen again while Sir Francis and his kind lived to prevent it.

The service was at length over and the worshippers were coming out into the sunshine. There was Martin Frobisher, and with him John Hawkins. Cheers went up for these brave men. And now. . .the moment for which they had all been waiting had come, for out of the church came Lord Howard of Effingham and beside him Sir Francis Drake himself.

Here was the idol of Plymouth—the one man among all these great men whom all longed to serve and to follow to the death. His beard touched the fine lace of his ruff; his sweeping moustaches curled jauntily; his full-lidded, twinkling eyes surveyed the crowd, accepting its homage.

"Sir Francis, God bless thee!"

"Sir Francis forever!"

He doffed his cap. Adventurer, charmer, showman, he bowed, and took his companion by the arm as though to introduce him to the crowd; the full lids were lifted as though to say: "You and I, men of Devon, must accept this man. You and I—for the sake of courtesy—will do him honour as the Lord Admiral of the Fleet; but we know, do we not, who will beat the Spaniard. We know whose courage, whose resourcefulness will bring us victory. And you, good men of Devon, while—for courtesy's sake— you will follow him, will truly follow me with all your heart."

A murmur ran through the crowd. Drake commanded and, as ever, Drake would be obeyed.

Drake said: "Homage to my Lord Howard of Effingham," and so the men of Plymouth would do homage to the noble lord. Had Drake said: "To the Devil with Howard. Follow none but your leader!" then there would have been mutiny in the Fleet.

A smile curved Richard's fine, thin lips. How stimulating to contemplate the power that was in this man to set the mood of a mob. The Queen was a woman, and a foolish one at times. Did she not realise how easily she might have lost her throne when she asked Drake to take second place to Howard? She still ran a risk. Noble birth alone could not defeat Spain's Armada. And if Drake was a parson's son of yeoman stock, yet had he the power, as no other had it, to make men follow him. Tradition demanded that the admiral of the fleet should be a noble lord and so here came my Lord Howard of Effingham to take the place which should have belonged to Sir Francis Drake.

Richard shrugged his shoulders and was turning away when he caught sight of two young women in the crowd whom he recognised as serving wenches in his own household. They were giggling and laughing together — two girls on holiday. The big buxom one was eyeing the young men; she had tawny hair cut short like a boy's and eyes to match. But for her short hair, she was a typical Devon maid. The second was a more interesting type. She was dark-eyed and her dark hair was cut short like her companion's. He was amused to see the way in which those dark eyes followed Sir Francis. What adoration! There was scarcely a woman in the town, he supposed, who would not adore Sir Francis, but this girl looked at him as though he were a saint rather than a handsome and charming adventurer. And who but a simple maid would think Sir Francis a saint!

Richard was mildly interested, for the girl had a faint trace of beauty; her face was unmarked by emotion; she was young — not more than fifteen, he supposed. It was a pity that Alton, the housekeeper, cut the girls' hair. Still, it was the woman's business to keep them in order, and he doubted not that she knew her business. She was a stern creature, with a trace of something vicious in her; he guessed that the girls had many a beating to endure, but no doubt they deserved it. Yet, it was a pity she had cut off their hair, for they would have been more pleasant to look at if they had had more of it; and he liked to look at pleasant things. He wondered lightly about them; he was not a sensual man. He had married a wife chosen for him by his grandfather, and he had felt no great emotion when she had died, nor any need to replace her. There was nothing monklike in his attitude to women; he had a friend in Pennie Cross, to see whom he rode there now and then. She was older than he was — charming, serious-minded, interested in matters which interested him. Theirs was hardly a passionate friendship. It was not likely therefore that he would look on the serving girls as Sir Humphrey would have looked. It was merely that the smile on the face of the little dark one amused him, and fleetingly he hoped that if punishment must be inflicted on the girls for coming into the town without Mistress

Alton's permission, the cane would not be allowed to fall too heavily on those slender shoulders.

He forgot the girls as he went for his horse. Looking about him as he rode away from the town, he could see the Tamar winding its way like a silver snake between Devon and Cornwall. The green banks of the lane were rich with bluebells, the red of ragged robin and the white of the stitchwort flowers. It was only a mile or so to his house at Pennicomquick. A pleasant sight was this house of his with its thatched roof, its gables and its latticed windows. It was spacious too, although not so large as Sir Humphrey's over at Stoke, and a comfortable place to live in. He shuddered at the thought of its being ransacked and burned by Spaniards. He rode through the gates, past the yews which Joseph Jubin his gardener had cut into the shapes of birds, past the lavender not yet in flower and the lad's love with its penetrating yet very pleasant odour.

Clem Swann, his groom, came out of the stables to take his horse, and Richard went into the house and up the staircase to his study. This study was a pleasant room with its big diamond-paned windows and oak panelled walls. There was a carpet on the floor and rich hangings on the walls; he could not bear to be surrounded by anything but the most beautiful that could be obtained. There was in this room a big oak chest of which he kept the key; there were shelves of books all exquisitely bound in calf; the stools were tapestry-covered, and there was one elaborately carved chair which, it was understood, no one should sit on but himself.

He realized that he was fatigued. It was the heat and excitement of the morning. He pulled the bell, and when Josiah Hough, his personal servant, appeared, he asked that wine be brought.

"Sir," said Josiah, as he set the wine on the table and poured it out for his master, "you have come from the town. Did you see Sir Francis, sir, might I be so bold as to ask?"

Richard raised his eyebrows. The servants were in awe of him and it was not often that they spoke without being spoken to; but he smiled lightly. This was indeed a very special occasion.

"I saw him, Josiah. The people cheered him mightily."

"The whole country seems in a sort of tremble, sir."

"Not with fear, Josiah. With excitement."

"There's some that say the Spaniards have the best ships in the world, sir."

"That may be, Josiah. But it's men not ships that win a battle. Their ships are like their grandees — very pleasant to look upon, full of dignity. Our English ships may not be so handsome, but sometimes it is better to move with speed than with dignity."

" 'Tis true, master."

Richard folded his long white hands together and smiled at his servant. "They have to face the English in their own waters. Have you any doubt of the issue? They have to face him whom they have named *El*

Draque — the Dragon. They fear him, Josiah, and he is no stranger to them. In their bigotry, in their fanaticism, they believe him to be a magician. Who else, they ask themselves, could score such victories over their Holy Church?"

Josiah drew back astonished; he had never before seen such passion in his master's face. He waited for Richard to go on, but at that moment the sound of sudden shrieks of laughter came floating through the open window.

"Who is that?" asked Richard.

Josiah went to the window. " 'Tis the two maids, sir. I'll put a stick about their shoulders. 'Tis young Betsy Cape and Luce Martin."

To Josiah's surprise. his master rose and came languidly to the window. He looked down on the two girls he had seen in the town.

"A saucy pair of wenches, sir," went on Josiah. "Betsy's a bold thing, and she's showing Luce the way to boldness. I'll have Mistress Alton whip them for shrieking below your window."

"Why do they shriek? It was obviously with pleasure. Do they not realize the import of such a time as this?"

"They realize only the import of a riband or a man's smile, sir."

Betsy's laugh rang out. Richard shuddered as though it grated on his nerves.

"Pray go and tell them to be quiet," he said.

Josiah went, and from the window Richard watched. He was faintly surprised that he should have felt this flicker of interest. He saw each girl receive a slap across her face. Betsy put out a red tongue at Josiah's back and little Luce clapped her hands over her mouth to stop herself laughing.

Even after they had gone into the house Richard continued to think of them. What did the future hold for such as they were? Marriage with one of Clem Swann's boys, life in a cottage close to the house, continuing to work for him mayhap, breeding children — boys who would fight for another hero like Drake against another enemy like the Spaniard; and girls to giggle over a riband and the smile of a sailor.

Then he forgot them. He took a book from the shelf and sat back in his chair. It was difficult to read when at any moment the first of the Spanish ships might be sighted on the horizon.

*   *   *

Luce Martin was fifteen years old. She had been sent to work at the house of Richard Merriman when she was thirteen. Her father was a fisherman and he lived in a little cottage in Whitsand Bay, on the other side of the Tamar. This made Luce a bit of a foreigner to the people of Devon. Living was hard to get; sometimes the boats went out and returned with little, and if they returned full of fish it seemed that then there was a glut. There were times when the family lived on buttermilk, with nothing to eat but scraps of rye bread. There were many brothers and sisters, so that even their mother had to stop and count them if she were asked their number; they came regularly each year. Luce was one of the middle ones; and when Mistress Alton, who herself came from the Whitsand Bay neighbourhood, offered to take her to the house in Pennicomquick to work under her, Luce's parents agreed with great eagerness.

So she had set out from her home with a small bundle containing her possessions, and for the first time in her life she was ferried over the Tamar; she walked the few remaining miles to her new home.

She had been afraid of Mistress Alton from the moment she had first heard her name, and she had not been reassured by her first meeting with the woman, for Mistress Alton was, in Luce's eyes, terrible to behold. A tall, thin woman with a mouth which scarcely opened even when she talked, and shut up like a trap immediately afterwards, she wore the neatest and most sober clothes Luce had ever seen, and her skin was hideously disfigured by a very bad attack of the pox. But she had a reputation for great piety, though this did not lessen Luce's fears.

As soon as Luce arrived she had been sent into the yard to strip. Her clothes were lousy. She was given garments to wear which had been chosen by Mistress Alton, for such a fastidious gentleman as Mr. Richard Merriman could not demean himself in the affairs of his servants, and he left everything of such a nature to his housekeeper. The clothes were of the same pattern as those worn by Luce's fellow serving maid, Betsy Cape. Then Luce's lovely long hair, which hung curling to her waist, was cut short.

Hair, said Mistress Alton as she cut it, was best cut short, and especially hair that was thick and curly, for that undoubtedly was a gift from Satan.

The Devil's name was more often on Mistress Alton's lips than that of God, who in her eyes seemed to be a superior, vindictive version of the Devil.

So here was Luce, barely thirteen and frightened, never having seen anything as grand as the house in which she now found herself, each day taught her duty to God and her master, but chiefly her duty to Mistress Alton.

Mistress Alton managed the house; she cooked and salted the food and bottled her preserves; she supervised everything that had to be done inside the house and was inordinately proud of her work. She never made a mistake; if mistakes were made, others made them; and faults had to be paid for. It was Mistress Alton's duty to see that they were, and the faults of Luce and Betsy were paid for with beatings administered with the thin cane which hung from the housekeeper's belt together with the keys of her cupboards.

Beatings, which were given for the slightest offence, took place regularly. When Bill Lackwell came to the kitchen to bring fish, and Mistress Alton fancied the girls threw saucy glances at him, they were beaten; once she caught Betsy kissing Charlie Hurly when he came with eggs from his father's farm, and Betsy was treated to a very special beating for that.

It was her duty, said Mistress Alton, to stop that sort of thing. When Betsy was beaten, Luce must be there to look on; and Betsy was always made to witness Luce's punishment.

"It will be a lesson to *you*, my girl!" each would be told.

They were obliged to strip to the waist for the caning, for what was the good of beating through the thickness of cloth? They must hold their bodices over their breasts though, for it was immodest to show them even to members of their own sex. If they dropped the bodice or it slipped out of place, they must be beaten for immodesty.

Mistress Alton kept them working hard. The Devil was forever at their elbows, Mistress Alton explained, waiting to tempt idlers.

So to thirteen-year-old Luce life was all work and beatings. She did not think there was anything strange about that; her father had been wont to beat her merely because he was in the mood. She was lucky, she knew, to get her food and clothing; but now that she was growing older she was a little resentful about the shortness of her hair, and Betsy fostered this discontent.

They slept together in an attic. In some houses all the servants would sleep together in one big room, but Mistress Alton would not have young girls and men sleeping together.

"My dear life!" she said. "What goings-on there would be indeed! I'd not get a wink of sleep for the watch I'd have to keep for wickedness."

Every night the girls were locked into their attic and the windows bolted. "And if," said Mistress Alton, "I should hear of you girls unbolting that window, I'd turn you out of the house, I would. There's some wantonness that can't be beat out, and that sort I would not stand!"

Luce and Betsy would lie on their straw pallets and talk until they fell asleep, which usually they quickly did being tired out after the day's hard work.

On that Whit-Sunday night as they lay together on their pallets waiting for the coming of Mistress Alton, Luce whispered: "Shall us both be beaten to-night?"

"Neither of us will," answered Betsy with such conviction that Luce raised herself to look at her.

"Why not?"

"Because her's too busy to think of caning us."

"How do you know?"

"Charlie Hurly told me." Betsy giggled. "He came up to the house this afternoon. I do think he came to see me. He was out there, trying to get me to go out . . ."

Happy Betsy! A life of hard work and continual punishment could not quell her spirits; she always felt herself to be on the verge of an adventure which involved her seduction, and this evil fate seemed to be what Betsy longed for more than anything.

"You'd taken a bit of the pie," Luce reminded her. "She saw it on your mouth and you'd spilled some on your bodice."

"Well, I got a cut or two for that. Besides, she's too busy, I tell 'ee. 'Sh! Here she comes."

The light in the attic was still good enough for them to see the housekeeper clearly. Betsy was right, thought Luce; something had happened. She looked excited. Luce guessed it was this waiting for the Spaniards to come.

Mistress Alton was wearing her best dress; her ruff was of cambric and her skirt more wired than the one she usually wore; but it was not her dress that Luce noticed so much as her face, for Luce had rarely seen the housekeeper look so pleased. Moreover, nothing was said about their misdeeds of the day, and there were no beatings on that Sunday night.

When she left them, Betsy said, smiling secretly: "I could tell 'ee, Luce Martin, where she be going."

"Where?" demanded Luce.

Betsy continued to smile. "Have you ever thought that there might be witches among us?"

"Witches!" whispered Luce.

"And living close to us. Do you know what witches can do, Luce? They can do anything . . . just anything at all."

Luce did not want to talk about witches; she wanted to continue with the thoughts which had been with her ever since she had seen Sir Francis come out of church. Listening to Betsy's continual talk of men and their ways had aroused Luce's curiosity; and there were things she wished to know and experience. She did not care to make herself understood to Betsy. Better for Betsy to think her cold and prim than that

Betsy should know the real reason why she hated it when she was teased about Ned Swann, who stank of the stables, and Bill Lackwell, who stank of fish. She did not like Ned Swann; still less did she like Bill Lackwell, whose grandmother was a witch. No; Luce's lover must not be as these. She wished for someone great and noble, someone handsome with a lace ruff and a jaunty beard—not Sir Francis, of course, but someone very like him.

Betsy went on with her talk of witches.

"They can rouse a tempest. They can strike down a man or woman with the pox or an ague. They can do devils' work. You're not listening. Why, *you* should listen. Bill Lackwell's got his eyes on you, and if he was to set his heart on 'ee, he'd get you. 'Course he would. Ain't his grandmother one of *them*?"

"I'd have nothing to do with Bill Lackwell."

"That's what you do say now. But what if she was to get to work on 'ee, eh? Witches can do anything. Then there's devils that can creep into your bed at night, and no bolts on doors and windows is going to keep them out. They can come in all shapes. Some come handsome—just the way a woman would look for handsomeness; some comes as toads and hares and cats and dogs. Some comes as the Devil himself."

Betsy's voice had risen to a shriek, and she paused for breath before hurrying on: "I'll tell 'ee something else. I'll tell 'ee why we've been spared the cane. It's because they're going off... They're meeting to-night. Charlie... he told me. They're going to take old woman Lackwell and look for the Devil's mark. . .teats where she feeds her familiar. . .and then they'll tie her up and duck her. 'Twill be the end of old Granny Lackwell, for if she do float then she be a witch and they'll take her to Witches Gibbet and hang her up by the neck; and if she do sink, well then, she'll be no witch, but she'll be drowned all the same."

Luce began to shiver.

"Don't I wish I were there!" said Betsy. "Why, if we've got one witch among us, then we may have others, and if we have, then we should look for them. It don't do to have witches round us. No wonder Charlie's father lost a whole litter of pigs last month. He says 'twas witches' work, and we ought to find them, if they do be among us."

They were silent.

Darkness fell and the stars came out; there was a thin rind of moon to shed a little light through the diamond panes of the window. They could not sleep, and at last Betsy began to talk of the Spaniards.

"They come to the towns and burn down the houses and ravish the maidens. Well, we couldn't be blamed for that, could we? But some says they ain't human. 'Tain't whores they do want to make of us girls, but Catholics. They give you the scourge and put on the thumbscrews and hang you up by your wrists; and if you was to turn Catholic before they burn you, they strangle you first. If you don't they just roast you alive. Listen. Can you hear those voices? That's them with Granny Lackwell." She leaped up and went to the window. "We couldn't climb out of this window, could we? But if that door was unlocked, I'd be out. I'd be down them stairs. Wouldn't you, Luce? Wouldn't it be worth a bit of trouble to see what they're doing to old Granny Lackwell?"

Luce nodded and Betsy began to giggle. She danced to the door.

"Why," she said, "if that door was unlocked, I'd open it and walk out . . . right down them stairs . . ."

She broke off. She had turned the handle and the door opened, for Mistress Alton had forgotten to lock it.

*   *   *

Half a mile or so from the big house and the cottages of Pennicomquick some fifteen men and ten women were gathered around an old woman. The light from a flare or two showed the clearing among the trees, and in this clearing was a pond of stagnant water. The faces of these people looked fantastic in the glow; lust of the hunt burned in their eyes, and mingling with it was a gleam of righteousness which made them enjoy their cruelty the more. The Church of England no less than the Church of Rome denounced all witches and sentenced them to ignoble death.

Women were whispering together: "I did see the smoke coming out of her chimney to-day. It did rise in shapes like serpents. 'Twas no ordinary smoke. 'Twas evil she was brewing in her cauldron, I'm sure."

"That cat of hers, 'tis no ordinary cat. 'Tis her familiar and she suckles it. We'll see her float, mark my words."

19

"And if her floats, what then?"

"What the law won't do for us we must do for ourselves. To the gibbet with her."

They were tying up the old woman now in the traditional manner—her wrists to her ankles; they were attaching a rope about her waist so that they could pull her out of the water and if possible prevent her drowning. They were eager to prove her a witch and hang her on the gibbet.

The poor old creature was moaning softly; a trickle of saliva ran from her lips; she was bemused with fear. She crouched on the grass, stark naked, her withered body seeming inhuman in the light from the flares. They had found a big wart on her back and had declared this to be the Devil's mark, so that there was ample justification for putting to the test one so branded.

The old woman's cat was mewing piteously. They had intended that he should follow his mistress into the water, and a stone was being tied about his neck; he scratched and clawed at his tormentors with what they were certain was more venom than could be displayed by an ordinary cat.

"Send the cat off first," cried a man. "Who knows? It might have powers to help the witch."

This the crowd agreed to do, and the cat was flung into the pond. It went to the bottom immediately.

"Now," cried Mistress Alton, who was well to the fore. "No more delay. Now for the witch. Tom Hurly, you'd better say a word or two before we does it, to show the real reason why we feel we've got to act."

Tom Hurly, a talkative man, was quite prepared to speak.

"We'll ask the blessing of God," he said, "for we know, every one of us, that 'tis His will we should down the Devil and all his friends. Oh Lord, let not this witch escape Thy Vengeance. Let her be shown for what she is by the test of water. Let not the work of Thine enemy Satan come to her aid. If she floats, then Lord, we'll hang her—with Thy help—on the witches gibbet. If she sinks we'll know her for innocent. In Thy Name we seek Thy Help in purging this our land from the Evil One."

Mistress Alton cried: "Come on, friends. In the Name of the Lord."

With a howl of triumph, her persecutors crowded in on the old woman, trying to hustle her to her feet. She could not stand, trussed as she was, and could only crouch on all fours, like an animal in pain.

And then, suddenly, into their midst came Richard Merriman. His presence was so unexpected that the men stopped what they were doing to take off their caps or pull their forelocks, while the women curtsied.

Richard looked with distaste at the naked woman and from her to her persecutors.

"You were making such a devil of a row," he said. "So it's a witch hunt."

"Well, sir," said Tom Hurly the spokesman, "this Granny Lackwell, she be a witch, sir . . ."

"Oh come, Hurly—just a wretched old woman, I am sure."

"No, sir. Not she . . ."

They all began to talk at once.

"My little Jane was took sick with fits, sir, when the old woman looked at her."

"Every pig in a litter lost . . ."

Richard stood there; very elegant he looked in his elaborate breeches slashed and puffed and decorated with gold lace; his doublet was cut in the Italian fashion — dazzling in its richness.

"You disturbed me," he said, "with your howling and shouts. As for the woman, she is no witch. I tell you she is a helpless old woman. Does anyone of you dare to contradict me? Let me tell you that it is not for such as you to take the law into your hands. Untie the ropes, Tom, and one of you take off your gown and wrap it about her. Mistress Alton, I would have thought you might have been looking to your duties rather than mingling with such fools. The two girls should not be allowed to creep out at this hour to witness such things. I am sorry that you do not take better care of them. The rest of you . . . have done with this folly. Take the woman back to her home. If you look for occupation, some of you might keep a watch on the sea. What if the Spaniards should land while you waste your time tormenting an old woman?"

They obeyed him, since it would not have occurred to them to do otherwise. They had always obeyed Mr. Merriman as their forebears had obeyed his.

Richard had no doubt that his orders would be carried out. He walked away.

Poor old woman! he thought. A witch? Well, he had saved her life to-night, but he doubted not that they would murder her one day. She was marked as a witch and it was a sad fate that awaited such a woman. He had been watching them to-night for longer than they realized. They interested him with their superstitions and their cruelty; it seemed to him that the two went often hand in hand.

He smiled, thinking of the two girls. They would be severely punished for this, and so they should be. But he suspected Betsy was the ringleader in this little adventure. Luce had not enjoyed it as her companion had. There was a different quality about Luce.

*   *   *

The uneasy weeks were passing. June had come, bringing with it the fiercest winds that could be remembered for the time of year. South-westerly gales were keeping the English fleet laid up in harbour, and the stores promised by the Queen and her Council in London had failed to arrive.

Sir Humphrey rode over from Stoke with his son Bartle to call on his friend in Pennicomquick.

Sir Humphrey was the acknowledged father of one boy — Bartle, who was six years old — and was the suspected father of many another child who pulled a forelock and scraped a leg or bobbed a greeting as it stood back from the pounding hoofs of Sir Humphrey's mare. Sir Humphrey was not displeased by the numerous progeny which were put to his account; and if his lady had given him only one son, that was surely a fault to be laid at her door, not his.

He enjoyed life; he was afraid of nothing so long as he understood it — and war, bloodshed and violence he understood perfectly; it was the supernatural which alarmed him. He would face any man with a sword or a blunderbuss; but witches worked in the dark; they attacked a man with a plague or a pox. He was talking of witches to Bartle as they rode over.

Bartle — even at six — was a boy of whom a man such as Sir Humphrey could be proud. He was tall for his years, fair-haired, rosy-cheeked and blue-eyed. He had his mother's looks and his father's spirit. He would be one for the women and the wine of life which was adventure.

Bartle could never hear enough of his father's exploits at sea. He would run his hands over the golden ornaments which his father had brought back from Peru and Hispaniola. He would wrap about him the rich cloth filched from the Spaniards, and he would strut. He was a man in the making.

There was no danger of the boy's turning out to be a scholar; his blue eyes were already turned towards the sea.

They had passed the Lackwell cottage and Sir Humphrey had called out to the boy not to look that way.

"That old woman could put a spell on you, boy. She could turn you from the healthy man you are going to be into a poxy go-by-the-ground . . . or even into a womanish scholar like our friend Merriman."

"I wouldn't mind that, sir, for I should then be able to please my tutor. I'd get through my tasks and not waste so much time on 'em."

"Don't say that, boy. That's tempting the Devil. Stay as you are, and don't give too much thought to your tasks. Just get the way to read and write, and the manners of a gentleman. That's all such as you and me want, boy."

"Look!" cried the boy. "There are ships in the Channel. Over there . . . Bolt Head way. . ."

Sir Humphrey drew up his mare. She stood obedient while he strained his bloodshot eyes, cursing them because they were not so sharp as the boy's.

"There, Father, look! One . . . two . . . three . . . Oh, sir, the Spaniards have come. Let us go to the town. I could do something. I could . . ."

"Be silent, boy. Come on."

They galloped, their hearts beating fast — relief, even joy, showing in their faces.

"The Spaniards have come!" shouted Sir Humphrey. "Out of your houses . . . you oafs . . . you lazy dogs! Now you will have a taste of a fight. By God, my sword will be red before this day is out."

Men, women and children came running from their cottages. Sir Humphrey pointed seawards and rode on.

Richard had come out to meet them. His face was calm and he was smiling in what Sir Humphrey often referred to as that "plaguey superior way of his."

"The Spaniards!" cried Sir Humphrey. "By Christ, man, they're here at last."

Richard continued to smile. "Nonsense, Cavill. It is only the victualling ships from Tilbury."

"By. . . God!" cried Sir Humphrey.

" 'Tis so, sir," shouted Bartle. "I can see the red cross of England."

Richard laid a hand on the boy's shoulder. "So eager, then, for bloodshed? Come into the house for a glass of wine."

They led their horses into the courtyard, where Clem Swann and Ned came to take them; then they went into the house. Richard rang the bell, which Luce answered. He asked for cakes and wine.

Mistress Alton brought the refreshment, with Luce in attendance. Mistress Alton's mouth seemed firmer since the adventure of Whit-Sunday night; there was a faint disapproval in her eyes, and Richard guessed that was for himself because of his leniency towards God's enemies. He smiled at her sardonically. Then his attention went to the girl, and fleetingly he wondered if her back still smarted from the whipping she must have received that night.

Sir Humphrey's attention went immediately to the women, for it was as natural for him to assess women as he assessed his horses. He knew the Alton type; she hated the thought of other people's love-making because she had missed having any of her own. A stick of a woman. No good, no good at all. But the girl? He had not noticed her before; she had always run at his approach, he believed. . . a shy, slip of a girl, hardly ready till now to satisfy his purposes. She was still young, but not too young. Rather like a comely boy with her hair short like that. Sir Humphrey decided to keep an eye on Richard's serving wench. Not that he would go out of his way. . .but if the opportunity came. . .well, he'd be ready for it. And Sir Humphrey was the kind of man whom opportunity invariably favoured.

When the servants went out, Bartle sat entranced, listening to the conversation of his elders.

"By God," Sir Humphrey was saying. "Drake is straining at the leash, man. Of course he is. Does he want to wait in harbour, cowering from the gale like a child behind its nurse's skirts? No, sir. He should out and at 'em! There's restiveness aboard. I know. Drake says, 'We'll go and tackle the Spaniard in his own seas.' But 'No!' says the Queen. And 'No!' says her Council. 'Stay close to the land and protect *us*.' By God, sir, that's not Drake's way. First to the attack; that's our Admiral. And he's right. By God, he's proved it. He's proved it a thousand times."

The boy jumped up and down in his chair.

"It would seem," said Richard, "that it is no good thing to have men of theories impeding men of action. Had he been given his head, I am inclined to think our danger would be past ere this. Sir Francis is manacled by instructions from London. He knows the course he wishes to take. *Fortes fortuna adjuvat*."

"What's that?" said Sir Humphrey.

"Bartle will tell you," said Richard; "or he should be able to."

But Bartle could not tell his father, and Sir Humphrey was not greatly disturbed on that score.

"Alas! Bartle, it would seem you are a sad pupil. I asked your tutor how you did, and he shook his head in a most melancholy fashion. You dream too much of adventure, of the sea, of bringing home treasure. Is that not so?"

"Then he dreams a man's dreams," said Sir Humphrey.

Bartle said: "The coming of these ships will mean that our fleet will sail to the attack." His face fell. "They will fight away from our coast...along the coast of Spain, mayhap in Cadiz Harbour. The Spaniards will see the fight instead of us."

Sir Humphrey let out a roar of laughter. "They'll never make a scholar of you, boy. He'd rather see a fight than know the meaning of a Latin tag, wouldn't you, son?" Sir Humphrey looked into his wine. "There's something that bothers me, Richard. You know...you shouldn't have stopped 'em the other night. Witches is witches, and the sooner we find out who among us is with the Devil, the better for us all."

Richard looked at Bartle. "You may find a peach or two in the gardens," he said.

"Nay!" said Sir Humphrey. "Let the boy stay. I don't want him made into a mincing dainty who mustn't hear this and who mustn't hear that. He knows there are witches, don't you, boy? And he knows what it's our bounden duty to do to them."

Bartle nodded. "I wish I'd been there," he said. "Why did you stop them, sir? The old woman is a witch."

"Utterly distasteful!" said Richard. "Good God, we must keep law and order in these parts. It is not for our yokels to take the law into their hands. She is just a foolish old woman who brews herbs and gives charms to lovesick maidens. I heard the shouting and went out. A most disgusting spectacle."

Sir Humphrey looked at his friend. Damn me, thought Sir Humphrey, if I'd be a friend of his but for living so close. Only half a man. Riding over to see that widow woman every so often. A dried-up old widow woman when there's a ripe young virgin under his very roof. Reading his books, scratching away with his quill, can't look on a witch being put to the test without finding it disgusting, distasteful. Give me a man!

Sir Humphrey said: "If there are witches hereabouts, they should be found and finished. We want no trafficking with the Devil."

Richard shrugged his elegant shoulders and gave Sir Humphrey another of his superior smiles. Then he turned the discussion back to the Spaniards, and they were on this when Sir Humphrey rose to go.

When Richard went with his guests to the gate, the girl Luce was in the garden. She had a basket of peaches in her hand, and she coloured and dropped a curtsy as they came out.

"Hey!" said Sir Humphrey. "What you got there, girl?" Richard watched him pretend to peer into the basket while he looked at the opening of her bodice.

"Peaches, sir."

Sir Humphrey took one, and dug his teeth into it. "Why, they're better than ours. Send me over a basket by the girl, will you, Richard?" He gave the peach to Bartle to finish, and slapped Luce's buttocks as she turned away. "Bring them over, girl, and don't give them to anyone but me. You understand?"

Luce looked from Sir Humphrey to her master. Richard nodded and she curtsied again before returning to the house.

When he had waved farewell to Sir Humphrey and his son, Richard came back through the gardens and, as he did so, saw Luce coming out to gather peaches for Sir Humphrey. Richard followed her over to the wall on which the peaches were growing. Luce blushed and fumbled to be so observed.

"Don't give him of our best," he said. "Let us save those for our own table."

She picked the fruit, and when the basket was full he took it from her.

"Go to the stables," he said, "and tell Ned Swann I wish him to take these over to Sir Humphrey."

She curtsied and he watched her as she went into the courtyard.

*   *   *

In the harbour torches and cressets lighted the sailors loading ships. The Spanish galleons had not come, but the English were going out to meet them, for Drake had won the day. First Howard had agreed to his plan, then the Queen and her Council had followed. Sailors were singing and whistling as they made ready. The suspense of waiting was over.

30

Mistress Alton had been taken sick. She lay in her bed, muttering prayers which she believed was the only way to counteract a spell. Old woman Lackwell had fixed her sore eyes on Mistress Alton on Whit-Sunday night, and ever since Mistress Alton had been sick. She was certain she had been "overlooked."

Life seemed good to Luce and Betsy without Mistress Alton to watch them, to complain and to cut them across the legs and arms with her cane.

Outside the sun was shining and the gardens were filled with the scent of roses and the lavender which was just breaking into bloom. Betsy sang as she and Luce went from the kitchen to the pastry, and from the pastry to the buttery and back to the kitchen:

> "Hyle that the sun with his beames hot
> Scorched the fruits in vale and mountain.
> Philon the shepherd late forgot,
> Sitting beside a crystal fountain."

She taught the words to Luce and they sang them together.

> "Sitting beside a crystal fountain
> In shadow of a green oak tree,
> Upon his pipe this song played he,
> Untrue love, untrue love,
> Untrue love, adieu, love.
> Your mind is light."

They danced round the kitchen, curtsying, dipping, touching hands, bowing.

Charlie Hurly looked through the window and was watching for some minutes before they saw him. Then he clapped his hands, and Luce blushed, while Betsy went to the window and put her hands on her hips, pretending to scold him. But he just laughed and beckoned Betsy out to the shed, for he had something to tell her; she scolded still more and said she would not go, but Luce could not help noticing that she was soon making an excuse to go outside and that she stayed there for a full quarter of an hour.

They had to take it in turns to go up to Mistress Alton's room for instructions. She lay on her pallet, her face greenish yellow, her dry lips muttering prayers to ward off evil.

In the courtyard Charlie Hurly was talking to Ned Swann about what was going on in the harbour; they were nodding their heads, looking grave, looking wise. Charlie would not have dared hang about like that if Mistress Alton had been about. Betsy would not have dared to stay chattering.

And that night, of course, Mistress Alton was unable to lock the two girls in their room.

*　　*　　*

The weeks of waiting were not yet done with. The fleet had set out only to be driven back by the gales. Every man and woman of Plymouth shared the impatience of the admirals, and railed against the Queen for her meanness in not sending more of the desperately needed stores. Rations were short on board the ships, and although Drake and Howard were convinced that the winds which were tormenting them were also plaguing the Spaniards, when the opportunity arose to leave the shores of Devon and go into the attack, ill-equipped as they were they were unable to do so. The caution of the Queen, and still more the stinginess of the lady, were preventing a quick victory. It was all very well to make fine speeches at Tilbury, but what folly to let her meanness set her throne and her country in danger!

But in the first week of that July, Howard and Drake could no longer wait; in spite of sickness aboard and shortage of food, they set out for the attack. But before long, back they came dejected and disappointed. The storm-battered Spaniards lay off Corunna, where they would have been at the mercy of the English, but — like a miracle that had worked in the Spaniards' favour — the north wind had suddenly dropped, and the English, in full sight of their enemy, lay becalmed until a south wind arose. They could return or wait — their food and water low, thanks to their Queen — on the pleasure of the winds.

Mistress Alton, now recovered from her mysterious illness, was certain what this meant. It was witchcraft. She knew, if others did not, how the tempest and calm could be controlled by witches. She went about muttering prayers all day; the cane was not used so frequently since she had risen from her sick-bed, but only because she had not the strength in her arms. She had never seen such an addle-pated pair as the two serving wenches had become. There was Betsy going out to get water without a bucket. As for Luce, you could speak to her and she would not seem to hear. These girls had been up to something, Mistress Alton was quick to note, for she was a woman who recognised sin the moment she saw it.

She thought of getting Clem Swann to give them a good beating for her; but she did not trust Clem Swann. He would be gloating over their white shoulders or mayhap trying to get them to expose their bosoms. For modesty's sake, she could not get Clem Swann to punish them; and as for getting him to beat them through their petticoats, that would be just a lark to them. Yet it was a sad thing to let sin go unpunished.

Sir Humphrey was of the same opinion as Mistress Alton regarding the frustrations at sea. This was witches' work. How else could it be explained? He wanted to take old Granny Lackwell and make her talk, make her expose her confederates. He argued the point with Richard; and it was maddening how a scholar could tie up a man with words. He was turning over in his mind whether he would not act in this matter in spite of his friend's disapproval, and one bright Friday afternoon, he decided to ride over to Pennicomquick and tell Richard so.

He did not, however, reach the house, for as he rode the few miles which separated his house from that of Richard, a rider came galloping towards him, and he saw that it was one of his own men whom he had sent that morning into Plymouth on an errand.

"Sir Humphrey," cried the man, "they are coming. Captain Fleming has just come into the harbour. The admirals were at play on the Hoe. The Spaniards are sighted off the Lizard."

Then Sir Humphrey forgot the danger of witches. He lost no time in galloping straight down to the harbour.

*   *   *

The days that followed saw the defeat of what had been believed to be the greatest armada the world had seen. Much of the battle had been witnessed from the Devon and Cornish coasts before the Spaniards fled up Channel towards the Isle of Wight, pursued by English ships in which men counted their ammunition and were close to starvation, living as they were on half rations. News travelled slowly and it was some time before the people of Plymouth knew the story of the fireships which had finished off the fine work of their seamen.

This was a proud story, but not so proud was the tale of men set ashore to die in the streets of sea-ports from wounds and starvation. Yet England was saved from Spain and the Inquisition in spite of her Queen, who, now that her kingdom was safe, sat shaking her ginger head at the cost of the operations, and grumbling because an ill wind had arisen and carried the battered and beaten ships with their treasure out of her grasp, so that the sea-bed garnered the riches which English seamen had won for their Queen.

Quiet had returned to the town of Plymouth. Nobody talked of the Spaniards now, except the penniless sailors who, their work done, were having to whistle for their pay. Danger of invasion had gone; danger of starvation was less exciting.

It was at the beginning of September when Mistress Alton brought the weeping Luce to her master and bade the girl tell him of her shame.

Richard could see the change in Luce. There were dark shadows under her eyes and her face was set into lines of anxiety.

She was silent, so Mistress Alton spoke for her.

"I have terrible news." The woman's lips could not hide the savage satisfaction she was feeling.

Richard raised his eyebrows. "Indeed? I should have thought it was good news by the look of you."

"Then, sir, my looks belie my feelings. This girl has brought shame on herself and me. On me because she was in my charge; but I lay sick and so she escaped to her wickedness. On herself because the Lord has decided that she shall answer for her sins here below. She thought to escape, but she has learned that sins must be paid for. I have whipped her; she still bleeds from the whipping. And now there is naught to be done but turn her out of doors."

"What great sin is this?" asked Richard, stroking the lace of his ruff with tenderness, as though he were more concerned with its set than with the troubles of a serving girl.

"She is with child, sir. The wicked wanton creature! She's been sneaking out at night to meet her lover, and now it seems he'll have nothing to do with her. So she is left to bring her shame to me."

36

"Who is your lover?" asked Richard.

Luce hung her head and would not answer. Mistress Alton's clenched fist punched the girl's back.

"Speak, you young hussy, when the master bids you."

Luce lifted her dark eyes to his face. "I . . . I cannot say, master."

"Has he bidden you to silence?"

"I . . . I don't know."

Mistress Alton let out a snort of laughter. "She cannot say his name. It seems he came to her at night. It was no fault of hers, she says. I have heard that tale before. They cast their eyes upon the men; they follow when they're beckoned, and then when they start to grow big, they play the innocent. 'I did not know. . . It was forced upon me . . .'Twas no fault of mine . . .'"

"Leave the girl with me," said Richard.

The woman hesitated, her mouth working, her eyes gleaming.

"Sir . . ." she began; but he lifted a hand impatiently.

"I pray you leave the girl with me."

When he spoke in that tone—gentle yet very firm with a faintly threatening note in his voice—no one dared disobey him. So Mistress Alton went reluctantly out.

"Now, Luce," he said, when she had gone, "come here. Sit down and tell me exactly what happened."

"I . . . I can't tell you, sir, for I don't rightly know."

"Now, please," he insisted, "that is nonsense. I am afraid you will make me angry if you persist in this silliness. Who is the man? Come along. You must know. Tell me his name at once."

"I . . . I dare not."

"You dare not tell *me*! Now was it Ned Swann?"

She shook her head.

"Luce, listen to me; tell me everything and, who knows, I may decide to help you. Do you think this man would consider marrying you?"

"Oh, no. . . no!"

"He is far above you in station? You must tell him then, and I doubt not that he will find a husband for you. Why, girl, it is not the first time this has happened. Dry your tears, I dare swear a man will be found to marry you."

She looked at him then, shaking her head; and suddenly, tumbling from her lips came the whole story.

It had happened thus:

On the first night of Mistress Alton's sickness, she and Betsy had left their attic and crept out of the house. That day Charlie Hurly had told Betsy that at midnight he was going to witness a very strange sight and he wanted her to accompany him. There were witches in the neighbourhood — many of them — and on certain nights they met to do homage to the Devil, to learn his secrets and to win great powers from him in exchange for their souls.

Betsy had promised to go. She knew that it was possible on this night, and it was too good an opportunity to miss. But when midnight came she was frightened, and she asked Luce to accompany her. Luce did not want to go at first but, after a good deal of persuasion, she did so.

After that the story became still more incoherent. It was obvious to Richard that Charlie had lured Betsy out in order to seduce her; it was small wonder that he was annoyed when she arrived at their tryst with her fellow servant.

Luce then assured him that she had witnessed strange and diabolical things that night, but nothing more strange and more diabolical than the thing which had happened to her.

Charlie had taken them to a clearing in the woods, and they had hidden behind trees and watched. Luce had seen wild figures dancing round a fire; she was sure they were not entirely human beings; some had the heads of animals, and they danced, taking partners and making gestures as though they were . . .

She faltered, but he helped her. "As though they were inviting each other to fornication?" he said.

She hung her head. "Please, sir, I can say no more. Turn me out . . . Let me starve . . . Let me beg . . . But don't ask me to tell you more, for I cannot tell it."

"Nevertheless," he said, "you will tell me, for I insist."

"I should not have left the attic, sir. I knew that was wrong. I knew that was wicked. I shouldn't have watched." She began to sob. "Then it wouldn't have happened to me."

"Go on," he commanded.

And she told him how suddenly she had found that Betsy and Charlie were no longer beside her; she was alone there among the trees, and before her eyes was taking place that weird scene in the clearing. But she was aware suddenly that she was not alone...for close to her was a figure, a figure clad in black from head to foot. She could not see his face, or indeed whether he had a face, as men had faces. She knew there were eyes that watched her; there were horns...Yes, she saw the horns.

"And, sir," she said, "I was took with trembling, for I did know..."

"What did you know, Luce?"

"I knew, sir, that I was in the presence of the Devil himself. He came to me...and I tried to run, but I was stuck there...like I was chained, sir...and he came nearer and nearer...and I couldn't cry out...nor could I move."

His smile was sardonic. "And then, Luce?"

"He picked me up and threw me over his shoulder."

"So he had a shoulder, then?"

"Yes, sir. I did feel as though I were thrown over his shoulder. I fainted, sir. I fainted right away. I thought, sir, I was being carried straight to eternal damnation as Mistress Alton is always talking of."

"And when you came to?"

"I was lying on the grass, sir. There at the edge of the wood where the bushes is thick...and I knew, sir, I knew what had happened to me."

40

He laid both his hands on her shoulders and looked into her face. "Luce, are you seriously trying to tell me that you believe it was the Devil? Come, girl. You know it was a man dressed up as the Devil. You know it. Admit it. I have an idea that you know who the man is."

"No, sir. I swear I don't."

"Do you swear it? Would you swear it on the Holy Bible?"

"Yes, sir, that I would."

"Luce, you try my patience sorely. It is a trick that has been played on you."

"I do not think so. For there was another time . . ."

"Another time?"

"He came to me in the dark of night when I lay abed."

"What, in this house? Why did you not wake Betsy?"

"Mistress Alton was sick. She was so sick that she wanted one of us to stay with her. So . . . Betsy stayed. I was alone that night. And I woke suddenly. It was dark . . . and I knew he was there."

"Did you faint that time, Luce?"

"No, sir. That time I did not faint. I . . . I was awake all the time . . ."

"And you persist that he was the Devil?"

"Yes, sir. I know he was the Devil."

"Now, listen to me, Luce. I can understand your believing this incredible thing on the night in the wood, but not . . . oh, certainly not . . . when he came to your room. Think of all the men hereabouts who

41

have looked your way and desired you. You must be aware of them."

She shook her head. She was crying silently, the tears spilling over onto her bodice. He looked at her swollen face with distaste and walked away from her to the window.

"I will give you a word of warning," he said. "Tell no one else this incredible tale. If you do, I fear there may be trouble for you . . . greater trouble than this bearing of a child whose father you do not know."

He turned to look at her standing there so miserable, so abject.

"There are some who would say I should send you back to your parents. Would you like that, Luce?"

She began to sob aloud.

He spoke more gently. "Don't make that noise, child. Go now. I shall not send you home if you do not wish to go. Instead, I will do my best to find a man willing to father your child. Come. You have been foolish—for you know you were wrong to leave the house when Mistress Alton forbade you to leave it—and this is the result of your folly. Try to remember that what has happened to you has happened to others before you. Go now. I promise to help you."

He watched her stumble from the room, and he thought how different she was from that graceful girl whom he had seen outside the church on Whit-Sunday morning.

*   *   *

That was the story of Tamar's conception.

Richard was as good as his word. He chose Ned Swann as a likely husband for Luce, but Ned was reluctant to take her. He had heard whispers as to the paternity of the child that made the marriage necessary.

The Lackwells were not so particular. Bill Lackwell had often cast a lustful eye on the girl, and as Richard offered a small sum of money to go with her, Bill decided it was not a bad match.

So Bill married Luce and almost a year after Luce had watched Sir Francis Drake leave the church with Lord Howard of Effingham, her baby was born.

Tamar was a dark-eyed girl with the marks of beauty on her even in her earliest days. She was a bonny child, and some said that she was actually Bill Lackwell's daughter; but there were many who did not wish to rid themselves of the belief that she was the child of Satan.

CHAPTER
TWO

Tamar, being more than ordinarily intelligent, quickly became aware of the difference between herself and other children, for, by the time she was five years old, Luce had three more to litter the one room of the Lackwell cottage. Tamar looked on gravely at the scenes which took place before her young eyes. She had seen the birth of one brother and the death of another. She had sat solemnly in her corner watching, for no one turned her out, and it was then that she first became aware of that awe — which in time grew to fear — with which she was able to inspire those about her.

She made a little corner for herself near the fire — when there was one — the cosiest spot away from the window where the cracked oiled paper, which did the service of glass, let in the draughts. She collected coloured stones and made a boundary with them about her corner.

"Nobody ain't coming inside these stones," she said; and she had said it defiantly, expecting Bill Lackwell to kick the stones from one end of the earthen floor to the other, and to pick her up by her rags and lay about her with his calloused hands before he put her outside the door. But he did no such thing; he merely looked away from her, while her mother watched her with terrified eyes.

Tamar was triumphant. Nobody moved the stones. When the other children came to take them their mother called them away — even their father growled at them; and Tamar kept the cosiest corner in that miserable room to herself.

Tamar was interested in everything that went on in the cottage and outside it. The other children seemed to think of little beyond whether they would eat or whether they would get one of their father's cruel beatings; it was true that Tamar did not have to think of the latter, as Bill Lackwell never touched her, no matter what she did, but food was a matter of great importance to her.

On a stool, from which she rarely moved, sat old Grandmother Lackwell. She could hardly walk now, for when she had been dragged from the cottage to be tested that Whit-Sunday night, her leg had been broken; she could only drag it along as she walked, and that with great pain. She would sit brooding — just sitting, her rheumy old eyes half closed, not seeing the cottage or its inhabitants, as though she were not there in that room but miles away.

Tamar was interested in the old woman; she sensed in her that distinction which had unaccountably been bestowed on herself. The old woman did nothing for her keep, except now and then sell some of the herbs which grew in the patch round the cottage; she would send her customers out with instructions what to pick, and when they had done so, they would bring them into her. Then she would tell them what to do with these plants and what to say while they were doing it. She hardly ever received money, but a few days after these transactions, a gift would be laid at the door — rye bread or an egg or two. Bill Lackwell or Luce took them in and they would all share, no thanks being given to the old woman; but everyone knew that it was due to her that they came.

But, reasoned Tamar, these gifts came too rarely to buy for the old woman her seat in the overcrowded cottage. Yet she was never spoken to harshly, never asked to move. They were afraid of her, as they were beginning to be of Tamar.

One day the child sidled up to the old woman.

"Granny," she said, "tell me about the herbs that grow in our patch."

Then one of the skinny hands touched Tamar's thick black curls.

"Fair and beautiful," mumbled the old woman, so that Tamar had to move close to her to hear what she said. "You will know what you have to do when the time comes."

So Tamar, pondering these words behind her ring of stones, knew that she was a very important person and one day would be more so.

She lived her own secret life. When it was warm she slept out of doors. She liked that, and was sad when the colder nights came to drive her under the Lackwell thatch.

Luce was no longer a slim young girl, but a tired woman, weary with constant child-bearing — her body thickened yet scraggy from the state of semi-starvation which was invariably her lot. The hair, which Mistress Alton had said was a gift from Satan, was now long, but it had lost its lustre and fell untidily to her waist. Out of the horror she had experienced during her first months as Bill Lackwell's wife had grown a dull acceptance of her fate.

She watched her eldest daughter with apprehension. Tamar was named after the river near which her conception had taken place; for such a child, Luce had felt, should not be named with a name that might belong to any child. She had anxiously awaited that moment when the perfectly formed feet might change to cloven hoofs. They remained perfect human feet. She felt the shapely head for those excrescences from which horns might be expected to grow. There was no sign of these. Tamar might have been anybody's child, except that from an early age that brightness of eye, that shapely oval face and the perfectly moulded limbs, as well as a quickness of perception, distinguished her from others. The beauty was an accentuation of that which had been Luce's in the days when she had served under Mistress Alton; but the other qualities did not come from Luce.

Luce wanted to love this daughter, but it was impossible to overcome her apprehension concerning the child, and Tamar could not help but be aware of this.

The little girl had been healthy from the day of her birth; she had remained unswaddled, for in Bill Lackwell's cottage there were no swaddling clothes. This meant that her young limbs were free to kick and feel the fresh air, and certainly to enjoy a modicum of cleanliness which was denied more well-cared-for children.

And so she grew — knowledgeable, longing to use her bright intelligence, missing little that went on around her. She saw the cruel treatment of her half-brothers and sisters by the bully Lackwell; she saw her mother suffering also from his violence, she saw their reconciliations and she knew what frequently happened under the rags on their bed of straw. She saw her mother change gradually from a shrivelled, bony woman to a big one, and she knew what that meant.

She was six years old when the difference between herself and others became fully apparent to her.

Betsy Hurly sometimes came to the cottage. Betsy had done rather well for herself, for she had induced Charlie Hurly to marry her and was now mistress of the Hurly farm. The noisy, full-blooded farmer's wife still hankered after adventures which varied only in a few details from those which had excited her before her marriage.

One day she came to the cottage when only Luce and the old woman — with Tamar sitting in her corner surrounded by her stones — were there.

Betsy brought an air of well-being with her, and in her quick way Tamar was immediately aware of how poor the place was when Betsy sat in it with her coarse worsted garments, which, while not as becoming as those worn by the gentry, looked rich compared with the rags of the other three.

Tamar, polishing her stones, was aware of everything. Outside the cottage, Annis waited. Annis was Betsy's eldest daughter — a few months younger than Tamar. Tamar looked at the child through the open door of the cottage, and Annis put out her tongue. But Tamar was more interested in the grown-ups than in the child.

Betsy was saying: "Come on, Luce. You could if you wanted to. You know how to do it. Where's the good in pretending you don't? I know too much. Don't forget you told me about it. 'Tain't much I'm asking. I'll pay thee well for it."

Luce kept her eyes down. "What is it you want, Betsy?"

Betsy said in a solemn whisper: "Jim Haines. Have you seen him, Luce? Nigh on six feet. What a man! But, my dear life, he don't see none but that young dairy-maid. I do want his affections turned to me."

"But, Betsy, you shouldn't want such things."

"Don't 'ee talk nonsense, Luce Lackwell. Should I be like you . . . let Bill Lackwell beat you sick and then give you child after child as you can't afford to feed?"

" 'Sh!" said Luce.

But Betsy would not be silent. "Well, you did have a bit of glory once, didn't 'ee? I bet *that* were a bit different from Bill Lackwell, weren't it?"

Betsy's eyes slewed round to Tamar, who seemed to be absorbed in her stones.

"Wasn't it, Luce? A bit different, eh?"

"Yes, it was then."

"Must have been. My dear soul! I reckon it must have been just about better than anything."

Luce nodded.

"But it brought you to this. I reckon you'd have had Ned Swann but for *someone's* taking a fancy to 'ee."

Luce said, "Don't say such things. 'Tis like asking for a judgment."

"You'm right. But where's the good pretending you've never had naught to do with such things? Where's the sense? You could give me a charm and bring Jim Haines straight to me arms."

"No, Betsy. 'Twouldn't be right."

"Wouldn't it then? I can tell 'ee Charlie has his larks."

"Come out to the patch," said Luce. "I knows I shouldn't. I know naught of such things. But I heard what the old woman told somebody t'other day."

Betsy glanced towards the old woman, who had sat impassive during this discussion.

"Her don't hear," explained Luce. "Her's very deaf. You have to go right up close and shout to make her hear."

They went out to the patch. Tamar stared after them while Annis looked into the cottage. She again put out her tongue at Tamar, who regarded her with solemn eyes.

"Come here," said Tamar.

"No, I won't."

"Then go away. I don't care."

"I won't."

"You're afraid."

Annis had fair hair and grey eyes; she was quite pretty, but beside Tamar she looked insignificant.

"If you wasn't afraid," said Tamar, "you'd come in."

Annis stepped gingerly into the cottage and cautiously approached the stones.

"What's them?"

"Stones."

"What for?"

"Nobody mustn't come farther than here."

Annis knelt down and looked at the stones; then she looked at Tamar, who smiled suddenly and, picking up one of the stones, gave it to Annis.

When the two women came back into the cottage Betsy looked at her daughter and turned pale. "Annis!" she cried. "What are you doing in here, then? I'll take you home and tan the hide off 'ee."

Annis got up from the floor and ran out of the cottage. Tamar watched her, then started up. "She's got my stone. Give it back. Give it back."

Betsy was out of the door; she had Annis by the shoulder; she shook her until the child's face was red. "Drop it. Drop it quick."

Annis dropped the stone and in triumph Tamar seized it.

"Take that!" said Betsy, and slapped her daughter's face. "And now come home." She pulled at the child's arm. "Good day to you, Luce."

"Goodbye, Betsy."

Tamar looked at her mother, but Luce would not meet her eyes.

I'm different, thought Tamar. Nobody slaps my face. Nobody talks of tanning my hide. I'm different. I'm Tamar. They're afraid of me.

*   *   *

Down at Sutton Pool people stood about on the cobbles watching the departure of Sir Walter Raleigh and his five ships which were going to explore the Orinoco in the hope of bringing back gold for the Queen.

There was less enthusiasm at such spectacles than there had been a few years ago. Plymouth could not forget the horrible sight of those brave seamen, the heroes of the defeat of the Spanish Armada, now starving in the streets, begging their bread — some cruelly wounded — their services ignored, and what was more important to them, unpaid for by an ungrateful Queen and Council.

These men would have long since died but for men like Drake, Hawkins and Frobisher, who had provided much out of their own pockets, starting a fund for mendicant seamen, building a hospital for mariners; and Sir Francis, when he had left his house in Looe Street to live in Buckland Abbey, had continued with his scheme for bringing water to the town. Now it was conveyed there from the west stream of the River Plym. No wonder they worshipped this man. It was already said — in spite of the digging operations which were to be seen —

that Sir Francis had gone to the river and, bidding it follow him, had galloped into Plymouth. They preferred to think of their benefactor not only as a good brave man, but as a wizard.

And now, with the departure of Sir Walter, there was not the same enthusiasm as when Sir Francis sailed. Adventure was in the blood of these people who lived along the seaboard, but they hated injustice, and they could not forget — being constantly reminded by the sad sights about them, as they were — the callous behaviour of their Queen.

Tamar was there by the Pool. The noble ships rocking so proudly on the water delighted her and she wished that she were sailing with the expedition. It even occurred to her to hide herself in one of the ships. Then she remembered that old Granny Lackwell would be in the cottage alone to-day. Tamar was impulsive, and once an idea had hit her she was eager to put it into practice. She pushed her way through the crowd and ran all the way home.

The old woman was sitting in her accustomed place. Tamar went close to her and shouted in her ear.

"Granny, it's Tamar."

Granny nodded.

"Granny, I've come to ask you things."

She nodded again.

"Why are they afraid of you and me?"

Granny laughed, showing black stumps which fascinated while they horrified the child. "Why are your teeth black?" she asked; but she realised at once that that was a question which could wait, for it had nothing to do with the mystery she was so eager to uncover. "How was I born?" she said quickly.

Old Granny became excited. Her hands were shaking. Tamar looked anxiously about her, for she knew that whatever revelations might take place could only do so if the two of them were alone together.

"Did a man lie with my mother, as Bill Lackwell does under the rags . . . or was it on the grass?"

That made Granny choke with laughter.

"Speak, Granny, speak! I shall be angry if you laugh. I want to know."

Granny sat very still; then she turned her head to look at the child.

"On the grass," she said.

"Why?"

Granny shook her head.

"They like doing that, I think," said Tamar gravely, for she could see that she must continue to prompt the old woman if she were to get her to reveal anything. "It was because they liked it," she went on. "And then my mother grew big and I came out. But . . . why are they afraid of me?"

Granny shook her head, but Tamar lightly slapped the old woman's arm. "Granny, I must know. You are afraid of me. My mother is afraid of me. Even Lackwell is afraid of me. He is big and strong; he has a belt and hard hands, and I am little — see how little I am, Granny! — and he is afraid of me. They are afraid of you too, Granny. It is something you have given me."

Granny shook her head. "I didn't give 'ee nothing. 'Tweren't me."

"Then who was it, Granny? Speak . . . speak. I'll hurt you if you don't tell me."

Granny's eyes grew frightened. "There now . . . there, little beauty. Don't speak so."

"Granny, it was the man on the grass. He gave me something. What is it?"

"He did give you fair looks."

" 'Tain't hair and eyes, Granny. Lackwell wouldn't care about they. Besides, they're afraid of you, Granny, and you'm ugly. You'm terrible ugly."

Granny nodded. She signed, and the black cat at her feet jumped on to her lap. She stroked the cat's back. "Stroke it with me, child," she said; and she took Tamar's little hand and together they stroked the cat.

"You're a witch, Granny," said Tamar.

Granny nodded.

"Granny, have you seen the Devil?"

Granny shook her head.

"Tell me about being a witch. What *is* being a witch?"

"It's having powers as others ain't got. It's powers that be give to the likes of we. We'm Satan's, and he's our master."

"Go on, Granny. Go on. Don't stop."

"We'm devil's children. That be it. We can heal . . . and we can kill. We can turn milk sour before it leaves the cows and goats, and we can do great things. We have Sabbats, child, Sabbats when we do meet, and there we do worship the horned goat who be a messenger from Satan. There's some as say he be one of us . . . dressed up like . . . That may be so, but when he do put on the shape of a goat he be a goat . . . and we do dance about him. Ah! I be too old for dancing now. My days be done. I'm good for naught but to tell others what to brew. 'Twas the night I was took for the test. They'd have done for me then . . . but for a gentleman that stopped 'em. I've been sick and ailing since. But I be a witch, child, and there's none can deny me that."

"Granny . . . am I a witch?"

"Not yet you ain't."

"Shall I be a witch?"

"Like as not you will . . . seeing as you come into the world the way you did."

"How did I come into the world? On the grass, was it? Was my father a witch?"

Granny was solemn. "They do say, child, that he was the greatest of them all . . . under God."

"An angel?"

"Nay. Put thy hand on Toby's back. Come close to me, child . . . closer . . ."

Tamar stood breathless, waiting. "Tell me, Granny. Tell me."

"Your father, child, was none other than the Devil himself."

*   *   *

The hot sultry July was with them and Tamar was scarcely ever in the cottage, coming in only to snatch a piece of rye bread or salted fish. But if the old

56

woman was alone she would sit with her and they would talk together, for Tamar wished to know all the dark secrets of Granny's devils' world.

Not that Granny was easy to understand; sometimes she mumbled and, even standing so close and suffering the full force of her tainted breath, Tamar could discover very little. But she knew the great secret. People were afraid of her because she was Satan's daughter.

She ran through the grass delighting in its cool caress on her bare feet; she would whisper to the trees: "I am the Devil's daughter. Nothing can hurt me because he looks after me."

She loved the green solitude of the country, and it was her pleasure to collect strange plants and bring them to the old woman to ask what magic properties they contained; but it was the town itself which offered her the greatest delight. She would spend hours lying stretched out on the Hoe, straining her eyes across the sea, trying to picture what lay beyond that line where the sea met the sky. She would stand in the streets, watching the people, listening to their talk; the market delighted her and sometimes there was food to be picked up. There were times when, attracted by her grace and beauty, strangers would throw her a coin. She would watch the men load and unload ships.

There was an ancient seaman who sat on the Hoe with her and told her about his adventures on the Spanish Main. She asked question after question, delighting to listen as he did to talk. They met many times and it seemed to her that he held a new world in his mind to which his voice was the key. But one day when she saw him, he looked away and pretended he did not see her; then she ran to him and tugged his arm. He did not shout at her or curse as he knew so well how to curse; he just turned and would not look at her, gently disengaging himself and hobbling away with his crutch as well as one leg would let him. She knew what had happened; he had discovered who her father was, and he was afraid.

She threw herself down on the grass and sobbed angrily and passionately; but when she saw the old sailor again she stood before him and lifting her flashing eyes to his face, she cursed him. He turned pale and hobbled off. Now she felt triumphant, for she knew he was more afraid of a dark-eyed little girl than the Spanish Inquisition.

One exciting day news came that the Spaniards had landed in Cornwall, that Mousehole was in flames and Penzance under attack.

Tamar watched the ships set out from the Sound to go to the aid of the Cornishmen. They were stimulating days to a child who knew herself to be feared as much as the Spaniards.

August was hot and all through the month Drake and Hawkins were preparing to sail away, and Tamar was there to watch them when they went.

She would never forget the day when the town learned of the death of Drake and Hawkins. Then she saw a city in mourning and longed to be loved as these men had been. It was better to be loved than feared, she felt, for being feared gave you a lonely life.

She listened to people's talk of Drake, for no one talked to her. Her loneliness was becoming more and more marked as she grew older.

Once in the cottage when only her mother and the old woman were there with Tamar, Luce talked of Drake.

"I saw him many times," said Luce, in an unusually talkative mood, no doubt due to the death of the hero. "I remember once...it was in the time of our greatest danger. The whole place was waiting... waiting for the Spaniards. That was in the days when Spaniards *was* Spaniards."

"Yes?" said Tamar eagerly.

"It was like a sort of fever in the place. The Spaniards had big ships, they said, and ours was little 'uns. That didn't matter, though. We had *him*, you see."

"And he was better than anyone else!" cried Tamar.

"They did go to church...him and a great lord. I went to see them...with Betsy. I was different then..." Her eyes filled with tears as she smoothed her rough hands over her rags. "Yes, I were different. I had me hair cut short like a boy's. Hair like mine was a gift from Satan—so Mistress Alton did say."

"A gift from Satan!" cried Tamar, touching her own abundant curls.

"And she cut it off...like a boy's. Betsy's too...though Betsy's weren't what mine was."

"Go on!" begged Tamar.

"We went to the church and *he* were there. I saw him. He came out with the noble lord, and women wept to see him and men threw their caps in the air. 'God speed to you, Sir Francis!' they did shout. And now he be dead. The bonny beauty of him rotting on the sea-bed. I never did think that he would die and I be here."

"Tell me more," said Tamar. "Tell me . . . tell me. . . . Tell me about those days and Mistress Alton."

Tears began to run down Luce's cheeks.

"I thought about him too much. 'Tain't right to have the thoughts I had. 'Tis tempting the Devil. That's what it was. I didn't ask much. . . . I only asked a little."

"That's silly," said Tamar. "You must ask for a lot. I shall."

Luce turned to her daughter. "You must not go out at night. You must stay in. I wouldn't like what happened to me to happen to you. Be careful. I wouldn't like you to be caught too young."

Tamar's eyes flashed. "I'd have none of that."

"You don't know what you do say, child. 'Tis something that none of us know about until too late."

"I should know."

"Be careful. It can happen sudden like, and then there's the rest of your life" — she looked down at her garments — "the rest of your life in tatters and rags. You'm caught, and it can happen sudden-like."

"Not to me!" declared Tamar. "There is nobody clever enough to catch me!"

*   *   *

Once more big ships were in the harbour. Drake was no more; Hawkins had gone; but there were other West Country men waiting to step into the shoes of these men. One of these was Sir Walter Raleigh and people were talking of him now as Drake's Heir. All through the spring, while Plymouth mourned Drake, the fleet was assembling in the Sound. Lord Howard was there and this was yet another great occasion. But the change in the times was obvious to all. Men were no longer flocking to serve in the ships, and Raleigh brought strangers to Plymouth — men who did not speak with the soft Devon burr — sullen strangers who had been pressed into service.

The people murmured. It had not been thus in the days of Drake, who had had to refuse men the honour of sailing with him. What a tragic change this was — when men deserting from their ships were hanged on the Hoe as an example to others of like mind.

It was a day in June. The fleet was ready to sail and Tamar was on the Hoe to watch its departure when close to her she noticed a boy who was so much older than she was that he seemed a man. She knew him for Bartle Cavill, the son of Sir Humphrey. He was thirteen years old, tall, with eyes as blue as the sea, and a shock of yellow hair. She noticed how he gazed at the ships with yearning in his eyes; and understanding that feeling — which was hers also — she moved nearer to him.

She saw that his breeches were puffed and ornamented with mulberry-coloured silk, and she loved its colour and softness. She had to touch the silk to feel if it were as soft as it looked, so she stretched out a hand and felt it. Yes, it was even softer than it looked. There were bars of different colours. Was the green as soft as the mulberry? She had to test it.

But he had become aware of her hands upon him; swift as lightning he caught her by the arm.

"Thief!" he cried. "So I've caught you, thief!"

She lifted her great dark eyes to his face, and said shyly: "I was only feeling the silk."

The blue eyes seemed more brilliant than the sea itself.

"You're hurting me," she said.

"That is my intention!" he retorted. "You'll know what it means to be hurt when they hang you for stealing."

"I stole nothing."

"I'll have you searched. Stand away. Don't dare come close to me, you dirty beggar! What insolence!"

"I'm not a beggar, and I'm not a thief. It is you who should be afraid of me."

"I'll have those rags stripped off you and searched. I'll see you're whipped before they hang you. I'll ask it as a special favour to myself."

She had twisted her arm suddenly and freed herself, but he caught her by her hair.

"See that man hanging there?" he demanded. "He deserted his ship. That's what happens to dirty beggars who steal from their betters."

"I have no betters," she said with dignity while she screwed up her face in pain, for he seemed to be pulling her hair out by the roots.

62

His eyes blazed with rage. "Insolence! You'll be sorry for this."

"You're the one who'll be sorry. You don't know who I am."

He looked into her face and laughed. "So it's you . . . the Devil's own, eh!"

She was shaken, for she saw no fear in his face.

"Now do you know who *I* am?" he asked.

"Yes, I do."

"Then you know I use no idle words. I'll have you whipped for your insolence."

"You wouldn't dare. No one would dare. I . . . I'd. . . ." She glared at him. "It would be the worse for you if you hurt me."

He let her go and she ran, and, turning round, saw that he had not moved, but was standing still watching her.

She walked on with slow dignity, but as soon as she felt he could see her no more she broke into a run. She was trembling with fear and hatred, because she was not sure whether or not he had been afraid of her.

* * *

Soon after that she heard that Bartle Cavill had run away to sea, and she was relieved. Afterwards life went on as usual. She was growing up; she was now ten years old.

There seemed less excitement in the town nowadays. King Philip had been dead for a year, and there no longer seemed any great danger of raids on the coast. Just before his death it had been brought home to the King that he would never realise his ambitions. Plymouth had not even seen the ships of his Adelantado, which had come to invade, for a kindly storm had wrecked them in the Bay of Biscay. Such a disaster to ships — as grand and formidable as those of his great Armada — meant the end of his attempt to subdue England. But on the high seas rivalry continued.

Somewhere out there, Tamar sometimes thought, was Bartle Cavill. Perhaps he had left his ship by now and was storming some city; perhaps he was cutting his way through the jungle; perhaps he was being tortured in a dungeon. All of these things might have happened to him. She thought of him with great hatred, not so much for the words he had used to her but for the contempt he had shown her in his brilliant blue eyes.

Her lonely life continued. No children played with her, but she did not wish to play their games. She was learning a good deal from Granny Lackwell, and when people came to the cottage for herbs, Granny would say: "The child will pick them for you. The child knows."

Then Tamar would enjoy afresh that strange power which was hers.

But one day she learned that people hated her because they feared her. The most terrifying experience of her life so far was awaiting her.

It was dusk of an evening in summer and she was walking to a favourite haunt of hers — a shady spot with many trees which overhung a large pond. She often came here; she liked to sit by the pond and watch the birds and insects; she had learned to imitate the calls of the birds so that they answered her; and she liked to watch the ants in the long grass and the spiders in their webs. Sometimes she would dabble her feet in the water. It was a pleasant spot for a hot day such as this had been.

But as she came under the trees she heard a sudden whoop above her, and several small figures — some smaller than herself — dropped from the trees. The children of the neighbourhood were upon her.

She was felled to the ground at once, and although she kicked fiercely and tried to free herself, they were too many for her — and some were quite big boys. While they had her on the ground they blindfolded her by tying a piece of rag about her eyes, and she knew then that they were afraid that she would recognise them. She exulted in that because it showed that they were afraid of her.

"Let me go!" she cried. "I'll curse you. You'll be sorry. I know who you are. I don't have to see you."

They said nothing. One of them kicked her; another punched her back. She felt sick and faint, for although she had often witnessed physical violence she had never before experienced it.

She kicked and screamed, calling: "You'll be sorry. I know you. I know you all."

Still her tormentors did not speak. They forced her to sit on the grass, and when they seized her hands and tied them to her ankles she knew what they planned to do to her.

Many hands touched her, scratching her, tearing her skin. She expected some power to come to her aid, but she had nothing . . . nothing but the strength of a ten-year-old girl to use against them.

A great shout went up from their throats and she felt herself thrown; the waters of the muddy pond splashed about her and she was sitting on its weedy bottom. They had not been able to throw her very far in, and she was only waist-high in the water.

The children on the edge of the pond forgot that she must not hear their voices and they began to shriek:

"She's sinking."

"She's *not*!"

"She'll float all right. She's the Devil's own daughter. He do look after his own."

One of the boys jabbed at her with a long branch of a tree; the skin of her leg was torn as he tried to push her farther out. She was past feeling pain, for she believed she was going to die, since, trussed as she was, she could do nothing to help herself, and the rag about her eyes — now wet and most foul smelling — prevented her from seeing about her.

The shouts went on.

"She's a witch all right."

Someone threw a stone at her. It missed and splashed into the water. More stones came and some of them hit her. She felt herself sinking into the mud. She was half fainting, yet her anger and her belief in herself kept her from doing so. To faint would be to drown, unless the children became frightened and pulled her out. But they would not be frightened, for there was no one to care if she was drowned. Old Granny might care; but the old woman was near death and hardly counted. Her mother? Perhaps she would be a little sorry, but mostly relieved; she would not have to watch her as she did now, waiting for some outward sign of the devil in her daughter. Everyone else would be glad. So there was no one at all who would be really sorry.

And as she gasped and spluttered, she was suddenly aware of silence. The children had stopped shouting.

Then a voice said: "You . . . you . . . and you there, go in and bring the girl out."

She was seized and pulled to the bank. She lay there gasping.

"Take that rag from her eyes and untie her wrists."

Black spots were dancing before her eyes now. The darkening sky seemed to sway above her.

A cultured voice said: "It's the Lackwell girl."

Then Tamar turned over and was violently sick. She groaned and tried to stand up. She saw that the children had scattered but that the man remained. She knew him for Richard Merriman, who lived in the big house.

"You're all right," he said. "Those young devils might have drowned you. Keep out of their way in future."

She heard herself stammer: "They were afraid of me. They had to bind my eyes."

She tottered towards him and he caught her as she almost fell. She was quick enough to see the disgust he felt at her nearness, and she was aware immediately of her verminous rags in contrast with his exquisite garments. With dignity she drew herself away from him.

"Thank you for making them pull me out," she said, and began to totter away.

"Here, child!" he called after her.

But she would not look back.

"What the devil!" he shouted.

The tears were running down her cheeks. She had been deeply insulted, first by the children and then by him; she was not going to let anyone see her tears.

She limped back to the cottage and Granny did her best to comfort her. Granny hobbled from her chair to make some special brew.

"There," muttered the old woman. "You'm doing well. 'Twas your first ducking and you stood up well to it."

When Tamar retired behind her ring of stones, she did not feel the pain of her limbs and the soreness of her wounds. She could only think of the man in the elegant clothes who had been disgusted to have her near him.

*   *   *

She thought of Richard Merriman a good deal after that. But for him she might have died, for they would have stoned her to death or left her to drown, as they often did stray cats and dogs; she was no more to them than an unwanted animal. Yet they were afraid of her, and that was why they hated her. Perhaps it was not such a good thing to be feared? How much better to be loved!

She must not be angry with Richard Merriman, though, for he had saved her. He could not help it if she disgusted him. She remembered how she had disgusted Bartle Cavill and her eyes blazed with hatred at the thought of him. I hope the Spaniards get him! she thought. I hope they brand him with hot irons and burn him for his faith.

She looked about her, waiting for the earth to open and the Devil to appear, waiting for some animal to come to her and speak with a human voice, and demand her eternal soul in exchange for what she asked. Nothing happened.

"No!" she whispered. "I don't want the Spaniards to get him, for he would never deny his faith and they would burn him alive and I would never seen him again." And she wanted to see him again, so that she could show him in some way how she hated him.

As for the other man, Richard Merriman, she must show her gratitude to him, since he had saved her life. The daughter of Satan must acknowledge her debts.

There was a spot on the cliffs where it was said that it was possible to find seagulls' eggs, although it was rarely anyone went in search of them as the climb was dangerous and the slate and shale cliffs offered scarcely any footing; but the eggs would be all the more appreciated if they were hard to get.

She grew excited at the project. When she took the eggs to him, she would say very haughtily: "You do

69

not like the smell of me, sir, but perhaps you will like the taste of these. They are for you because you saved my life."

The sun was high in the sky when she set out. As she walked to the lonely spot, she kept clear of all trees, for she would never again walk unwarily under trees; she kept turning to make sure she was not being followed. The climb was long and steep, and several times she nearly lost her footing; the birds whirled about her head — gulls and cormorants — shrieking, screaming at her as though indignant at her intrusion. But she was not afraid of the birds.

She pulled her way up, hanging onto the tufts of coarse ling, cutting her feet on jagged rock, scratching her legs on the gorse; once or twice she almost fell, but she went on triumphantly.

Looking down at the rocks below, it occurred to her that if she fell it would be to death; but that was how she would have it, for he had saved her life, and she wished to risk it again in making her thank-offering.

The wind tugged at her thick hair. It was as verminous as her rags, and she hated it to be so; she longed for a gown with puffed sleeves and a skirt cut away to show a splendid undergown. But one thing she had learned from her ducking was that although her clothes smelt of the mud of the pond, many of the lice attached to them had lost their lives in the water. If she dipped her clothes in a clear stream, and her hair too, she might leave some more of the irritating creatures behind; and a clear stream would not leave a smell upon her and her garments as the pond had.

She knew of such a stream; it was in the grounds surrounding none other than the house of Richard Merriman himself. Before she took the eggs to him she would wash her hair and her clothes in the stream.

Such thoughts made her laugh out loud. He would see the change in her. In her imagination the dip in the stream would do more than rid her rags of their pests; it would transform them into silks and velvets.

She went on with vigour, eager to be done with the difficult task and get to the easier and more pleasant one of cleaning herself and her garments in the stream. She clutched at a clump of ling which came away in her hand, but she was able to save herself just in time, though in doing so she scratched her arm badly and it started to bleed.

But she did not care, since she had found her first seagulls' eggs.

Getting down took far longer than the ascent, as now she had the eggs to consider, and she could not have borne the disappointment if she had broken them. She had tied each one separately and skilfully into her rags, for she needed all the help her hands could give her. Gingerly she came, the soft curls at her forehead damp with the sweat of her exertion; and dirty and dishevelled, she eventually reached the grounds about Richard Merriman's house.

The stream at this point was about six feet wide and someone — long ago — had put stepping-stones across it. It was sheltered by trees and shrubs; the grass grew long with weeds and wild flowers between, for Joseph Jubin, at his master's orders, had left this part of the grounds uncultivated.

Delighted to find that only one of the eggs was cracked, very carefully she placed them on the grass while she took off her rags. When she dipped them into the stream the colour of the water changed to a dark brown, and she laughed in quiet pleasure to watch.

She spread them out in the sun, and, cautiously tiptoeing into the stream, she dipped her hair in the water. The cold water took her breath away. She sat down in the stream and rubbed the dirt off her body. Washing seemed a more daring operation than climbing steep cliffs in search of seagulls' eggs.

Stretching herself in the sunshine, waiting for her rags to dry, she thought how pleasant it was to be naked, for thus she would look the same as everyone else. Mistress Alton would look no better, stripped of her good clothes; nor would the wife of Sir Humphrey Cavill, that fine lady who was Bartle's mother!

Her damp hair fell to her waist and she spread it round her to make it dry more easily while she sat hugging her knees, thinking how pleased he would be with the eggs, which must surely be a delicacy even for him. And as she sat there her eyes caught the pale crimson of the betony flower and with a little cry of delight she leaned forward to pick it. He should have that flower, for it would keep evil away from his house.

Neither her rags nor her hair were quite dry, but no matter, she was all impatience now to take him his gift and could wait no longer. She went swiftly towards the house, looking up in admiration at its gabled and diamond-paned windows. It was the most beautiful house she had ever seen; it seemed more beautiful than Sir Humphrey's over at Stoke, because she could never get near enough to Sir Humphrey's to see it as clearly as she could see this. There were big dogs at Cavill House that snarled and snapped and pulled at their chains; and the servants would have no hesitation in turning them loose on anyone like herself who went too close.

She laid the eggs outside the door and put the crimson flower on top of them. Then she lifted the great knocker and let it fall. She heard the sound echoing through the hall and stood there waiting, in spite of her natural boldness, with a quaking heart.

The door opened, but it was not he who opened it; it was a young girl with short hair — cut like a boy's; and she was wearing what seemed to Tamar a very fine gown.

The girl stared at her in dismay. She looked at the eggs on the doorstep and whitened as though Tamar were an emissary from the Devil, which she probably thought the child was.

"What do you want?" asked the girl nervously.

"Your master," answered Tamar boldly.

"You . . . you want to see . . . the master?"

Tamar drew herself up with dignity. "Tell him to come here," she said.

But now Mistress Alton had come to the door. "What's this? What's this?"

The cane and the keys at her waist swung out, and Tamar was aware of them while she kept her eyes on the woman's face.

"I want your master," said Tamar.

"You want...what?"

"The master. I got something for him."

Mistress Alton's lips tightened. "I never heard the like! The impertinence. It's that black-eyed daughter of a black-eyed witch! You get out of here and take your filth with you." Her hands reached for her cane.

"I've come to see your master. You'll be sorry if you hurt me."

"You can strike me dead," said Mistress Alton, "but I'll not have you set your evil feet in this house. What's all this mess on my doorstep?"

" 'Tis no mess," said Tamar firmly. " 'Tis what I've brought for your master."

"You've brought... *what* for the master?"

"Seagulls' eggs and a flower for luck. I got them myself. Look! I climbed high for them."

"Take those things away."

"I won't. They're for him."

Mistress Alton's face grew red with rage and before Tamar realized what she was about to do, she had stepped forward and stamped on the eggs.

Tamar stared down at the havoc and let out a little cry of anguish; then she rushed at the woman and, catching her skirts in both hands, kicked her.

74

"Help! Help!" cried Mistress Alton. "I'm set upon. You Moll . . . don't stand there gaping. Get someone quick. My dear life, don't you see the witch is trying to do me some harm?"

At this point Richard Merriman came into the hall, his eyebrows lifted, his eyes puzzled. Tamar released the woman and looked at him through her tangled locks.

"What does this mean?" he asked coldly.

"This . . . witch . . . came here to harm you . . . to harm us all!" cried the housekeeper.

"What a small witch!" he said.

"She was putting eggs on the doorstep. It was a spell, that's what it was. I know their wicked ways."

He had approached to look at the eggs.

Tamar cried out shrilly: "They were seagulls' eggs. I got them for you. It was because you saved me. I went high for them. And the flower was for good luck. It will keep evil away from your house."

"Ah," he said. "You're Luce's girl. What is your name?"

"Tamar."

"A good name," he said; he was smiling. "It was good of you to bring the eggs. I thank you."

"But they are broken. She stamped on them."

"I thank you all the same."

She picked up the flower.

"This is for you too. It will keep evil away."

He took it. "So you pay your debts, then?" he said. And he continued to look at her. Then he seemed to rouse himself from his thoughts; he was haughty and dignified again. "Take her into the house and give her some food," he said. "Give her some clothes too."

"I can't have those rags in the house, sir," declared Mistress Alton. "She should strip outside and put on what I can give her there."

He shrugged his shoulders. "See that she has all she wants to eat."

Tamar lifted her eyes to his face; she was completely fascinated by his clothes, his voice and his manners.

He looked at her again. He said: "Yes, it was good of you to think of bringing me the eggs. Come to the house when you are hungry. Mistress Alton will always give you food when you need it."

He continued to look at her while a faint smile touched his mouth. Then he turned and went away.

"Don't dare set foot in this house," said Mistress Alton. "Don't dare bring your bugs in here. Go round to the back and I'll throw something out to you. You take those rags away with you when you go."

And so, Tamar, as her mother had done when she first came to the house, stripped outside and put on the clothes which were given her. She was a new Tamar now; the clothes were too big for her, but that did not matter, for they were fine good clothes.

Then she was allowed to sit on a stool outside the back door when Moll handed her a bowl of soup.

She had never before had such a glorious adventure, and all the time she ate, occasionally letting her hands stroke the rough worsted of her gown, she thought of Richard Merriman, of his beautiful voice and his rich clothes; and then it seemed to her that he had looked at her in an odd fashion, as though he, like others, realized that there was something strange about her.

*　　*　　*

Tamar was just past fourteen when Simon Carter the witch-pricker came to Plymouth.

The old Queen had been dead a year now and a new King had come from Scotland to rule the English and the Scots. Tamar knew this because she never lost an opportunity of listening to the gossip in the streets. She would stand close to men talking outside taverns; she would lie on the Hoe where the seamen gathered, and listen to their talk, keeping her face turned away so that they might not recognise her for the Devil's daughter.

She learned that it was a good thing that they had this James to rule them, for now that the two countries were united under him there would be no more trouble between them. He was a learned man — people were beginning to call him the British Solomon — and, being a fervent believer in the powers of witchcraft, he had determined to do all he could to drive it from his realm.

There were many witches in Scotland, it seemed, as well as in the North of England — far more than there were in the South — and on the continent of Europe there were more than in England and Scotland together. Witches had had an easy time in England compared with their lot in other countries. In their allegiance to the Devil, they denied the Holy Church of Rome and were considered heretics, the greatest criminals of the day. In Catholic countries there was one death only for heretics — the faggots to follow torture.

Tamar heard terrible stories of what happened to witches in other countries and she was glad of that shining strip of Channel which separated her native land from them.

The new King, it appeared, had undeniable evidence of bold witches who had dared work against his own person and that of his Queen. These witches had all but succeeded in drowning Queen Anne when she had set out from Denmark for her marriage to the Scottish King. Twice the Queen had attempted the journey and, just as she was within a few miles of the Scottish coast, a tempest had arisen and blown her squadrons on to the coast of Norway. When the disaster had been repeated, one of her captains admitted having taken on his ship a man who had a witch for a wife; and when a third attempt to reach Scotland was frustrated, there was no doubt in the minds of many that they were the victims of witchcraft.

The witch-wife of the sailor was burned alive with many of her companions, and when the King of Scotland himself set out across the sea to fetch his bride to her new home, his ship was all but wrecked off the coast of Norway.

Convinced that these tempestuous voyages, which had almost resulted in the death by drowning of himself and his Queen, had been the Devil's work, the

King had started an enquiry into the matter as soon as his marriage had been celebrated on Scottish soil. Many well-known witches were seized and under torture confessed to what they had done.

They had baptized a cat, making mock of one of the holy ceremonies of the Church; and then they had stolen parts of the bodies of dead men, and these they had attached to the cat's legs. With the cat they had gone to the end of Leith pier, from where they had thrown the cat into the sea.

The cat had been a strong swimmer and had reached land in spite of its handicaps. The witches declared that this had told them that the new Queen would make port safely. The witches explained that the great Earl of Bothwell had been in communication with them; and it was rumoured that he attended their Sabbats, dressed as the Devil, and that he put on the power of the Evil One with his accoutrements.

The Scottish witches were strangled, and burned till there was nothing left of them but ashes.

This had happened more than ten years ago, and now this King with his wife and family had gone to London.

There were others besides witches to flout the authority of the State. The Puritans, Separatists and Brownists were now continually talked of. Tamar heard terrible stories of the ills these people suffered and had been suffering for years.

Persecution was rife throughout the land; not the hideous bloody persecution which had caused the name of Queen Mary to be spoken with shuddering contempt; but persecution all the same. In Plymouth men had been seized, torn from their families and thrust into prison because they had failed to attend the established church and wished to worship God in their own way. The prisons of London and most other cities were full of such men; they were left to starve in the pits and little eases of those prisons; they were set upon with cudgels and beaten almost to death; some were hanged.

Tamar, at fourteen, was budding into rare beauty, and although she was completely unlettered, her intelligence was fine and quick. She wished, therefore, to know of these matters of religion; and she was saddened because, being suspected of connection with witches, she was hardly ever spoken to.

She knew something of witchcraft, for she had been an eager pupil of Granny Lackwell, who still sat on her stool in the cottage; Granny was getting old now and at times she would sink into a stupor and so remain for hours at a time; she would talk incoherently of flying through the air on a broomstick, of her conversations with Toby, her familiar, and a man in black who, she professed, came to visit her. Tamar had never witnessed any of these visits, and she was inclined to believe that Granny Lackwell was not right in her head.

Bartle was back from his sea voyage — a young man of twenty — tall and strong and very proud of a scar he bore on his cheek. His skin was tanned a light shade of brown which made his blue eyes quite startling. Tamar heard that he was such another as his father and that all the maidens of the town and the surrounding villages were ready to come when he beckoned. It was said that there would be many a child with the Cavill blue eyes roaming the streets and lanes in a year or two.

Once Tamar met him on the Hoe. His lips curled in recognition as she ran past him.

And now. . . Simon Carter the witch-pricker had come to Plymouth. Soberly dressed as became his solemn mission, he carried a Bible in his hand; and with him came a group of men to help in his work.

He stood in the square and told the people of the great work he was doing for God and the King. The country was suffering from witches. He could recognise a witch when he saw one, merely by looking at her; but he believed in justice, so he condemned none before they had been put through the test.

"If any of ye know a witch, do not hold back that knowledge. And if any of ye have suspicions that your neighbour traffics with the Devil, then come forth and name them."

Tamar stood on the edge of the crowd, alert, ready to run if any should look her way.

Simon Carter was a man who knew how to talk to simple people.

God, he explained, was all-powerful, but there was one — turned out from Heaven — who under God was greater than any. Goodness must prevail, because God was the greatest power in the world; but evil unchecked could do great harm. Nor was God one to save from witches those who by their own folly — and

he was not sure that he should not say wickedness —
abstained from denouncing these creatures. For to
give oneself to the Devil was to work against God.
They were all God's servants, were they not? Then let
them show it by giving the information he sought.

"Good people, have your crops ever failed you and
you wondered why? Have your animals died of strange
sickness? Have you ever been taken with fits and
vomiting and strange sickness? You have! Then, my
friends, you may take my word for it, you have been
the victims of a witch's spleen. Think, men and
women . . . think of those who live around you. Have
any of them ever done strange things? Have you seen
animals slink into their houses? Have you seen them
collecting strange herbs and brewing odd
concoctions? Have you ever seen or heard them
muttering to themselves? Have you seen them going
into the country at dark of moon? Come! As you
would serve your King, as you value your health, your
good living and that of your little ones . . . come and
tell me of those who lead dark lives among you."

Tamar slipped away from the crowd. The streets
were deserted. It seemed that everyone was in the
square. She knew that she was in danger. The old
woman was in danger, and if they tortured her she
would say those queer, incoherent things which she
had said to Tamar. There was nothing she could do,
for how could she take the old woman and hide her? It
would be impossible to move her from the cottage.

She did not go back to the cottage, but lay
stretched out on the grass, looking at the sea, trying to

think clearly, to make some plan to save herself and the old woman.

But the desire to know what was happening in the town was too strong to be resisted, and she went back.

Already Simon Carter had six women gathered together in the Town Hall.

He talked continually.

"Witchcraft, my good friends, is more often found in women than in men. The incubus and the succubus and any devil of Satan's kingdom loves best the women. For women are weak creatures, more given to wickedness than men. They lack the brighter intellect which God has given men; they are more easily persuaded to wickedness. Strip the women of their clothes. My good friends, we will now search for the Devil's mark. He stamps them with it to mark them his forever. He will often put it in the most secret places of the body, so that it is necessary for us to search most diligently."

One woman was protesting; she was young and not uncomely. But one of Simon Carter's men had pinioned her, while another tore her garments from her.

"And what," continued Simon Carter, taking the woman nearest him and forcing her on to her knees while he jerked her face roughly upwards and pulled at her nostrils to peer up them, "and what, my innocent friends, do these creatures do besides the evil tricks they play on you? They wallow in filth, my friends. They entertain strange creatures in their beds. There is the succubus who visits men and draws from them the seed of life; this they pass on to the incubus who visits these women and plants in them the seed contaminated by devils." He pushed the woman to the ground. "Come, woman, don't be shy. Let your evil mind believe that I am the toad you welcome to your bed . . . the devil who comes to pleasure you . . ."

He gave a shout of triumph, for he had found what he called the Devil's Mark. It was behind the woman's knee in the hollow where the leg and thigh join. He chuckled with glee. Each witch he brought to the gallows meant fifteen shillings in his pocket.

"Now, dear people, you shall see how I prick her. She won't bleed, this one, for she has the witches' mark on her. How do I know? Because, men and women, the divine power has been given me. I see a witch; I prick her for the sake of justice. But I know a witch when I see one. Oh, my brothers and sisters of this fair city, you will rejoice in remembering the day that Simon Carter came among you to rid your town of this curse."

He dug a pin into the wart.

"No blood!" he cried. "This is devil's work. If I prick any godly member of this city with a pin, what happens? The blood will spurt. But prick a witch and all the Devil's help cannot save her. She will not bleed, because she is of the devil, and her flesh and blood obey not the rules laid down by God. This witch shall hang on that fair stretch of green which overlooks the sea. Ye shall watch her carcass rot, and then, dear friends, when you have seen how justice can be done, you will bring more and more witches to me."

Tamar could bear no more. She had listened to the horrible obscenities of the lookers-on. She was bewildered, for the name which had been called on more than any other had been that of God.

Nobody noticed Tamar; everybody's eyes were on the naked women; they could only gloat while the searchers handled their victims, crudely exposing them to the eyes of the watchers while they muttered words of righteousness.

Tamar fled and did not stop running until she reached the cottage. Her mother was there with several of her half-brothers and sisters; she ignored them and went to the old woman.

"Granny! Granny!" she cried. "The witch-pricker is in the town. You must make a spell quickly. You must not let him come here . . . or he'll get you . . . he'll get me!"

The old woman was taken with great trembling; her jaw fell and her eyes closed; she sagged on her stool.

The others took no notice.

*   *   *

A few days later the witch-pricker came to the cottage with two of his men. A crowd from the town followed them.

Tamar heard them coming and made for the door, but she was too late; she could not run away without being seen, and she knew that to attempt to do so would call attention to herself.

Both Luce and Bill Lackwell were in the cottage with three of the children.

Simon Carter threw open the door and stood looking in.

"Ah!" he said, looking straight at Granny. "There sits a witch! 'Twouldn't be necessary to look for the mark on her. Never saw I a witch who was more clearly a witch."

Tamar in her corner, surrounded by her stones which she knew would have no power to protect her now, stared at Granny.

The old woman had recovered a little in the last few days; she had been able to open her eyes, but not to speak. The right side of her face was drawn down and she could not move her right arm or leg. Poor Granny! It was small wonder that Simon Carter was so sure she was a witch.

The two men seized her and pulled her off her stool. She fell forward, a dead weight in their arms.

"She's dead," said one of the men; and it was true.

They let her body slip to the floor.

"It's a trick!" cried Simon. "She's called the aid of her familiar. Take that cat and wring its neck. There's devilry in this place. I can feel it, I can smell it. The Devil is right here . . . close to us, good people. Keep your thoughts holy. Say the Lord's Prayer. That will drive him away quicker than anything. Now we must make sure this woman is dead, for witches play tricks, friends."

They pulled open her rags and felt for poor Granny's heart.

Tamar could not take her eyes from Simon Carter. His mouth was a straight line; his eyes glinted like points of light beneath his bushy brows which almost hid them. He was very angry. A dead witch meant a loss of good money and he had made the journey for nothing.

"Good people," he said, "the Devil has taken this woman. It has pleased him to cheat us of justice." He turned his eyes on Luce, who was cowering against the wall. He continued to stare at her.

Someone in the crowd peering in at the door began to whisper.

"Didn't Luce Lackwell . . . you remember . . . Wasn't it said . . . ?"

Simon Carter, his ears as sharp as his eyes for the hunting of a witch, had swung round.

"What was that, dear friend? The woman there . . ."

A woman was pushed forward. "Well, 'twas said . . . I couldn't swear to the truth of it . . . but 'twas said . . ."

"Come. Speak up, woman dear," begged Simon. "Remember your duty to God and your country."

" 'Twas the woman Luce Lackwell . . ." She pointed at Luce. " 'Twas said she were took by the Devil . . ."

Simon had turned to Luce, his mouth curved in a hopeful leer.

"This woman?" He lifted Luce's hair from her face and peered into her eyes. "You cannot hide it from me. I have seen it in your eyes. There is the guilt. So 'twas you, woman, witch woman, who raised the spell that sent yon older witch to the Devil her master? Come, my men, search for the mark. I'll warrant you we'll find it in some secret place, for she is a woman of secrets, this one."

Luce screamed as they tore off her clothes. In a few seconds they had her naked before them.

Tamar could not bear this. She had to get out of the cottage — not so much because escape was imperative to her safety, but because she could not bear to watch her mother's shame.

She sidled to the door, and so intent was the crowd on watching Luce and the prickers that they did not notice who she was or what she was doing until she had broken through them.

Someone said then: "That's the girl . . . the result of her mother's evil union. Don't let her go. She should have the test."

Tamar ran as fast as she could; the thud of footsteps behind her terrified her, but she was fleeter than any of them and no one had any intention of missing the sight to be seen in the cottage.

At length it seemed that Tamar was free of them. The sun beat down on her and she felt sick and faint, gasping as she was to regain her breath. She did not know where to go until she remembered the stream which was in Richard Merriman's private grounds. She thought of this man now in her extreme need. Not that he had taken very much notice of her when he had seen her; but there had been something in his look which made it different from the looks he bestowed on other children of the place. A faint curving of the lips which might have been a smile. She had often been to his house and received food and clothes, and she guessed that Mistress Alton would not have given those to her if she had not been afraid of offending her master by refraining from so doing. She felt that this gentleman was in some way her friend, so she would hide herself on his land while she thought of something she might do.

She lay down by the stream, cupping the water in her hands and splashing it over her heated face. She listened for the slightest sound, but all was quiet, and when it began to grow dark she hid herself among the bushes and slept.

She awoke at dawn and her longing for food was almost more than she could bear. Wild plans for returning to the cottage came to her, but with them came also the memory of those men who had done shameful things to her mother; she saw the lustful faces of the watchers.

She could not go back to the cottage. Then a wild idea came to her.

There were occasions on summer days when Richard Merriman walked in his garden. This was usually in the late afternoon. Once she had climbed the big oak tree against which she now leaned and she had seen him; after that she had often looked for him and seen him — always at the same hour.

If he came to-day, could she go and ask him to help her? He had saved her life when the children had thrown her into the pond, so perhaps now he would help her to escape from the pricker. Of course it might be that he would hand her to those men, but she did not think so; he hated unpleasantness, and those men, and what they did to women, were unpleasant. She was desperate, for she could not stay here without food much longer, and she could think of no one else whose help she could ask.

How much happier she felt now that she had a plan! First she would wash herself and her garments, for if she were going to ask such a favour of him it would not do to offend him by her smell.

She looked at the sky and guessed that by the time her clothes were dry it would also be the time for him to take his walk. She took off her gown — she wore nothing beneath it — and tried to rub it clean in the stream. It was not very satisfactory, but was the best she could do. She spread it out on the grass and washed herself.

She lay in the sun, her wet hair spread around her, and thought of what she would say to him. Perhaps she would hide behind the bushes in his garden and call to him and, when he was close, whisper: "I am in danger. The witch-pricker is after me. You saved me once. Will you save me again?"

She was sure he could hide her if he wished to, because he was more powerful than anyone she knew; and she believed that he would help her because of the way his lips curled when he glanced at her.

And sitting there, ruminating, she did not hear footsteps approaching until it was too late; then turning she saw, with a horror that numbed her, that between her and her gown spread out on the grass stood Bartle Cavill.

She felt her heart stop and go racing on. There was something in his look which horrified her even as she had been horrified when those men had laid their hands on her mother. Lust had shown in the faces of those men who had looked on her mother's nakedness; the same lust was looking out of those dazzling blue eyes now.

"Well met!" said Bartle with a mocking bow.

She did not move; she tried to cower behind the covering of her hair.

He took a step towards her, the lust deepening in his eyes.

"I have just visited my neighbour — rather a prosy bore. I did not know that such a charming encounter awaited me."

"Keep away!" she said.

"That I declare I won't. It's Tamar, is it not? The witch's girl! By God, you are a beauty without your rags, Tamar."

"Stay where you are . . . or I will put a spell on you."

"If you have such powers, why are you so scared, Tamar?"

He caught her arm and she tried to spring up; but he pulled her down and they rolled over and over on the grass. He was panting and laughing.

"You were waiting for me!" he said. "Yes, you slut, you were. I declare! What immodesty! You trespassed on Merriman's land. Do you know you could be hanged for that?" He tried to kiss her, but she was wriggling madly. "Damn me, if I won't have you hanged for trespass. But no! You waited for me. That was a pretty thing to do. And you took your clothes off. Really, Tamar, it was no use trying to hide yourself with all this beautiful hair . . . You have been a most immodest creature . . ." He yelled suddenly, for she had dug her teeth into his hand. "So you would bite me, eh? It will be the worse for you if you try those tricks . . ."

She spat out his blood.

"I hate you . . . I hate . . ."

"Keep still, you little Devil's imp. Keep still."

With all her strength she kicked him wildly, but the kick went home; she scratched his face and, seizing his nose, she twisted it as though she would wrench it off.

He cursed her, but momentarily she had the advantage, for her violence had had the effect of making him loosen his hold of her. She was up. He caught her ankle, but she swung herself free. Her chance had come. She picked up her gown and sped across the grass in the direction of the cultivated gardens. She had had a good start and she reached them first. Relief filled her heart then, for there, examining his shrubs, was Richard Merriman.

Panting, she threw herself against him.

"Save me!" she cried. "Save me!"

Bartle had pulled up and stood still, breathing heavily and looking like an angry and frustrated bull, while Tamar buried her face in Richard's coat.

"What the devil's this?" began Richard. But there was no need of explanations. One look at Bartle was sufficient to see what he was after, and the child was none other than Luce Lackwell's girl, for whom the witch-pricker was making a search.

"Don't let him...get me..." panted Tamar. "Don't let him...please...Hide me."

"Why have you come back, Bartle?" said Richard, trying to gain time, wondering what he was going to do with the child.

"I found her on your ground...trespassing, the young devil! She was lying naked on the grass. She saw me come here and she knew I'd go back that way. She was waiting for me."

"I wonder why she took such pains to wait for you and then run away?" said Richard lightly.

"He lies!" cried Tamar.

"Put your gown on, girl," said Richard; and he put her from him.

She blushed and stood behind him while she put on the damp gown.

"Pray, sir," said Bartle with an attempt at a swagger, "there is no need for you to look so shocked. I doubt if I'd have been the first."

"You lie!" flashed Tamar.

"The girl repulsed you—that much is evident," said Richard. "I wish you would not bring your buccaneering manners into my gardens."

"It was just a bit of sport," said Bartle sullenly.

"And after you had had your sport, I suppose you would have handed her over to the witch-pricker."

"Good God, no! I should naturally have hidden her."

"Providing she had been your willing slave! That was your noble plan, I doubt not."

"Oh, she would have been well enough. If she is a virgin, as she protests she is, that state would not have lasted long. And why should not I have been the first?"

Richard looked down at Tamar. "Do not tremble so," he said.

"Give her to me, sir," said Bartle. "I swear I'll hide her. I'll put her somewhere where she can't be found till Simon Carter has gone."

"*No!*" cried Tamar.

"She seems to be as much afraid of you as of Simon Carter. You have been guilty of most discourteous and ungentlemanly behaviour."

"Damme, sir, the girl would have been all right. A little reluctance at first is natural. Many's the time I've found it so, and then it's all hell let loose to turn them off."

"I repeat that you have been unmannerly. Would you like a chance to mend your ways? You know how distasteful to me is the violence of low-born creatures such as this man Carter. Moreover, this one is only a child. I do not think she should be handed over to the pricker."

"I have no wish to hand her over." His mouth curled as he gazed on Tamar's flushed face. "I can think of more pleasant ways for dealing with such a little beauty."

"Don't be afraid," said Richard, looking down at Tamar. "He is a strutting coxcomb who has recently discovered that he is a man and yearns to prove it on every conceivable occasion. Let's forgive him, for now we need his help. Go to the front door, Bartle, engage Alton in conversation and see that you keep her so engaged while I slip up the back staircase with the girl."

"With all my heart, sir."

"And in five minutes come to my study."

Bartle swaggered off, but not before he had thrown a sly glance at Tamar which seemed to say, "You have not seen the last of me!"

"Now," said Richard, looking down at her, "do not speak. Walk behind me, try to make sure you are hidden. Let us hope none from the house has seen this pretty scene from a window."

She followed him to a door at the back. He looked inside, turned and nodded; then swiftly and silently he led the way through a dark passage to the back stairs; they mounted these and were soon in his study.

There was kindness in his eyes as he looked at her.

"You are exhausted, child," he said. "When did you last eat?"

"It was before the pricker came to the cottage."

"Don't be afraid. I will ring for my personal servant. Josiah Hough is a good and obedient man. You need fear nothing from him."

She watched him with wondering eyes as he pulled the bell rope. He seemed god-like to her, all-powerful, kind but in an aloof way, completely incomprehensible.

Josiah appeared; he made no show of surprise at the sight of Tamar in his master's study.

"Bring food and wine at once, Josiah," said Richard. "If any should ask whom it is for, say it is for me. But be quick."

"Yes, sir."

The door shut on him and Richard turned to Tamar. "You are in grave danger, child. I will not attempt to minimize it, because you know full well what it means if this witch-pricker gets you. I am going to hide you."

"You are a good man," she said.

He laughed. "Nay," he said; " that is not so. It is not kindness in me. No matter. You tremble still. It is because you think of that young oaf. Think of him merely as a lusty young man — that is all. He can be trusted not to betray you. I shall not leave you alone with him. I trust his honour in all things but those in which his manly lusts are concerned. If he gives a promise, he will keep it."

Josiah came in with the tray, and when he had gone Richard made her sit at the table. She had never sat at such a table before, and she rubbed her finger wonderingly along its smooth surface. She stared about the room and dropped her eyes to the carpet. She had never imagined a carpet, though she had once heard her mother talk of carpets. Everything was strange, like a daydream, but she was not afraid; as long as he was near her she would not be afraid.

There was a knock on the door and Richard let in Bartle.

Bartle looked at her, but she kept her eyes downcast and began ravenously to eat the food; she found that once she had started she could not care for anything else — not even if the witchprickers were at the door or Bartle in pursuit.

"Pretty manners!" sneered Bartle, indicating Tamar.

"Almost as pretty as your own," retorted Richard. "She knows no better. You should."

"Oh, hang me, sir, draw me and quarter me! A witch's girl! A stay-out-late! A girl who sleeps in hedges! If she's not asking for it, who is? She ought to think herself honoured that I waste my time on her."

"She seems oblivious of the honour," said Richard. "And even when it was almost forced upon her she did not appreciate it. But, Bartle, let us be serious. You know that all this talk of witchcraft wearies me. Of course you are not with me. You are as superstitious as any. Well, let us hope you will grow out of it. In any case, you will help me with this girl for your own reasons. Well, we both have our reasons. Now, promise me you will say nothing to anyone — not even your father — of the girl's being here. Give me your word as a gentleman."

"I give my word. Now have I your leave to retire?"

Richard nodded.

Bartle went on: "Good day to you, sir. Good day, Tamar." He threw her a kiss. "To our next merry meeting. May it be as merry as this one." He held up a hand. "See! It bears the mark of your teeth to remind me of you. Your gown is ugly. I hate your gown. I like you so much better without it."

The door shut on him and they heard him singing as he went downstairs.

Richard looked at Tamar. What can I do with her? he asked himself. How can I hide her? He shrugged his shoulders. In spite of his outward calm, he was excited. Life had been monotonous since the sudden death of that dear friend of his, the widow who had lived at Pennie Cross.

Tamar was eating noisily. Her eyes met his and she smiled.

Her trust in him was complete; and sensing it, he felt a pleasure which surprised him.

*　　*　　*

Tamar remained in Richard's study for two days before her presence was discovered; and she had herself to blame for that.

She was not yet accustomed to the grandeur of the room, and she would walk about it, touching the furnishings and the table, the bookshelves and the oak chest. She sat on the stools and the chair; she gazed in wonder at the tapestry. There was, moreover, a glass mirror with a most elaborate frame and this gave Tamar the first clear sight of her face; it was so fascinating to see herself as she appeared to others. Indeed, she was so completely occupied with the novelty of being in such a, room that she forgot her fears. Her curiosity was to betray her.

Beyond the study was Richard's bedroom, and she was eager to see this for she was sure it would be wonderful. She had never seen a bedroom used solely for sleeping in; beds to her were pallets of straw on the floors of cottages.

And so, the desire to see a real bedroom became too much for her. She went to the study door and peeped out into the corridor. There was no one about, but from the bottom of the stairs she heard the sound of voices. That came, she guessed, from the servants working in the kitchen.

She tiptoed along the passage until she reached the door next to that from which she had come. She lifted the latch and went in. This WAS his bedroom.

She had only meant to peep, but she could not resist further exploration. There was the bed, its tester and headpiece covered with such intricate carving that she must go near to examine it. The posts were carved with equal beauty. She felt the curtains gleefully and thought how wonderful it would be to sleep in such a bed, to pull the curtains so that she would be shut in a little room of her own. On the floor was a beautiful carpet of Oriental design; not that Tamar knew anything of its origin; she only knew that it was beautiful. There were what she thought of as carpets on the walls, all cleverly worked in *petit point*. There was a mirror of burnished metal in a frame which she thought of as gold. She ran to the chest and knelt to examine the figures carved upon it. She would have enjoyed opening the chest and peeping inside.

And then, suddenly, she felt a chill of horror run down her spine, for she knew, by instinct, that someone was at the door watching her.

She swung round, but she was too late to see who had been there. She only heard the rustle of garments and the sound of quick, light footsteps. Terrified, Tamar dashed to the door, but no one was in sight.

*　　*　　*

Tamar heard the shouts in the distance. They came nearer and nearer. Now they were right outside the house.

Richard ran into the study; she had never before seen him in a hurry.

He said: "My child, they have come for you. They are almost here."

In terror she flung herself at him and clung to his doublet. He disengaged her and put her from him, frowning.

"You must stay here," he said. "Don't move. You understand? If they see you, you are lost."

She nodded.

He left her and she leaned against the door, an awful sickness coming over her. She saw herself seized and stripped; she felt the horrible pins jabbing into her. She saw them dragging her to the Hoe, and her body swinging on a gibbet. Tamar . . . dead . . . and the crows pecking at her.

Then she heard Richard's voice; strong, it seemed, and her spirits rose. He was not an ordinary man; he was a god. He was as different from other people as she herself was.

He was leaning over the balustrade of the gallery and looking down on to the hall in which the crowd had assembled.

"What are you doing in my house?" he demanded. "How dare you come breaking in like this? I'll have you whipped, every one of you."

Then Simon Carter spoke in his loud yet gentle voice.

"Be calm, dear friend. We come on a peaceful mission. You know me. I am Simon Carter, and I am here to rid our land of those who do evil in it. We have, two days since, hanged a witch, but before she died she told us of her sins. She had lain with the Devil, and of this unholy union a child was born. This child — Satan's own daughter — must be put to death at once. The town is unsafe while she lives. Nay, the country is unsafe. I have reason to believe she is here, and I must beg of you, good sir, I must entreat you, kind gentleman, to let nothing stand in the way of our taking her."

"Who gave you this news?"

"Those who did would wish that their confidence was not betrayed. I am a respecter of wishes. I respect all those who work in the service of God. It is only those who consort with the Devil that I am here to denounce and punish with death. We know the girl to be in this house. I must, in the name of God and the law, ask you to give her up to me."

"And if I refuse? And if I say she is not here?"

"Dear good sir, we should have no recourse but to search the house. It goes not well with those who obstruct the King's justice."

"So you have come here to take a child and ill-treat her."

"This is no human child, sir. This is the very spawn of the Devil. We are all born in sin, sir, and it is for us to wash ourselves clean of it in our passage through life. But this creature was born in filth, with all the wisdom of hell in her head. Her mother hangs rotting in the sun. I have learned much of her evil ways. We persuaded her to confess her sins. Ah! I have much evidence to take with me when I leave your fair county. The *old* witch worked a spell under our very eyes. She assumed death, but we have strung her up all the same, and she now dangles beside the other. Now, the child, sir . . . I give you a second or two to produce her . . . then we search the house."

There was a short silence. Tamar, cowering behind the door, had heard every word.

They were coming up the stairs. They would take her, for even he could not save her. He was only one; and they were many.

Then he spoke:

"You make a great mistake in coming here for the child. Why should the Devil take a poor silly serving wench and get her with child? Such would be without sense. Is the Devil senseless? If he is like a lustful man and nothing more, you waste your time in seeking out his creatures. Come! Why should the Devil get a girl

102

like Luce Lackwell with child? Why? Why? Do you agree that it is an action without purpose?"

"This man prevaricates," cried Simon Carter. "Let us waste no more time with him. Come, my friends, search the house!"

"Be careful!" commanded Richard. "My friends down there—you who have come to take a child and submit her to indignity before you murder her—take care that I do not have you all thrown into prison for trespass."

"Master!" cried a man in the throng. "We but want the young witch. Give her to us, sir, for that's all we do want."

"You fools!" cried Richard. "Can you understand nothing? Have you not noticed all these years how I have watched over her? Ask the women of my kitchen. She has come here regularly for food. Clothes have been given her. Ask the girls, ask my housekeeper if I did not say that she was never to be turned away. You are stupid people. Is it not clear to you now? You were so anxious to give the girl a devil for a father that you did not see what was under your noses. What has the girl done but be the victim of a filthy story? Her mother lay with the Devil. Is that so?"

There was silence.

"Is that so?" he shouted.

There was still no answer from below, and he went on in a loud and ringing tone: "I demand to know. Is there any other charge against her but that of her mysterious coming into the world? Speak to me there!

103

You, Hurly. Don't stand gaping at me, man. What charge against the girl?"

"Naught, sir," stammered Hurly, "save that she be the child of the Devil."

Then Richard laughed loudly. "Naught save that! Well, I have the girl here. And here she stays. Have you forgotten that Luce was my serving wench? And a comely one. Think you that I, having lost my wife, have always lived the life of a celibate? Think again, my friends; and this time think with good sense. Luce's daughter is also mine. This girl here in my house is where she has a right to be, since she is my daughter."

"I had the woman's confession!" screamed Simon Carter. "She was at the witches' Sabbat and the Devil pursued her!"

"She dreamed that. I visited her in her room. There was to be a child, so I married her off to Lackwell. Is that such an unusual story, so difficult to believe? Now, Simon Carter, get you out of my house, and if you are not gone in half a minute, I'll have you clapped in gaol. The magistrates of this town are friends of mine. I'll see they show you no mercy. And that is for all of you. Go! Unless there is any among you who dares doubt my story!"

He paused. No one spoke.

"Go then!" he shouted. "But one moment. If any one of you dares harm my daughter, let him know that he will have me to answer to for his offence."

He stood there, watching them turn sheepishly away. He did not move until the last of them had disappeared; then he stood for a moment looking down with disgust at the mess they had made on the tessellated floor of his hall.

He went into his study. He looked at Tamar and she looked at him. Her eyes were wide with faint wonder and disbelief; his held a hint of amusement.

Tamar thought: It is as though I have never really seen him before . . . nor he me.

CHAPTER
THREE

When Richard took Tamar down to the kitchen, the two serving girls, Moll Swann and Annis Hurly, were there with Mistress Alton.

Richard said mockingly: "Mistress Alton, I don't doubt that you heard the noise those people were making."

The housekeeper nodded slowly, being too bewildered for speech. Her mind was full of images—the master and Luce Martin! The sly wanton, so mild all the time that she and the master...And that black-eyed creature the result! It was more than she could believe. She had known, of course, of the master's visits to the lady of Pennie Cross, who had recently died; but that lady was of the gentry. The master's lapses in that direction were deplorable but understandable. But Luce Martin! That slut! And she had always thought the master so fastidious. What could you know of anybody?

As for the two girls, they could only stare. They had been expecting to see Tamar searched, pricked and hanged; and instead, here she was standing before them.

"If you heard the noise, you doubtless heard what was said," went on Richard. "Then you will know of the relationship between this child and myself. I wish her to help in the house as her mother did, so I shall leave her with you. Teach her to become as thrifty a housekeeper as yourself." He paused at the door. "And, Mistress Alton, I pray you, do not cut off her hair."

Mistress Alton said afterwards to Betsy Hurly, when she came to talk over the affair, that she felt as though the wind had been taken out of her sails by what she'd heard him say to the crowd, so that she felt becalmed. But for that she would have told him she was not going to stay in his house and train his bastards.

As it was, the housekeeper merely nodded and he went out, leaving Tamar in her care.

Tamar advanced towards the table. There was silence in the kitchen. If they were bewildered, she was more so. She had just heard a most astounding revelation, and she knew that if she could have chosen her own father, she would have chosen him. But she did not really believe he had spoken the truth. He had said what he had said because he knew that it was the only thing that could save her. Tamar herself was certain that no human being was her father; and although it would be pleasant to be connected with the gentry, how could she abandon her belief in the secret power which could only come to her through the Devil?

And now, remembering that power in her which set her aside from all others, she was able to face the

107

hostile eyes of the woman whom — ever since she had so callously smashed the seagulls' eggs — Tamar had known to be her enemy.

Mistress Alton's lips were moving; she was saying the Lord's Prayer, so Tamar knew that she herself was not the only one who refused to deny the Devil's part in fathering her.

The two serving girls were waiting for the housekeeper to speak, and Mistress Alton knew that she must exert her authority before those two. She still wore her cane dangling from her waist, and she used it frequently, but not so frequently as she had done on Luce and Annis' mother, Betsy. She was shorter of breath now, and those two were apt to giggle when being belaboured. That was humiliating; still, they were afraid of her tongue, if not of her cane.

"So you've come to work for me in the kitchens, eh?" she said, playing for time.

"Not for you," flashed Tamar. "For him."

"We will see. What are you girls standing about for? Moll, take the key and go to the bolting house. Bring flour and put it into the pastry. I'll be there to do my baking very soon... so look sharp. Annis, take the girl and draw some ale. I could do with a drop myself after all I've been through."

Annis came reluctantly towards Tamar.

"Go on! Go on!" cried the housekeeper, sitting down heavily upon a stool and mopping her brow with her apron. "I was all of a tremble," she told Betsy Hurly afterwards. "So I was to have in my kitchen, at best a bastard, at worst a witch!"

Annis took Tamar into the buttery, where Tamar looked eagerly about her, and Annis looked eagerly at Tamar.

"So this is the buttery," said Tamar, dipping her brown finger into a pot of butter and tasting it. She watched Annis draw ale. Then she took that from her and tasted it.

Annis giggled.

"Did she cut your hair like that?" asked Tamar.

Annis nodded.

Tamar tossed her own luxuriant locks. "She cut my mother's. My mother told me."

"The master said not to cut yours."

"If she had tried, it would have been the worse for her."

Annis shivered; then she saw that Tamar's eyes were full of tears. Tamar dashed them angrily away. "I was thinking of my mother . . . in the cottage. They did terrible things to her . . ."

Annis could cry easily. She picked up a corner of her apron and wiped her eyes.

"Why do *you* cry?" asked Tamar curiously.

"She was your mother, even though she was a witch."

Tamar smiled to herself. The world had ceased to be full of hostile people.

"Don't cry," she said. "I won't hurt you. It's only those I hate who need to be afraid."

They had been a long time in the buttery, but Mistress Alton said nothing about that. She was still, as she said, made all of a tremble by this savage creature who had been brought into her kitchen.

*   *   *

Tamar shared a room with Annis and Moll. Moll was only ten years old — Clem Swann's girl — and she went to sleep as soon as her head touched the straw. But Annis lay awake. So did Tamar.

"Tamar," whispered Annis, "be you really a witch?"

Tamar was silent.

"You know most things, I reckon," said Annis. "Do you know how to make milk turn sour and make cows so that they won't give milk?"

Tamar still said nothing.

"I remember you," went on Annis. " 'Twas when my mother came to ask yourn for a charm. 'Twas years ago. I took a stone from 'ee and you thought I'd stole it. You looked like a witch then. My mother said she could see the Devil looking out of your eyes. Natural eyes couldn't look so big and blazing, she said. She got my father to use his belt on me for touching that stone. I ain't forgot."

Tamar contemplated this new friend of hers and felt protective towards her. Apart from Richard Merriman, the girl was the first one who had ever shown friendliness towards her, and she liked friendliness, particularly when it was given with a certain awe and reverence.

"I didn't mean you to get the belt," said Tamar. "But you ought to have give up the stone when I asked for it."

"Was it a magic stone, Tamar?"

110

Tamar did not answer.

Annis moved nearer to her. "You don't think Moll's awake, do 'ee? I'll whisper...in case she is. Could you give me a charm, Tamar, some'at as would make a man turn towards me?"

Tamar shivered, for Annis's words had brought her encounter with Bartle very near. She lay silently thinking of it, seeing him clearly, that smile on his face, the lips half parted, the eyes of blazing blue.

She let herself imagine being caught by him, and she could smell the hot grass, feel his breath on her face...just as she had when he had tripped her and fallen on her, pressing her down on the ground.

She said sternly: "Why do you want a man turned towards you?"

"Why? Because I do. 'Tis natural like."

"But...you *want* that?"

Annis rolled over and lay staring into the darkness. "Wouldn't matter telling you. I 'spect you do know. 'Tis John Tyler, who do work on the farm with Father. He's terrible handsome. You wait till you see him. Well, John ain't the man a girl can say 'No' to and..."

Tamar drew away; she was alarmed by the excited note in Annis's voice. Annis...a girl younger than herself...and already that which had almost happened to Tamar had happened to her; and it seemed as though she had been far from reluctant.

"You did...that?" said Tamar, shaken out of her role of wise woman.

111

" 'Twas only once. I'd gone over to see my mother and father and to give a hand in the dairy. . . and John, he walked back with me . . . and then well, he being the terrible handsome sort of man a girl couldn't say 'No' to. . . But that Bess Hollicks in the dairy. . . it seems she were after him too, and she'd been down to see old Mother Hartock in Looe Street down in the town, and she got this charm that would take him from me. Old Mother Hartock be caught now. She were one of the first the pricker took; but that don't help me, for the charm do still work; and it be her he takes into the barn. . . not me."

"Did he. . . force you?" asked Tamar, her voice trembling.

Annis laughed softly in the darkness. "Well, I did make a show of being frightened like. . . but I'd always had my eyes on John."

There was a short silence, then Annis said: "Will you give me a charm, Tamar? Will you make a brew for me? For it does seem to me that if you don't I shall never know another man. . . for I do know there be no one in the world for me but John."

"Yes," said Tamar. "I'll make a charm for you. But, Annis, have you thought what happens to girls? Remember my mother. She got a child and then she was married to Bill Lackwell."

"Oh, but she were different. 'Twas the Devil. . . I didn't mean that, Tamar. It sort of slipped out. 'Twas the master. . . not the Devil. But I dunno. Couldn't expect the master to look at the likes of me. If I had John's child, he'd have to marry me."

"Suppose he didn't?"

"He'd have to. . . seeing he works for my father. Besides, John's a good man. He did tell me so. He told me in the barn. He said, ' 'Tis wrong and 'tis wicked, Annis, and I don't want to do it to 'ee, but for the life of me I can't stop myself.' Now, that do show goodness, to my mind. I prayed in church for forgiveness of my sin, I did. 'Dear Lord,' I said, 'I didn't want to sin, but it was so that I couldn't help it. . .' "

Tamar listened to all this, entranced. No one of her own age had ever chatted to her as this girl was chatting. She wanted to stretch out a hand and, taking Annis's, say: "Don't you ever be afraid of me." But caution restrained her; she loved her power too much to throw it lightly away.

"I don't know as I ought to brew for 'ee, Annis," she said.

"Why not?"

"'Tis wrong for 'ee to go in the barn with John Tyler, and I won't help wrong."

"You're a *white* witch, then?"

"I don't want to hurt nobody. . .'cept they hurt me."

" 'Tis a good thing to take John away from Bess Hollicks, for she ain't a good girl. She don't ask the Lord's forgiveness for *her* sin, I reckon."

"Annis, I'll make a brew for 'ee."

113

"Oh . . . Tamar, will 'ee then?" Annis giggled her pleasure.

"And when you've drunk it, he won't have eyes for anyone else."

There was silence. Annis was thinking what a fine thing it was to have the Devil's daughter working and sleeping beside a girl, so that she could take advantage of the Devil's power without giving up one little bit of her soul for it!

As for Tamar, her thoughts were mixed. She did not know whether she was glad or sorry, happy or unhappy.

*   *   *

The house absorbed her. So many things to learn. So many things she had never seen before.

Friendship with Annis grew. She had gathered the herbs which she would brew to make the charm, though she warned Annis that she must not be impatient, as some of the ingredients were not easy to come by. She needed a hair grown on the nethermost tip of a dog's tail, the brains of a cat or a newt, the bone of a frog whose flesh had been consumed by ants, to say nothing of herbs which did not grow by the wayside. These must be collected before she could begin to brew.

Mistress Alton saw the girls whispering together and made the sign of the Cross, while she went about muttering the Lord's Prayer.

Betsy Hurly came to the kitchen to chat with the housekeeper. Betsy—now a comfortable matron— had aged quickly; she no longer indulged in amorous adventures, and had become a friend of Mistress Alton's. They enjoyed many a gossip together concerning the scandals of the neighbourhood, from which occupation they both derived much pleasure. Mistress Alton was prepared to forget that Betsy had once been what she called "a flighty bit of no-good," because of the news she brought; as for Betsy she had been delighted to find a place for her daughter, and she was ready to forget the cruelty she herself had suffered at the housekeeper's hands.

"Well," said Betsy, sipping her ale, "so you've got that young savage here, I see."

"I was all knocked of a heap," said Mistress Alton. "They came to take her. . . as was right and proper that she should be took. . . and when I heard what *he* had to say. . . well I was as I told you, like a ship without a sail. Bold as brass he said it, leaning over the balustrade. I had the door half open, so I saw. Bold as brass he says, 'She's my daughter,' he says. 'Luce was my serving wench. . . and a comely one. . .' Fancy that Luce! Can you believe it?"

"No, I can't. And what's more I don't. You forget how Luce and me was together. I remember the night. . . I remember her lying there. There was mud on her skirt. . . and bits of leaf clinging to it. She was staring wild like. . . and I got it out of her. She said: 'Big he was. . . and he had horns at the top of his head. His eyes was like a man's eyes. . . shining through the black. I fainted. . . but I knew I'd been took. I knew I'd been ravished by the Devil.' Were that going with the master? Why, 'twould have been a different story then, I reckon. We'd have had her giving herself airs. There was that girl over at Stoke, remember: Sir Humphrey fancied her and for a week or two she couldn't spare a nod for the likes of we. That's how it is when gentry fancies a girl. But the Devil . . . that's another matter."

" 'Sh!" said Mistress Alton and recited the Lord's Prayer right through. Betsy followed her, stumbling. Then, feeling herself reinforced against possible evil, the housekeeper gave vent to her feelings: " 'Tis terrible. What would happen if I lifted my arm against her? I reckon it would be struck stiff like. My father was struck that way by a witch. Right as rain one day, and the next he fell down . . . never spoke again. We knew he'd been overlooked, for he'd had words with an old woman on the road. We boiled his urine up in a pan over the fire, knowing that, as it boiled, that witch would feel her inside burning. We knew she'd have to come to make us stop, and it would be the first as came to the house after the pan began to boil. It were a steady sort of body that come, and we'd never have thought it of her. We hung her, but even that didn't do no good. She were dead, but 'twere a lifelong spell she'd laid on Father, and he never spoke again."

"Mistress Alton, you do terrify me!"

"And 'tis right that you should be terrified, with witches among us."

"But . . . how could the master . . . ? He be a clever man . . . a gentleman . . . How could he say such things?"

"There's some as gets too clever. It goes to their heads and then they start acting queer. Do you remember the night when we put . . . or was about to put . . . old woman Lackwell to the test? Do you remember how it was him as stopped us?"

"I do indeed," said Betsy.

"It's too much of these books, that's what 'tis . . ."

Tamar knew they talked of her. She watched them maliciously, trying to frighten them with a flash of her black eyes.

Life had changed, but the power was still with her and she was not going to relinquish it without a fight.

One day, when she was set to dust the woodwork of the gallery, she went into the master's study. No one was supposed to go in there except Josiah Hough, but Tamar had once spent two days and nights in there, so she did not think that she need obey the rules which other people must.

What interested her most in this room were the books. She had, when she had been a prisoner here, surreptitiously opened one or two of them, but the letters were quite baffling to her, and no matter how she stared at them or from what angle she studied them, she could make nothing of them. She had felt angry, because power meant so much to her. She believed that if she looked at a book and asked the Devil's aid, he would make her able to understand.

Now, dusting the rail of the gallery, she thought of the books, and the temptation to take another look at them was irresistible.

There was no one in the room, so she sped to the bookcase and opened one at random. She turned it round, staring at the letters.

She was still as ignorant as she had been before. She slapped the page in anger. Earnestly she desired to be able to read the letters, as once she had desired to make herself clean.

Richard came in quietly and found her; he looked very angry.

"What are you doing?" he demanded.

"Looking," she explained.

"Have you not been told that you are not to come here?" he asked coldly.

"No," she answered. "The others have, but I have not been."

"No one from the kitchen is allowed to come in here. Please go."

Her heart was quaking, but she stood boldly before him.

"You are clever," she said. "It is not proper that you should have a daughter who does not know what books mean."

He laughed suddenly, and she saw now that he had ceased to be angry.

"You mean you want to read? Do you think you possibly could?"

"If I wished," she said.

"You must not give yourself airs because I allow you to work in my kitchens."

She repeated stubbornly: "It is not proper for you to have a daughter who does not know what books mean."

"Nonsense!" he retorted. "Very few girls . . . highborn girls at that, not bastards like yourself . . . are taught to read."

"Perhaps they don't want to," she said. "If they did . . . and were clever enough . . . they would learn."

"You are persistent, Tamar," he said.

She smiled dazzlingly, for she could see that he was just a little interested.

"Listen to me; if you were obliged to learn, you would hate it. It is not easy."

"I like to learn. I learned all Granny could tell me."

"This is very different from listening to the chatter of an old woman."

"Old men chatter very like old women."

He looked at her sternly and then suddenly burst into a laugh. "Do you refer to me as an old man?"

"You are not very young."

"And you suggest that *I* should teach *you* how to read?"

"I am your daughter. You have told everybody so. It is not proper that I should not know what these books mean."

He came close to her and looked into her face. "Listen to me," he said. "I will show you that you can never learn to read."

She smiled. "I will show you that I will."

"You will come here for an hour every morning, and I myself will attempt to teach you. I will do this for a week, and at the end of that time you will have discovered that you cannot learn to read and write."

"And write too!" she cried gleefully.

"Do not smile so complacently," he said. "I am a very impatient man and I cannot endure stupidity."

She said: "I am very clever and I will show you how I shall learn."

"We will start to-morrow," he said. "Come here at ten of the clock."

She went out smiling, but in spite of her victory she felt very sad. She could very easily have wept; she did not know why, except that he made her very sad and happy all at once.

* * *

But her learning did not end in a week. Richard was to discover he had no ordinary pupil, and in spite of himself he was aware of a faint excitement when the girl was with him. He was amused by her concentration, delighted to see *her* delight when at length, after what seemed like hours of struggle, she ceased to make her capital J's round the wrong way.

At the end of the week, he said: "Not very amusing, is it?"

She agreed that it was not. "But it will be," she added, "when I know it."

He was secretly pleased that she wished to go on; he enjoyed teaching, and teaching such a strange creature was particularly interesting.

"I'll give you another week," he said grudgingly.

One day he spoke to her very sternly. "I saw you gathering weeds the other day. I suppose it was for some charm or other. That was a very stupid thing to do. Don't you realize what a narrow escape you had?"

"Yes," she said.

"If you got into trouble again, it would not be so easy to get you out of it. Moreover, I might not feel inclined to do so. I did so in the first place because it seemed to me no fault of your own that those fools were after you. But, in the face of what happened, deliberately to go out . . . collecting herbs . . . making charms . . . That I consider the height of folly."

He dismissed her, and she was very sorry that she could not please him in this matter, but she had to keep her promise to Annis, so she went on gathering what she needed for her brew.

The day came when the potion was completed and Annis drank it. She had had to make it at twelve noon, although it should have been midnight; but as they were locked in their room, this could not be.

"I have said a special word about the time," she explained.

"Do you think it'll make any difference?" asked Annis anxiously.

"No. I said that it was because of Mistress Alton, and you can depend upon it those who are helping us will understand."

Annis was delighted. She found it hard to wait until she could see John Tyler again.

Bartle and his father rode over to Pennicomquick, and supper was served to them in the winter parlour, where Moll and Annis waited on them. Richard did not wish Tamar to do so. Tamar went out of the house and into the gardens; she was trembling at the thought of Bartle's being in the house.

It was the silliest thing she could have done, because he saw her from one of the windows, and, making an excuse to the two men, came out to her.

"Hello, Devil's daughter!" he said.

"Don't you dare come near me!" she snapped.

"Have you no kiss for me? 'Twill be a farewell kiss. I am sailing to-morrow."

"I'll never have anything but kicks and scorn for you."

"That's a fool's prophecy. . . doomed to be false."

"I am no fool."

"Tamar, you are the greatest fool in Devon. You might have been my mistress by now. Think of the honour of that to such as you!"

"I see only the shame."

"Think also of the beautiful foreign girls who will be enjoying me. That is what you have to think of, Tamar, until I come back. I have made a vow. When I come back it is the Devil's daughter for me. She may be a little unwilling at first, but afterwards. . . afterwards. . . you will see, Tamar."

"I hate you. I shall always hate you."

"Another false prophecy. And you have changed. Yes, you have. You've got new airs. . . new graces, but damn me, you're as pretty as ever! No! You're more pretty."

She walked past him into the house. She was confident in the knowledge that he dared not touch her now. Life had changed for her. She was learning to be a scholar and a member of the gentry; and at the same time she was not losing any of her magical powers.

Bartle sailed away next day, and for that she was thankful. Now she could enjoy listening to Annis's stories of her love affair with John Tyler.

"Why," said Annis, "I met him there in the hayfield, and I said to him, 'How do 'ee do, John?' and he looked sort of sheepish like, as he has been since he forgot me for Bessie. He said, 'I be well, Annis. And how be you?' And I said, just as I'd said when I drank the brew like as you told me, 'Beautiful and desirable in your eyes, John Tyler.' 'What be that, then?' he asked. I said, ' 'Tis goodbye you've said to your tumbles with Bessie, John; from now on there's no one in this world for you but me.' He said, 'Why's that, then, Annis?' Then I told him. 'For this, John. I've bewitched 'ee. I've taken the draught as Tamar did brew for me. She's charmed you, John.' 'Well, then,' he said, 'there's naught as we can do about it.' So we went to the barn and all is well between us two."

Listening, Tamar was filled with pleasure. She was going to be able to read and write; she was going to be able to talk as easily and cleverly as did the gentry. She was going to be one of those people whom she admired — with this difference: She could work spells, and they could not!

*   *   *

Tamar was sixteen years old. She had grown taller and plumper in the last two years — the two most important years in her life so far.

There had been no kitchen work for Tamar for a long time. She was accepted as the daughter of the house now. In spite of himself, Richard could not control a growing delight in her. For one thing she was so beautiful — and he had always been susceptible to beauty in any form — so that it was a source of delight merely to look at her. For another she was intelligent; she could amuse and amaze him. She had learned quickly and in a few months after those first lessons she was reading and writing. He had told her then that he did not wish her to waste time in the kitchen; if she cared to study, he would help her.

She did care. She cared deeply.

"You have much to learn besides reading and writing," he said. "You must learn to walk with grace, to act with dignity, to be always poised. And there is your speech. That offends me greatly."

After that she must sit before a mirror mouthing words, taking each vowel and consonant and repeating it until she could say it in a manner which pleased him. She was now speaking in an accent similar to his own, with little trace of soft, cooing Devon in it.

She loved gay colours, and in the blues and scarlets which she favoured her dark hair looked darker, her flashing eyes more bright. When she rode out — for among other things she had learned to ride — people turned to look at her, and swore she had a touch of the Devil in her. She was too beautiful and too clever, they said, to be all human. Look how she had escaped pricking and death, and look what she had made out of it!

Tamar ignored them; she was secretly pleased that they should continue to regard her as the possessor of supernatural powers.

Richard deplored this in her. He would have her sit and talk with him; since the death of his friend in Pennie Cross he needed someone to whom he could talk of the subjects which interested him most and, to his astonishment, Tamar was filling that need. It seemed amazing to him that he could talk thus to the girl who a few years ago had seemed such a little savage.

Sir Humphrey once said: "Merriman, you dote on that girl." He nudged Richard. "Damme! If you hadn't told us she was your daughter, I'd say she was your mistress. Not sure I don't believe it now."

"Nonsense!" he had retorted sharply. "I'm interested. Who could help being interested in a girl like that? Think of her upbringing and look at her now. She's damned unusual."

Sir Humphrey had gone off chuckling.

The fact was that Richard was growing more interested in Tamar than he had thought it possible for him to be in any person. That was why it disturbed him deeply that she could cling so stubbornly to the belief in her supernatural birth. And the reason? Because he feared for her. He feared that if she were in danger again he might not be able to save her, and the thought of losing her, as he said, depressed him; but that, he knew, was a very mild way of expressing what he would feel.

Again and again he remonstrated with her; he was coldly contemptuous; he told her she was being stupid; but nothing he could say could turn her from her beliefs.

One November day he called her to his study.

She noticed that a faint colour burned under his skin, and she knew that something had happened to perturb him.

"Tamar," he said, "sit down, child. I want to talk to you. I've just had news of a diabolical plot in London. It's going to have far-reaching effects on the whole country, you will see."

"What is this plot?" she asked.

"A plot to blow up the King and Parliament, and so rid the country of its rulers at one blow. This is going to mean fresh persecutions."

"Who did this thing?"

"Oh, it was a foolish plot . . . doomed to failure. As I've heard it, a Robert Catesby — a Northamptonshire man and a Catholic — gathered together some fellow Catholics, engaged a man called Guy Fawkes, a soldier of fortune, to secrete himself in the vaults of the Houses of Parliament with a barrel of gunpowder and matches. One of the conspirators warned a friend not to attend Parliament on November the Fifth — the day for which it had been arranged — and so suspicion was aroused, the vaults searched, the plot discovered.

Such folly! This is not the way to get that freedom to live and worship which I long to see in this land."

"Freedom to live and worship," she repeated; and added mischievously: "And to believe in witches . . . if you wish to?"

"How you cling to that stupid belief! There are times, Tamar, when I despair of you."

"It is such a distinction to be the daughter of the Devil. I cannot give it up. And whatever you say, Granny Lackwell's charms did what they were supposed to do. The sick were healed. Some fell sick when she had looked at them . . . or had bad luck."

He looked at her wearily, but even so he could not help smiling at the lovely, animated face. "Sometimes the charms worked," he said; "sometimes they did not. When they did not, it was forgotten; when they did, it was remembered and talked about. That was chance, my dear. We have talked of this many times. But this plot . . . it is going to mean new and severe laws against the Catholics. We shall probably have Catholic-prickers among us as well as witch-prickers."

"At least you need have no anxiety for me when these new prickers come."

He looked at her quizzically. "I fear you are a wild girl, Tamar, and I confess you give me some anxiety. You have learned much, and quickly—no one would guess that you were not born into your present position—and yet you persist stubbornly in clinging to superstitions regarding yourself which can bring at best discomfort, at worst disaster."

"I know," she answered, "that there is a mystery surrounding my birth. You forget that I saw my mother's face when it was referred to. She would not have made up a story about being seized by the Devil in a dark wood."

"There is something I have to say to you, Tamar. I did not mean to. . .yet; but I see I must. I shall have to tell you something of myself. First, I am collecting information of a certain sort. When I have all I need I may have it printed as a book."

"What kind of book?" she asked.

"A book of all times — past and present, of bloodshed and horror."

"Why are you compiling this book?"

"I think it may be because I wish to show what I have found, to others. . . .Perhaps also that I am seeking something myself."

"What do you seek?"

"I am unsure. It may be a religion. . .or it may not be a religion at all. In preparing what I have so far done, it has been necessary for me to have personal experiences and study a good deal. Oh, Tamar, I have often wanted to speak to you of this. There was a time when I would talk of it to a very good friend of mine. Alas! she is now dead, and it is as though you have stepped into her place. . .in one respect. You are eager to know what takes place about you — I do not, of course, mean actual happenings, but in the minds of people, in the trend of the age. You are quick to see a point. Yes, you are a comfort to me."

128

She was astonished. He had never talked of affection before. A great happiness came to her. She admired him more than anyone she had ever known.

He went on: "There are so few people to whom I could speak of such things. Our friends the Cavills? Well, they are our friends because their lands are not very far distant and it is easy to ride over and be neighbourly. In a way, too, they fit into my picture. They are so much a part of the times in which we now live. Father and son, they are perfect physically; they delight in exercising the body rather than the mind. How like the father the son is! They are buccaneers, both of them. They delight in taking with the strength of their hands what is not theirs, and making it their own."

Tamar felt her cheeks grow hot, as they did whenever Bartle's name was mentioned. She knew she would never forget him and those terrifying moments he had given her; sometimes she dreamed of him. He was far away now; he had been away for two years. Let him stay away.

"Buccaneers, yes!" she said. "Although I confess to a certain liking for Sir Humphrey which I cannot give to his son."

"Sir Humphrey has grown mellow. At Bartle's age he was just such another as Bartle. They have the essence of manhood, and they, Tamar, are the ideals of our times. Such men as they are making our country great, and they will continue to do so. They lead the way to that dominance which our country will attain. Do not despise Bartle too much for what he tried to do to you. Rejoice that he did not succeed. But for Bartle and his kind we should have the Spaniards with us now, and these persecutions of witches and Puritans, Separatists and Catholics — in fact, of all who do not conform to the way laid down by the State and Church — would be a hundred times more rigorous, a thousand times more bloody. You have heard a good deal of the Inquisition in Spain. Let us rejoice that our country has nothing so evil as that. Still, we suffer here, as all the world suffers. I see no way out of suffering until we have learnt tolerance. A man must choose his own religion. Persecution does not — as authority fondly believes — stamp out; it nourishes. King Philip could not drive our men off the seas because of the terrible cruelties he inflicted on those he captured. Men rallied to the ships to fight the Spaniard for revenge as well as gain. My dear child, there are more poor deluded witches in this country since our prickers and suchlike came to seek them out than there ever were before."

"Richard," she said, for as she had explained to him she could never bring herself to call him "Father," and within a month of her coming to his house she had called him by his Christian name. "Richard, how can you know these things?"

"That is at the very root of what I wish to tell you now."

She waited and after a brief hesitation, as though even now he were reluctant to speak of these things, he began to tell her:

130

"It is a tale of persecution that I wish to tell you—persecution at which I have been a looker-on all my life. A terrible thing happened to me when I was eight years old, and this brought me close to what I have come to see as the scourge of the world, the great impediment to progress. I must tell you of this, Tamar, because it has made me what I am.

"My father was a gentleman of the Court of Queen Mary. . . that Mary of the bloody persecutions. She married, as you know, King Philip of Spain, and when the King came to England, there was a beautiful lady in his retinue with whom my father fell in love. They were married; and when the King returned to Spain, it was necessary that my mother should go back with him, as she was not strong enough to endure the damp of these islands. My father went with her to Madrid and there I was born.

"We were a very happy family until the time when I was seven years old; then my father was arrested and brought before the Inquisition. I had very early become aware of this evil thing; I had seen the furtive horror in people's eyes; but it was only when it touched my own family that I understood what it really meant. My father was taken in the night, and I saw him only once afterwards. That was a year later. I hardly recognised him; his ruddy complexion had become yellow, and he had great difficulty in walking, for he had suffered much torture in the gloomy chambers of the Inquisition.

"A boy of my age should not have been there, of course; but there was fear in our house. My mother lay in her sick bed, and there were leeches ready to say that she was unable to attend; therefore her absence was excusable. But I must not be absent, for if I were, that would be noted, and I should be marked as one who was not being brought up as a good citizen and Catholic.

"Tamar, the memory of that day is always with me. It never fades. Early in the morning I was awakened by the muffled pealing of the bells. I was aroused by the servants, hastily dressed and hurried into the streets.

"The *autos-da-fé* are great holidays in Spain. The population turns out in its best clothes. There is all that pomp and ceremony in which no Church delights as does the Church of Rome.

"I was taken to the gates of the Inquisition so that I might be there to see the tragic procession file out to its doom. Among these miserable men and women was my father. He was dressed hideously in a loose yellow gown; this *sanbenito* was embroidered with busts surrounded with flames, and the flames pointed upwards; figures of horrible devils had also been worked on it, and these were shown as fanning the flames. This particular type of *sanbenito* told the onlookers that my father was one of those condemned to be burned alive. I cannot convey to you the horror of it all, and when I thought of it later, it seemed to me that more horrible than anything, more horrible than even the vile torture to which these people had been submitted, was the religious pomp with which these foul ceremonies were conducted. The working people must be present on pain of having suspicion fall on them; their presence was commanded by their Church. Here was a scene more revolting, I imagined, than those played out in the amphitheatre of Rome under savage Nero and Tiberius. The Romans committed cruelty for what in their view was sport; the Spaniards delighted in it none the less, but they tried to hide their delight in a cloak of piety. In later years I came to believe that the Spaniards were guilty of the greater sin.

"Most of these victims were members of the upper classes; doubtless this was due to the fact that the Inquisition seized all the possessions of those it murdered, and the Inquisition was determined to remain rich and powerful.

"To the *Quemadero*...the place of fire...where the Grand Inquisitor rose and addressed the crowd, enumerating the sins of those about to face most horrible death.

"Then were the fires lighted, and I looked on, Tamar, at those poor bodies, shattered by the rack, burned by fiery pincers, waiting for the final torture which would at last bring a merciful death. Some were strangled before they were burnt—those had turned Catholic at the last moment; the others were roasted alive because they clung to their own faith. My father was of the latter, and I was there...to witness his death..."

Tamar could only look at him, her eyes filled with horror and compassion that blazed into sudden hatred against the tormentors of his father. She could find no words to say to him.

After a pause he continued: "Well, that was many years ago. There have been thousands to suffer torture as my father suffered. Even in this country the scourge of the Holy Roman Church was felt. Fires have blazed at Smithfield and no man has felt safe from his neighbour.

"I was smuggled back to England when my mother died. I had faithful servants — men who had followed my father to Spain and were themselves in fear of the Inquisition, and would, no doubt, have fallen victims to it; the temporary leniency shown to them was due to the fact that there were richer prizes to claim more immediate attention. In England my family owned great estates, and I was brought up by my grandparents in the Protestant religion.

"This seemed a kindlier religion; and one must have religion in this mysterious world into which we come without our own volition, struggle for a few years and then pass on. It is the passing on which makes us long for faith, for we cannot bear that we should die and be no more. Yes, this was a happier reign. Men of England were sickened by the fires of Smithfield, and the men of England are made of different stuff from those of Spain. We do not love solemn ceremonies; we love gay days and holidays; we like our streets to run with wine — not blood. Slow to anger, yet, when aroused, pertinacious in the extreme, we are quick to forget; there is no race in the world as ready to forgive a wrong as the English, providing sufficient time has elapsed for it to be comfortably forgotten. I was happy to be in such a country; but as I grew older I began to hear an echo of those cruelties springing up again in this land. Perhaps they had never really died. The Queen was head of the Church, as her father had made himself, and there were some who would not accept her as such and wished to bring about a greater reformation of the Church.

"I saw the beginning of fresh persecutions. Now it was the Puritans and Separatists who suffered. I saw men thrown into gaol...kept in noisome prisons. This was, I assured myself, leniency compared with Spain's horrible methods; still, it was persecution. And one day in Smithfield, I saw two Anabaptists burned to death—the first to suffer since Elizabeth came to the throne; but nevertheless I could feel little satisfaction in a religion which could permit such things...even if infrequently.

"I gave myself up then to the study of men and their various faiths since the beginning of time. Among these was the faith of witchcraft."

He paused to pour himself a goblet of wine. Then he looked straight at Tamar.

"Yes," he went on, "I dabbled in witchcraft, for I found it closely connected with the religion of this country. On the Continent horrible torture is inflicted on witches, who are mostly women— sometimes deluded, sometimes completely innocent of the delusion that they possess the powers of evil. And these tortures are inflicted in the name of God.

"Why, I asked myself, do these people confess to witchcraft in some cases before they are put to the torture? Because they believe in it. They die for their faith just as my father died for his. Your attitude, Tamar, has been of great interest to me. You were brought up to believe yourself a child of the Devil, and from this you derived great satisfaction. And even now that you have the benefit of some education, you cling to your beliefs. Small wonder that the ignorant refuse to renounce theirs."

"It is very well for you to disbelieve," she interrupted him. "But I saw Granny Lackwell's charms work. There *is* some power beyond the reach of ordinary men and women, and witches can find it."

"Tamar, I studied witchcraft, and I found it to be linked with the religion of this country before St. Augustine came here with Christianity. Witchcraft as practised to-day has its roots in the days when our forefathers worshipped Woden the All-father, Thor the Thunderer, Tyr the god who gave men wisdom and cunning, Freya the goddess of battle. Witches, it is true, never mention these gods; indeed, they know nothing of them. It is centuries since St. Augustine came here, and then alas! Christianity was *forced* on the inhabitants of this land. That is at the root of all religious conflict. Those in authority will not allow free-will. Through the ages the so-called Christian Church has fiercely, and with bloodshed and torment, denounced witchcraft because witchcraft is a part of a rival faith.

"I have attended witches' Sabbats. I have gone masked in a goat's head. I have seen the dances round a bonfire, and I have recognised these dances as being the same as those performed in this land before Christianity was forced upon its people. In those days our population was very small and there was a desperate need to increase it. These dances, which were in those days performed round the figure of a horned goat, were known as fertility dances. Now they seem lewd in aspect, because their meaning is not understood. They were meant to rouse the participators to an urgency of desire, for it was felt that the greater the desire, the more chance there would be of fertility, and that the children conceived on such nights would be strong—great men to lead their country in war, fine women to breed again such men.

"The witches who dance on their Sabbats do not know all this. They believe that it is the Devil who has called them out to dance. They have been told so, and they are ignorant and credulous. The Church—fearing them—has said: 'You are base. You are possessed by the Devil.' And these people, who would find life drab indeed without their belief in their own supernatural powers, cannot give them up. They are ready to die for them. Imagination can work miracles; it can make the weak-minded see what is not there."

Tamar was looking at him strangely now. He knew that she was picturing him, masked, dancing at a witches' Sabbat, and she was beginning to understand how that which had up till now seemed incredible had come about.

"Yes," he said, with a faint, ironic smile, "now you begin to see. I told no lie when I acknowledged you as my daughter before those people. You *are* my daughter.

"I am not what one would call a sensual man; nor have I lived the life of a monk since the death of my wife. There have been occasional light love affairs, and you have heard of my dear friend now dead. I had seen your mother in the house. She was a dainty creature. She had a quality which was, alas! too slight to grow. I think I probably desired her without realizing that I did, although I did not think very much about her. Others had noticed her also. One was our friend, Sir Humphrey. I guessed that ere long she would fall to him unless some obstacle was put in his way. I had little intention of making that my business, and if Luce had not gone to the Sabbat you would never have been born.

"Those ancient dances were calculated to warm the coldest heart. There are strange chants. There is magic in them—so the witches think. They arouse the dancers to a frenzy. There is fornication on such nights, and each man or woman who participates believes that, through her partner, she has communication with the Devil. In the days when the gods and heroes of Asgard were worshipped, the horned goat represented fertility; in these days the old beliefs are forgotten and only the ritual remains. The Christian interpretation is put on the goat, and that is

138

that he represents the Devil, for men of one faith readily believe all others to be of the Devil. We have seen that even a variation of the same faith suffers the same condemnation. But I must explain to you.

"I wore the black robes which those attending associate with the Devil. There were horns to my cap. I had joined in the dance which to them was witchcraft, but which to me was the fertility dance of my forefathers. It is calculated, as I said, to arouse desire in the coldest man or woman; and this it does. That much is preserved. I was caught up in the primitive urge of my forefathers; and there was Luce in the woods.

"I did not foresee the terrible thing which would happen to her because of this. My conscience at that time worried me little. You know that I found a husband for her. It did not seem to me that what had happened to Luce was worse than what happened to so many more. I meant to take her into my confidence, to talk to her in some way as I have just talked to you, to explain to her that it was I who had seduced her. I even thought of keeping her here as my mistress. She was a dainty creature. I found her stupid, and I had no patience with stupidity. I married her off, and that, I felt, was all that was needed. When I heard that she talked of what had happened that night, I dismissed her as a little fool. I had tried to warn her, but it was impossible to do so without disclosing the identity of her seducer. You are shocked, child. You look at me with horror."

"I saw them come to the cottage...I saw them take her."

"I know. I have thought of it often. It was a terrible end for a girl such as Luce had been. I have made excuses for myself, but I see now that what I did to her was far worse than anything Sir Humphrey could have done. I want you to see me as I am. Have no illusions. I sheltered you when they pursued you because of my guilty conscience, not because I had any feeling towards you as a daughter."

"Yet I do not forget that you acknowledged me as your daughter before all those people when I was in my greatest danger."

"That was when I knew they had hanged her; and but for me that would never have happened to her."

"It is all violence and death!" said Tamar. "Perhaps now I understand you more than I did before."

"And to understand me is to despise me?"

"No. I think to love you as well as admire you. You did a great wrong to my mother...a very wicked thing. But you were sorry and you took me in and you told all those people that you were my father. How could I despise you?"

He said: "If you had not been beautiful, intelligent and amusing, I should doubtless have left you to work in the kitchens."

She did not speak and he said: "Please say what is in your mind."

"It is that you think me beautiful, intelligent and amusing."

She ran to him and flung her arms about him.

"My beloved daughter!" he said.

And she lifted her face to his. "I never thought to see you weep," she said.

He held her close to him and she felt his lips on her hair.

He put her from him suddenly, as though ashamed of his emotion.

He poured wine into two goblets and handed one to her.

"To Tamar!" he said. "To my daughter. My daughter . . . who now believes that the Devil is exonerated from all responsibility in her birth."

"To you, dear Father," she replied.

He understood the look in her eyes. He said as he put down his glass and took her by the shoulders: "Now you know the truth."

But she continued to smile her secret smile.

"They were afraid of me," she said. "I was protected in my childhood."

"You were protected by the belief of those about you."

"I have seen charms work," she said.

He sighed, and she continued:

"They would say that the Devil was in you that night. And indeed, you will admit that you behaved in a way which was not usual with you."

"I see," he said slowly, "that nothing I can tell you will shift your belief."

She embraced him once more, holding her cheek against his.

"I am glad though that he chose you. I am glad that it was your body he entered."

"Alas!" he answered, "I see your faith is unshakable." He turned her face up to his. "Tamar, can't you give it up?"

Slowly she shook her head.

*　　*　　*

Plague came to Plymouth.

In the streets men and women lay dying, calling for help which none dared give. On the doors were large red crosses, warning all to keep away. At night the pest-cart went through the streets. "Bring forth your dead!" was the mournful cry.

The surrounding villages were more fortunate than the town. It was in the cobbled streets with filth running in the gutters that the dread disease flourished. But fear was in every mind; each watched himself or herself for the dreaded signs — the shivering, sickness, headache, and delirium, which must shortly be followed by the fearful sign on the breast which was the grim herald of death.

Into the Sound one hot day came a ship; she rested at anchor while she sent a rowing boat ashore. No citizens were on the quay to greet those three men who came in that boat. The men came ashore, fear in their hearts. It did not take them long to discover why they had received no welcome. They quickly saw the red crosses on the doors, the inert figures of those who had lain down in the streets to die.

They went back to their boat with all possible speed and rowed out to their ship.

* * *

Annis knocked at the door of Tamar's room.

Tamar had her own bedroom now. It contained a four-poster bed, a carved chest, a wardrobe and a press; she had a chair with a tapestry back and there was the great luxury of a carpet on the floor. She delighted in these things to such an extent that Richard had said she must have them. Indeed, she had not yet grown accustomed to them, and would walk round her room examining them, rejoicing in the knowledge that they were hers. There was also a mirror of burnished metal, and in this she enjoyed studying her face; for her beauty delighted her more than her other possessions.

Annis was excited, Tamar saw at once.

"Mistress Tamar, I must tell 'ee what I've found. 'Twere in the barn...our barn, you know... John's and mine. I did go home and, natural like, I did look for John. He weren't to be seen, so I just put me head in at the barn...for memory's sake, you might say...and there I did see men! There were three of them...all lying down, starving like, they seemed. Queer sort of men. One said: 'Mistress, for the love of the Lord bring us food and drink.' And he said it twice before I could understand...he spoke that queer. I didn't know what I should do. I were scared out of my wits."

"Men?" said Tamar. "What sort of men?"

143

"Strange sort of men . . . and such a way of speaking! I was hard put to it to understand what it was they were saying, and it was guess work that told me. I could see they were starving. I could see they was well-nigh done for."

"Why did you not go to your father or mother?"

"I don't rightly know, 'cept they'd have drove 'em off the farm. Father, he won't have strangers there. He says they steal his roots and corn and suchlike. They'd be stealing the pigs' food — that's what Father would say. I didn't know where to turn, so I come to you."

Tamar smiled, well pleased. She revelled in admiration, and that of Annis was so wholehearted.

"I'll go and see for myself," she said. "I'll ride over. You can follow me. If these men are starving, they'll need help quickly. But we have to be careful, Annis. We don't know who they are."

"I thought mayhap *you* would know," said Annis.

Tamar wrinkled her brows in concentration. "I feel they are good men," she said. "Men we may have to help."

"I'm glad of that," said Annis, "for I might have told me father."

"First of all, I will see them," said Tamar.

The wind pulled at her long black hair as she rode over to the barn. She liked to wear it loose, so that she should be known and recognised at once. She enjoyed Mistress Alton's horrified glances at the offending glory.

Tamar had grown proud in the last few years, for she had risen too quickly in too short a time. In one

144

stride she had left poverty for luxury, physical misery for comfort; she was Richard Merriman's acknowledged daughter, but she was not going to lose one whit of the special prestige among the ignorant which the belief in her satanic parentage had brought her.

She reached the barn, pushed open the door and stood looking at the three wretched men lying in the gloom. Their plight was pitiful, but her eyes had been accustomed to look at such sights.

"Who are you?" she asked.

One of the men who seemed stronger than the others raised himself a little.

"Lady, my name is Humility Brown, and I and my friends have not eaten for . . . we forget how long. For the love of the Lord, bring us food and drink, or we perish."

The man's voice was cultured, which enabled her to understand what he said, but even so it was obvious that he came from another part of the country.

"Tell me first what you do here."

"We rest and shelter against the weather."

"How did you get here?"

"We came off the ship *Adventurer*. We were on our way to Virginia in the New World."

"But where are your shipmates?"

"They would not take us back. We came ashore for stores . . . three of us . . . and when we reached the town we saw its plight. We returned to the ship, but they would not take us back aboard. There was naught we could do . . ."

Tamar slipped outside the door and shut it. These men had been in the polluted town. It might be that already they carried the terrible infection, the token already on their breasts.

She ran to her horse and mounted. She knew that the villages were free of the plague because they had cut off all communication with the stricken town.

She met Annis on the way back.

Annis cried: "Mistress, you saw them? You are going to help?"

"Annis!" cried Tamar. "You must not go near the barn. What shall we do? Those men have been in the town. They left their ship to buy stores and came to the town, so their shipmates would not have them back; but you and I, Annis, have been near them."

Annis began to shiver, but almost immediately she lifted her big grey eyes to Tamar's face and answered cheerfully: "Mistress, *you* can make us clean. We shall be safe because you will see to it."

Tamar's dark eyes were wide, her cheeks flushed. "Why, yes. We shall be safe. I shall see to that. Annis, if I told you to go into the barn and have no fear, would you go?"

"If you would set a charm on me so that I'd come to no harm, I would."

"Then I will. This is what I will do. You can go to the barn now, but do not go inside. Stand outside and let no one enter. I will bring food for the men. I will save their lives, and then no one will doubt my power. But, Annis . . . we shall not tell the master of this until it is done."

Annis nodded.

"Now to the barn. Remember! Stand there and let no one enter. If any come, you must tell them that plague victims are inside. Wait there . . . till I come."

Tamar galloped back to the house, where she went to the kitchen and collected food and wine. She found a piece of charcoal which she took with her when she rode back to the barn, where Annis was standing, placidly obedient to her mistress's command.

"You can go now, Annis. Wait for me at the end of the field."

Annis ran off and Tamar opened the door of the barn.

"Humility Brown," she said, "are you there?"

"Yes, lady."

"Here is food and drink. I will put it by the door. Have you strength to reach it?"

"Yes. And may the good Lord bless you for ever."

"I will bring more food and drink to-morrow. If there is anything else you want, you must ask me for it."

Humility Brown said with much emotion: "My friends, here is an angel from Heaven. Food, friends. This is an answer to prayer."

Tamar shut the door, and she wrote on it in charcoal: "The Lord Have Mercy On Us."

Anyone approaching would know what that meant.

*   *   *

Tamar was eighteen — wilful and proud. Richard often felt misgivings regarding her. The emotion she aroused in him astonished him. He was beginning to care more for this wild, natural daughter of his than he had ever cared for anyone in the whole of his life.

Her beauty enchanted him; her tortuous nature alarmed him. He had seen her tender and kind, cruel and haughty. She was half cultured, half savage. Her wits were sharp, her mind clear, but nothing he could do or say would rid her of this ridiculous belief in her own supernatural powers. She had, he supposed, found this belief too persistent in her lonely childhood to be able to relinquish it now that she had a comfortable home and an affectionate father to care for her. She was not one to wish to rely on the protection of others.

He had arranged that she should meet all the eligible men of the neighbourhood, but none of them pleased her. There were several who, despite the dark stories which still circulated about her, were so fascinated by all that charm and beauty that willingly would they have married her. But she gave herself the airs of a princess and laughed at the arrangements he would have made for her.

It was not that he wished to lose her; he found her company too entertaining for that; but he had discovered in himself parental feelings which he had not suspected he possessed, and he really wished to do what was best for his daughter. It seemed to him that she would be happier if she were married; he longed to see her with children of her own. If she married and reared a family, she might give up some of her wild ideas; she might accept him as her father, and her own birth as a purely natural event. This he greatly desired, since her persistence in her absurd belief, which proclaimed the savage in her, was at the root of his uneasiness.

Bartle Cavill was home from another voyage, and Bartle was possessed of a pride that equalled Tamar's own. It was clear that he was far from indifferent to Tamar, and Richard would not be displeased by a match between them.

Well, there was nothing he could do but wait and see. To-night he was giving a ball for her. The first ball he had given. Why not? She was eighteen; and he wished all the gentry of the countryside to know that he looked on her as his daughter — illegitimate, it was true, but illegitimacy must be winked at when a man had no legal heirs. Tamar would be rich one day and a fortune would wipe out the stigma of illegitimacy.

From his window now he could see her talking to Humility Brown, who was working in the gardens.

He smiled. Her conduct regarding those three men from *Adventurer* had been brave in the extreme; and yet it may have been her superstitious belief in herself rather than bravery, which had made her act the way she had. He himself had not heard of the affair until it was all over. She had fed those men, who had not been suffering from the plague at all, but from starvation. She had — in that bold, proud way of hers — taken them under her wing. There were only two of them alive, as they had not been discovered in time to save the third — Humility Brown and William Spears. William was working at the Hurly farm and was living in one of the farm cottages with other workers. Humility was working in Richard's own gardens and had been allotted one of the outhouses adjoining the house, for, as Tamar had pointed out, Joseph Jubin really needed assistance.

Tamar's delight in Humility Brown seemed admirable; but was it, Richard wondered. She was a minx, deeply conscious of that rare beauty of hers, and Humility Brown was a Puritan. Her pleasure in saving the man's life shone in her eyes every time she saw him; Richard guessed that Humility did not feel pleasure in Tamar's presence . . . Or was it that he was *afraid* he might feel pleasure? He was a minister from the town of Boston in Lincolnshire, and as fanatical in his beliefs as Tamar was in hers. It was said that there were more Puritans in that part of the country than in any other, and that persecution was more persistent there. Many of Humility's sect had fled to Holland — that centre of Protestantism — and lived there for some time. Richard found conversation with the man interesting, and was often turning over in his mind whether he might not find him some employment more suitable to his learning; but Richard knew himself; he had often decided he would do such-and-such and through sheer inertia had failed to make the necessary arrangements to bring these plans to fruition.

Now he began to wonder what Humility was saying to Tamar.

*　　*　　*

Tamar stood watching Humility weeding a flower bed. There were beads of sweat on Humility's brow,

150

and not only his physical exertions had put them there; he always felt uneasy in the presence of his employer's daughter.

"Humility," she persisted, "you are afraid of me."

It was a matter of great secret delight to her that he should want to ignore her and yet find this impossible.

"Nay," said Humility; "I do not fear thee. In my mind's eye I see the Cross, and while I keep that in my mind and heart, I fear nothing."

"Ah, Humility, you are a good man, and I am glad I saved your life. You thought me an angel when I brought you food. Did I look like an angel?"

Humility lifted his eyes to her lovely, laughing face.

"To a starving man, any who brought food would seem like an angel."

"Even if she came from the Devil?"

Humility said a prayer, not aloud; but she knew he said it by the way in which his lips moved.

"What did you think when you heard who I was?" she demanded.

He went on muttering, and she stamped her foot.

"Answer me, Humility! Have you forgotten that I am the mistress here?"

"I would," he said, "that you had allowed me to work on one of the farms . . . or in the town."

"But I saved your life. It is for me to say where you shall work. Humility, if you do not answer when I speak to you I shall have you punished."

"Your father is a just man. I do not think he would agree to punishment which was unmerited."

"If I asked him, he would."

He smiled. "I should not fear punishment," he said.

He continued to weed while she watched him. He both delighted and angered her . . . delighted her because he was a continual reminder of her power, angered her because there was a power in him that rivalled her own.

The minister from Boston was a man yearning to be a martyr. He was the sort who would suffer a thousand tortures and deem himself honoured to die for his faith. He believed the power of God was in him as firmly as Tamar believed she possessed certain powers which were a gift from the Devil.

She knew why he looked at her quickly and looked away. He was a man, and he found her beauty encroaching on his notice; he found her, as most men did, desirable.

It was pleasant to be desired, though she had no wish at present to gratify any man's desires, since she was unsure of her own feelings in this matter; but whereas she could feel fear when the glinting eyes of Bartle Cavill were fixed upon her, she could feel amusement when this man looked quickly and looked away.

He was older than Bartle. He would be about thirty years old, she imagined, which seemed very old to her when she considered the man in the role of a lover. She could guess what sort of life he had led; he was a Puritan child of Puritan parents. Puritans believed that ministers should live frugally, as Jesus Christ had done when He was on Earth. Humility had been brought up to believe that it was sinful to laugh, to enjoy more food than would keep him alive, and as for dancing or making love — these would be mortal sins. She knew that with her flaunting beauty, her quick and ready laughter, her awareness of her own attractions, she must seem like the Devil incarnate to such a man.

She liked to be near him when he was working, just to tease, to taunt. She wished him to know that he was as vulnerable as other men.

She would not have dared to taunt Bartle in such a way.

"Why do you frown at me, good Humility?" she asked. "Why do you stare at my hair as though you hate it?"

"You should cut it short or hide it under a cap."

"Why so? Do you think it is a gift from the Devil?"

He did not answer and she went on imperiously: "Answer when I speak to you. Do you think it is a gift from the Devil?"

Then he said: "That may well be so."

"I thought that God made all beautiful things."

He tried to plead with her, as he had on other occasions: "Do not be deceived. Mend your ways. Renounce the Devil. Embrace the true faith. If you would save yourself from eternal damnation, give up your evil ways."

"Was it evil to save your life?"

"If you called in the aid of the Devil, I had rather you had left me to die."

"It did not seem so when I came to the barn. You called out to me most piteously. I'll warrant you'd have taken food then if imps from Hell had brought it to you."

"You deceive yourself, daughter."

"Don't dare to call me daughter. You know whose daughter I am."

"I know that your birth was the result of sin."

"What if I were to tell your master that?"

"I would tell him so myself."

She gave him a grudging smile of admiration, for she knew that he spoke the truth. He was brave; she must concede that. That was why she felt herself forced to taunt him; his bravery was as great as her own; his belief that he was right as firm as that she held.

"You would, I believe," she said. "Some masters would have you beaten for it. But he is a good man . . . a far better man than you will ever be, Humility Brown."

He was silent.

"Oh," she went on angrily, "he does not go about thanking God that he is saved, that he is so much better than those who risked their lives to save his. He is a good man, I tell you, and if you dare say you are a better, I will whip you with my own hands."

It was at such times that he had the advantage. He was calm, and she could never be calm. He was cold and sure; she was fiery and passionate, though equally sure.

"And you would not care if I did!" Her eyes flashed. "But there are some things I could do which would make you care. Humility Brown, you are a coward. You are afraid to look at me. You take sly glances and look away. Have a care, Humility Brown! I might yet take you to eternal damnation with me. You think me beautiful. Your lips might deny that, but your eyes do not. I might decide to show you that you are but a sinful man, Humility Brown. You have heard talk of who is my real father, have you not? It is true, you know, that I am the Devil's own daughter."

Laughing, she ran into the house and called to Annis to come to her room and help her to dress for the ball.

*   *   *

She knew that Annis's repeated assertions, that she looked more beautiful than ever to-night, were true.

The dress was of scarlet, blue, and gold — her own choice of colours. The scarlet overgown opened in front to show the deep blue gold-embroidered skirt; her ruff was of finest lace — an upstanding collar that ended on the shoulders, leaving her bosom exposed after the fashion for unmarried ladies. She wore her hair loose, hanging down to the waist. There would be no one else at the ball who would wear her hair as she wore it.

Annis chattered gaily. Annis was now her personal maid, for Tamar, wishing to be known as a lady of fashion, must have such a maid of her own. Richard would have provided her with a trained one had she asked, but loyalty was strong in Tamar, and she wished to remove Annis from the housekeeper's tyranny. Indeed, Annis was more to her than any maid could have been; Annis was her friend.

"You're more beautiful than anyone has ever been," declared Annis. " 'Tis no wonder folks say beauty such as your's ain't of this world."

"You're fond of me, Annis; that's why you think so." It might be true, but Tamar was well pleased with the maid's words all the same.

"Others think it, mistress," explained Annis. "John, he said to me, 'Annis,' he said, 'Mistress Tamar have a beauty which is not of this world.' I spoke to him sharp-like. I said, 'John Tyler, have you been so bold as to cast your eyes that way, then?' And he said, 'Nay, Annis, I dare not. But there ain't another like her, and they do say as there's hardly a gentleman as claps eyes on her that wouldn't give his fortune to marry her, witch though she be.' I said, 'You'd better keep your eyes on me, John Tyler.' To which he answered, 'How could I help doing that, since her give you a charm herself to make me?' "

"Ah!" laughed Tamar. "So that charm still does its work, eh?"

"It does it beautiful, mistress. John's well-nigh beside himself for me some days."

Tamar studied this maid of hers who had experiences such as she herself had not. She thought of Humility Brown, and immediately another figure entered her thoughts — a young man with the most brilliant blue eyes she had ever seen. Then there was another picture in her mind, a picture which had been responsible for many a nightmare.

I hate Bartle Cavill, she told herself.

In the gallery the musicians were already assembling.

"Be quick," said Annis. "You should be there with the master to greet the guests."

Tamar hurried down. Richard was waiting for her at the bottom of the staircase.

She curtsied gaily.

"How do you like me, Richard?"

"You look very beautiful, my dear."

"Then you are not ashamed to own me as your daughter?"

He refused to pander to her demand for compliments. "There is a wildness in your eyes," he said. "What are you plotting this night?"

"I make no plots."

"Perhaps I should make some for you. It would please me very much to see you married."

"I am happy as I am."

"You should marry and have children. It is the duty of a father to choose a husband for his daughter."

She smiled demurely. "You have talked to me so much of the necessity to allow people free-will that I cannot believe you would go against your principles."

"I am very fond of you. It might be that I should consider it my duty. . ."

She took his hand and kissed it. "And I love you dearly," she said. "Nevertheless, I would not allow any to choose for me, or to arrange a marriage I did not want."

"I should not attempt it. But I do confess I should enjoy seeing you and your family riding over to Pennicomquick from Stoke. . ."

"From Stoke?"

He laughed. "I was thinking of Bartle. I am sure he would very gladly marry you."

"Bartle!" She spat out the name. "I would rather die than marry Bartle. He is coarse... vulgar... lecherous. I wonder that you dare mention his name to me."

"Hush! I crave your pardon. All the same, I think you are hard on the young man. He is brave; he has had many adventures and would be ready to settle down and live the life of a landowner with a family to bring up. Oh, I know he frightened you badly once. He was a clumsy boy, that was all."

"A lustful, lecherous beast!"

"I am sorry. Forget what I said."

"I shall... with all speed."

She was trembling, for the guests were arriving, and among the first were Sir Humphrey and Lady Cavill with their son Bartle.

Sir Humphrey's eyes admired Tamar; Lady Cavill kissed her in that half fearful way which Tamar was accustomed to; Bartle bowed over her hand, his eyes brilliant, shining with that blue fire which lit them whenever they fell upon her.

Haughtily she turned from him and talked to Sir Humphrey.

Other guests were arriving—all the gentry within riding distance. Richard had decided that Tamar's first ball should be worthy of his daughter.

When the guests had danced and were eating the rich foods which had been prepared for them—

venison and pies with clouted cream, roast meats of all varieties, to be washed down with wine and ale — morris dancers appeared with gay ribbons in their garments and bells attached to their legs, and they performed before the guests to the playing of musicians in the gallery.

Tamar was gay that night. She told herself it would have been a perfect evening but for the presence of Bartle. When he tried to speak to her she eluded him, and it delighted her to see how this angered him. Deliberately she coquetted with a tall and handsome young man whose large estates lay alongside the Plym. That young man was so fascinated by his beautiful hostess that he asked her to marry him. Then she was immediately sorry, for she had not wished to tease him — only to escape from Bartle.

But close on midnight, when the great fire in the centre of the hall had burned low and some of the guests were half asleep on their stools, indolent with too much rich food and wine, Bartle cornered her. She leaned against the oak panelling of the wall and studied him insolently. He was handsome enough in his swaggering way; his face was red and his eyes had never seemed so blue.

"What Devil's game do you think you're playing with me?" he demanded.

She lifted her hand to brush his aside, but he caught her in a grip which hurt.

"Release me at once or I'll have you thrown out," she retorted.

159

"It would be wise if you did not goad me too far, as you have been doing this night," he warned.

"I . . . goad you? I can assure you that no one could have been further from my thoughts this night . . . than you!"

"That's a lie and a poor one."

"You have a high conceit of yourself."

"I wonder, does it match yours?"

His eyes explored her face and rested on her bare bosom. She flushed hotly.

"Tamar," he said, "why put off what must certainly come to you?"

"What do you mean?"

"You surely have not forgotten that I made a vow concerning you?"

"Alas for you and your vows! I am not a poor child whom nobody cares for now. You would have to answer to Richard."

"Not if you came to me of your own free-will."

"You would wait a long time for that!"

He brought his face close to hers.

"My dear Tamar, I do not intend to wait. I shall be leaving England in a week. Before that day I shall have what I have long desired."

"You talk without sense."

"We shall see."

"If you dared to try to do to me what you tried once before, I would have no hesitation in killing you."

"But how would you manage that?"

"I should find myself unable to surprise you if I told you that."

160

"I believe that you have the Devil in you."

"That is the first thing of sense you have said to me to-night."

"But," he went on, "there will be no forcing. It shall be of your own free-will—I promise you that."

"Oh? And have you fixed a day for this voluntary surrender?"

"The day—or night—does not matter, but it shall be before I leave. That I have determined on."

She tried to remain calm, but she was uneasy, and she knew that he was aware of it. She forced herself to laugh, but her laughter was stilled abruptly when he said: "Simon Carter is in Plymouth. The witch-pricker has returned."

"Well?" She knew she had turned pale.

"That frightens you, does it not? Well it might! What if I go to him? What if I tell him that I have seen you making spells? What if I tell him I have seen you changing to a hare?"

"You would be a liar, and that would not help *you*, would it?"

"He would come to you, Tamar. Nothing Richard could do would prevent your being searched. Remember when you were on the point of being searched and pricked before, the only charge against you was your mother's statement that the Devil was your father. Richard declared *he* was, and therefore there was naught against you. But if you had been seen weaving spells . . . consorting with your familiar . . ."

"You . . . beast!"

"I would be kind, if you would but be kind to me. Tamar, why should I want to betray you? It would not be once or twice with me. I know that. To look at you tells me that."

"So," she said, her lips trembling, "you can pick a bedfellow as Simon Carter can pick a witch!"

"Leave your window open. I know which room is yours. I will come to you when the house is quiet. Then you need have no fear. If any attacked you, if any said a word against you, my sword would be ready to defend you . . . for ever, Tamar."

She was staring at him in silent horror, and he went on insolently: "Why, I might even marry you. Richard thinks it is time you married, and he is prepared to be very generous towards the man who marries the witch he is pleased to call his daughter."

"I would rather die than marry you."

"You talk too lightly of death."

"Please let me go. I never want to see your face again."

"You have grown haughty. How will you like the indignity of the search? How will you like to have those foul men exploring your body? How will you like to hang on a gibbet?"

She said coldly, her eyes glittering: "I would prefer torture and death to what you suggest."

He released her then.

His eyes followed her wherever she went for the rest of that evening; when he took his leave they mocked her. She saw his swaggering confidence; he was certain that she would give in to him.

162

He whispered to her: "Two days in which to come to a decision. No longer, I warn you. Time is precious."

When Annis helped her to undress she made the girl talk of her love affair with John Tyler. She listened with close attention and plagued Annis into giving details which made the girl hang her head and blush.

Then she laughed aloud, dismissed Annis and, throwing herself on the bed, she drew the curtains, shutting herself in.

But she could not shut out the image of Bartle's blazing eyes. And when she slept she dreamed of his pulling aside the curtains and forcing himself upon her. Humility Brown too was in the dream: she forgot what part he had played in it.

*　　*　　*

A hundred times Tamar relived that day when she had heard the shouts of the people, with Simon Carter at their head, as they came to the house to take her.

Surely Bartle would not betray her to that man. Once he had helped Richard to hide her. But that was only because he wanted her for himself. He was without pity; he was graceless; he was a boorish lecher; and how she hated him! He wished to treat her as he treated the native girls in those towns which he pillaged and burned. He was a buccaneer, a pirate, for all that he was considered one of King James's brave seamen.

Annis brought her a letter from him. Annis was all secret smiles. "Mistress, I have something for 'ee. 'Tis a note from a gentleman. He bid me give it to you and lose no time. He said 'twere important. Oh, mistress, what a handsome gentleman he be! The sort a woman would be powerless to resist. He gave me a kiss and said he'd warrant I was a pretty bedfellow to some lucky shepherd. I did feel myself shake, mistress, when he did lay his hands upon me."

"Be silent!" cried Tamar shrilly. "You are nothing more than a slut, Annis. If John went with another, you'd be to blame. And it would not surprise me greatly."

"Oh, mistress, you'll not take off the spell!"

"Unless you mend your ways, I swear I will. Now give me the note and leave me. I wish to be alone."

She read it through as soon as Annis had left her.

"I must see you at once," he had written. "It is important. Come to the garden and talk to me. I will wait in sight of the house, so, my chicken-hearted virgin, you need not be afraid. If you ignore this summons, you will be very sorry indeed. I am waiting now and it will not be wise to keep me waiting long. From him who is soon to be your lover."

She went to her window. He was down there, and he looked up and waved impatiently. She saw Humility in the distance.

Hastily she went down.

Elegantly dressed, Bartle was strolling about the gardens. As she approached, he hurried towards her, bowed and kissed her hands.

"Come into the enclosed garden," he said. "That fellow will hear everything if we do not."

She followed him, for she did not wish Humility to know of her predicament. Doubtless he would be pleased if he learned that the witch-pricker was about to be set on her trail.

The garden was secluded, surrounded by a high hedge, and bordering the paths were evergreens cut into fantastic shapes. Soon it would be spring and the first shoots in the flower beds were beginning to show themselves.

Bartle smiled at her mockingly.

"So," he said, "you spoke truth. You would rather die than give yourself to me."

She did not answer, but merely lifted her head and haughtily looked away from him. He took her by the shoulders and forced a rough kiss on her mouth. Her eyes blazed and she kicked him as she had once before. He ignored that, but he released her, though he stood barring her way at the gap in the evergreen hedge which was the only way in or out of the garden.

"We did not come here to fight," he said, "but to talk. Why, my dear Tamar . . ."

"Not *your* Tamar! . . . Never yours!"

"A little too soon perhaps. But this time to-morrow I shall call you my Tamar, and mayhap you will be glad to be so called."

She shrugged her shoulders. "I can see no object in your detaining me here."

"That is because you are so hasty. You never wait to hear: you speak . . . without thinking. You give an opinion on my plans before you have heard them. If I married you, which I have told you I am quite prepared to do and for what reason, I should have to subdue that high temper of yours. I should have to mould you into a meek and loving wife."

"Don't dare to insult me thus. I wonder you are not afraid I shall bewitch you."

"If it had been possible for you to harm me, you would have done so ere this."

"Let me pass, or I shall call to the gardener to come to my rescue."

"What! That meek Puritan! If he dared oppose me I'd slit his throat — and he knows it. Listen sensibly, girl, to what I have to tell you. To-night I shall come to your room. Leave your window open, as I shall come in that way."

She flashed at him: "My window will be barred and bolted to-night . . . and every night until that happy day when you sail away from Plymouth."

"I think, Tamar, that your window will be open to-night."

"Why so?"

"You would rather die than give me what I ask, and you have proved that to me."

"And you have proved your words were idle. You were not going to set Simon Carter upon me. If you were, why have you not done so — as you threatened to do — by this time?"

"Because I have vowed to have you for myself. You yourself are prepared to die rather than concede me what I ask. But are you prepared that others should die?"

"What others?"

"He who calls himself your father."

"I do not understand you."

"Do you not? What if I informed on Richard Merriman?"

"You are completely mad. How could you? And why?"

"The witch Luce said that the Devil was her lover. Richard says *he* was her lover. It is possible that he went to the meeting of witches — because it was at such a meeting that Luce was ravished . . . so she said. You, my beauty, were the result of that unholy union, as you know. I might suggest that Richard is a witch. I might suspect him and, having such suspicions, I should do my duty and go to the pricker and tell him of them. Let him find a mark . . . any mark . . . and I'll warrant that will be the end of Richard Merriman."

"You are vile and I loathe you!"

"Yes. I knew you would. But if you will not love me, then must you be taken loathing me. It will be a change. Too many women have loved me to madness."

"You are a conceited villain."

"I know it well," he mocked.

"Bartle, you would not do this. You cannot mean it. He is your friend!"

"Ah! Now you look at me with soft eyes. Now you plead. Tamar, witch or woman, I have sworn to have you. Never before have I had aught to do with witches, but you have been in my thoughts ever since I found you naked on the grass. I am ready to do anything . . . anything . . . barter my soul for you if necessary."

She felt tears starting to her eyes. "Let me go!" she cried.

He caught her arm as she tried to run past him.

"Leave your window open to-night. I promise you such joy as you have never dreamed of."

She ran past him and into the house.

*   *   *

She had gone to bed early. She had dismissed Annis, who was quite bewildered. Something ailed her mistress, she knew. Annis wondered what could ail one who had all that Tamar had. And now handsome Bartle Cavill was coming to woo her, and with those two, as Annis said to John Tyler, " 'twould mean a marriage ring and a marriage bed, not a heap of hay in a barn."

Tamar lay shivering. The door was locked and she had drawn the curtains about her bed; they stirred lightly in the breeze from the open window.

The decision had been made for her. He had threatened Richard, and for Richard's sake she must do this thing which was horrible and loathsome to her. It was worse than rape, because it would be done with a semblance of willingness.

"He is a fiend!" she muttered.

She had ill-wished him, but that was of no avail. She had tried to work a spell; but she believed he must have some protection against such things, some secret knowledge which he had picked up from foreign magicians on his travels.

She was dizzy with fear — or excitement.

Any moment now she would hear him, climbing into her bedroom. He would pull aside the curtains and stand there, mocking her in his triumph.

Only for Richard, would she do this. He had saved her life and now she would save his by giving more than her life, for had she not been willing to lose it rather than give in to Bartle for her own sake?

Outside the window she could hear the sounds of the night — the hoot of an owl, the sudden barking of a dog. It sounded as though witches were riding through the air on broomsticks, but it was only the wind in the chimney.

He had not yet come.

She thought — and, to her surprise, the thought angered her: Perhaps he did not mean it. Perhaps he will not come. He was merely teasing. Did he not say once that he would carry tales of me to the pricker?

In the midst of her fearful apprehension she was conscious of a twinge of disappointment.

It is because I wished to make a sacrifice for Richard, she told herself quickly. Even in this most evil thing there is some goodness, for I should have done it for Richard's sake. Had Richard known what wicked bargain Bartle had made with me, he would try to prevent my carrying out my share in it. Richard would let himself be taken by the pricker for my sake. So shall I find satisfaction in giving myself to Bartle . . . for Richard's sake.

And now she could hear a new sound outside her window.

She lay very still. She could hear the thud as he landed on his feet; she could hear his breathing, heavy with the exertion of the climb.

Very slowly, it seemed to her, the curtains were parted. She could not see his face; there was not enough light for that; she was only aware of a broad figure bending over her.

"Tamar!" he said; and his voice was higher than usual, yet thicker, unlike its usual timbre, but she knew it for Bartle's.

She shrank as his hands touched her.

"So," he whispered, "you were waiting for me? I knew you would be."

CHAPTER
FOUR

The memory of that night would not leave her.

He had refused to go before dawn was in the sky, and she had no means of making him. There was nothing she could do but lie, quiet and submissive.

She had wept in her anger and he had kissed her tears. But his tenderness quickly changed to mockery.

"You deceive yourself, Tamar! You are as eager for me as I am for you. I certainly shall not go until it pleases me to do so. I meant to stay all through the night. That was our bargain. What a demanding witch you are! Most women ask for a jewel; but you submit for a man's life!"

"You have humiliated me," she answered. "Is that not enough? Go now, I beg of you."

"Come! You know that when you beg me to go, you are really begging me to stay."

"You lie! And stop talking. What if your voice should be heard?"

He put his mouth close to her ear. "They would say 'Tamar has a man in her bed! Well, what do we expect from such as Tamar? Perhaps it is the Devil she has in there? No, not her own father . . . merely some imp from Hell!'"

"If they came and found you here...?"

"Well then, I should tell them how I came to be where I am. I should say, 'I came through the window. Tamar opened it for me.' That is the truth, you know. When I parted the curtains of your bed, you were waiting for me. Can you deny that?"

"You are a devil, I believe."

"Then we are well mated. Of course we are. We know that now. Oh, Tamar, how I love you. This is the beginning. Leave your window open to-morrow and I will come again."

"That was not in the bargain," she said quickly.

"Bargain? Who talks of bargains? You know why I am here."

"Yes! Because you are a traitor...a false friend."

"What! To Richard? I'd never have betrayed Richard, sweetheart, and you knew that all the time. I was merely giving you the excuse you wanted for surrender."

"I loathe you. I hate you. You are worse even than I believed you to be. Go at once...At once, I say!"

But he had crushed her against him, laughing softly, biting her ear. "You knew I would never have betrayed Richard. He is an old bore, but I'm fond of him. It is not for filthy prickers of the lower orders to use their pins on men of our station. I said what I did to give you an excuse. You knew it. You cannot deceive me. And you were delighted."

She had felt that the humiliation was more than she could tolerate.

When at last he had gone she leaped out of bed and bolted her window. He stood below and bowed mockingly.

Annis was astonished when, pulling back the curtains later that morning, she found Tamar fast asleep, pale-faced and exhausted.

Tamar opened her eyes and looked at her maid.

"Why, mistress, what ails you?" cried Annis. "You look . . . different . . ."

"Don't be a fool. How could I be different?" She rose, her mind full of what had so recently happened to her. "Don't stand there staring at me!" she shouted to Annis. "Help me to dress."

She slapped Annis when the girl fumbled with the fastening of her gown, and, seeing the tears well up in Annis's eyes, she herself began to weep while she embraced her maid.

"Annis, I'm sorry. You're right. I'm not myself."

Annis was all smiles immediately. "I was clumsy. It was just that I couldn't bear you to be cross with me. What ails thee, dear mistress? What has happened to 'ee this night?"

"This night!" cried Tamar. "What do you mean by that?"

"Nothing," said Annis quickly. " 'Twere just that you did seem strange like when I left you for the night, and now you be stranger still."

Tamar kissed Annis's cheek. "Do not speak to me of it," she said. "I am well. I did not sleep well; that is all."

Annis nodded, and it was clear to Tamar that the girl thought she had been up to some Devil's work during the night. And that, Tamar told herself fiercely, would have been a deal more to my liking than what has befallen me.

Bartle dared to ride over to Pennicomquick that morning. "To drink a goblet of wine with the mistress of the house," he told Tamar when Annis brought him into the room.

Tamar regarded him icily. He looked as debonair as ever. There was no novelty for him, she supposed, in such nights.

"How dare you show yourself here!" she demanded.

"I would dare much to see you. I thought you would receive me warmly after last night."

"We were not friends before. We are greater enemies now."

"You cannot be my enemy, and I would never be yours. Oh, Tamar, you are so beautiful and I adore you. I have come to make honourable amends. I have come to ask you to marry me. Custom demands that I go to Richard and tell him what I wish and how I hope he will decide I am a good enough match for his daughter. But that, I know, will not do for Tamar. She must be wooed, then won. Ha! Not so. She must be won, then wooed. So I come to you, Tamar, before I go to your father."

"I would choose my husband and, if I lived until I were fifty and there was no one else in the world, I would never take you."

"Let us have done with quarrels. Let us be reasonable. We are both expected to marry, so why not each other?"

"Because a woman should not marry a man she hates."

"You mean you really hate me?"

"I mean it from the bottom of my heart."

He had become haughty now; he walked to the window and looked out. She remained by the table; and they were thus when Richard came into the room.

Bartle left Plymouth a few days later. Tamar did not know why she felt she must go and see him leave; but she did.

There was the usual bustle such departures always brought with them down there on the causeway. Ships being loaded, sailors shouting to one another, anchors being lifted, sails set.

She had hoped Bartle would not see her, but his sharp eyes found her. He came to her and stood before her, smiling down at her.

"So you have come to see me off on my voyage?"

"To assure myself that you had really gone," she answered caustically. "It gives me great pleasure to know that I shall not see you for a long time."

"I shall soon be back, sweetheart," he said: "and then . . ."

"I beg of you, make no more vows. I assure you there shall be no repetition of that shameful night."

"My lovely Tamar! I shall carry your image in my heart. I expect a dull voyage, for there can be little pleasure for me outside your bed."

175

He caught her up and kissed her full on the mouth. Then he put her down, bowed low and left her.

She walked up to the Hoe that she might watch the ships until they were specks on the white-flecked sea, while anger, humiliation and something like regret filled her heart.

* * *

When she arrived back at the house she saw Humility Brown at work in the garden. She went over to him; by taunting him she thought to regain her self-respect.

"Good day to you, Humility Brown."

"Good day," he answered. But he did not look at her.

She said sharply: "When I speak to you, pray do not go on with your work. Look at me. Smile! Say 'Good day' as though you meant it."

He looked at her gravely, and she felt herself blushing hotly, for she thought he saw the change in her, and visions of Bartle and herself would not be shut out of her mind.

"Do not stare!" she said.

Then he did smile. "I am admonished for not looking, and when I look that does not please you. You are in an ill mood to-day."

"What is that to you?"

"Nothing; but that I am sorry to see you put out."

"*You* . . . sorry for *me!*"

"Ah yes. I am deeply sorry for you."

"And why, pray?"

"Because guilt lies heavy on your soul."

176

"Who says so? Can you see guilt in my face?"

"You have forsaken true goodness for the evil power which comes to you through the Devil. You have asked for beauty to tempt the senses of men, and it has been given to you."

"It was given without my asking," she retorted. "And does it tempt your senses, Humility Brown?"

His lips moved in silent prayer.

"Stop that!" she cried. "Stop it, I say!"

"My poor erring daughter," he said, "give up your sins. Wash your soul pure in the blood of the Holy Lamb."

She laughed. "Is that what you have done? But you have no sins, I suppose . . . and never have had!"

"We are all sinners."

"It surprises me that you should put yourself into that class. Oh, Humility Brown, sometimes I wish I had left you to starve in the barn."

"Aye! And so do I! Then I should be past my pains . . . safe in the arms of Jesus."

"It might be the fires of Hell for you, Humility Brown."

He bowed his head and once more sought refuge in prayer.

"Oh, I meant not that!" she cried in repentance. "You are a good man and the gates of Heaven will be flung wide for you, I doubt not."

"Daughter," he cried, "repent. Repent while there is yet time."

"Repent of what?"

"Of your sins."

"It might be that I have sinned through no fault of my own."

"It is only the Devil's own who are forced into sin. The Good Shepherd protects His sheep."

"Are you sure of that?"

"As sure as I stand here."

She was silent. It was Humility who spoke first. He leaned on his spade and looked at her earnestly.

"You are a sinner," he said; "that I know. You defy the Holy Gospel. There are many who think you have dealings with witches. You are in peril. Your soul is in danger."

"What can I do about that?"

"Wicked as you are, I know I can trust you with a secret. I will show you how much I am prepared to trust you if you care to let me do so."

She was interested; for the first time since that memorable night, she had forgotten Bartle.

"You would never betray friends," he said, "even though you thought what they did was folly."

"I believe that to be so," she said.

"You are generous and there is kindness in you . . . kindness towards the weak; such kindness was the kindness taught us by our Lord Jesus Christ. Because you possess it, I believe there is hope for you. But you are vain and proud and, I believe, wicked in some strange way. But because of your kindness I wish to save your soul as once you saved my body."

"You must tell me what you mean by that."

"Some of us are meeting together. We meet in secret."

"I see."

He went on: "You know what I mean. William Spears and I, and others here who wish to worship God in the right way, have fixed a meeting-place where we forgather."

"That is a dangerous thing to do, Humility. If you were discovered, it would mean prison — perhaps torture and execution."

He smiled and his smile illumined his face so that it seemed almost beautiful.

"You are a fool!" she said angrily, in sudden fear for him.

"I am the Lord's," he answered.

She was emotional that morning and her eyes filled with tears.

"You are a brave man. I beg of you, take care. I would not care to see you come to harm after I took such pains to save your life."

"We meet in a hut . . . Stoke way. It is on Sir Humphrey Cavill's estate."

"Have a care! Sir Humphrey would have no scruples about denouncing you if he discovered. He is a bigot . . . and so is his son. They are without pity . . . without . . ."

"I know it," he said. "And this we all know: We meet in the name of Truth, in the name of the Lord. We know the risks we run and we are prepared to run them. If the Lord should see fit to make our presence known to those who would persecute us, then we are all ready to accept persecution for His sake."

"Why do you tell me this?"

"That you might join our meeting and perhaps find peace there."

"*I* . . . meet with *Puritans*!" She smoothed the rich stuff of her dress and looked down at it lovingly.

"You would learn that it is folly to lay up for yourself treasures upon earth. You would learn that you should repent of your sins."

She turned from him and hurried into the house. She knew that she would go and see their secret meeting-place. She needed the excitement of new experiences now that Bartle, whose loathsome presence had provided them, had gone away.

* * *

Tamar went once to the meeting-place. Such affairs were not for her. She was like a bird of paradise among sparrows. She sensed the hostility of the Puritans towards her. What, they were asking themselves, was Humility Brown about, to ask a witch to their meetings?

When Humility preached that night he said: "There is none among us who could not reach salvation, an that one wished it."

That she knew was for her.

But she stood apart from them — apart from them as she had been from the people amongst whom she had lived during her childhood. Only Humility wished to befriend her. She listened to his preaching; she watched the earnestness of his expression. He was a bolder man here than in the gardens; there he seemed aptly named; here he was a leader.

She felt a new pride in the fact that she had saved his life. She could look scornfully round her now at the faces of his followers and remind herself that not one of them would have dared to do for him what she had done.

She did not go again to the meeting-place.

Simon Carter had now left Plymouth, and the crow-pecked bodies of several men and women hung rotting from the gibbets.

But for me, thought Tamar, Richard might have been one of them!

Then she must think again of that night which she knew would be the most memorable of her life because it was the most shameful. When she looked out to sea she thought of Bartle. Where was he now? Somewhere on the Spanish Main? Perhaps he had reached land; perhaps he was tricking some other woman to shame as he had tricked her. She might turn angrily away from the sea to the land, but the green grass and the trees reminded her of the day when he had found her naked on the grass and had pursued her. There was no escape from thoughts of Bartle.

Annis came to her room one day; it was easy to see that something was on Annis's mind.

"What is it, Annis?" asked Tamar.

Annis cast down her eyes. "Trouble, mistress. That's what 'tis."

"I know," said Tamar. "You are going to tell me that you are with child."

Annis lifted her wondering eyes to Tamar's face. "You knew afore I did myself, I reckon, mistress."

Tamar could not resist the pleasure of allowing her to think so.

"That this should happen to *me*!" sighed Annis.

"Well, Annis, there was many a meeting in the old barn, I believe."

"You took the spell off, then, did 'ee, mistress?"

"You cannot do what you have been doing so often, with no result. You must tell John and he will have to marry you."

Annis began to cry.

" 'Tis like this, mistress. John, he be sharing a cottage with Will Spears and Dan Layman. John couldn't marry a wife and take her to share with they two."

"But, Annis, John will have to ask for a cottage of his own now."

"There be no empty cottage."

"Your father and mother would let you live at the farm. They surely would when they know how things are."

"My mother said she'd break my neck if aught of this sort ever happened to me. Me father said he'd give me the whipping of me life."

"That's what they said before it happened, Annis. They'll know they will have to look after you now. They'll have to help you and John."

Annis began to cry bitterly. " 'Tis John himself, mistress. You see, I did tell him the charm would look after that there . . . and it looked as though I were right. It certainly looked as though it were. I dursen't tell him. That be the plain truth."

"Annis," said Tamar in exasperation, "you are a little fool!"

"That's what most of us women be, I reckon!" said Annis.

"Please stop crying, Annis. I will think of something to be done."

Annis knelt at Tamar's feet and embraced her knees.

"You'll take it away, mistress. They do say 'tis a thing a witch can do."

"No," said Tamar. "I cannot do that."

All hope faded from Annis's face.

"It would be wrong to do it. But never fear, I will make a plan for you. I will see that you come to no harm. You must trust me."

"Oh, I do, mistress," said Annis fervently, "with the very soul of me!"

*　　*　　*

Richard said to Tamar: "Do you know what that fool Humility Brown is doing? He is arranging meetings of the Puritans. Moreover, he is going about the place converting people to his faith. It is a highly dangerous thing to do!"

"He is a very brave but very foolish man, I fear," said Tamar.

"I will speak to him. Ring the bell and ask one of the maids to fetch him."

"I will go myself and bring him to you," she said.

She went into the garden.

"Humility Brown, your master wishes to speak to you. You may well look startled. He has discovered that you are holding meetings and, not content with putting yourself in danger, you go about asking other people to do the same. He is very angry with you."

"If they wish to save their souls, it is of no concern to any but themselves," he said. "The life of the body is transient; that of the soul eternal."

"Well, you must now come and give an account of yourself. I would have you know that I have not betrayed you."

"I did not think for one moment that that was so."

"Thank you," she answered. "Now come this way. Your master does not care to be kept waiting."

She could not help thinking how noble the man looked as he stood before Richard, how cleverly he answered the questions put to him. A brave man . . . this Humility Brown! She compared him with Bartle, and her mouth tightened at the recollection of that which she had tried so hard to forget.

"You are, I know," said Richard, "convinced that you are right. But you are defying the law of this land, and how can that be right?"

"I know of one law only, sir . . . the law of God."

"It would seem," said Richard coldly, "that whether God is on your side or on that of the Church of England is a matter of opinion. But I did not send for you to discuss that. What I wish to say is this: You, my good man, may be made of martyr's stuff, but think you that you do right to involve others?"

184

"If they wish to save their souls alive, they must worship God in the only true way," said Humility. "The Carpenter's Son preached simplicity, but in the Church of England ceremonial rites are practised which are little short of popery. Where does the Church of England differ from the Church of Rome? It would seem in this only: One has a King at its head; one a Pope."

"You attach too great an importance to the method and ritual of worshipping God. I have little patience with those who would send to their death men and women who have a way of worshipping God which differs from their own. It seems to me the utmost arrogance to say, 'You are wrong because you do not as I do!' Arrogance is a sin, is it not? And one Catholics and Puritans are guilty of . . . and all other sects with them. Jesus said, 'Not everyone that saith unto me, Lord, Lord, shall enter the kingdom of heaven; but he that *doeth* the will of My Father.' Are you not guilty of the sin of pride when you continually thank God that you are not as other men are? What if I informed against you and your meeting?"

"If you feel that is your duty, then you should do it."

Tamar said: "Richard, you have always declared that men should be free to worship God in whatever way they wish."

"I have said that and I believe it." He turned to Humility. "All I wish to do is to beg you to have a care."

"I will, sir. And I think you would benefit if you came to our meetings."

"What!" cried Richard. "You dare ask me!"

"You have a soul to save, sir."

"He is a better man than you will ever be, for all your piety!" cried Tamar.

"I did not say that he was not," said Humility.

"But you thought it. I saw it in your eyes."

They made a striking contrast — Tamar and Richard in their gay garments; Humility in his sombre attire.

"It is not sufficient for a man to have a kind heart," said Humility. "It is not sufficient to be courageous and tolerant. It is imperative to worship God in the right way."

"You mean in the Puritan manner," said Richard with a touch of sarcasm.

"That is so, sir."

"You may go now. And remember my warning."

"I thank you, sir."

He bowed gravely to Tamar and to Richard; but as he was about to leave he turned to Tamar.

"Repent," he said. "I beg of you, repent before it is too late. I shall pray for your souls, for you are both in need of salvation."

As he went out Tamar looked at Richard.

"I never knew a man so sure," she said.

"A fanatical fool!" said Richard.

"Yet I have a certain admiration for him."

"That may be because you are also fanatical, also foolish, my dear." He smiled grimly. "He the

Puritan . . . and you the Pagan. And who should be bold enough to say one is right and one is wrong? A cleverer man than I am."

"You are cleverer than any of us and you are the one with doubts." She paused reflectively. "I shall be a little angry if he comes to harm. I did not save his life to have him throw it away."

"If he comes to grief, it is his own fault. My sincere hope is that he does not bring trouble to others in this place."

Tamar went to her own room and had not been there for many minutes when there was a knock on her door.

It was Annis, looking happier than she had for a long time.

"I did see Humility Brown coming from master's study."

"What of that?"

"I was wondering . . . be master saved?"

"Saved from what?"

"Be his soul saved? Has Humility saved it for him?"

"Your master's soul has long been saved. He is the best man in the world, and as such will enter the Kingdom of Heaven before any preaching Puritan!"

Annis would not contradict her; but Tamar saw disbelief in the girl's eyes.

"You, Annis, have been taking a good dose of Mr. Humility Brown, I do believe."

"Oh, mistress, I did mean to tell 'ee. It did happen these several days gone. We'd been to the meetings,

John and me together like...and then...we found we was saved."

"You and John...Puritans!"

"That be the size of it, mistress."

Tamar was angry. She had always felt Humility to be a rival, and Annis belonged to her. She could not help looking upon this as desertion.

"So," she said with a sneer, "'you and John are safe for Heaven, eh?"

"Yes, mistress, we be safe. We only has to worship God as 'tis laid down we should and we be saved."

"As laid down by Master Humility Brown, I suppose."

"That I wouldn't know, mistress. 'Tis as laid down...that's all I do know."

"You will not wish to continue to serve me, then."

Annis paled. "Mistress, I would never wish to be parted from you."

"Puritans should have naught to do with those who are in touch with the Devil."

"Oh, mistress, 'tis not so. You be good...though not saved yet. I do pray you'll be saved...every night I do. Why, I'd rather not be saved than leave 'ee. Nobody ain't ever been so kind to me as you have. I'll give up they meetings if you do forbid me to go."

Tamar laughed in triumph. "No, Annis. You may continue to be a Puritan if you wish it. It makes no difference to me. I am still your friend."

"Well, mistress, 'tis John really. He went to the meeting and got himself saved. He did come to me and say, 'Annis, I be saved, and you'd better be saved too. I shouldn't like to think of your soul in eternal torment, that I shouldn't.' And I said, 'Well, John, 'tis share and share alike with us, and if you be saved then saved I'll be.' So he took me along to the meeting and there I was saved too. Mistress, Master Brown do talk so beautiful . . . he do carry you away, he do. But John says what we've been doing in the barn is sinful like, and now we'm saved we mustn't do it any more."

"You'll have to marry at once, Annis. Puritans must not behave as you've been behaving."

"I know, mistress, but I think the dear Lord will forgive us, for He will know how for the life of us we couldn't say no to it afore we was saved."

"Did you tell John you were with child?"

"In a roundabout way, I did. I said, 'John, if we be saved, we should marry, for we've been sinful and marriage is the only way out of sin like ours.' But John said, ' 'Tis so, Annis. 'Tis fornication that we've been at, and Master Humility Brown did say bitter things about fornication. 'Tis a big sin all right.' ' 'Tis only marriage, John,' I says, 'that'll put us right and save our souls from torment.' John said, 'Aye, 'tis so, but I've been sinful with two others, Annis, so 'tis a terrible problem which the Lord has set before me.'"

"But did you not tell him that there was to be a child?"

"I couldn't find it in my heart to do it, mistress."

"You must do so, Annis, and when John says he'll marry you I'll see what I can do for the pair of you."

"Mistress, you be very good to me. I do hope you'll get saved, for I'm wondering what Heaven will be like without you."

"You need not concern yourself with me," said Tamar. "Depend upon it, when my time comes, I shall know how to take care of myself."

Annis nodded her agreement.

*　　*　　*

Annis was weeping bitterly, her head in Tamar's lap. A terrible tragedy had overtaken Annis.

John—the most simple of all the new Puritans—had talked too freely. He had been arrested and taken to the gaol.

When Annis heard the news she was overcome by her grief. In six months' time her baby would be born, and it was unlikely—judging from what had happened in similar cases—that John would be free in time to marry her before the child's birth.

"What'll they do to John?" she wailed. "Mistress Alton has had her eyes on me . . . smiling in a sly, secret sort of way as though to say, 'I knew it would happen to 'ee, Annis Hurly!'"

"Take no notice of that old woman," said Tamar. "You anger me. Why did you not tell John at once so that he might have married you before this happened?"

"I don't know, mistress. I must have been half mazed."

"You must indeed. But your master will be able to help you. I'll have a word with him. I'll warrant John will soon be home and then I swear I'll make him marry you. If you won't tell him, I'll tell him myself."

Annis continued to sob wildly.

"Oh, mistress, you're that good to me!"

"More good to you than Humility Brown with all his fine preaching? But for that man, John would not be in prison to-day. Have you thought of that?"

"He says 'twas God's will, mistress."

"God's will!" snapped Tamar. "Mayhap you should ask God to help you now. . . God or Humility Brown."

"Nobody was ever as good to me as you, mistress," said Annis plaintively.

Tamar went down to Richard.

"You have heard this news?" she asked.

"That fool John Tyler talked too much. He has a head on him like a bundle of hay."

"Richard, what can you do for him?"

Richard shrugged his shoulders. "I think it will be seen that a simpleton such as John Tyler can hardly be dangerous."

"It is necessary that he does not stay away too long. He has to marry Annis."

Richard gave a burst of ironic laughter. "The men and the maidens!" he said.

But she was quick in their defence. "Humility Brown would doubtless say: 'He that is without sin among you, let him first cast a stone.'"

Richard smiled apologetically. "I crave your pardon. . . and theirs. Tell Annis I will do all that can be done."

"I have already told her that."

He raised his eyebrows. "How odd it is that you who persist in your relationship—and shall I say allegiance—to the Devil, should spend so much time bothering yourself with the troubles of others!"

"If Mistress Alton casts her sneering eyes on Annis, I shall take her cane and beat her with it. Why do we not get rid of that woman? I hate her."

"Sometimes I ask myself that. But she is a good cook and she has learned my tastes. It would not be easy to replace her. I fear I have not the necessary energy to try."

"Let her be then, but let her remember her place. I'll not have Annis made more unhappy than she already is. I want you to see what can be done about John's release. I know you would help me in any case, but I want you to help quickly. I want him to marry Annis. She loves him and will look after him—he needs looking after, it seems. And there is something else. Annis is afraid of her mother and father. She dreads having to live at the farm with them, which is what she and John would have to do if they married. I want to keep Annis with me. She has been with me so long, and I could not fancy replacing her. So I want you to have a cottage built for them. There is a spot not far from the Swanns'. They could live there and John could go on working at the farm and I could keep Annis. Will you do this, Richard?"

He hesitated: then he burst into sudden laughter. "You take my breath away."

She kissed him in her impulsive way. He was enchanted, while he still wondered why this should be so.

"You will, then," she said. "I knew you would. Now will you please ride into the town and see what you can do about John's release?"

She went down with him to the stables and watched him ride off.

*　　*　　*

Events did not slip into the pleasant pattern which Tamar had planned. For one thing, Richard could not obtain John's release. John had talked seditiously; he had talked against Church and State.

Tamar soothed Annis as best she could. "You must not fret, girl. He'll be out soon."

But he did not come out and the weeks stretched into months. Mistress Alton was now watching her slyly.

"A nice state of affairs!" said Mistress Alton to Moll Swann. "Slip into sin and slip into prosperity, so it would seem. The reward is to the wicked. Have a bastard, and a cottage shall be built for you."

The housekeeper made a face at Tamar when Tamar's back was turned, and only Moll — who was little more than half-witted — and Moll's sister Jane could see her. That was all she dared do. She had been afraid since Tamar had come into the house that the girl would prevail on Richard Merriman to send his housekeeper away. Sometimes Mistress Alton felt that it was only her excellence in running his house

and his hatred of being disturbed which were
responsible for his keeping her on; she knew she
must tread warily, but for the life of her she could
not stop herself tattling about Annis. How she wished
she had Annis in the kitchens. She would have shown
her what she thought of her. As it was, she could not
stop talking about her.

"That Annis," she said to Moll and Jane, "got too
big for her boots when the *mistress* of the house, the
master's *daughter*, took it into her head that she must
have a maid to wait on her. Maid indeed! Now we see
Annis getting too big for her petticoats, besides her
boots!"

Annis was afraid to go home. Her father had
threatened, if she did, to tie her to the whipping-post
in the yard and give her the biggest whipping of her
life; her mother had said she would help him. Mistress
Alton, licking her lips, tried to beguile Annis into
going home; but Tamar saw that this did not happen.

Tamar was fierce in her defence of Annis. She
hated both Mistress Alton and Humility Brown, who
were harsh in their condemnation; she wondered at
this time how she could ever have thought Humility
noble.

She stopped him at his work one day when she was
coming from the stables.

"How dare you look as you do at Annis?" she
demanded.

He did not answer.

"I hate you when you look like that. Scornful . . . as
though . . . as though you would rejoice to see Annis

burning slowly in horrible flames that are fanned by devils."

"That will doubtless be her fate."

"I could not accept a God who allowed that."

"You blaspheme," he said.

"Mayhap I do. And you are a tyrant . . . So are all like you. Can you not understand that Annis is a broken-hearted woman?"

"She is a fornicator. She has sinned and cannot hope to escape her punishment."

"She *is* being punished. She loves John Tyler, and they keep him in prison. She is afraid of what they will do to him. She is afraid he will not be released before her baby is born. Is that not enough punishment for anything she has done?" He did not answer, and she went on: "It is you . . . *you* . . . who should be in prison. Not John Tyler. You tricked him into going to your meetings, and he is punished while you go free!"

He said: "If it were the will of God that I should be taken, then it would be I who was in gaol at this moment."

"You madden me! So it is God's will that Annis should suffer thus?"

"How could it be otherwise? Sin brings punishment, and she has been guilty of the greatest sin."

"Have you never committed such a sin?"

He flushed scarlet and looked at her in horror.

"No!" she cried. "*You* have not! You are not man enough. You might take sly glances and think . . . and hope . . . but you escape sin because you are not a man but a . . . a Puritan!"

"You make excuses for your maid, and perhaps . . . yourself."

Her rage was uncontrollable at that moment and, lifting her riding whip, she struck at him. The lash came down on his hand as he stepped back, and, watching the red weal spring up, she was instantly sobered and ashamed.

"You . . . you maddened me!" she said.

"The Devil was at your elbow," he said; and it seemed to Tamar that he regarded his hand with a certain satisfaction.

Her anger returned. "If you dare talk to me in that strain," she said, "I will do it again . . . and again!"

Then she turned and ran into the house.

*   *   *

Annis's child was a boy, and she called him Christian. "In the hope," said Annis tearfully, "that he will grow up better than his sinful parents."

John was released a month or so after the birth, and he and Annis were married at once, settling into the new cottage near the Swanns'.

The villagers grumbled that the Tylers were the luckiest pair to be met with for many a mile, and it seemed that rewards went to the sinful. That was not what Preacher Brown taught. It was not what the Church taught either! It was easy enough to see what had happened. Tamar had brought this about. Tamar was pleased. Of course she was! Another baby born

196

out of wedlock! Another to be brought up in the service of the Devil!

As for Mistress Alton, she was almost beside herself with annoyance. She chattered to anyone who would listen. It was only when people demanded to know how she could continue to work in a house whose mistress she believed to be a witch that she began to ask herself what she would do if she were turned away. Then she was a little subdued.

Humility Brown was even more dismayed than Mistress Alton. All during the months of Annis's pregnancy he had tried to persuade Tamar not to give the cottage to the Tylers, and she, being contrite because of the mark her whip had made on his hand, was polite to him until the weal had gone. When it had completely disappeared there was many a stormy scene between them.

"What would you do if you were in my place?" she demanded. "Tell me what I should do if I were a good Puritan."

"Pray for the girl."

"Prayers would not build her cottage." She laughed mockingly at him. "My words shock you. You expect the heavens to open and some terrible blight to fall upon me. Annis has sinned, you say; and I will say to you what I have said to others: 'Let him who is without sin cast the first stone.' Would that be you, Humility Brown? I believe it would be. Humility! That should not be your name. Pride should be your name. For the pride of those who are saved, such as you, seems beyond the pride of the damned such as I suppose I am."

"You condone sin," he explained. "There are deserving couples in this place who marry in purity. Could you not have given one such couple a cottage?"

"But I love Annis and Annis is in trouble. But how could you understand that? You never loved anything but good — never hated anything but evil. You would turn Annis out, would you not? Send her home to those wicked parents of hers, whom doubtless you consider good people. It seems to me that your Church has led you a long way from the teachings of Jesus."

"You would glorify evil," he said. "There is no denying that."

With rising temper, she left him.

$$* \qquad * \qquad *$$

One summer's day Bartle came home. Down in the town there was the excitement and bustle which the return of the ships never failed to produce.

The day after his arrival he came riding into the stables at Pennicomquick. Tamar heard the clatter of hoofs and she hurried to her window, for the news of his return had reached her immediately on his arrival and she had been expecting his visit. She saw him leave the stables; she saw him come striding across the lawns in his arrogant way, towards the house. He looked up at her window and she hastily withdrew. She was astonished to see how her hands were trembling as she pulled at her bell-rope.

198

Annis came, for Annis still worked for Tamar, bringing her baby, who was now a year old, with her from the cottage each day. Christian was at this moment toddling on the lawn, for he was just learning to take a few unsteady steps by himself.

"Annis," said Tamar, "if anyone asks for me, say I am not at home. That is all."

Tamar went back to the window, standing cautiously away, and she saw Bartle approach the child. Little Christian toddled willingly towards him, and Bartle lifted him, and as he held the child high above his head, Tamar heard Christian's shrieks of joy.

Then she stepped back quickly, for Bartle had looked from the child to the window.

He had not been five minutes in the house when Annis came running up.

"Mistress, the master sent me up to find 'ee."

"I told you to say I was not at home."

"Mistress, 'twas a lie. I could not say it."

Tamar laughed angrily. "Here is more of Humility Brown's work! You cannot tell a lie when I bid you!"

"Well, mistress, I did say I would come to your room and, if you were here, tell you that you were wanted below. And, mistress, 'tis a gentleman as the master says you'll be pleased to see."

"I know who is there!" she cried.

Annis kept her eyes downcast. She was a good Puritan now—she and John together—and any manifestation of the peculiar powers of her mistress, while exciting her as they always had done, filled her with apprehension. Humility Brown preached against witchcraft even as the prickers did; and yet one whom Annis loved equally with her husband and child was of that strange and frightening community.

With a suddenness typical of her, Tamar's anger changed to understanding. She laid a hand on Annis's shoulder and said: "I saw him from the window. There was no craft in it; and since you do not wish to lie, you may say that I am here, but that I do not wish to come down."

Annis, smiling gladly with that simplicity which always touched Tamar, went out, but in a little while she was back.

"The master says it is Mr. Cavill returned from the sea, and he thinks that will make you change your mind."

"Go and tell him that that does not make me change my mind."

She stayed in her room for more than an hour and it was only when she had seen Bartle leave that she went downstairs.

Richard was there, sitting thoughtfully in the window-seat of the big room, looking idly out of the window. He raised his eyebrows when he saw her.

"That was most discourteous of you!" he said.

"I had no wish to see him."

"He is our neighbour and there is friendship between our families. He has been away a long time. . . two years, I believe; and when he comes to see us you send down such a message!"

She shrugged her shoulders.

"Tamar," he went on, "why do you continue to hate that young man so vehemently? Can you not forgive him for what he tried to do to you so long ago?"

"No, I cannot."

"But it is so long ago and he was but a wild boy then!"

"He is a wild man now."

"I wish you would marry. You are twenty years old, and that is a marriageable age. You see the happiness of Annis and her John. You are fond of little Christian. Have you no desire to have children of your own?"

"I think when the time comes for me to marry, I shall know. If it does not come"—she shrugged her shoulders again—"well, then I shall not marry." She turned on him fiercely. "Why do you always think about my marrying when Bartle is here?"

"Perhaps because I feel he would make a suitable husband."

"How can you think that? What is your opinion of me, that you think him a match for me? He is nothing but a buccaneer, a pirate! Oh . . . all very legal, because it is only Spanish ships that he robs, Spanish towns that he fires, only Spanish virgins whom he violates! Or are there others who suffer at his hands?"

"I fear you are determined to hate him. It is that pride of yours, which will always be your biggest enemy. You are so sure that you are right when you set yourself to judge such as Bartle, to protect such as Humility Brown; but, do you know, your sense of right and wrong is governed by your emotions? Bartle is a buccaneer; therefore to be despised.

Myself, Annis, John Tyler, have all been guilty of sin, but us you fiercely defend. I wish very much that you would try to be a little more reasonable with Bartle."

"He does not need my kindness!" she said.

The next day she was riding on the moors, thinking of him — as she had not ceased to do for one moment since his return — when she heard the sound of thudding hoofs behind her; and there was Bartle himself.

She drew up and faced him. He had aged a little. He was nearly twenty-seven years old — a man in years. There were more lines about his eyes; his skin was more deeply bronzed; the scar on his cheek seemed less prominent than it had; but his eyes were the same brilliant blue that she remembered. They mocked her now, and she felt the old excited hatred rising within her.

"Well met, Tamar."

"I doubt that it is well."

"What a greeting for your lover!"

"You are no lover of mine!"

"Have you forgotten that night we spent together?"

"I have done my best to wipe the shame of it from my mind."

"At least," he said, "you speak too vehemently for indifference." He smiled. "And that gives me hope."

"Hope? Of what? That you may trick me as you did before?"

"Come, Tamar. Be true to yourself. You saw through the trick. I was merely being generous . . .

giving you a chance to surrender, not for your own sake — for that you were determined not to do in spite of the fact that you found me irresistible — but for the sake of another."

"Your conversation tires me. I am riding back now."

"No," he said. "You will stay awhile and talk with me. Shall we dismount? Let us tie our horses to yonder bush. Then we can make plans more easily."

"I have no plans to make with you."

"That's a pity, for I have plans, and it would be as well for you to know of them."

"I shall not join in them. Nor shall I dismount."

He leaned over and, catching her bridle, laughed up into her face. "You are afraid to dismount. You are afraid that I shall seize you as I almost did that day. . . do you remember when you saw me go to Richard's and were so beside yourself with your desire for me that you stripped and lay in wait to seduce me?"

She looked at him haughtily. "Why do you do everything to increase my hatred for you?"

"Because your hatred is the measure of your love."

"You appear to think you have learned much subtlety from your Spanish conquests. Let me tell you that you are completely ignorant of me and my feelings."

"A Spanish woman and an English one are much the same under the skin, you know. One can divide them into types. . . the clinging types, the meek types.

Then there is your own type, Tamar. The wild ones needing to be tamed."

"Your stupid talk sickens me. I am not a horse to be broken in."

"No indeed. As I told you once before, you are a woman who must be wooed . . . now that she has been won."

"Do you think that, because you once handled me shamefully, it gives you the right to speak to me thus?"

"Ah, Tamar, how I wish that you could see your face. You are excited . . . You are hoping that I will take you now as I did before. Even while you are just a little afraid . . . you hope. Look into your mind, my beauty, and tell me what you see there. Tell the truth. Tell how every detail of our love is cherished in your heart. You have remembered . . . all the time I have been away you have remembered, as I have."

She let her whip cut across her horse's flanks so that it reared and broke away from his hold on the bridle. It galloped off, but Bartle was soon beside her.

He shouted: "I thought the child in the garden was ours."

She looked straight ahead.

"I was disappointed," he continued to shout.

She slowed down her horse to fling at him: "I should have killed myself before I would have borne a child of yours."

"You talk too lightly of death, just as you talk too fervently of hate."

"Go away! Leave me alone."

"I must talk to you."

"You could have nothing to say which could be of the slightest interest to me."

"You are afraid of me."

"I know you so well. You are a brute, a raper of women, a buccaneer, a robber. All that you are I loathe and despise. And I do not trust you. You have more physical strength than I have, and I would not care to be alone with you in lonely places."

She heard his guffaw.

"Oh, Tamar," he cried, "have I ever forced you? Did you not receive me into your bed without a protest?"

She felt hot tears of shame pricking her eyes and she angrily whipped up her horse.

"Come!" she whispered. "Gallop faster. Let us put a great distance between him and us."

But the sweating horses kept level.

Bartle shouted: "Tamar, never fear! It is going to be you and I together. . . for as long as we live."

When they had left the open country behind them and were in the narrow, hilly lanes, it was necessary to walk their horses, and he talked to her with seriousness.

"Tamar, listen to me. I grow old and I must marry. My father is anxious to see my children before he dies. I have thought of this matter while I have been away. I love the sea; but I love you more. You are like the sea, Tamar. . . uncertain. . . beautiful and tender to some, wild and stormy to others. I want you, Tamar."

"You waste your words. And if you would ask my advice I would say this: Yes, you should marry and produce children. There are many girls in this countryside, as well-born as yourself, who would make excellent wives. One of them would doubtless be glad to put up with your crude manners and infidelities, for the sake of one day becoming Lady Cavill."

"I want none but you."

"That may be so, because it would be characteristic of you to want what you cannot have."

"I should not be continually at sea," he said. "We could watch our children grow up. What say you, Tamar?"

"I say you are a fool. In the opinion of your family, I should not be considered worthy of you, and in my opinion you are not worthy of myself. So much unworthiness could not make for happiness, I feel sure."

"My family would forget all those strange stories of your birth once you married me."

"They will never be forgotten."

"Only because you give yourself such airs. You ride about with flying hair so that you may look like a witch, apart from all other witches, with a beauty that fires the blood of men and sickens the hearts of women with envy."

"So you would marry me, knowing me different from other women?"

"I want to marry you," he said firmly.

"Bartle." Her voice softened slightly. "You believe, do you not, that I am no ordinary mortal woman? You believe that I have a power which is not of this Earth. Do you believe that the Devil forced me on my mother that night twenty-one years ago?"

He avoided her eyes. "How should I know what to believe?"

"And yet . . . you would marry me. You would ask me to be the mother of your children!"

"I would," he said solemnly. "There are two loves in my life," he went on slowly, "and I understand myself sufficiently to know that there always will be. One is the sea. You know I ran away to sea when I was fourteen. That was against my father's wishes. I knew that he might disinherit me for this, as he had threatened to do, but I did not care. I had to go to sea. I did not care that for a time I should live the life of a common sailor. I knew my life was in danger; I knew I faced death; but that was what I wanted. And you are my other love, Tamar. Untamed as the sea . . . and as dangerous. I know it, but I must have you. I faced continual dangers on the sea, and I will face them in union with you . . . woman . . . witch . . . devil . . . whatever you be."

She was moved, for she had never before known him speak with such seriousness. Moreover, she could not help feeling proud to see him so humble before her. In some measure that made up for the shame he had inflicted upon her.

She said, and her voice was more gentle than it had ever been when she was addressing him: "If what you say is true, then I am sorry for you. But I will never marry you. You must content yourself with your other love, the sea. You are a fool, Bartle, and I could never love a fool. If you had been kind to me, I might have felt some friendliness towards you; and if you had continued to be kind I might even have married you. Violence . . . shameful violence . . . such as you have dared to show towards me, would never win anything but my contempt."

"So you continue to hate me?"

"I can never love you."

"You forget I have felt you tremble in my arms."

"With hate."

"No," he said, "with passion."

"If that were so, why should I not take advantage of what must seem to you this great and magnanimous offer to make me your wife?"

"Because you do not know yourself. You are determined to hate me, and you cling to hatred as a drowning man clings to a raft, knowing it will soon be swept away from him."

"Know this," she answered. "You have done to me that for which you will never have my forgiveness. You know that I am not like other women. You have said yourself that I have the Devil in me."

He smiled at her—his eyes blazing with that sudden heat of desire which seemed to scorch her, so that for one wild moment she thought it might melt her repulsion and turn it into a fierce capitulation.

Alarmed, she said: "There is nothing more I have to say to you."

And she rode on ahead of him.

* * *

All through that autumn and winter Bartle haunted Pennicomquick. Richard and Tamar were entertained by his family at Stoke. Sir Humphrey had grown very feeble now and watched, with impatience, what he thought to be the courtship of his son and Richard's daughter. He did not like the fact of the girl's illegitimacy, but he was by no means insensible to her charms. She was tall and finely built; he could imagine her producing fine sons; and since Bartle seemed set on having her, Sir Humphrey wished they would not delay in marrying, for if he were to see his grandchildren before he died, there was not much time to be lost.

Tamar, studying the old man, thought: That is what Bartle will be like in thirty years' time. Too much good wine: too much rich food; too many women; a wound or two from a Spaniard's sword, which had seemed to heal, but which left their mark; lecherous eyes for a pretty maid; a wistful eye for the gap between her youth and his age; quick temper; legs swollen with gout. Yes, Bartle would be just like that in thirty years' time. They were of a kind — country gentlemen and buccaneers!

Yet her feelings towards Bartle changed during those months. There were times when he ceased to mock, when he talked of his adventures; often this would be when she sat with him and his family and

Richard in the panelled hall with the Cavill ancestry looking down from the pictures in the gallery above. Then he would make vivid the life at sea which he had so enjoyed, the hundred dangers he had faced, the stories of boarding the Spanish quarry and looting her hold of its treasure. Sir Humphrey would join in with anecdotes from his own adventures, and between them they would turn the hall into a ship for Tamar, and she would feel that she sailed with them upon an ocean. She saw, through their eyes, the Spaniard on the horizon, heard the shout aboard, "A sail! A sail!" She could hear Bartle's voice, his eyes flashing: "Dowse your topsail! Salute him for the sea. Whence is your ship?" And the dreaded yet longed-for answer: "Of Spain. Whence is yours?" She saw the ship shot through and through; the fire that had started in the hold. She saw the surgeon looking to the wounded when the darkness fell. Bartle's voice again: "Keep your berth to windward and see that we lose her not in the night!" She saw the resumption of the fight next day and heard the sound of drums and trumpets, the cry of "St. George for England!"

She was fascinated, in spite of her determination not to be. How his eyes sparkled as he talked; they took on that vivid shade of blue which burned in them when, she knew, he most desired her. He was a man such as Humility Brown could never be.

At Christmas time there was lavish entertainment at Stoke; and the guests of honour were Tamar and her father. There were hunting parties when Tamar and Bartle rode side by side and were always first at the kill. He was more gentle and no longer referred to that night when he had forced himself upon her. He had taken heed of her words; and she was warming towards him.

When he came upon little Christian toddling in the gardens, he would stop and speak to him; he would bring him sweetmeats and fruit, and the child would crow with pleasure at the sight of him. He would take the little boy in his arms and throw him into the air; he would set him upon his mare and hold him there while the mare walked about on the grass. The child adored him.

Annis — now expecting another child — looked on with tears in her eyes.

"He is a good man," she whispered to Tamar; "for only good men are kind to children and the weak."

Then Tamar forced herself to remember an occasion when he had not been so kind to the weak. But was she right in harbouring resentment? Should he not be forgiven if he had repented of his harsh treatment of her?

He was the wooer now. He implied when he entertained her at his father's mansion: This is what I have to offer you. This house and estates will be mine one day.

When they rode to the hunt together he was telling her: We should have a good life together.

When he made much of little Christian he meant: See! How happy we should be if we had children of our own!

But Tamar could not easily forget her distrust of him. There was too much that she could remember vividly.

I do not trust him! she insisted to herself.

And yet, the days when she did not see him were dull days. She was softening towards him and might have softened more, but, naturally, he could not for long keep up this model behaviour.

Several times he had seen her talking to Humility Brown, and on these occasions had spoken slightingly of the man, whereupon Tamar had characteristically sprung to his defence.

One day, at the beginning of the spring, Bartle came to Pennicomquick and found Tamar in the gardens conversing with the Puritan; and when later she and Bartle were riding out together, he said: "You seem very taken with that fellow."

"Taken with him?"

"You cannot hide your feelings from me by repeating what I say. You are *taken* with him! I could see that by the way you looked at him."

"You see too much, Bartle, since you see what is not there."

"You were coquetting with him. By God, you were! Forcing him to look at you, standing there smiling provocatively. You have a fancy for him!" Bartle's face was flushed and distorted with his jealousy. "I believe he is your lover."

She answered coldly: "I had thought your manners improved of late. It seems I am mistaken."

"You cannot deny it. You prevaricate. You cannot hide the truth from me."

"And even if your foul suggestion were truth, why should I wish to hide it from you? What concern would it be of yours?"

"So all this time while I have been playing the mild-mannered suitor, he has been revelling in the pleasures of your bed!"

"If you were nearer, I would strike you for that."

"You need not be so concerned to protect the honour of your sly-eyed Puritan. I always did suspect the meekness of such fellows. They use it to disarm foolish females like yourself. Tell me, does he begin your pleasures by praying first?"

"Stop it!" she screamed at him. "I hate you! What a fool I was to imagine that you were slightly less hateful than I had believed you to be! How dare you utter your coarse thoughts aloud to me! Do you imagine all men are as depraved as yourself!"

He was solemn suddenly. "Tamar, I was wrong. I see it. Forgive me."

"That I will not do. I cannot endure your conversation. Save it, please, for your low-born sailors. I speak to whom I will, and at this moment I do not wish to speak to you."

She was about to whip up her horse when he laid his hand on the bridle.

"Can you not forgive a jealous lover?"

She looked haughtily beyond him. "I can forgive no one who dares say such things."

"Listen, Tamar. I was wrong. I was foolish and jealous. I did not like to see you smile at anyone but me."

"Say no more," she said. "And pray take your hands from my bridle. I wish to go home now."

"First say you forgive me. Say all things are as they were between us."

She met his eyes coolly. "Very well. We were but friendly because our fathers' houses are close, and our fathers wish us to be."

She saw that fierce, angry passion blaze into his eyes.

But he said no more and they rode back to Pennicomquick.

Next day he rode over again. She saw him in the garden with young Christian and noticed how handsome he was, how tall, how strong, and how puny Humility Brown seemed when compared with him.

The child was smiling with pleasure as Bartle lifted him up. He loved children and softened when he was with them — but not too much. He was one of those men who had the power to attract children even when he reprimanded them or scarcely seemed to notice them. He would make a fine father — a father children would be proud of. She pondered: I am twenty, and whom else could I marry if not Bartle? Love, though, should be soft and tender — not fierce, demanding, fostering those tempestuous quarrels which were continually springing up between them. No, she could not love Bartle, but he excited her.

She went down to him and they played with the child together. Humility walked by on his way to the potting sheds, and she smiled at him as he passed; she was thinking of the contrast between him and Bartle, but Bartle saw the smile and misconstrued it. His expression changed, and Tamar felt her anger rising.

Bartle said: "There is to be an expedition at the beginning of the summer. I am asked to captain one of the ships."

"That should be exciting for you," she answered.

"It will. One grows tired of a landsman's life."

They went into the house and she was astonished at her depression which the prospect of losing him had brought with it.

*　　　*　　　*

She thought afterwards how different their lives might have been if they had not, at that point, taken a certain turning.

She was wild, passionate and unaccountable; she had forgotten that Bartle was similar.

If pride was her besetting sin, impatience and violence were his. He was a man of deep and sensuous passions, and he had been celibate too long. It had needed only the smile she had given Humility Brown—that most inoffensive of men—to rekindle the violent passions Bartle had been suppressing all these months.

He sought her out. He must speak to her. Would she walk in the grounds with him?

He took her to that spot by the stream which they both had cause to remember so well; she knew as soon as they reached that spot that she had the old Bartle to deal with. Gone was the tender lover, striving to please; there remained the sensual man determined to have his way. The very manner in which he took her by the shoulders was brutal.

His eyes blazed and she flinched before the passion in them. He kissed her hard on the lips and his kisses were a burning prophecy; he was going to kiss her whether she wanted him to or not.

All her old fear rose within her and, with it, came her passionate hatred.

"Release me at once."

But he kept his hands on her shoulders and looked into her face.

"Did you know," he said, "that that man, Humility Brown... *Humility* Brown!... dared to hold meetings at a hut on my father's lands?"

She felt a flutter in her stomach.

"Oh yes," he went on; "that sly creature dares to collect his flock together in a hut there. The meek man is a sinner; he is breaking the law. There are some fine new penalties imposed for such law-breakers."

"Why do you tell *me* this?"

"Wait and you will hear. One of my grooms has become a temporary Puritan at my request, and he has told me when the next meeting is to be; so you see I am in the secret."

"I asked you what this has to do with me. What are you threatening to do?"

"As a good servant of my country, what do you expect me to do?"

"You could not do it, Bartle!" she cried. "All those people who have lived among us . . . our friends!"

"Law-breakers! And Humility Brown the biggest one among them. He'll be thrown into gaol. I heard some tales of what they are doing to these people. They leave them to rot in prison. They starve them and beat them. It might even be the rope for such a hardened criminal as Humility Brown! Who knows? Perhaps even the faggots . . ."

"You shall not do this!"

"Why not?"

"I shall stop you. I shall warn him."

"I'll have him taken up in any case. He could not deny what he had been up to."

"Are you really as cruel as you would have me believe?"

He shook her and his eyes blazed forth their passion . . . a passion of hate for Humility Brown, a passion of desire for herself.

"I do not like your feeling for this man," he said.

"You are mad."

"I have seen you together."

"He is a humble gardener. What should I want with him?"

"I am not blind. He is a man of learning. He works in the garden because he lost everything on a ship bound for Virginia. He is biding his time until he can set out again . . . then doubtless he plans to take you with him. Richard invites him to his study. He talks

217

with him. Theirs is not the relationship of master and servant."

"Could not Richard be interested in a servant?"

"Does he invite other servants to talk with him? Nay! Richard and his daughter have an interest in the fellow which I do not like."

"I hate you, Bartle."

"Is that because you love him?"

She brought up her hand to strike him, but he caught it.

"You are hurting me," she said.

"I intend to. You will learn how I can hurt those who insult me by preferring a meek-tongued preacher to a man. When they hang him, I will take you to see the spectacle. I'll warrant there'll be a goodly crowd to cheer him on to hell."

"Bartle," she pleaded, "you don't mean that you will really do this cruel and dastardly thing?"

"You will see what I can do for my country."

He watched her slyly and she should have been warned. When he released her and began to walk away, she ran after him.

"I beg of you not to do this, Bartle."

He turned and smiled slowly, and his smile made her tremble, for she was reminded of another occasion.

He said, "Sweetheart, I can refuse you nothing. If you were to beg of me . . . prettily enough . . . I might reconsider my decision."

He put his arms about her and held her in a grip so tight that she felt as though the blood were being squeezed out of her body.

"For a consideration," he went on, "there is nothing on earth that I would not do for you."

"What . . .?" she began weakly.

"Leave your window open to-night, and I'll swear by God and my fathers that the Puritans shall meet wherever and as often as they like without interference from me."

She looked at him scornfully. "Do you think I would be deceived again and by the same trick?"

"The other *was* a trick, I grant you. I would not have betrayed a friend like Richard. I am fond of Richard. But Humility Brown? Why, I loathe the man; I despise him; and the way in which you smile at him alone would make him my enemy."

"Are you determined to make my hatred burn more fiercely?"

He answered: "If I cannot have you in love, then will I have you in hate; for have you I will, one way or the other."

"Then it is no use my pleading with you?"

"There is only one way."

She tossed her head angrily and walked into the house.

*　　*　　*

She lay waiting for him.

There was, she told herself, nothing else she could do. He had tricked her before, but this time he meant what he said. He was brutal; he was callous; he was lecherous. How could she ever have thought of marriage with him?

"I would rather die!" she said into her pillow.

What else could I do but this? How could I let Humility Brown be betrayed? Others would be involved too.

She closed her eyes and tried to see Humility standing in one of the pits of the prisons, knee-deep in water, fighting the rats which tried to attack his starving body. But she could only see Bartle coming towards her, whispering her name.

I hate him! she insisted. This is terrible and shameful. But it is better that this should happen to me than that my friends should lie neglected in prison and then perhaps be taken out to violent death.

He was coming now. It was happening as it had happened before. The curtains parted and she heard his light laugh in the darkness.

His hands were caressing her.

He said: "So, sweetheart, once more you are waiting for me."

* * *

"I hate you! I hate you!" she told him. "I shall hate you for ever for what you have done to me."

He mocked her as he had done before.

"How you longed for me! Do you think you hid your feelings from me? I am too clever for you. Tamar, I know too much of women. Why do you persist in telling me you hate me? You long for me. You burn for me. You knew I cared nothing for Puritans. A plague and a pox on them! I care naught. Let them meet every day. Let them pray till they are hoarse. I'd never betray them. Do I look like a man who would bestir himself to betray miserable Puritans?"

"I believe you would be capable of the utmost cruelty."

He smiled. "Oh, it was a wonderful night, was it not? Better than the first . . . when perhaps you might have been a little reluctant."

"You are coarse and crude and I hate you."

"Constant repetition is not so emphatic as you appear to believe."

"With me it is."

"Marry me, Tamar. I promise to be as faithful as I can."

"Marry you! I would rather die."

"What if there should be a child? Then you would be ready enough, I'll swear."

"If there were a child it would make no difference."

"We will wait and see. When that sly-faced housekeeper starts peeking and prying, I'm ready to wager you'll not be so reluctant."

"You forget that I hate you."

He sighed. "So you have said. When, Tamar, will you be truthful, frank and reasonable? When may I cease thinking up these elaborate schemes so that we can be together?"

"There will never be another time."

"I hope there will be a child," he said. "My God, how I hope for that! There will be time to know before the ships sail. If there is a child, I know you will change your mind. You will be obliged to. It will be a good excuse for you; and how you love excuses! For the child's sake, you will agree to marry me, just as you so charmingly agree to make love with me, first for Richard's sake, then for that of Humility Brown!"

"Marriage with you!" she sneered. "I laugh to contemplate it, though mayhap I should not laugh, for what a bitter tragedy it would be! I should do you some mischief before I had lived a week with you."

"Never fear! I would subdue you. I would have you meek and loving . . . a perfect wife before the week were out."

She felt bruised and wounded, humiliated beyond endurance. He did excite her; she knew the truth now, which was that she half hated, half delighted in his love-making; and that was a shameful conclusion for her to come to.

She was all contrasts during the weeks that followed. She was terrified that there would be a child and yet, at times, she longed that this might be. She pictured herself saying to him: "For the child's sake, then . . ." And she thought of all the attendant excitement which would follow such a decision.

But then her pride arose — that she, whom people had been afraid to cross, even when she was a child, should be so treated, so humiliated, as though she were any low serving girl to be taken at the master's caprice!

No! Fiercely she hated him and what he had done to her; and now again she was terrified that there would be a child.

There was no child.

She mocked him when he came to the house.

"When do you sail?"

"Perhaps," he said, "the next time I sail will be with you up the Thames to London Town."

She laughed exultantly. "I think," she said, "that when the ships sail out you will be with them."

"Oddly enough," he answered, "I would rather marry you. I have had my fill of the sea; you, I have just tasted."

"I hate your coarse words, and I should never have consented to marry you even if there had been a child. But there will be no child."

She laughed loud and long to see his dismay. He understood at last that she had meant what she said when she had told him she hated him.

*   *   *

He sailed away that summer, and she told herself that she was glad.

But when—only a few weeks after he had been at sea—a ship came limping into the Sound with the news that it was the only one which had escaped after an attack by Algerian or Turkish pirates, she was on the quay with the rest of the town; and her pride suddenly broke when she heard that Bartle was one of those who had not returned.

CHAPTER
FIVE

It was Tamar's wedding night.

She was twenty-three years old — old enough to be married — and she thought of the last three years as dull and uneventful.

She had been twenty years old when she had heard that Bartle was lost. The men from that ship which had limped back to Plymouth explained that they had been outnumbered three to one in the Bay of Biscay, and aboard the attacking forces were fierce pirates — Turks or Algerians. Bartle's ship had been fired and all loot taken before it was sunk. It was a fate he had risked many times and now it had overtaken him.

She was numb and listless during those days which had followed. She could not analyse her feelings for Bartle. Her hatred had been fierce because he had so deeply humiliated her. Twice he had tricked her; twice he had cheated her; and he had mocked her mercilessly. He was every bit as cruel as the men who had killed him, and yet . . . how could she understand this feeling which was now hers? Why was it that she hated the bright and shining water which had taken him? Why was it that all the excitement had gone from her life? Was it because there was no one in it who seemed worthy of her hatred?

Whenever a ship came in, she was one of the first to take her stand on Barbican Causeway. She would shade her eyes and watch it as it came towards the land. Surely he must have escaped! He was too young to die. And it was impossible to imagine him dead. She would never be able to do that.

She was restless, yet subdued. There were times when she seemed not to hear, if people spoke to her. Richard was anxious about her, suspecting that she regretted not having married Bartle.

She would not let herself believe that she yearned for that tempestuous existence which marriage with him would have been. How ironical that by marrying him she could have saved him from taking that fatal journey. That first shameful occasion, so she had believed at the time, had saved Richard's life; the second, Humility's; and now, there could be no doubt that, had she given herself to Bartle for ever, she would have saved his.

Often she was at the Tylers' cottage. Annis had another boy now, and at Humility's suggestion they had christened him Restraint. In the old days Tamar would have laughed at that, for the healthy boy, pulling greedily at his mother's breasts, seemed to her most incongruously named. But she had, she realized, little laughter left in her.

Annis in her cottage home, with John a devout Puritan and most faithful husband, was a contented woman. It was irritating to contemplate such contentment, and to envy Annis her home and children just as she envied Richard his calm outlook on life, Humility his faith. This was a strange state for a girl to be in, particularly when a little while ago her life had seemed to be all excitement and pleasure.

Shortly after that day when Bartle had sailed away, Richard put into action a plan which had long been in his mind. He had always taken a keen interest in Humility Brown and had not cared to see him doing rough work under Jubin; he had, therefore, decided that it would be a good plan if Humility—who was a good penman and general scholar—took some of the burden of his estates off his shoulders. Humility was naturally delighted with the change of occupation; and Richard pointed out that he must leave the draughty outhouse for which he had been so grateful when he had first been given work, and one of the attics should be made ready for him. This would not only be more comfortable, but more in keeping with his new status.

It was now that a change seemed to come over Humility. He glowed with something more than his faith. He had some of his meals with Richard and Tamar, and it was one day when they were at supper in the winter parlour that he explained his newly found elation.

"I am a happy man," he declared, his eyes shining with gratitude as they rested on Richard. "I had thought my desires were sinful, but now I know them to be favoured by the Lord. When my friends sailed away to Virginia and left me behind with Will Spears and Spears' boy, I was filled with regret and, in spite of constant prayers, I could not purge my mind of sorrow because I had missed an opportunity of reaching the new land. 'Humility Brown,' I said to myself, 'if it had been God's will that you should have gone to Virginia, do you think He would have sent you into plague-stricken Plymouth?' I knew that it was God's will that I should not go to Virginia then. And I prayed nightly that I might be resigned to my fate. But I hankered. I yearned. I thought of my friends, leading the new life in the new country where they did not find it necessary to creep away and in secret worship God. Oh, to be free and unafraid and to lift up mine eyes to the hills and say 'Holy, Holy, Holy. . .'"

Tamar watched him critically. A born preacher, he was ever carried away by words, and that was a vanity in him surely. He loved the sound of his own voice as dearly as she loved the sight of her face. She would taunt him with that one day when she felt in the mood to do so.

Humility caught the look in her eyes and said: "Forgive me. I grow excited, I fear. I *am* excited. My mind is filled with what I believe to be a message from on High. I have a notion that it may well, after all, be God's will that I go to Virginia. Sir, you have made it possible for me to feed and clothe myself and, by your generous payment, to save money which will enable me to go to the promised land."

"So," said Richard, "that is what you plan. To save, and when you are ready and the opportunity comes, to sail away."

Humility's eyes gleamed. "Ships often come to Plymouth. It is possible to get to Virginia if you have a little money. I rejoice. I see that the Lord did not intend me to miss the promised land."

"Perhaps," said Tamar with a sparkle of her old mischief, "you have been delayed as a punishment, but it may be that, like Moses of old, your sins have been such that it is considered just that you never reach your promised land."

"That may well be," agreed Humility.

"Then you must have sinned greatly — and I wonder how."

That evening she threw off some of her listlessness. She was interested in something once more: Humility's going to Virginia!

She would interrupt him at his work as he sat, quill in hand, and make him talk about Virginia. He was easily tempted to such talk, and it amused her afterwards to see his remorse for the wasted time.

"To steal time," she teased remorselessly, "is as bad as stealing goods. You know that, Humility?"

"You are a temptress!" he said.

And she laughed. Then he whispered a prayer.

"Shall you wear a hair-shirt for this?" she asked; and she was pleased because she could feel amused, teasing Humility Brown.

But when he did not appear at meals next day and she understood he was fasting, she felt sorry for what she had done. Then she discovered that as well as amusement she could feel regret; and it seemed significant that Humility Brown should be

228

the one to make her feel that life was not so dreary after all.

Sometimes they would have serious conversations together. He seemed more human now that he had a goal to work for, and she took an interest in his mounting savings. She would have liked to have given him money, but she knew he would not accept that. He worked assiduously. There never was such a worker, Richard declared, never such a man for denying himself comfort.

"If he were not such a fanatic he would be a great man, I think," said Tamar.

"Great men are often fanatics," Richard reminded her.

Annis and John were saving too. Their simple faith shone in their faces. They were going one day, under the guidance of Humility Brown and accompanied by most of those who joined with them to worship God in secret meeting places, to the new promised land.

"So," Tamar had demanded angrily, "you would leave me, would you, Annis?"

But Annis shook her head. "Mistress, perhaps you will be among those who go with us."

"I? Why. . . the Puritans would not have me."

"They would, mistress, if you were a Puritan."

"You talk like Humility Brown!" snapped Tamar.

"Ah, mistress, if you could but know the peace and joy that has come to me and John! We be saved. Think of it. Happiness has come to us, mistress. I pray on my knees every night that it will come to you."

Tamar left the cottage that day and rode on the moors. The wind caught her long hair as she rode. Here was the spot where Bartle had caught up with her; here he had seized her bridle and laughed up into her face. Now. . . she was alone on the moors and he was alone on the bed of the sea.

She dismounted and tied her horse to a bush. Then she threw herself on to the grass and sobbed brokenheartedly. She thought of Annis and John Tyler, and mostly she thought of Humility Brown. What was it these people had that she had not? Faith! Belief that their souls were saved. Belief in a future life so that what happened here on Earth was of no moment. What an enviable state to be in!

When she was back at the house, she pinned up her hair — not in an elaborate style, but looped over her ears and made into a knot at the nape of her neck. The effect was startling, for she looked almost demure. She was aware of the look of approval which crossed the face of Humility Brown when he saw her.

Annis too was pleased to see her thus. They sat by the chimney-piece in the cottage, and the children — Christian, Restraint and Prudence — played at their feet.

"Annis," said Tamar, "can you truly say that you have never been so happy in your life?"

"I truly can," said Annis.

"But why should a *new* way of worshipping God make you happy?"

"Because 'tis the only true right way," answered Annis.

"Are you right . . . I wonder?"

Annis knelt at Tamar's feet. "Mistress, come to us. Come to our meetings. Listen to the good words and then see if you cannot find the peace which has come to John and me."

"Annis, you must know that when you are in your meeting-place you may be discovered at any time. That may mean prison. John may be taken from you and the children. How can you be happy living in perpetual fear?"

"If John were taken we should know it was the will of the Lord. Good would come of it, for the ways of God are good."

"You might be summoned for failing to appear at church."

Annis nodded and smiled blissfully.

"Annis, sometimes I think you are a fool. Yet you have found happiness and I have not; and since happiness is what we all seek, it must be the wise who find it."

"Mistress, cut yourself off from the Devil. You can do it. I know you are a witch, mistress. You have the powers of witchcraft, but you have never used them for ill; you are a white witch, and prayer could release you from your bondage; it could bring you safe to the arms of Jesus."

Her lips curled. "You talk like Humility Brown."

She could not understand what happened to her during those years — perhaps it was because that which came to her came gradually. She was not wild Tamar one day and Tamar saved the next. Each week saw a little of the old wildness passing, a little of the new quietness gained.

Humility talked with her long and earnestly now that she had ceased to mock him. Who was she to mock? These people had faith, and faith gave them the contentment which she lacked and longed for. She was restless, searching for something which she could never have now that Bartle was dead; and when Bartle was here she had not wanted it.

She was twenty-three and unmarried. Soon she would be qualifying for the title of "ancient maid." She longed for children. Annis had another now — little Felicity. Four children for Annis and not one for Tamar! She was fond of Annis's children and made excuses to visit them at the cottage or have them at the house.

But Tamar was not the sort to live through another woman's experiences.

She wanted this faith; she wanted to escape from restlessness; she longed to be saved so that what happened here on Earth was of no importance since her eyes would be fixed on the happy life to come.

She told Humility this, and he went down on his knees and thanked God.

Tamar's conversion was more enthusiastic than anyone else's, for she could never be half-hearted about anything she took up. Richard watched her with some amusement and a little alarm. He warned her that it was purely dissatisfaction with her present life which was at the root of her acceptance of the faith —

not her belief in it. But she turned from Richard; she turned to Humility.

She listened to him as his followers listened; he was a leader among men. His voice had a power and charm all its own. She saw the goodness in him.

"Oh, Humility," she cried. "I know that what happens to me here matters not. It is the life to come for which we must prepare ourselves."

He embraced her and they knelt in prayer together. The miracle had happened. Tamar was saved.

And then, one day, Humility said an astonishing thing.

"Tamar." He had ceased to call her "daughter." "Tamar, it is the greatest joy the Lord could have given me, to see you turn towards the Truth. You are at peace now. That is natural. But I have had a revelation concerning you. It is this: You are unfulfilled. You are meant to be the mother of children. You are released from the bonds of Satan. God is good; He is all-powerful and through His divine help I have been enabled to free you, for the power of the Devil compared with that of God is like a candle flame to the sun. I could lead you to contentment, to true happiness — which is the suppression of self in the service of God. Would that you would place your hand in mine and I might show you the way."

She held out her hand and he took it.

"Tamar, I did not intend ever to give way to the carnal lusts of the flesh . . . nor will I. But I have seen a new life opening before me. In the new land to which I hope to go, we shall need children . . . good, strong, noble children of the Puritan faith to carry on the work we have started. Each woman should do her share; she must give herself a chance to show her fertility. Each man must do likewise. There need be no lust in a good man and a good woman coming together in matrimony."

She drew away from him. "What do you suggest?"

"That you and I marry and, in the grace of holy wedlock, have children to the glory of God and our faith."

She felt the hot colour in her face. She was shocked by the suggestion; yet this was the answer to her problem. She longed for children, and in having Humility Brown's children she would help to populate the promised land to which one day they would go.

At last there could be a purpose in living. Perhaps for this reason Humility Brown had been sent to Plymouth; perhaps for this reason she had saved his life. At this moment it all seemed so right, so simple and natural.

"I will marry you," she said.

Afterwards she thought of what must be lived through before she reached that happy state of seeing her children round her, contented in a strange land, and she was afraid.

Dreams came to her as she lay in bed. Once she imagined that the curtains round her bed parted. That was a fancy; but she pursued it, and Bartle was standing by her bed. He said: "How can you marry that...Puritan! I will not let you!" And in the dream she felt his hands caress her.

Then she jumped out of bed and prayed solemnly and earnestly for the purification of her body and the salvation of her soul.

Queer dreams persisted—fearful dreams of anger and passion.

What have I done? she asked herself. How can I marry Humility Brown?

Richard was against the marriage, and he said so firmly. It was like mating a bird of paradise with a crow.

"You have hurried into this with your usual impetuosity. I know you well—better than you know yourself. You have been depressed—not yourself—and you have been searching for a new interest in life. All this talk of going to Virginia has fired your imagination. I would to God..."

"Yes?" she said.

"It was nothing."

"Tell me. I want to know."

"Oh, it is foolish of us to make plans for others. I was merely wishing that I had insisted on a father's right, and married you to Bartle. He would not then have gone away and..."

He stopped, for she had buried her face in her hands and was sobbing bitterly.

"Oh, Tamar, my dearest..."

"It was just that I could not bear to hear you say it was my fault he is dead."

"Of course it was not your fault. If you did not want to marry him, you were right not to. What has happened to you, Tamar? You have changed so."

"I don't know what has happened to me," she said.

"I beg of you, my dear, consider this marriage and what it will mean. Consider that seriously. Let us go away for a sea trip. We'll hug the coast and sail up the Thames to London. Or shall we take our horses and ride?"

She shook her head. "My mind is made up. We want children...Humility and I. And Richard, when we go to Virginia, *you* must come with us. I could not bear it if you stayed behind." Her eyes shone suddenly. "You are rich. You could finance such an expedition. Richard, could you not tear yourself away from this life—which is not, I believe, very satisfactory to you—and start a new one?"

He answered: "You spring such questions on a man at a minute's notice."

"It would be wonderful!" she cried. "We would all sail out of the Sound together...with our stores and all that we should need for our new life. There could not be a more exciting and wonderful adventure than sailing away into the unknown."

Richard let her talk, but he remained uneasy. It seemed to him that a girl should be thinking of her life with her husband rather than a life in new surroundings. Something had happened to change Tamar. Could it be that she had loved Bartle? She was like a person trying to get intoxicated in order to

236

drown a sorrow. Was the hope of children and the new life in Virginia, the wine to make her forget?

As the day fixed for her wedding grew nearer, her mood changed. She rode out to the moors, her hair flying, and it seemed to Richard, watching her, that the old Tamar was not far away. It would not have surprised him if she had decided against the marriage after all. She almost did, when Humility wished them to set up house together in the outhouses, which he suggested could be made into a cottage home for them. Then how her eyes flashed! That was folly, she insisted. They should go on living in the house. If he were to save every penny he could, those pennies should not be spent in the vanity of setting up a home. It would seem that he had forgotten the Virginia project.

"Tamar," said Humility, hurt by the change in her, "it is good that a man and his wife should set up home together . . . however humble that home may be. I do not wish that you should continue to live under your father's roof."

"And there," she answered, "you show your pride. You will have to accept these conditions. You must remember that our plan is to leave this country as soon as it is possible to do so. Did we not plan to marry that we might have children to populate the new country?"

"That was so."

She gave a sudden spurt of laughter. "It is as easy to get children in a comfortable house as in a draughty cottage, I do assure you."

Humility grew pale with alarm. He saw that the Devil was very close to her, and he realized that Tamar was not completely saved. Moreover, he guessed that it would take a lifetime for him to achieve that desired result.

He had to agree. No new arrangements, then. Her room was big enough for both of them. He would share her bed, which was large and comfortable, until they were sure of a child, and when that had happened he could go back to his attic.

He could not understand what was going on in her mind. He did not know that she was most defiant when her fear was greatest. Her frank way of discussing what he felt should not be discussed by unmarried couples worried him. Yet, he assured himself, it was his duty to humour her until he could control her, which, he doubted not, he would be able to do with the Lord's help when they married.

So he must agree to this unnatural arrangement. Well, to some extent she was right. Soon they would be sailing for Virginia.

As the wedding day grew nearer, so did Tamar's fear grow greater. At the back of her mind was a belief that Bartle would reappear; he would explain that some miraculous and incredible thing had happened—the sort of thing which could only happen to Bartle—and he had come back. His blue eyes would flash, and he would have a blackmailing scheme to lay before her which would involve her breaking this incongruous betrothal and marrying him. She would no doubt be forced to do it for the sake of someone other than herself.

But the wedding day came, and she married Humility Brown; and now the house was still and she lay in the bed with the curtains drawn about it, just as she had lain and waited for Bartle.

She could hear the sound of a man's breathing beyond the bed-curtains — but it was not Bartle; it was her husband, Humility Brown.

He had parted the curtains as they had been parted on those other nights and she could see him as only a shape beside the bed — not the big broad shape which she had seen before, but the thin figure of her husband.

How different was this night from those others! Humility did not come eagerly to her; he did not whisper in that passionate voice; he did not caress her with urgent hands. He knelt by the bed and prayed.

"O Heavenly Father, it is because I believe it to be Thy will that I kneel at this bedside to-night. I pray Thee bless this woman, make her fertile, for, O Lord, it is for that reason I am here this night . . . not for carnal lust . . . but for the procreation of children as is laid down in Thy law. Thou knowest how I have grappled with myself . . ."

Tamar could listen to no more. How dare he call her "this woman"! He was not here for love of her, but in the hope of begetting children that they might do their share in populating the new land.

But her anger was lost in the numbness of regret, of a longing for another man, as Humility rose from his knees and came to her.

* * *

A month after her marriage to Humility Brown, Tamar knew that she was pregnant. Now her depression had lifted; she was glad she had married; this new adventure was going to be worth the step she had taken to achieve it.

She lost no time in imparting the news to Humility, and the first thing he did was to go down on his knees and thank God, but when he arose she imagined that he was not so thankful as it had first appeared.

She understood why, for although to Humility, who believed himself to be wise, she was a mysterious creature of odd and unaccountable moods, she was able to read him as easily as a printed sheet.

She was to have a child; the purpose of their nightly embraces was achieved; therefore until after the child was born these must be suspended. How could it be otherwise as, he had so often declared to God in her hearing, they took place for only one reason? That was in the nightly prayer he said at her bedside.

"God has answered our prayer!" he said.

"Now," she told him with a trace of malice, "you may with good conscience go back to your attic."

He was taken aback, but she went on quickly: "That would be wisest. It would be unfortunate if, after all your protestations, you were to give way to carnal lust—which you might well do if you continued to share my bed."

240

He despaired of her, she knew. She had no modesty, he told her. He pointed out that she said, without thinking, whatever came into her mind. He hoped that one day she would learn from Puritan women to veil her thoughts — even from herself.

She smiled. The last month had brought her soul no nearer to salvation, she feared. It had been very close, she knew, when she had promised to marry him, but alas! it grew farther away.

He went back to his attic and she was relieved; she was mistress of her own domain once more; she had the child safe within her, and that was all she wanted of him.

She would have Annis sent to her room, or go herself to the cottage. They would bend over their sewing and talk incessantly of the baby. Tamar even learned to take a pride in her work, which astonished her, for she had never before been attracted to the needle. She sat and dreamed of the baby, and she believed that she was happier now than she had ever been; she ceased to think of the journey to Virginia, for her only thought was of the child.

How slowly the months passed! Springtime, and it would be December before her baby was born!

Annis said one summer's day as they sat in the garden with their sewing: "It does seem a miracle to me that you and Mr. Brown should be joined together. We did always think 'twould be a *grand* marriage for thee. One of the gentlemen from hereabouts as was mad for 'ee. And then you marry the Puritan! Of course, a finer and more noble gentleman never did live, I do know; and I said to John, I said: 'Happy should a woman be in such a union, but . . .'"

"But?" demanded Tamar sharply; and Annis flushed and became intent upon her work. Tamar burst out: "A woman should be happy in such a union, but I am no ordinary woman, am I, Annis? No, I am not! Do not look alarmed. We know—you and I. Oh, Annis, sometimes I think I am bound to the darkness by silken threads which are so light that no one can see them, and only I am aware of them."

"Ain't you saved, then, mistress?"

"No, Annis."

"Oh, 'tis a terrible hard job to save 'ee. The Devil holds fast to his own. But you ain't bad. That's what I say to John: 'There's witchcraft in her, but all witchcraft ain't bad.' If it do help people, how can it be bad?"

"You are a dear creature, Annis."

"I have no wish but to serve you all the days of my life, mistress."

"You are my friend too, Annis."

Annis moved nearer to Tamar. "I did think at one time it would have been Master Bartle Cavill as you would have took. My dear soul! Think of it! If he'd lived and you'd have married him you'd have been Lady Cavill now. You'd have been the Lady of the Manor. I can picture 'ee, sitting there at the head of the table like . . . in your gowns of silk and velvet."

"Yes, Annis."

Annis faltered, remembering that it was sinful to talk of worldly pleasure. "I fear I be a sinful woman," she said. "I'll never learn to be a good Puritan. I be vain and overfond of this world's glories. It'll be a terrible hard struggle for me to climb the golden stairs."

"You'll climb the stairs, I promise you," said Tamar. "As for your sins, no questions will be asked."

Annis opened her eyes very wide. "You couldn't fix that, mistress, for the Devil wouldn't carry no weight up there."

Tamar laughed. "All this talk of Heaven wearies me. I want to be happy here. Oh Annis, I wonder what my baby will be like. A boy or a girl? A girl, I hope, for if it is a boy he might be like Humility . . . and if a girl like me. How wonderful to see yourself in miniature . . . another Tamar . . . but with a Puritan instead of a Devil for her father!"

She laughed so loudly that Annis was frightened, for, as she said to John afterwards: "Women can be awful strange in the waiting months."

The child was born on a snowy December day. Annis was with Tamar, for she had acquired in the last years some competence as a midwife. Richard had engaged the best physician in Plymouth; but it was Annis whom Tamar wanted with her.

The child was a boy, and Tamar, as she lay in what seemed like the best of all worlds, since there was no pain in it and her baby was in her arms, believed that this was the answer to her problem. She had found happiness at last.

He was dark-eyed, that boy; and already there was a good thick down on his head. She laughed with joy to look at him.

Annis said: "Why, mistress, you can't be disappointed in such a bonny boy, for all that you did want a girl."

"I . . . want a girl! Nonsense! I wanted nothing but this one!"

She was absorbed in the child. She had his basket beside her bed, and none but herself must attend to his wants. She would not swaddle him, for she remembered that she herself had not been swaddled, and she did not wish to shut his beautiful limbs away from her sight.

Annis shook her head. That was wrong. He would catch his death.

"He will not catch his death. I will keep him warm. I want him to grow up beautiful like his mother."

"But, mistress . . ." cried Annis, distressed.

"I know what is good for my child." Her eyes flashed and it seemed to Annis, as she told John afterwards, as though the Devil looked out of them. John said: 'Annis, I do know she be the wife of Mr. Brown. I do know she have been good to 'ee. But she can work spells. Didn't she give you one to work on me? And spells ain't Christian, Annis. I would wish to see thee clear of her.' At which Annis's eyes flashed almost as fiercely as those of her mistress, and she answered: 'I'd cut off me right hand rather than leave her, John Tyler.' And John was afraid to say more, for he knew that Annis did not mean she would only give up her right hand for her mistress. And when you have the true faith and you have been saved, you do not want to hear your wife utter blasphemy.

So Tamar brought up her child in her own way, and he thrived; but when the time came for naming him, there was conflict between his parents.

"We will call him Humility," said his father. "Such a name will be to him, as my thoughtful parents knew it would be to me, a constant reminder that he must live up to that quality."

"I will not have him called Humility!" declared Tamar.

"Why not, wife?"

"I have planned to call him Richard, after my father."

"Perhaps I may allow you to call our next boy by that name. Although I would suggest something more appropriate to accompany it."

"What?" she cried. "Restraint? Charity? Virtue? I do not love your Puritan names."

"Do you not then love these qualities in a human being?"

"I do not like them attached as a name is attached. There is something smug about the thing. As though to say, 'I am humble' or 'I am full of restraint.' 'I am charitable and virtuous!' Actions, not words, should proclaim these qualities."

She saw by the flush under his skin that he was trying hard to control himself.

"We will call him Humility," he said. "My dear, the first duty of a wife towards her husband is obedience."

"*I* am no ordinary wife and I would thank you not to speak of me in such terms. This child is mine and I alone will choose his name."

"I regret I must be firm in this," he said. "Had you asked me in humility, I might have allowed him a second name, and, as you wished to name him after your father and that is a pleasant and agreeable thought, I might have given my consent. But in view of your rebellion, your careless words, I can only forbid the use of the name, and I must. . . ."

"Pray, do not preach to me!" she cried. "If you attempt to, you will stay in your attic altogether and there will be no more children. That would be a pity, as I wished for more."

"I do not understand you, Tamar."

"No, you do not understand *me*. But understand *this*: The child will be named Richard."

"I cannot countenance such unwifely behaviour," he said; but he stopped short, looking at her.

She was very beautiful with her long black hair upon the pillows, her big luminous eyes flashing, her breast bare in the low-cut bed-gown.

*　　*　　*

Little Dick was three years old and Rowan just born when the Indian princess came to Plymouth.

Tamar had left Rowan in the care of Annis and had taken Dick down to Barbican Causeway to see the ships come in.

The little boy, dark-eyed and vivacious, was entirely Tamar's child. She rejoiced to watch him; so must she have been when she was his age. She was determined

246

that none of those hardships which she had had to face should fall to his lot. There seemed hardly anything of Humility in him; indeed, the boy avoided his father whenever possible. He was afraid of the pale, stern-faced man whose every sentence seemed to begin with "Thou shalt not. . ."

He loved the sea, and was never tired of watching it and listening to the tales his mother told him of the Spaniards.

She had taken him down on this occasion, little guessing that such a romantic figure would be on board. There she was — a lovely, dark-eyed girl, a princess from the promised land itself, with straight black hair and strange clothes. Nor was she the only visitor from that distant land, for she, as a princess, had brought her train with her — Indians in brightly coloured clothes that accentuated the darkness of their hair and eyes.

The princess was Pocahontas, now called Rebecca, since she had embraced the Christian faith and had married an Englishman. When the spectators had recovered from their surprise, they welcomed her warmly, for they knew something of her romantic story. Captain John Smith had been in Plymouth a year or so ago, talking to the people. He had, he explained, been travelling through the West Country; his plan was to get people to accompany him to the New World. He scorned those who went in search of gold, for did not many of them return disappointed? There were, he assured them, greater prizes to be taken: trade for England; the development of uncultivated land; an empire. He had been treated badly in Virginia and was anxious to explore new territory. He talked of the place he had christened New England. There was fish in those seas as good — nay, better — than anywhere else in the world. There was one cape which had been called Cape Cod because never before had so many fish been seen as were swimming in the water surrounding it. Corn could be grown there; cattle raised. He explained that he was eager to take out a band of men, and was recruiting for his ships.

Richard had entertained him at Pennicomquick, where Captain Smith had told many a story of the New World; and although Humility had dreamed of going to Virginia, he did not see why New England should not be equally suitable.

Those had been exciting months while Smith made his preparations.

But Richard was against their going. He pointed out again and again that they would be leaving a life of comfort for one of hardship. There might be famine. Had Tamar considered that? Had she imagined her little Dick crying for food? Let those go who found life here intolerable — for they had little to lose. But for those who enjoyed the comfortable life, there should be much consideration before lightly giving it up.

Humility longed to go, for he saw the hand of God in the coming of Captain Smith to Plymouth.

Tamar had then been aware of a growing perversity in herself, which at times made her want to oppose this man whom she had married. She said: "Don't

248

you always see the hand of God when something turns up which you want? It was always Virginia . . . Virginia . . . Virginia . . . I thought that was the place. This New England is virgin soil. Shall we take our child to possible starvation? You may go, but you will go alone."

And then the matter was decided for them. One of the Plymouth ships, which had set out for the New World in search of gold, came back empty and with tales of hardship. Interest in the expedition dropped. Tamar became pregnant again. And when Smith sailed with the two ships which were all he could muster, the family at Pennicomquick was not with him.

But Smith had made known in Plymouth the romantic story of Pocahontas, and when Tamar took the little boy on her horse and rode slowly homewards she told it to him.

"Captain Smith had gone into a strange land, my son," said Tamar, "and with him were many who wished to make the land their own. But there were people—already in the land—people like those you have seen to-day, and they did not wish the white men to take their land from them. And one day Captain Smith was caught by the Indians and they were going to kill him, when the Princess you have seen to-day stepped forward and, just as they were about to kill him, threw herself upon him, so that they had to hold back their blows. Then she begged the King, her father, to save his life; and this he did. So she is remembered in this land as the little girl—for she was only twelve years old—who saved the life of an

Englishman and was a friend to the English. Now, my little Dick, you will be able to tell your grandfather who it was you have seen this day. What is her name? Do you remember?"

"Pocahontas," said Dick; and his eyes were bright. He was filled with excitement by what he had seen. One day *he* would be one of the adventurers of the sea.

There was nothing of his father in him; and she was glad.

*   *   *

The coming of the Princess excited them.

Humility, his eyes blazing with fervour, declared that this was yet another sign from God. Relations between the Indians and the white settlers were such that an Indian Princess had married a white man and become a Christian and was not afraid to visit the country of the white men. That was a sign. There could be little danger from Indians where such conditions prevailed.

Humility was eager to set out. He declared this was due to his desire to break away from a country whose rulers forbade men to worship God as they wished. But, Tamar asked herself, was that the only reason? Humility did not like their present domestic arrangements, which, she was ready to admit, were unusual and would make a man of Humility's pride uneasy.

No wonder he was eager to get away.

"I would never leave Richard," declared Tamar. "Wait, and he will come with us. He needs a good deal of time to come to such a decision. Moreover, if he came with us, we could go in comfort. He is a rich man and he could use his wealth to give us a well-equipped ship. We cannot go to a strange land and start a settlement there without a good deal of wealth. Believe me, for I know that when the time is ripe Richard will come with us."

Richard went on to talk of comfort *versus* hardship. Was it fair, he demanded, to take women and children to savage lands?

"God would look after them," said Humility.

"The Spaniards, pirates or Indians might arrive on the scene before God," said Tamar, goaded into flippancy by her husband's piety, as she so often was.

Humility prayed silently, and, watching him, Tamar asked herself once more, as she had asked so many times: Why did I marry this man? How could I want to hurt him as I do if I loved him? And yet . . . ever since I saved his life I have been aware of him. I am as happy with him as I could be with any.

"I thought," said Humility, "that you were as eager for this project as I. You talk of risks. Here we risk our lives. We never know when we shall be sent to prison and left to die there. Continually we break the laws of this land. We need only an informer among us, and disaster would be upon us. In the strange land we might find other dangers, but we would hold our heads high and fear none."

Tamar was swayed. "That is so," she agreed. "Richard, there is much to be said for freedom, even if it brings other troubles with it."

But Richard would not be convinced.

"Consider this matter," he said. "You would have me sell my lands, equip a ship, and take with us all our wealth to this new land. Think! First we must make a perilous journey. We must face storm and tempest. Worse still, this ocean we must cross is infested with pirates of all nationalities. Such a ship as ours would be an easy victim. There would be money aboard . . . goods; and pirates would know this. We should have to face death . . . horrible death . . . perhaps worse than horrible death. There may be Spaniards who would hand us over to the Inquisition; Turks who would take us down to the Barbary coast and make slaves of us. As Humility would say, that might be the will of God. But I would not wish such things to happen to myself or Tamar or the children. Dick is three years old; Rowan a baby. Let them grow older. Wait. Let us discover more of this land before we leave the evils we know for those we can only conjecture."

"Just think!" said Tamar. "If you would equip a ship we could begin preparing to-morrow."

"That is why I feel we must give this matter the deepest thought. There is always safety in waiting."

So they waited and the uneventful life continued.

They heard that the little Princess had died at Gravesend just as she was about to return to her native land. She had been unable to endure the damp air of England.

Richard said then that he had been right to oppose the venture.

252

"Their climate might have the same effect on us," he said.

"Men and women are like plants. They cannot easily be uprooted."

Then Tamar knew that she was to have another child, and temporarily she lost all desire to wander.

* * *

Tamar nearly lost her life when Lorea was born. She lay in bed only half conscious of time and place. For days she remained thus, and in the weeks that followed a listlessness settled upon her.

She heard the voices of those about her without hearing their words: Annis's high-pitched and full of tears; Richard's solemn and full of sorrow; Humility's sad, yet resigned; then Dick aged five and Rowan three, were frightened and bewildered.

She had never been inactive for so long, and inactivity gave her time for thought. She was most unhappily and unsuitably married. How could she ever have been so foolish as to imagine she could have lived a quiet life, that she could have been the meek, submissive Puritan wife of a man like Humility? Often she felt sorry on his account for having married him, and determined to do her best to hide her revulsion.

They had three children now; Humility would not feel he had justified his marrying until they had twelve. Nine more ordeals such as this one she had just passed through! She sighed. Well, it was her duty, and she was committed to it.

Dick and Rowan were *her* children, with rosy cheeks and bright black eyes and dark hair—high-spirited wild young things. She wondered about the new child, little Lorea, born small and puny, not like her brother and sister, who, almost from their birth, had amazed everybody, so that people like Annis and Mistress Alton thought that some devil's power had been used by their mother to make them stronger, more bright and beautiful than others of their age.

When she rose from her bed after the passing of weeks, her mirror showed her how pale and thin she had become. She would sit in her room, deep in thought. Humility was delighted with her. He had returned to her room, as it was time, he said, to get themselves another child.

The memory of the ordeal was still very vividly with her, but she submitted.

Humility went down on his knees and praised God.

"I thank Thee, Lord, for showing this woman Thy ways at last . . ."

Dick and Rowan were bewildered by the change in her; she was too tired to play the games she had once played. They accepted the change, as children will, more readily than the grown-ups. They had lost their bright, gay and exciting mother; and in her place was a quiet stranger.

Little Lorea was a sickly child, over whom all shook their heads. Her poor, pathetic face looked out from the swaddling clothes, and she never smiled; she hardly ever cried.

Humility would sigh, looking at her; he would murmur: "If this be the will of God, then must we bear it."

He turned stern eyes on his two elder children. Violence was something he could never employ, but he saw clearly the need of correction where those two were concerned. Dick, for his sins, was often shut into a dark cupboard, because that, Humility had discovered, was what he feared more than aught else. Rowan, who was always hungry, was sent fasting to bed.

A change had come over the household.

The Devil is in chains! thought Humility.

The summer came, and in the long, hot days Tamar sat out of doors. Then the colour returned to her face and she was aware of a deep delight in the smells of the sun-baked earth and the scent of the flowers. The smell of earth reminded her always of Bartle; she remembered it so well from the day when he had tripped her up and forced her down — and, ever after that, the smell of earth was a smell which excited her; and after those days out of doors, she would feel a little resentful towards Humility. She could not help it if she dreamed of a passionate lover who came to her, most dishonourably it was true, but with what passion, because he desired her, not children!

Then came a day when Dick and Rowan were lost.

They had been caught laughing during prayers that morning and had been called to their father and told to repeat the Lord's Prayer. Humility shared the current belief that inability to say the Lord's Prayer was in itself a confession of wickedness, for there was some magical quality about the words, so that they would not come fluently through impure mouths. When the children faltered, Humility, in deep sorrow, talked to them of the hell which awaited all sinners. Dick, for instance, would be perpetually in the dark, unable to see anything but the eyes of devils who would torment him and pull out his flesh with hot pincers while he burned eternally. Rowan, who was greedy in the extreme, would be sat at a table containing all the food she loved best, and every time she reached out a hand to take some of it, it would be snatched from her. She would starve, but not to death, for she too would suffer the pains of burning for ever.

The thought of burning eternally did not greatly worry the children; they had never been burned. But the thought of being shut in a dark cupboard with devils terrified Dick. Rowan, more sturdily practical than her brother, could imagine no greater torment than going hungry.

In the days before Lorea's birth they might have gone to their mother for comfort, but they sensed, with the quick perception of children, that their mother had changed, and that their father now ruled their lives.

Hell and the supposed horrors devised by their Heavenly Father were in the far distant future; but right before them were the punishments of their earthly one. The dark was not to be faced; and if Rowan was going without her usual food she might as well do it out of doors where there were berries and nuts and plants which were good to eat.

So they ran away.

Tamar was with Annis when the news was brought to her. She had been standing by the basket in which lay her youngest child. Every day Lorea's face took on a more deathly hue. How many weeks of life were left to the child? she wondered.

Annis looked up from some garment she was stitching, and her eyes betrayed the sudden fear which had come to her.

"What ails you, Annis?" asked Tamar.

Annis hesitated, but Tamar insisted that she tell, and at last it came. "I thought, mistress, that you was back with the Devil. I thought you were going to work out one of your spells to save the child."

Tamar's eyes gleamed, but just at that moment Moll Swann came in to say that the children were not to be found. Moll had searched everywhere in the house and grounds. Moll was afraid they were lost.

Then in a moment Tamar threw off the inertia of months as though she were tossing aside a garment.

"Let everyone search," she said. "They must be found at once."

"Where be you going, mistress?" asked Annis.

"To find them," answered Tamar. "Go to the stables and tell them to saddle my horse."

She was in her habit and away in a few minutes, her hair blown loose in the wind as of old. Hundreds of thoughts filled her mind as she rode on. Her children had been frightened because they had missed the mother they had once known; and they had been unable to endure their life at Pennicomquick as the children of Humility Brown. She understood that, and she was to blame.

She rode hard and straight to the spot where the children were — there would be some who would say there was witchcraft in that. Was there? she wondered. Or was it that she herself had taken them there so many times? It was a small grassy plateau on the cliffs, from which it was possible to see, in all its beauty and promise of adventure, that shining expanse of channel. Here she had often told them stories of the sea; and the stories she had told had been those Bartle had told her.

When they saw her coming with her hair flying and the colour in her cheeks, they gave shouts of joy and ran to her.

Dick said: "Rowan, she's come! She's come!"

Tamar held them fiercely against her and she knew that they also meant that she had come back to them. The mother they had once known had returned.

They were delighted to have been found. The dark of the night would have been as frightening as the dark of a cupboard; and starvation in the open air as bad as starvation at home.

She set them on her horse and they went slowly back; but the journey did not seem long to them, for they were all so happy to be reunited.

The children had lost their fears, for their real mother was back and she would protect them from their Puritan father.

The household was in a turmoil when they arrived. Richard saw the trio entering the stable-yard, and knew what had happened. Tamar's health had returned, and with it the true Tamar. The period of submission had been due to her decline in health after the birth of Lorea; just as her conversion had taken place after some deep mental disturbance. He watched the meeting between the returning party and Humility.

Humility had been anxious. He was fond of his children, Richard knew; perhaps he was proud of their fine looks and healthy bodies; but because he was proud of them he considered it necessary to be the sterner with them. Now, though, he had to face their mother, and she stood before him like a tigress with her young.

"Praise be to God!" cried Humility. "The children are safe."

Tamar did not answer. She lifted the children to the ground and called to the gaping Ned Swann to take the horse.

"Dick," said Humility, "Rowan, I can see that you are ashamed of what you have done. That is well. But do not think this can go unpunished."

Tamar said: "They have been sufficiently punished and shall be punished no more."

"Wife," he said, his eyes on her flushed face and wild hair, "you have brought them home. Now you will leave them to me."

"No," she answered, "*you* will leave them to *me*."

She felt the children's hands in hers, clinging hot and tight.

"Annis!" she cried. "Annis, food for the children . . . quickly."

Glances were exchanged among the watching servants. Moll whispered to Jane: "The mistress be back, then." Mistress Alton gave one fearful look at Tamar and began to mutter the Lord's Prayer; and Tamar, watching them, laughed inwardly. They were thinking that the Devil had been in chains, but he had broken free.

Well, at least Dick and Rowan were happy.

"Come, my darlings," she said. "And promise you will never leave your mother again, for she will never leave you."

And they kept their tight grip on her hands as they went past their father, but they could not help throwing triumphant glances at Humility as they did so.

Tamar made them eat in her room instead of in their nursery. As they ate, they told her how frightened they had been, and how they hoped that no one but their mother would find them.

Annis, standing by the baby's basket, shook her head. *She* knew how it was that their mother had been able to go straight to the place where they had been. Annis thought: It is good to have the children home safe, though the Devil is back!

Tamar, reading her thoughts, went over to the basket, and as she stood beside Annis, looking down at the sickly baby, wild thoughts came to her, and with them all the old belief in her powers. She *knew* that she could snatch this child from death.

She picked up Lorea. "Annis," she said quietly, "bring me warm water quickly. Waste no time."

Annis muttered fearfully: "What be you going to do, mistress?"

"Do as I say!"

When Annis returned, Tamar had cut the swaddling clothes from the baby who lay in her lap, her poor, cramped limbs caked and foul with the muck of months.

Annis shrieked; the children stopped eating. "Mistress, you will hasten her to her grave."

"Nay," said Tamar. "I will snatch her from it."

Tenderly and carefully she washed the baby while Annis, standing by, handing her what she asked for, heard the strange words she muttered as she patted and dried the skin which had a look of bad cheese. Then she wrapped the baby in a shawl and held it against her, crooning over it. Annis swore afterwards that from that moment the colour of the baby's face began to change.

Then she fed the baby. It took a little milk and was not sick. All that night Tamar kept her children with her—her baby at her breast, the other two on either side of her.

Humility came in, but she sent him out, and he dared not protest. Annis lay at the end of the bed, and there was no sleep for either her or her mistress that night. Every time the child awakened, Tamar fed her.

Annis was sure she was watching magic. As she said to John later: "It was magic for sure, but *good* magic. Couldn't have been aught else."

"Nay," answered John, " 'was devil's work, for God meant the child to die and she saved her, so how could that be good?"

But Annis believed that the dear Lord would understand and not be too hard on a woman whose sin was to save through witchcraft the baby He had decided to take.

The next day was warm and sunny and Tamar took the baby out into the shade of the garden. And Mistress Alton, watching from the windows with Jane and Moll, was certain that this was witchcraft.

In a week from that day when Dick and Rowan had run away from home, little Lorea was kicking her legs in the sunshine — puny still, but moving slowly away from the grave.

Tamar was triumphant. Her little girl was saved. She herself had worked the miracle and all her old power was back with her.

*　　*　　*

Richard saw trouble coming, and spoke of it to Humility.

"Man, you must have a care. From the way things are going I see more and more restrictions coming, more and more persecutions of such as you."

Humility answered as he answered all warnings: "Whatever should come to us would be through the will of God."

Most of the Puritans were attending the service of the Established Church. That was necessary to avoid suspicion. But Humility refused to go. Nothing had happened so far, for nobody had informed against him; but, Richard pointed out, that state of affairs might not last.

"What," he asked, "if you were taken off to prison? You would not escape as easily as John Tyler did. Oh, we are fortunate here, I know. The law is not so strictly enforced in this part of the country. But . . . Humility, if you were taken, I doubt if they would ever set you free." Humility was about to speak, but Richard interrupted impatiently: "I know what you will say. 'It is the will of God!' But what of your family? What of Tamar and the children?"

"They are well looked after here," said Humility. "As you know, I have never supported my family. That I was prepared to do, but Tamar is proud. The life I could offer her was not good enough. She would not renounce her comfort for her duty."

"It may have been the comfort of her children she was thinking of," said Richard coldly. "And it occurs to me that your pride is as great as Tamar's."

Humility was astonished. Richard smiled. It amazed him that Humility—a man of learning and some culture—could be so blind regarding himself, could walk contentedly in the narrow channel he had cut for himself . . . a channel which was bounded on both sides by the strictures of the Puritan faith.

"I . . . proud! Pride is one of the seven deadly sins. If I believed I possessed it . . ."

"I know," said Richard. "You would fast and pray. But sometimes when a man is aware of great goodness in himself he can be blind to that little which is in others. But let us not talk of this. I wish you to take more care, for there are trying times ahead of us."

But what was the use of talking to Humility? He could only fold his hands in prayer and continue in his way of life, so putting himself in perpetual danger of arrest, imprisonment and even death.

Richard was right. The King was not pleased with his Puritans. He had returned from Scotland and had not liked the way the English kept their Sundays. He wished them to attend church, but once divine service was over, there was no need to be glum. In fact, loyal subjects were ordered *not* to be glum.

A proclamation was read throughout the land.

It was His Majesty's pleasure that his people should not be disturbed or discouraged from any lawful recreations, such as dancing, either of men or women, archery, leaping, vaulting or any harmless recreations. Morris dances should be danced and maypoles set up. These sports were within the law.

There was another point in the proclamation. Some people were to be excluded from Sunday sports — those who did not attend service in their parish church, or attended for only part of the service. The name of any man or woman guilty of this should in future be announced from the pulpit.

Richard said to Humility: "Mark my words, this is the beginning of new persecutions."

In East Anglia, where the Separatist movement was at its strongest, persecutions were at their height. In London, where some bold Separatists were preaching their creed in the streets, there were riots and bloodshed. In Devon things were quieter, but to Richard the rumours were like the rumbling of a storm which was coming closer.

And one day two ships sailed into Plymouth Sound, and with the coming of these two ships came raised hopes and new plans to every Puritan who met in secret in that meeting-place which had been founded by Humility Brown.

These ships were the *Mayflower* — a vessel of some one hundred and eighty tons — and her smaller companion, the *Speedwell*.

Here was a great occasion for the town of Plymouth; but for no one more than for Humility Brown and William Spears, because aboard these ships were men they had once known, men from their own county.

Humility had rarely been so excited as he was on that day. Where these men went, would he follow. He was certain now that God had meant him to be left behind so that he might save many souls and take them to the promised land.

Miles Standish, a friend from his past, was delighted to see him. They had long talks together, and Standish gave Humility details of provisions which must be taken on such a trip if there was to be any hope of survival in a new land. Humility listened eagerly, made many notes; and was more than a little sad not to be of their number.

"But," he said to Standish, "I am wrong. I am wicked. It is not for me to rail against the fate which God has ordained for me. I am not ready yet."

"Yea, Humility, my friend," answered Standish. "It is clear that the Lord did not intend you to come with us. The captain of the *Speedwell* is faint of heart and declares his vessel to be unseaworthy. We might have taken you and your family and friends, but as the *Mayflower* goes alone, we have to take on board all those passengers whose hearts do not fail them. Everything must be carried in one ship instead of two, as we planned. Your turn will come, my friend, I doubt not."

It was a moving sight to watch that lonely ship sail off into the unknown. Crowds stood on the Hoe while the *Speedwell* lay in the Sound and the *Mayflower* sailed with those men and women who had said their last farewells to their native land, that they might find a new life, a new country where they could worship God in peace.

* * *

After the Pilgrim Fathers left Plymouth, several years passed uneventfully. There was now a new King on the throne — King Charles the First — but with his reign persecution did not end.

Humility continued to hope that the day was approaching when he would follow in the wake of the Pilgrims; Tamar swayed between him and Richard;

266

and it was not until a series of disasters occurred that Richard began to change his mind.

The first of these disasters concerned the Puritans. Several of them, it had been noted, were neither attending Sunday service in the church nor Sunday sports; their clothes were too sombre for fashion; they were, in short, living the lives of Puritans and breaking the law of the land.

Josiah Hough discovered that a trap had been laid to catch the Puritans at worship when they met in their barn on Thursday night at eight o'clock. He immediately brought this news to Richard, who lost no time in imparting it to Humility Brown.

"I beg of you, do not go there on Thursday," he said, "and warn all your friends to stay away."

"This," said Humility, "is the protecting arm of God. He does not wish us to rot in prison. He has other plans for us. More and more I am convinced that He wishes us, when the time is ripe, to sail for the New World."

So that Thursday there was no meeting at the barn, and those who had surrounded the place, hoping to make arrests, were so angry that they burned it to the ground.

"You have escaped this time," said Richard. "Let it be a warning to you to take double care in future."

A few months passed during which the Puritans seemed to have been forgotten, for a new witch-hunt was engaging attention.

In Devon this began with Jane Swann. Jane was a pretty girl—golden-haired and blue-eyed, a quiet, good girl. Ned Swann and his wife had been two of the first to turn Puritan, and their girls had been brought up almost from babyhood in the faith. Moll was slow-witted, but Jane was a bright girl and pretty enough in her quiet way to attract the attention of the young men of the neighbourhood.

One afternoon she was gathering wood in a lonely copse which adjoined the Hurlys' farm when she was overtaken by a man. She knew this man to be a merchant of Plymouth, a man of some substance, an ardent church-goer of pious reputation. He stopped and talked to the girl and she, believing him to be all that she had heard, had no fear of him until he made a suggestion which terrified her. She turned to run, but he caught her. She threatened to expose him if he hurt her. He laughed at that.

"Do you think any would believe the word of a girl like you against mine?" he asked.

Poor Jane was bewildered by her fear. She quickly realized that she would be forced to sin; defiled, shamed, damned for ever, she would have to confess at the meeting-place before all the Puritans. To a girl of her upbringing, death seemed preferable, for she would have no wish to live after such shame had overtaken her. She fought with all her might against this man as he tore her clothes from her and flung her to the ground.

He cursed her, but she screamed the louder. He silenced her with a blow that partially stunned her, and proceeded then with his evil work.

He had forgotten that the copse was so close to the farm, and suddenly he heard a rush of footsteps through the undergrowth, and there, standing before him were Peter Hurly and his young brother, George.

The greatly respected citizen was caught in the very act; furiously angry, overcome with shame, he scrambled to his feet and made off—but not before he was recognized—leaving the half-conscious girl lying on the ground.

The boys helped Jane to her feet, and as she could not walk, between them they carried her back to the house at Pennicomquick.

Tamar was horrified at the story they had to tell.

"Bring her to my room," she commanded. "Poor child! I will look after her. And let everyone know what sort of a man this is! He must be punished for this. We will see that he falls from that high pedestal on which he has set himself."

Tenderly she looked after the poor, shocked girl, and all the time she was thinking: This might have happened to me! And the memory of Bartle all those years ago was as vivid as ever.

She herself lost no time in spreading the story of what had happened to Jane; nor did she omit to mention the name of the culprit. "Who could be trusted after this?" everyone was asking.

Mistress Alton blamed the girl, for she persisted in her belief that evil was only suffered by those who deserved so to suffer; but Tamar stood over Jane like an angel with a flaming sword.

It was deeply gratifying to learn that Jane's ravisher was now shunned in the town, that he had ceased to be regarded as a respectable merchant and would not long be a wealthy one, for people did not wish to trade with one who had so deceived them as to his real character.

Poor Jane was recovering under Tamar's care, for Tamar impressed upon her that what had happened to her was due to no fault of hers. "Indeed," said Tamar with flashing eyes, "what happened to you might have happened to any of us!"

Even Humility admitted that what had occurred was Jane's misfortune rather than her fault. He spent long periods praying with her for the purification of her soul, although he thought that only a life of extreme piety could make her pure in the eyes of Jesus.

And one day Jane went out and failed to return.

She was missed early in the afternoon, and when night came and she was not back, Mistress Alton narrowed her eyes and grumbled to Jane's sister Moll: "You can depend upon it, I was right. When that sort of thing happens to a girl there's more in it than meets the eyes. Oh, they are all very innocent when they are caught. It was rape, of course. It is always rape! Mark my words, young Mollie, your sister went out to meet that man and was willing enough until the Hurly boys surprised them. And it wouldn't be such a big surprise to me now if they'd gone off together where they can sin undisturbed."

Tamar went down to the kitchen. "Has Jane returned?"

Mistress Alton smiled her secret smile. "She's well away by now. Like as not they're riding away on the other side of the Tamar. Or mayhap it's across the Plym they've gone. But gone they have . . . and you may be sure they've gone together . . ."

Tamar faced the woman. "I tell you it is not true. I have never seen anyone so distressed as Jane was when the boys brought her home."

"Distressed! Oh . . . aye! They're all distressed when they're caught. And to be caught like that . . ."

"How dare you blame *her*! She was forced. I have talked long with her. *I* could not be mistaken."

"You are too kind to the girl. Forced! Nobody ever tried forcing me."

"That," said Tamar as she swept out of the kitchen, "does not surprise me."

Tamar did not sleep at all that night. She felt convinced that something terrible was happening to Jane; and she believed that she knew this through her secret powers.

Humility, who was sharing her room, hoping for a fourth child, begged her to rest; but she would not rest. She paced up and down the room.

In the early morning, as soon as dawn began to show over Bolt Head, she dressed and went out. That was how it came about that it was Tamar who brought Jane back to the house.

Jane was hardly recognisable as the girl who had left the house yesterday. Her face was red and swollen—blistered and burned. Her bodice had been ripped off her shoulders and there were angry scars on her neck and chest. Across her back were burns which may have been made with a poker or a bar of redhot metal. Tamar could not believe that this was Jane until the girl spoke.

Feeling sick with anger and indignation, Tamar picked up the girl and carried her back to the house, for Jane was in a state of collapse; she had come within a quarter of a mile of the house, but could drag herself no further.

The gentleness of Tamar's hands were a vivid contrast to her angry, flashing eyes. She knew that a cruel and wicked revenge had been taken on an innocent girl.

Jane regained consciousness only to swoon with her pain. Her fair, once lovely, hair had been burned away at one side of her head. She murmured: "They made me say. . . They made me say. . ." And then she would slip into unconsciousness.

Tamar took Jane to her room, and, waking Humility, made him get out of the bed, on which she laid the suffering girl.

Humility stared at Jane. "What has happened to her?"

"They have tortured her. Oh, for the love of God, don't start praying now. Get Richard and get Annis. Tell her to bring warm water. . . and some wine to revive her. Quickly. . . Quickly. This is no time for prayers, but for action."

Jane was moaning softly in her agony.

"Oh, dear Jane," murmured Tamar while the tears ran down her cheeks. "I will save you. I will ease your pain."

Richard came in and stared at the girl. "Good God!" he cried. "What have they done to her? I will send a groom for a doctor at once."

"I have the ointments to heal these burns," said Tamar. "They are as good as any doctor's. Where is Annis? Oh . . . Annis . . . water . . . warm water . . . and my box of ointments."

"I will see that the doctor is called at once," said Richard; but Tamar laid a hand on his arm.

"We do not yet know the full meaning of this. She muttered something as I carried her in . . . something about a witch. If possible . . . let no one know she is here. I tell you I can do more for her than any doctor."

Annis, her eyes wide with horror, came in with the warm water and the ointments.

"She *must* have a doctor," said Richard. "The girl is near death."

"I saved Lorea, did I not? I tell you I know more than doctors."

Richard could see that there was little a doctor could do for Jane except soothe her burns, and that Tamar's ointments and lotions would do equally well. There had been some treacherous work here, and the fact that Jane had mentioned witches gave a clue to what had been done to her . . . and with what excuse.

Jane moaned softly while the wounds were bathed and Tamar applied the ointments. Wine was forced between Jane's lips; and Annis was bidden to tear up linen so that Tamar might bind the wounds.

Tamar and Annis sat up with Jane, for Tamar refused to have anyone with her but Annis. She wanted Annis's absolute belief in her ability to cure the girl — a belief which the others would not feel; and this lack of belief, Tamar felt, might thwart her success. She felt that, given an atmosphere of confidence and her herbs and ointments, together with magical words, she could carry this thing successfully through.

Soon after Jane had been found, a story was circulating about her. Jane Swann was a witch. She had admitted it. The respected merchant, desolate at losing his good name and his position in the town, had, with the concurrence of some of his friends, captured the girl and questioned her. One or two accepted tests were forced upon her, and after a while she broke down and confessed "the truth."

The merchant — according to this story — had not been in the woods that day. His wife had testified to that. There were others ready to testify. It was said that Jane Swann was in the habit of going into the woods, where she behaved in a very lewd fashion with her familiar — a devil. This devil was at times invisible, but, like all such devils, could change into any shape he chose. One woman swore that on another occasion, as she had walked through the copse, she had seen a girl whom she now believed to have been Jane Swann lying in the grass naked from the waist down, and by her lewd motions it was clear that the girl was having sexual connection with an invisible creature. The woman had watched, and after a while had seen a shape, formed in smoke above the girl, which disappeared into the sky. The girl then got up, rearranged her clothes most demurely and walked away. On this tragic occasion the two boys had seen what the woman had seen; and the girl, knowing that it was too late to hide herself — she had, of course, been unaware that she had been watched before — had pleaded with her familiar for help; whereupon he had changed himself into the shape of the merchant, and, after he was sure that the boys had recognized him as such, had made off. Then the girl told her tale of force and violence. Of course she had seemed stunned! Of course there were bruises! Was she not, on her own confession, a witch? Why, after the confession, she had flown off on a broomstick. There were many who swore they had seen her flying through the sky.

Such was the lying tale which had been put about, and that had restored the merchant's honour.

Richard had already warned Mistress Alton that she would be turned out immediately if she told anyone of Jane's presence in the house. It was thus possible to keep the whole neighbourhood — with the exception of the girl's parents — ignorant of where she was.

After a few weeks of Tamar's nursing, young Jane had recovered from the terrible shock sufficiently to tell the full story of that night of brutality.

Her enemies had watched her leave the house, had stunned her and taken her to a cottage in the town. Here she was made to sit before a fire; her bodice was torn from her back and a red-hot poker applied while she was ordered to confess the story which had been prepared for her.

She was, in spite of the awful agony, able to withstand the torture; it was only when they forced her face downwards on to the fire that she had shrieked for mercy and had given way.

There had been a man present who had taken down her confession in writing, which she had had to repeat at the dictation of her tormentors.

She had become unconscious when they had left her lying on the floor. They intended, she had gathered, to take her in the morning to the Hoe, to proclaim her wickedness to the world and hang her. Believing her to be half-dead already, they had taken no precaution against an escape; but after an hour or so, Jane's young body had somewhat recovered. She prayed for strength, and, feeling that anything was preferable to the ordeal she would have to face on the morrow if she stayed there, had managed to stumble to the door. She was surprised to find that she only had to unlatch this and walk out. And this she did, for the man who had been set to guard her had drunk heavily and was snoring loudly.

It had taken her many hours to crawl towards Pennicomquick, tortured as she was by the cold air making her wounds smart; and it was only her belief in the divine assistance for which she had prayed that enabled her to cling to consciousness as long as she did.

Tamar's one thought was of revenge. She longed to confront that evil man with his sins. But Richard argued with her until he made her see that her interference could only make matters worse for Jane. To let it be known that Jane was safe was to condemn her to the gibbet.

"Oh, Tamar," he said, "the times in which we live are dangerous ones . . . violent and dangerous. Think of the injustice of this! A poor Puritan maiden, wandering in the woods . . . and that to happen to her!" He was silent suddenly, staring before him. "Your mother . . ." he went on quietly, "she . . . wandered in the woods one night; she was seduced by one no better than this merchant . . . and that night her feet were set on a path that led her to the gallows. Who am I to condemn others!"

Tamar went to him and laid a hand on his shoulder. "You were not as this man," she said. "You were thoughtless, careless . . . He is wicked. I will not have you compare yourself with him. Oh, Richard, when I think of what has happened to Jane . . . I want . . . I want to go away. I think of those men and women who sailed from here on that ship. The *Mayflower*, was it not? Think of the dangers they must have faced. Spaniards . . . pirates . . . violence . . . But Richard, if they reached a new country—a country where this which has happened to Jane could not happen . . . then was it worth while."

"Yes," he agreed, "that would be worth while."

"Richard, you too are beginning to think of escape. Yes, I see you are. To a land where meeting-houses are not burned down, where innocent girls are not treated brutally."

They said no more at the time; but that tragic affair was the beginning of Richard's change of mind.

There was continual talk of witches now. Someone saw old Sally Martin at her cottage door talking earnestly to her cat; another saw Maddy Barlow suckling a rabbit. Smoke was seen coming from chimneys, forming itself into shapes of devils. No one dared pick any wild grasses and plants which were well-known remedies for certain ailments. If they were seen picking these things it was very likely that they would be accused of witchcraft. There were furtive glances everywhere. No one was safe from suspicion—neither men, women nor children. Tom Lee, the blacksmith's boy, said, after he had recovered from a fit, that he had been walking in the copse near the Hurly farm when he met an old woman who cursed him before she turned into a dog and ran away. He had clearly been overlooked, said his parents. By whom?

"There is a big witch community among us," it was whispered. "Who knows who these witches are? Children are not safe from their parents, parents from their children; husbands and wives may have the Devil between them."

One day Betsy Hurly, coming to see her daughter, with whom—now that Annis was a wife and mother—she had become reconciled, saw

Jane Swann at the window of Tamar's room. Betsy slyly said nothing of what she had seen, but went out of the house and spread the story all round the place.

The news spread like fire in the wind. Jane Swann was at the house of Richard Merriman. She was in that room which was occupied by Tamar Brown.

Betsy could not stop talking. "My dear, she couldn't hide that she was a witch. Awful she looked. I see her yellow hair showing from under a bandage. Nobody ain't got hair quite Jane Swann's colour. There she was at the window. And what's more . . . I did see *her* . . . Tamar herself . . . gathering herbs . . . her hair wild like as she do love to show it. Muttering she were as she picked the devil's plants."

It was felt that something had to be done and, once more, as had happened years ago when Tamar was fourteen years old, a group of people marched on to the house of Richard Merriman to take a witch. And once more Richard spoke to them; but on this occasion Humility Brown stood beside him.

"Good people," said Richard, "it is true that Jane Swann is here. We have nursed her back to health. You know she was forced in the copse, and you know by whom. She was then taken and most cruelly tortured. We are trying to nurse this poor sick girl back to health. I beg of you to go away and leave us in peace."

They murmured together.

"How do we know he ain't a witch? There be witches among gentry . . ."

"Where be the other one, the black-haired witch? She be the one we ought to be bothering ourselves with."

Then Humility spoke: "Friends, I see among you some who have prayed with me. I have prayed with this poor girl and I believe her story to be true. You know, my friends, that if there were a witch in this house, *I* should know it, and know also my duty, which would be to hand this witch over to you. And do you doubt that, however painful my duty, it would be done?"

There was a short silence. Then a voice said: "You be bewitched, minister. You married a witch."

Humility's eyes flashed wrath. "Purge yourself of your desire to see violence!" he cried, pointing to the man who had spoken. "Ask yourselves this: 'Does the sight of blood please us?' If you look into your hearts and answer that question truthfully, then, friends, you will know that your chances of salvation are slight indeed. I would beg of you to pray with me . . . to ask that your sins may be forgiven. This girl, Jane Swann, was cruelly handled by her ravisher. I saw her with my own eyes when she was brought in by the boys. Peter! George! Stand forth and bear witness. You saw the girl bruised and stunned. Did you not?"

The boys came forward. They said: "Yes, Mr. Brown, we saw her."

"Thank you, George. Thank you, Peter. And these good people think you were deceived, boys. But *I* saw also. That is what they forget. The Devil might deceive *you* into thinking you saw bruises, but would God allow His servant to be so deceived? Nay, the Devil has power, but he is like a man in chains before the strength of Almighty God. If any of you think aught evil goes on in this house, then take me, for I have then deceived you, friends. Take me and crucify me on the nearest tree. Drive the nails into my flesh . . . into my hands, through my feet. Cry, 'Crucify him!' And give me vinegar and gall to drink. Ah, my friends, would that I were worthy of such a death!"

He went on weaving spells through his words, at which the crowd grew quiet, and some wept, while others fell on their knees. And what had begun by being a demand for a girl's life had by his magic oratory been turned into a prayer meeting.

But that was not an end to the matter. On that occasion after prayer with Humility the people had gone quietly away, but they continued to speak together of the witchcraft they feared was in their midst.

It was remembered that Tamar had saved her baby when the child was all but in the grave; it was even said that Lorea had already been dead, and that, by pledging the little girl to the Devil, her mother had brought it to life. They remembered how Simon, the pricker, had wanted to search Tamar and how she had prevailed on Richard Merriman to call her "daughter," and how she had put a spell on him as she did on all men . . . even Humility Brown.

She was more clever than a witch; she was the Devil himself, for the Devil was doubtless like God — three in one, an unholy trinity.

She had turned many people to witchcraft. Look at Annis — getting a cottage, and John Tyler to marry her, even though it was a bit late. Richard Merriman had always been a strange man, and he grew stranger. They had even made Mistress Alton one of them. For did she say anything about that witch, Jane Swann, being in the house? She would have been the first to see justice done before they had made a witch of her.

One night there was an attempt to burn down the house, but the fire was noticed almost at once and put out.

Richard was very thoughtful after that. He made enquiries about chartering ships, and he discussed with Humility what would be needed to fit out an expedition and sail away in the wake of the *Mayflower*.

* * *

John Tyler was arrested for questioning, and all those Puritans who had been attending Humility's meetings were thrown into a panic. They had heard of the way confessions were extracted, and they were afraid that, meek and gentle as John Tyler was, he was hardly the sort to stand up to such questionings. Humility, as the leader, suggested giving himself up; but Richard pointed out the folly of that. If Humility admitted to holding meetings in the place, there would be countless arrests.

Richard himself went to the magistrate in Plymouth, a man whom he had known as a friend.

Richard was frank; he knew that the Government was eager to send men out to the New World to colonize under the English flag. On the Continent, recusants were punished with great severity; but all the English Government wanted to do was to get rid of them. It was ready even to assist those Dissenters who wished to leave the country. So Richard was able to secure John's release by explaining that he was making arrangements to charter a ship in which the Puritan community planned to leave the country for ever.

After that, Richard knew he was committed to proceed with this scheme which he had at first been inclined to treat as a fancy. He went into serious negotiations for a vessel of some one hundred tons, and was arranging with a certain Captain Flame to take her across the ocean.

More people were flocking to the meetings, excited by the rumours of emigration. Life was hard, and wonderful stories were circulated concerning the New World.

And then, as though momentous events could never come singly, a strange ship was one day sighted on the horizon. It was not an English ship — that much was apparent to eyes trained to look on English ships. It was a long, lean galley that cut through the water at astonishing speed and made straight for the Sound.

Bustle and excitement filled the town. Men got out their old guns, and sailors sharpened their cutlasses. But what was there to fear from one ship? Unless, of course, there were others following. The fleet was not in home waters and the sudden violent attack by the corsairs of Brittany was remembered.

Some of the old sailors declared the swiftly moving galley to be a Turk.

Tamar was on the Causeway when the galley came in. A sudden intuition had come to her; and her eyes sought one man among those lean and emaciated figures, but she could not find the one she sought.

But now the men had shipped their oars and were leaping out, embracing those about them. One of them stooped and touched the cobbles with his hands; then knelt and kissed them. In their rags of all shapes and colours, these men were scarcely recognizable as Englishmen; their skins had been burned to a dark brown; their beards were unkempt; and their bare backs showed the marks of the lash and other tortures.

And last to come ashore was the man for whom Tamar had looked. He could not remain unrecognized, this lean, emaciated giant, for his startlingly blue eyes betrayed his identity. He was laughing now; his teeth gleaming white in his lean, brown face, in which the bones seemed ready to pierce the skin. He was looking about him, and Tamar knew he was looking for her.

She ran to him. He caught her and held her; and she felt once more that excitement which she had not known since he went away.

The most bewildering and exhilarating moment of an eventful year was upon her. Bartle had come home.

*   *   *

He was back in his house at Stoke. Already he had lost that unkempt look. It was said that he and the men who had escaped with him were holding a prolonged feast at his house; he was going to keep them with him, for the ordeals through which they had passed together had made them his friends for ever. His cousin, who had inherited his title and estates when his father had died and he was believed lost, was still at the house, but he was preparing to leave.

Sir Bartle was the hero of the day and the toast of the county. Few men could have lived through what he had lived through; fewer still could have successfully escaped and brought his men home to safety.

It was a stirring story which Bartle and his crew had to tell. A few days out of Plymouth they had found themselves surrounded by Turkish galleys. Some of their crew were drowned, while others were taken prisoner and made to row in the galleys — a hardship such as only the strongest could endure. They were chained to the ship — six at one oar — and given only just enough food and drink to keep them alive. Any faintness or lack of energy was severely punished by the boatswain, who walked the gangway brandishing his lash, bringing it down when the mood took him, lacerating the flesh of his slaves. To this life had proud Bartle been condemned. The galleys only put to sea during the spring and summer, and in winter were laid up, when the galley slaves were confined in a foul prison until they should be needed again.

This life had Bartle and his men somehow miraculously endured for sixteen years; and during the last four Bartle had conceived and prepared the plan of escape, which, with the help of his fellow slaves, he had put into effect.

Discipline in the prison was lax; there were few jailors to be spared — and, seizing an opportunity when a galley lay provisioned for the sea just beyond the walls of their prison, the men had broken out and, experienced as they were in handling this type of craft, were able to make good their escape.

It was a story of adventure, suffering and courage, which was typical of the seamen of the time. They accepted hardship and death as natural; for, as Bartle said, there was not a man of them who did not know before he set sail that he must face them.

Tamar felt that her outlook on life had changed with the coming of the galley. She had been prepared to accept life with Humility; she had been excited by the proposed emigration. But now. . .Bartle had come home.

It was late the very same day of his return that Bartle rode over to Pennicomquick. There had been just that one embrace down on the Causeway; then the crowd had surged round Bartle and she had taken the opportunity to escape, for her one wish at that moment had been to get away, to be alone, to think of the great upheaval which had so suddenly threatened to take place in her life.

She saw him arrive and went down to meet him.

He sat his horse, looking down at her. He had trimmed his beard and was wearing some of the elegant garments which he had worn before he went away. They hung loosely on his thin frame, but they gave him great dignity.

"So," he said, his blue eyes blazing, "you married the Puritan!"

"Yes."

Then Bartle laughed and his laughter was loud and mocking.

"Why should it amuse you so?" she asked.

"Why indeed! The witch . . . and the Puritan!"

"I have three children," she said.

"I congratulate you. How many sons?"

"One son; two daughters."

"A matron now," he said.

She thought: He has not changed at all. I hate him now, just as I always did.

At that moment Ned Swann came from the stables and Bartle dismounted.

" 'Tis good to see you home, Sir Bartle," said Ned.

"Thank you, Swann," said Bartle with one of his charming smiles.

"Come into the house," said Tamar. "Richard is eager to see you and hear of your adventures."

He did not take his eyes from her as they went into the house, where Richard received him warmly.

"Bartle . . . I never thought to have this pleasure . . ."

"Nor I, sir."

"Bartle, my dear boy, come here. Let me look at you. The strength of you! To endure *that* for sixteen years!"

"I'm made of sturdy stuff. I said: 'By God and His Mother, I'll break out of this prison if I kill twenty guards to do it."

"And did you?" asked Tamar.

"No," he answered. "Only ten."

Humility came in, and Bartle bowed mockingly. "Why, 'tis the gardener fellow." He looked haughtily down his long nose, while his sensuous lips curled. "I remember you, fellow."

Tamar flushed. Richard said: "Have you not heard? Humility is my son-in-law."

Bartle answered insolently: "Strange things happen at home and abroad, it seems."

Then he sprawled in a chair and drank freely while he talked. He talked of his life as a galley slave, of blood and sweat and the loyalty of his men. He had hardened and coarsened during the years of slavery; his talk was spattered with violent oaths, which made Humility flinch every time they were uttered.

"Mind you," he said, "I did not suffer so acutely as some. I became a Moslem. That gave me a better life. I have scars — I could show you my back — scars that I'll carry to my grave. But I came off lightly. There were some who were beaten to death. Not me. I bowed down to Allah and saved my skin."

Tamar saw that Humility was praying. Bartle saw it too.

"What do you whisper, man?" he demanded.

"Prayers," said Humility.

Bartle was immediately truculent. "I shock you. That is so. My good fellow, you could not endure a day in the galleys, with all your prayers to help you. Why, 'twas a plaguey sight easier to arrange an escape as a good Moslem. A Christian could never have done it. By Christ, I tell you that, had I stuck to my faith and said my prayers, I and my men would be getting ready now for another season in the galleys. It was a far better thing to become a temporary Moslem than that."

"Of course!" said Tamar, looking scornfully at Humility; but as Bartle laughed she gave him a haughty stare; then it seemed to her that she was no longer a woman in her thirties, the mother of three children; she was a young girl again, trembling because a man who had once been her lover had come back.

Richard told Bartle of the proposed expedition to the New World, to which Bartle listened with great interest.

His eyes glittered as they rested on Tamar. "So you are leaving this land. You are going to seek your fortune elsewhere." He lifted his glass and kept his eyes fixed on Tamar's face. "The best of good fortune to you. May you get the good luck you deserve."

Tamar bowed her head because she feared what this man might arouse in her; she said she must leave them, as she had to see to the children. But Bartle said he wished to meet the children, and there was nothing she could do but bring them down.

Dick—who had already heard of his miraculous escape—stood before Bartle, his cheeks rosy with excitement, his dark eyes shining with admiration. Rowan climbed at once on to his knee and, when he asked for a kiss, would not stop kissing him and pulling his beard. Only little Lorea, who was different from the others, hung back shyly; but when he held out a hand and drew her to him even she was overcome by that fascination which he obviously had for all children.

Over their heads Bartle's eyes held Tamar's and they seemed to say: "These should have been ours. The Puritan should have had no hand in making them."

She hurried them away as soon as she could. She was between laughter and tears. She was alive again . . . because Bartle had come home.

* * *

She was afraid to ride out on the moors in case he should follow her there. There were too many vivid memories crowding back. She only dared talk to him when other people were present.

Each day she saw him it was brought home to her how little he had really changed. His eyes mocked her as they had mocked all those years ago. She saw their burning brightness when they rested on her; their contemptuous hatred when they looked towards Humility. One day, she thought, he will come to me with a proposition, as he did before. It will be, "If you do not . . . I will . . ." Yes; he had changed very little.

She tried to shut out from her mind all thought of anything but the expedition. She would sit with Richard and Humility making lists of provisions. It was spring, and they would sail before the summer was over.

Bartle was charming Dick and Rowan; and even Lorea could be induced to ride on his shoulders. Annis's children ran at his heels begging to be allowed to ride on his horse. They all adored him. From the windows, Tamar often watched him, sprawled on the lawn with young Dick beside him, and she knew from the absorbed expression on the boy's face that he was hearing some wild tale of the sea; and she knew that Bartle was thinking: This boy might have been mine.

How glad she was that soon they would sail away from England, away from surroundings which echoed with memories, away from Bartle.

She had lied to Humility, telling him that she was once more pregnant. She could not bear him near her now. She felt that it was better that he should keep away altogether than that, when he knelt by her bedside and prayed for her fertility, she should shout at him something which she would later regret; she might even convey to him that she found him repulsive, or confess her relationship with Bartle before their marriage.

In the quiet of her room, her window barred and bolted, she would say: "I hate the man. I was settling down peaceably before he returned, but now he is back to plague and bewilder me. What a good thing it is that soon I shall sail away and never see him again.

There is no safety from him. He bows formally, but there is nothing formal in the glances he gives me. He is planning all the time how to shame me. I can sense it!"

It was early summer. Their ship — the *Liberty* — lay in the harbour.

In her cottage Annis was packing together her most cherished possessions, telling her children of the new life which would be theirs in the wonderful land across the sea. The Swann family would be going, and forty others. Mistress Alton had begged, with many tears and much humility, to be one of the party. She was suspected of witchcraft after Jane Swann had been tortured and she had said nothing of the girl's presence in the house. What would become of her, she wanted to know, if she were left behind? The answer was obvious. She would be homeless, and to be homeless and suspected of witchcraft was a pitiable plight for any woman to find herself in.

Richard and Tamar had despised this woman; they knew her for a bigot capable of spying and great cruelty. Yet she had become a Puritan and had as much right to make the journey as any other. So even Mistress Alton was preparing to go.

And one day Richard and Humility called Tamar to them.

Richard was very excited. "It seems we have had a very narrow escape. This man, Flame, whose credentials seemed so excellent, is, I hear, nothing but a pirate. He and his men are a band of scoundrels. Their plan undoubtedly was to take us out to sea, murder the lot of us, steal our possessions and go off with the ship on errands of piracy. We have indeed had a lucky escape."

"Glory be to God!" said Humility.

"Does this mean another postponement of our journey?" asked Tamar. "It must, since we shall have to find another captain and crew. And whom can we trust? Captain Flame seemed such a good man."

"There need be no delay," said Richard. "I think we have found a captain and crew whom we can trust."

Tamar looked at him expectantly.

"Bartle," said Richard, "has promised to take the ship to the New World."

CHAPTER
SIX

So the *Liberty* was to set sail with Bartle in command. Now she dipped and rose with the tide as she waited on the whim of the winds.

All that morning the last of the stores had gone aboard; legs of mutton minced and stewed and packed in butter and stored in earthen pots; roast beef in vinegar; gammons of bacon; oatmeal and fine wheat flour; wines and ales; butter; ginger; sugar; currants; prunes; cheeses; and the juice of lemons to ward off the scurvy.

The crew, the captain and the master were all on board; the chirurgeon with his physic; the cooper and the carpenter with their tools. The boatswain had tested the tackling and sails; and his mate was waiting to haul up the anchors; the cooper and the carpenter were talking together.

Tamar stood on deck with her children and Richard. Humility was leading a band of Puritans in the singing of psalms; they had just finished praying for a safe journey.

Looking back at the land where she had lived her life so far, Tamar was filled with emotion; and yet, she was not sorry to be going . . . now.

The children were hopping about beside her. Even Lorea could not keep still. Dick was shrilly pointing out the parts of the ship to Rowan. He called her attention to the sails and the rigging. His friend the boatswain had shown him the needles and twine he used for mending sails. "If we had a big storm, the sails would get torn. Then we might have to take to the boats. We may be drowned."

"I wouldn't," said Rowan. "I'd be in the captain's boat."

"So would I," cried Lorea. "I'd be in the captain's boat. So would you, Mamma, wouldn't you?"

Tamar did not answer; she was looking back at the land.

"It's hardly likely we'll get across without one big storm!" said Dick importantly.

And the girls squealed with delight.

Bartle was in deep conversation with the master of the ship.

"He's telling him how to trim his sails!" cried knowledgeable Dick. "He's telling him to what port we're going and to what height!"

Richard said: "You seem to know a good deal about sailing a ship, young Dick."

"Oh yes. Sir Bartle told me. When I grow up, I shall sail with Sir Bartle."

Tamar smiled: "Dear Richard," she said, "how glad I should be to see you as gay and carefree as the children. It has been a wrench, I fear, to sell as much of your land as you have done, and to leave your native country."

Richard shrugged his shoulders; but she knew that he was thinking he would come back home. He had not sold his house, but had handed it over to a distant cousin to hold in trust till his return. If he did not come back, the house would be his cousin's. But Richard was certain he would come back.

The children were dancing round Bartle now.

Tamar saw his hand rest lightly on Dick's shoulder. Dick was asking more of his continual questions.

Richard followed her eyes. "Do you still hate him?" he asked.

She did not answer.

"We have to remember he is our captain now," said Richard. "We have to obey him without question."

"Ah," she answered lightly. "His orders will be for his crew, not for his passengers."

They were silent. The tide was on the turn.

They heard the raucous voices of the sailors and younkers shouting to each other; they heard the singing of a shanty. Then the windlass was heaved round; anchors were being lifted; the yards braced. The sails were now set and the *Liberty* was slipping out of the Sound.

* * *

They had been two days at sea and the wind was freshening. Many of the passengers lay sick in their cabins — so sick that they wished themselves back at home.

Tamar was not sick; she had come on to the upper deck to escape the confined lower quarters and to get a breath of fresh air.

The children were below in the care of Annis; she hoped they were sleeping. Even Dick was a little tired after all the excitement of the last two days.

And as she stood there, Bartle joined her at the bulwarks.

He stood very close to her. "I always planned to make a voyage with you," he said. "But I did not think to bring your husband with us."

She did not answer, but moved away from him. He slipped his hand under her arm and drew her closer to him.

"A stiff gale," he said. "And an overgrowing sea. How like you this, Tamar?"

"It is early yet to say," she answered.

"Early indeed!" He put his lips close to her ear. "Whither are we going, you and I?"

"To the New World, I thought. That is, if you can be trusted to make the voyage."

"But where else do you think? To joy, to pleasure? To continue this miserable frustration?"

"You should know."

"So I thought, but it would seem to be you who calls the tune."

"How is that?"

His voice was hard and angry. "For sixteen years I suffered such misery, such agony, such humiliation as you cannot conceive. That would not have happened . . . but for you. But for you those sixteen years might have been spent at home . . . with you and our children. But your pride and your folly ruined not only my life, but your own. Do you think

I forget that? Do you think that I shall allow you to forget it?"

"You went to sea at your own desire," she said coldly. "You have said that you knew what risks you ran. Was it my fault that the Turks took you? Even had I foreseen it, should I have married you, loathing you?"

"You wanted me. It was only your pride that prevented your admitting it. You are a proud and foolish woman, Tamar, and I will never forgive you for what you have done to us." His voice was tender suddenly. "Why, there are tears on your cheeks."

"Tears!" she cried angrily. "It is the spray. I think I shall go down to the children."

"You will stay here."

"If I wish to go, I shall go. No one shall order me."

"*I* shall order you."

"Ah ! The Captain in command!"

"Exactly. Any who dares disobey him is clapped in irons."

"You would dare to clap me in irons!"

"If it were necessary."

She burst into laughter; he laughed with her.

"You pretend you do not wish to stay," he said, "and yet you cannot tear yourself away."

"What of your duties to your ship? Should they not be engaging your attention?"

"The ship is well looked after."

"What are your plans?"

"To take the ship to the New World."

"I meant . . . concerning yourself . . . and myself?"

She heard his deep, throaty laugh. "My plans concerning you have changed little since I first clapped eyes on you."

"I am waiting. What is it to be? 'If you do not invite me to your cabin, I shall put the whole ship's company in irons. I shall murder them all . . . or hand you over to the Turks!'"

"You put ideas into my head," he warned.

"I have a husband who shares my cabin," she reminded him.

"May God damn the Puritan!" he said. They were silent for a while before he continued: "When I was in captivity, the only way I could endure my life was by imagining another life side by side with my wretched existence. When I was working in the galleys, I pictured myself riding over green turf with you beside me, and that we laughed often together over the follies of our youth. I dreamed that we rode home to Stoke and our children came to meet us. It was a life worth living, and even you — proud as the Devil with your black witch's hair flying in the wind — were contented."

She murmured: "I am sorry for what happened to you, but the fault was not mine. It was yours . . . *yours* . . . It began that day when I was fourteen. Had you but been kind to me when I most needed kindness, ours might have been a very different story. But what use to reproach ourselves? We are as we are and nothing can change us. You are brutal, and you will always be brutal. It is no use crying for a tenderness which only kindness will nourish."

"The fault was yours!" he cried. "Do you think I could not have caught you? A little girl of fourteen! It was because I saw real fear in your eyes that I let you go. As for those nights...Why did I force you to do what you did? Because you were longing for me to do so. Because you deceive yourself, it is easy for others to deceive you. Do not think that you will ever escape from me. Do you think I would let your marriage to a Puritan stand in our way? I will tell you something, so that you will understand to what lengths I will go. Captain Flame is a much-maligned man. He is a good captain, a worthy man. But there could only be one captain in charge of the ship which carried Tamar away, and that was myself. So...I saw that this was so."

She turned and looked at him in amazement.

"Is there no end to your villainy?" she demanded.

He laughed significantly.

"Only one," he said.

*   *   *

They had been a month at sea, and Tamar knew with that sure intuition of hers that they were heading for emotional disaster.

Everything that Humility did or said irritated her beyond endurance. Her feeling for him was turning to hatred. She laughed inwardly to contemplate the struggle he was having with himself, confined as they were to the close quarters of their cabin. He believed her to be in a state of pregnancy and he longed for her; she would hear him, praying in the bunk above her own, and she knew she was the subject of his prayers.

It was thoughts of Bartle that disturbed her. She felt that he was in as complete a control of her destiny as he was of this ship. She knew that he was only awaiting his opportunity.

He would humiliate the Puritan whenever he could; and his crew followed his example. When Humility approached a group of sailors, their language would become a shade more obscene. Humility, now as ever conscious of his duty, had ignored their insults and their gibes and had done his best to make Puritans of them.

The conditions of life at sea were having their effects on all those unaccustomed to them. The roughness of the weather, the constant fear of sighting a hostile vessel, the monotony of the diet—all these things, though novelties at first, were beginning to upset the passengers.

The children were the happiest. They suffered less from the rigours of the weather, and as long as they had something to eat they were happy. Annis's five eldest—Christian, Restraint, Prudence, Felicity and Love—made themselves useful looking after the babies; the young ones—Charity, Patience, Joshua, Moses, Matthew, Ruth and little Miriam—played those games in which Dick was generally the leader.

And even watching the children, Tamar knew the tension was increasing. Dick was growing more and more like Bartle; this likeness was not, naturally, one of feature, but of gesture, mannerism and forthright way of speaking. Dick had begun to imitate the Captain in every way he could.

Even now at this moment, Dick was playing Captain, and he had the other children about him, to each of whom he had assigned some role as member of his crew.

Dick, rosy-cheeked, his eyes flashing, was shouting orders, and that manner of standing, legs apart, was Bartle's; that throaty voice was Bartle's.

"A sail, a sail! How stands she, to windward or leeward?"

Annis watched them with her. Annis muttered to herself and cast anxious glances at her mistress.

"And what ails you?" demanded Tamar. "You look sick and sorry, Annis. One would think you had not hoped and planned for this... for years..."

"I'll be glad enough when we touch land," said Annis, "the new land... Aye! I'll be glad enough then. 'Tis this long sea journey, mistress. So full of perils... I do shake and shiver in my bunk at night when the ship do roll and I hear the shouts of the men."

"Give chase and fetch her up!" cried Dick. "Come, man! Why do you stand gaping there. By God, I'll clap you in irons. Every man to his charge. Dowse your topsail and salute him for the sea. Whence is your ship?"

Rowan, who had been given the role of Spanish Captain cried: "Of Spain. Whence is yours?"

"Of England!" cried Dick. "Give him a broadside and run ahead. St. George for England!"

"Will you be quiet!" cried Annis. "You and your talk of Spaniards. No wonder we're all wrought up."

Dick said scornfully: "It might happen. You've got to be ready. Sir Bartle says..."

But Annis turned away impatiently; her fearful eyes met those of Tamar.

"The boy worships the Captain," she said; and she shivered.

"Annis," said Tamar, "what ails you?"

"You asked me that before, mistress. 'Tis just that there be something about the ship..."

"And its Captain?" asked Tamar.

"Aye. Its Captain and its crew. My dear life! I wouldn't care to be the one to cross Sir Bartle."

"Why not, Annis?"

"Because I believe I've seen the Devil look out of those blue eyes of his. He were always wild...even before he was took by the Turks, but he has grown wilder."

"It is mostly shouting," said Tamar, with an edge of scorn to her voice. "You can hear his shouting all over the ship."

" 'Tis the way of him. Is he kind to those men of his? No, he is not. He's a hard master; yet they're his men and they'd be for him, no matter what happened or what he did to them. There's magic in him. That's what I do feel...and it's the magic of a devil, for look how he do taunt a good man like Mr. Brown. He's put a spell on young Dick...and on all the children. You see how their eyes sparkle when he throws a word to them. If they can stand close to him, they're happy, even though he curses them. 'Tis a rare pity he can't be saved. He'd be a conquest for the righteous, he would, and a loss to the Devil."

"The Devil will never loosen his grip on that man!" said Tamar.

"I don't feel safe with all these rough men about," said Annis. "I've a feeling that one day. . . something will break loose. Do you see the way their eyes follow every female of us? Why, I reckon some of them men, in their time, have been to sea and ain't clapped eyes on a woman for months. 'Tis different like. . . with women aboard. And mistress, the Captain. . . he do have his eyes on someone."

"The Captain has his eyes on us all," said Tamar.

"But some more than others. There's Polly Eagel, for one."

"Polly Eagel!"

"That first baby of hers wasn't Tom Eagel's."

"Annis, please stop your tittle-tattle."

"Very well, mistress. I did hear that some of the poultry we've got penned up there on deck is pretty poorly. And there's a winnock in the litter of piglets. My dear life! Ain't there always a winnock in a litter—the little one who hasn't the strength of the others and gets crowded out like and sort of peaky?"

"Are you suggesting that the Captain and Polly Eagel. . .?"

"Not now, mistress. That was before we sailed. Well, you do know what Polly is with that flaxen hair and baby-blue eyes of hers. Oh. . . not now. There's only one that the Captain has his eyes on now, mistress."

"Well," said Tamar. "Go on."

" 'Tis that that frightens me, mistress. His eyes gleam so in his brown face, and the way he treats Mr. Brown frightens me. 'Tain't right . . . and yet I do know what it means."

"You see too much, Annis."

"That may be so, mistress, but I do beg of 'ee to have a care. You can't play with men like Mr. Brown, because they be too good; and you can't play with men like Sir Bartle, because they be too bad. When you start playing with men like that . . . something bad comes of it. That's what I be feared of, mistress. Something . . . bad!"

"But can you doubt, Annis, that I would be able to deal with whatever might blow up between those two?"

"Nay, mistress. You have your magic, but Sir Bartle too, he have a sort of magic. He has travelled the world and seen sights we have not seen. I did hear that the way those men escaped from prison were a miracle . . . no less. I did think when I watched him shouting to the men: 'Tis the Devil himself who sails this ship! And I asks myself if he bought his freedom from the Turk by setting himself in bondage to the Devil."

"Nay!" cried Tamar, laughing with sudden wildness. "He was the Devil's own before the Turk took him!"

The children came dashing past them.

"Try the pump! We are shot through and through. The ship's on fire!"

Tamar watched them without seeing them, thinking of the Devil who looked out of Bartle's eyes.

"God be thanked!" cried Dick. "The fire is out. Look to the wounded. Swabbers, clean up the deck. Keep your berth to windward. Repair the sails and shrouds. Mend your leaks. St. George for England!"

Something will happen soon, thought Tamar. It comes closer and closer.

*   *   *

When many of the passengers fell sick, Tamar took it upon herself to help the chirurgeon in curing them. She had her ointments and lotions, and there were many who had greater faith in her skill than in that of the doctor. Most of the sick were suffering from the effects of too much salted food, the fetid atmosphere of some of the quarters, the general insanitary conditions. Humility suffered with the others, but he would not rest. He would go the rounds of the sick and pray with them and talk to them of what work they would be expected to do in the new land.

Bartle sought every opportunity to talk to Tamar, and everything he said convinced her that he intended to ignore her marriage and to have her for himself. There were times when she wondered if he was planning to kill Humility. He had killed many men in his life — so what would one more matter to such as he was?

Her own feelings were difficult to define. She told herself that she was sorry for Humility, that she was filled with admiration for him as he went, pale and wan, about the ship, thinking not of his own suffering, but of that of others. Yet when she was with him she seemed to take a delight in taunting him, in trying to arouse his desire for her, and then remind him of her condition, as he supposed it to be; he irritated her beyond endurance; he maddened her. Bartle, she told herself, she hated; he was a bad man; he was cruel and wicked; yet when she saw him coming towards her, her heart would beat fast with pleasure; and she knew secretly — though she would not admit this — that Bartle's presence on board the *Liberty* made the voyage exhilarating and exciting for her.

"Ah!" said Bartle to her one day, stopping her as she would have walked past him, her box of ointments in her arms. "You should not have come on such a voyage. A woman . . . who is to have a child . . ."

"Who told *you* I was to have a child?"

He smiled insolently. "People talk, you know. John Tyler's wife knows; John Tyler knows also."

"I shall thank John Tyler and his wife to be silent about my affairs. As for you . . . you need not concern yourself with pitying me."

"I do concern myself with you. I shall always concern myself with you as long as we live."

"My child will not be born on this ship!" she said.

"Sometimes journeys such as this take a little longer than we bargain for."

"Nevertheless, my child will not be born on this ship!"

"How can you be so sure?"

"I *am* sure!"

"Mr. Humility Brown praises the Lord for the continued fertility of his wife! So Annis tells us. She also tells us something else. Annis wonders if her mistress may not have made a mistake. She wonders if it may be that there will not be a child after all."

Tamar flushed crimson.

"Ah," he continued, "you must not be angry with these Tylers — such honest, simple folk! Tyler is a talkative devil, and his wife gives him little chance to talk. So when the Captain does him the honour of plying him with questions, it is not easy for him to keep to himself what the Captain wishes to know."

"How dare you discuss me with these people!"

"Have no fear. This is our little secret. Humility Brown is your husband; he is a godly man; he shares your bed for piety, not for passion. Such a good man! No love-making for Humility Brown when the purpose of love-making is achieved."

"I have always loathed your coarseness. If you wish to please me, why not mend your manners?"

"If I wish to please you! Oh, how I please you! So much that you cannot bear to have this man near you when I come home. So you tell him that you are with child, knowing such a tale would keep the pious man away!"

She pushed past him and walked away, holding her head high; but she heard his mocking laughter following her, and she was more uneasy than ever.

* * *

It was on the night of the great storm that Tamar knew how Humility suffered.

The sea had been rough all that day, and towards nightfall all passengers had been ordered below.

Tamar brought the three children into her cabin and kept them close to her. Little Lorea was trembling; even Dick was afraid. It was a different matter to experience a real storm instead of pretending. Besides, he must stay below; Bartle had ordered him there. In the storms of Dick's imagination he had been on deck, shouting orders to his crew.

"How big is this storm?" asked Rowan.

"Not so big as the one Sir Bartle told me about," shouted Dick. "That was in the Bay of Biscay."

"I'm not frightened," said Rowan.

"Who said you were?"

"Well...most people are. Annis and John have been praying all the afternoon. What happens when the ship founders?"

"I doubt if Sir Bartle will let it do that."

"He said it was a pox-ridden old bucket—a god-forsaken old bucket. That's what he said it was. I don't think he likes this ship."

Dick laughed. "Captains always talk like that. They love their ships all the same. If it's wrecked, we shall all go in the shallop. Perhaps we'll be picked up by pirates."

Lorea began to cry.

"Be quiet!" said Tamar to the two elder children. "It is all right, my darling. We are not going to be shipwrecked."

"How do you know, Mamma?" asked Dick.

"Because the Captain would not let us be."

She noticed that all the children were ready to accept this.

The rolling of the ship was increasing. The wind howled menacingly, and all about the frail ship *Liberty* the waters seethed and pounded her timbers.

Humility stumbled in.

"This is a terrible night, wife. A terrible night. I have just heard bad news. A man has been washed overboard."

"Man overboard! Man overboard!" shrieked Dick.

"Can't they haul him in?" asked Tamar.

Humility looked at her and did not answer; he did not wish to say before the children that it was impossible to save the man in such a sea.

"One of the sailors," said Humility. "I heard some terrible curses on his lips but yesterday. How do any of us know what is in store for us?"

Tamar thought grimly that if the storm grew worse they would have a shrewd notion of what was in store for them. The *Liberty* was a frail ship; and the strongest ships could not battle indefinitely against storms such as this.

She thought of Bartle and wondered what he was doing now. She was angry suddenly. He would know whether they were in danger or not; he would not be in suspense.

310

She drew her children closer to her. Lorea began to whimper; the noise and fury and the mad rolling of the ship terrified the little girl.

Humility looked from his wife to his children; he said: "We cannot kneel . . . the ship rolls too much. But God will understand if we say our prayers as we are. He will forgive us this once. Come, children. Pray with me. We will ask God, if it be His wish, to bring us safely through this night."

Tamar said: "If it be His wish, then there is no need to ask Him. And if it is not His wish . . . then it is no use asking Him either. You waste your prayers."

"I like not, wife, to hear such unseemly words on your lips . . . at such a time."

"At such a time! Would you have me snivel, then, when I am in danger? Should I ask God's help then . . . when I have not done so at other times?"

"You wilfully misunderstand."

"No!" she cried. "I understand too well."

Yes, she was thinking, I understand that I hate you, husband. That I am ashamed to have married you and borne your children. It is Bartle I want . . . and I want him as passionately as he wants me. I may not love him. What a fool I was to wait for love! And what a time is this for thinking such thoughts! Who knows . . . in a moment . . . in an hour . . . before morning this ship may be rent in two and my body and Bartle's at the bottom of the sea.

And yet, looking at her husband, gripping the bunk against the heaving of the ship, while his eyes were shut and his lips moving in prayer, great waves of hatred seemed to flow over her — as great and inescapable as the wind that tore at the rigging of the ship and the waves that pounded her sides with malevolent determination to destroy her.

He had opened his eyes and she noticed that he glanced at her and quickly turned away.

He was thinking that she seemed younger than she had for some time — more like the girl she had been before the children were born, the girl who had watched him work in the gardens and had taunted him. Now her cheeks were flushed, her hair in disorder. She refused to cover it or braid it. He knew that she was goading him, luring him to sin. She was tempting him because she knew that the Devil was at his elbow whispering to him as he had once whispered to Jesus. The Devil was showing him his wife as he had shown Jesus the kingdoms of the world. "She is your wife," said the Devil. "Is it then carnal lust for a man to go with his wife?" "For such as I!" was his answer. "For such as I." "She is your wife, your wife . . ." persisted the voice in the darkness. "It was solely because I wished to procreate children for the New World that I took this woman, and I took her not for her beauty, but because she had a wayward soul which must be under constant surveillance, because she has a good, strong body that was obviously meant for the bearing of children. There was no lust . . . no lust . . ."

But when she looked at him with those smouldering lights in her eyes, she was telling him, "Humility, you deceive yourself. Lust there was, and one day you will stand before the throne of Almighty God and you will have to admit it."

He shut his eyes, shut out the sight of her beauty and her wildness and the wanton knowledge in her eyes. He prayed that the ship might weather the storm, that all might be saved to lead good lives in the promised land; and he prayed that he might overcome the temptation which this sensuous, wanton woman was holding out to him; he asked for the salvation of the ship, but his secret prayer was for the salvation of his soul.

*   *   *

After the storm there were a few days of calm. Now there was hardly a ripple on the water; and the sky was the same colour as the Captain's eyes. The boatswain and his mate sat on deck mending and patching the sails, repairing all the damage which the storm had wrought; the cooper and his mate were busy on their tasks. The cook and the steward were preparing delicacies, on the Captain's orders, for some of the sick among passengers and crew: a little buttered rice flavoured with sugar and cinnamon, a few stewed prunes, or minced mutton and roast beef.

Humility was holding a meeting on the top deck. Tamar could hear them, singing the psalms with feeling. They had come through the storm safely; they were still limp from fear and exhaustion. But this, said Humility, was a sign. The Lord had intended that they should make their homes in the promised land.

Bartle came and stood beside Tamar.

She turned and looked at him. "Rice with sugar and cinnamon!" she said. "And for your most humble sailors. It is a surprise to me to see that you could show such consideration."

"It is no pampering. Merely good sense. Those fellows — wet to the skin, shaking with cold — would fall into a raging fever but for the few comforts I can give them. Such delicacies as buttered rice and mincemeat, green ginger, a little fresh water brewed with sugar, ginger and cinnamon — to say nothing of a little good sack — can save a man's life. Whereas, give him salt fish with oil and mustard or salt and peas . . . and he'll not rally. Such fare is good indeed for ordinary occasions, but after such a storm, if I wish to keep my men with me, I must treat them to their delicacies. This crew of mine is too precious — every man of it — to risk such loss. What if we run into further storms? What if we meet with our enemies? Nay, mere common sense. God! How the preacher rants! Tamar, Tamar, why did you marry him?"

She turned away, but he laid a hand on her arm and, although she tried to shake it off, she could not do so.

"Life at sea," he continued, "is full of dangers. We should have stayed at home . . . both of us . . . Oh, not now. Seventeen years ago."

"How you hark back! I prefer to look forward."

"And so do I now. When, Tamar? *When*?"

"I do not understand you."

"You hold him off. You want me. But what is the use of wanting if we do nothing to ease our desire?"

"As I told you years ago, you have a great conceit of yourself."

"It is justified."

"Are you sure of that?"

"I am. You cannot bear to have him near you, so you lie to him. You tell him you are with child. And you lied for me. Oh, Tamar, I have gone without you too long."

"You might try Polly Eagel for a substitute."

"Who?"

"You feign ignorance, but I know of your adventures. I said Polly Eagel."

"I know her not."

"It is idle to pretend to me that you have not been her lover. I suppose you would have me believe that you have forgotten."

"It matters not whether or no you believe it. It is so. There have been so many, Tamar."

"And you think I should be happy to join such a crowd!"

"Whether you are happy joining it or not, you have already done so."

"There! You see, I can but hate you. You taunt me. You mock me. How could I love such as you?"

"And yet you do."

"Leave me, I beg of you."

"Not till you have heard my plan."

"What plan is this?"

"A plan for us two."

"Such a plan could not interest me."

"You repeat yourself. You have said that to me before."

"Then you invite repetition. You tire me. I pray you, leave me."

"And I pray you, Tamar, for your own sake, not to anger me. When I am truly in a rage, I am incapable of controlling my anger. You *will* listen to me. This is my plan. We shall reach our destination; our passengers will disembark; and you and I, with your children — and Richard if he wishes it — will sail for home. We will leave your husband here with his pilgrims. He shall have them and, as a reward for bringing him safely to port, I shall have you."

"An interesting plan," she said coldly. "But, as I told you, you would be foolish to include me in any plans you might make."

He came closer to her. "I would have you know that I am tired of waiting. We cannot go on like this. One of us . . . will . . . quite soon . . . do something to end this intolerable state of affairs."

She had begun to tremble. She could not meet his eyes, so she stared beyond him, across the translucent water.

* * *

It was night and there was tension throughout the ship. Even the sailors were subdued and spoke in whispers.

There were no lights on deck, nor on masts, nor at portholes. The Captain had ordered it so.

"Anyone showing a light," he had bellowed, "be it man, woman or child, will be clapped in irons."

At dusk a ship had been sighted on the horizon, and every seafaring man aboard had known her for a Spaniard.

Below, the passengers muttered together. The old ship was limping along, for she had suffered some damage in the storm. She was not equipped to fight; she carried men and women in search of a home, not a battle and plunder; stores and furniture instead of ordnance. And Catholic Spaniards could strike as deep a note of terror in any heart as could the barbarous Turk.

Annis came to Tamar's cabin, breathless in her agitation. Tamar could hear her panting in the darkness. Poor Annis! She was getting old; she had borne too many children, and of late there had been a bluish tinge about her lips when she was out of breath. Tamar remembered her suddenly as a little yellow-haired girl who had looked in at the Lackwell cottage door and put out her tongue. When death was near, she supposed, you thought back over the past.

Annis said, "Mistress, Mr. Brown is preaching to some on the lower deck. He be a very brave man, for if the Spaniards take him, it'll be burning alive after months of torture that'll be his lot. Sir Bartle — he's on the upper deck. He did ask me to bring you to him there, as he has something to say that is important. He says not to fail . . ."

Tamar put her cloak about her and went on deck. It was a cloudy night with a light fresh breeze which hustled the clouds every now and then bringing a group of stars into view. Bartle had seen her and came swiftly to her side.

"Tamar?"

"Yes, Bartle?"

"Thank God for the dark of night."

"Yes, thank God."

He put an arm about her and she did not resist; she thought of the mighty galleon that might at this moment be sailing towards them.

He said: "With the dawn we shall know. But there is some hope. She may not have seen us. I have changed our course. Tamar, you must not be taken by the Spaniards. Better that you should die by my hand than that."

"Yes," she answered firmly.

"Keep close to me, my love. When the dawn breaks, I wish you to be at my side. We never lived together, and it may be that now we never shall. But we can die together; and that we will do." He had moved his hand up her arm, caressing it. He drew her to him and kissed her with such tenderness as she had never known in him before. "What," he went on, "an unholy mess we have made of our lives! But it is too late for regrets now." He kept his arm about her. "You do not move away from me. I wish I could see your eyes. They are soft and tender, I'll warrant. They do not now flash with pride and anger."

"No," she said. "I do not move away from you now."

"And never will again?"

She did not answer, and he went on: "Tell me that marriage of yours was no true marriage."

"There are children to prove it," she said.

"There may be only a few hours left to us. Let them be truthful hours. What did you feel when you heard that I was lost?"

"Desolation. Yes; I know now that it was desolation. I sought for peace, and I thought that I should find it with Humility Brown."

"As we are given life here on Earth we are surely meant to live it. Why should we be born into this world with its trials and problems if we are to spend our time thinking only of another?"

"Oh," she said, "you are a pagan."

"I should never have thought of that if you had let me live my life. We should have married, done our duty to our line and home. We should have brought our children up to obey the Church and State. You are the pagan, and you have made a pagan of me."

They were silent and she felt his lips on her hair. Then he went on: "Where are we going, you and I? To death when the dawn comes? That will be easy. That will be quick. But if it is not death, what then, Tamar? Where are we going then?"

"We cannot think beyond the morning."

"Why can you be only gentle and truthful with me when we may have to die?"

"Why are *you* different now?"

"Oh, Tamar, let us think of what might have been! Seventeen years ago we had a chance to live. I went to slavery and torture; you to slavery of another kind; but both of our own choosing. We might have been together in our home. We might be there . . . now. Think you that any grass is as green as Devonshire grass, any air as temperate? Nowhere in the world is the sea quite the same colour as that which breaks about our shores. Nowhere else does the mist rise up — so soft and warm — and disappear so suddenly to let the sunshine through, the warm and kindly sun that never burns too fiercely. Yet you threw that life away. You banished me to slavery and yourself to life with a Puritan. I could hate you, Tamar, if I did not love you."

"I could hate you too," she said, "if I did not love you."

They kissed with passion now; and she saw herself regaining all that she had carelessly thrown away; she knew that their kisses were a pledge for the future . . . if they lived through the next day.

She heard Bartle laugh suddenly, and it was a laugh she remembered well.

"Tamar," he said, "we cannot die. We must defy the Spaniard. We have powder and shot, arms and fireworks. We'll give an account of ourselves. You will go to your cabin, take your children with you. You will stay there until I come. For come I will. I promise you I'll fight as I never fought before. I'll not die when I am just about to begin my life with you."

She clung to him. "We must not die. Of course we must not die!"

When dawn broke the whole ship's company was on deck.

Eager eyes scanned the horizon.

The Spaniard had disappeared.

*　　*　　*

The ship was moving forward.

"How long before we sight land?" Each member of the crew was asked this question every day.

"A week mayhap. Perhaps more...perhaps less."

A week! When they had been nearly three months afloat. Excitement ran high. All around them was the heaving water, but any day now land might be sighted.

The map which Captain Smith had made over ten years ago was studied with eagerness. The very names delighted them: Plymouth, Oxford, London; the river Charles and Southampton; and farther along the coast there were Dartmouth, Sandwich, Shooters Hill and Cape Elizabeth. Such names truly had a homely ring.

"See this point, Cape James. That was first called Cape Cod; it was named after the fish that abound there. We shall have fresh cod instead of salted herrings. There will be meat too. No more danger from pirates. No more fear of being captured by the Spaniards or the Turks...or the Dutch...or the French."

"What of the savages that were first here?"

"Oh...a friendly people. Did you not see the little Princess when she came to Plymouth?"

Tamar's uneasiness had grown since that night of fear. Bartle filled her thoughts — not this new country. She had avoided him since that night of mutual understanding, but she could not continue to do so. She could not banish Humility from her thoughts.

What had she done on that night? She had exposed her secrets to Bartle; she could no longer deny her feelings for him.

Yet she had her children. She was married to Humility Brown. How could she return to England with Bartle?

Humility was aware of the change in her. Her temper with him was shorter than ever; she seemed again and again to be endeavouring to make their life more difficult by picking quarrels.

If he were not such a good man, Tamar told herself, I should not feel I wronged him so deeply and I should not hate him so fiercely.

But hate him she did; she wished he were dead. What an easy way out his death would give them. She watched him speculatively. He looked very ill; the journey had tired him, strained him beyond his strength, for he was not a robust man. He fasted a good deal and she believed he did this as a penance; she believed he had been thinking what he would call "evil thoughts," and these thoughts would be concerned with herself.

Perhaps, thought Tamar, he is not such a good man as he thinks himself to be. If I could prove that to him I should not feel I wronged him so deeply in doing what I long to do.

The more she thought of him, the more irresistible was the desire to show him and herself that he was no better than other men. As the ship drew nearer to the New World, she thought continually of this.

322

One evening, when they were in their cabin, he looked at her intently and said: "Tamar, what has come over you? You have been slowly changing as we have made this journey. You have become more and more like the wild girl you were before your conversion. I feel you have need of guidance. I beg of you to let me give it to you."

"*I* . . . in need of guidance!" she cried. "Look at me! I am well. I never felt better. You look like a death's head. It may be *you* who need guidance from *me*!"

"I was speaking of spiritual guidance. The health of your body is good. But what of the health of your soul?"

Then came the climax to which she afterwards believed the whole of her life with Humility had been leading.

It was a calm night and she was lying in her cabin when Humility came in, as was his custom, to kneel and say a prayer before scrambling into the bunk above hers.

As she watched him, she was sure the Devil was with her, for she decided that now was the time to show him that, for all his fine words and great ideals, he was a man as other men were. She would make him see that he was a man, as Bartle was; the difference being that Bartle strode about the ship not caring who saw him for what he was; whereas Humility hid his inclinations with a cloak of piety. She had vowed she would tear that cloak from him; she would expose him, not only before her eyes, but his own. Then perhaps he would cease to mutter his prayers over her, to offer her guidance, to say in his heart, "Thank God I am not as other men!"

"Humility," she said; and she stretched out a hand to him.

The gentleness of her voice surprised him. The rushlight showed enough of her beauty to excite him. Her long wild hair fell about her shoulders and her breasts were bare.

"Wife," he said hoarsely, "does aught ail you?"

She took his hand. "I know not. Except it may be that I am not a wife. I am treated as a woman to have children, not as one to be loved. You pray before you embrace me. 'Make this woman fertile!' This woman! Fertile! Those are not lovers' words. I am not loved as other women."

"I have loved you," he said. "I do love you . . . as is meet for a man to love his wife."

She leaned forward and, smiling alluringly, put an arm about him.

"You *have* loved me with passion," she said.

He closed his eyes and she laughed inwardly at his cowardice. "I was dedicated to the Lord," he said. "Marriage was not for me. I had eschewed the lusts of the flesh. God blessed our union. Have we not had three children, and is not another on the way?"

She put her lips against his ear and whispered: "I wish to be loved for myself . . . not for the children I may bear."

"You are in great need of prayer, wife."

"Not I!" she said and her voice held a note of excited laughter. "But *you* are, Humility. Pray now. Stay close to me and pray."

"You are a temptress," he said.

"You must not be a coward, Humility. You must look at me. My nights are lonely because I have a husband who thinks of children and not of his wife."

"Why do you tempt me thus?" he asked wonderingly.

"Why indeed! Why do men tempt women or women men? Come nearer, Humility, and I will tell you. I have been left alone too long."

A madness seemed to possess her. Bartle and I are no worse than he is! she thought. None of us is very good . . . no one very bad. I'll not have him thanking God that he is better than others. He shall see here and now that he is not.

She did not love him; she hated him. She did not desire him; he was repulsive to her. But what at this moment she needed beyond love or desire was to show him the truth about himself.

"Come closer, Humility," she murmured.

* * *

She had not known how desperately he had fought against what he considered to be sin. He was no hypocrite, for firmly he believed all that he professed to believe.

She watched him staring blankly before him—his face pale in the wan light.

The desire to mock him was uncontrollable. "So, a man is a man even though he be a Puritan. He knows the same lusts as other men, and when tempted, he can fall just as others."

He covered his face with his hands.

"Would I had died *before* this happened. All the years of purity. . .wiped out. . .by a single act!"

She cried heatedly: "Do not deceive yourself. The temptation never arose before. If it had, you would have fallen into it. When you went to your attic, I was glad that you should go. I made no effort to detain you. If I had wished you to remain. . .if I had wished you to be my lover, have no doubts that you would have been. I beg of you, say no more, 'I am a better man than this one and that one.' For you are not! And it is better for a sinner to say, 'I am a sinner,' than for him to say, 'I am a righteous man!'"

His lips moved in prayer, but she could not stop her tongue.

"You ask the Lord to forgive you. For what? I am your wife. Why should it be righteous to shun me? Stop it! See yourself as you are. A man. . .no more, no less. You are a brave man, but others are brave. You are a Puritan, but others are Puritans. You are lustful, and so are other men. There is as much joy for you in your plain garments as there is for me in my colours and silks and velvets. You are not different from others. Know this: If at any time I had tempted you as I did to-night, you would have fallen. Do not judge others lest you be judged yourself."

He did not seem to be aware of her. He murmured: "I am unworthy. I have shown myself to be unworthy. I have fallen from God's grace and there is no health in me."

He went out and she lay thinking of him. Now he would know himself. When she told him of her future plans he would not be able to talk of her sin, for if he did she would remind him of his. Some would say he had not sinned, but he believed he had; and surely sin was in the motive rather than the deed.

But later she softened towards him. He was a good man; he was even a noble man. Perhaps when she saw him again she would try to persuade him that there could be no sin in normal acts. She would say to him: "If God did not wish us to act so, why should He have given us desires?" She feared she would not be able to comfort him, but the next time she saw him she would try.

She never saw Humility again.

John Tyler was the last to see him alive.

"It were early morning," said John. "I couldn't sleep, so I came on deck to see what I could see. I thought mayhap I should be the first to sight land. And there he was . . . Mr. Brown . . . leaning over the side, looking at the water. I said: 'Good morning to 'ee, Mr. Brown. A fine good morning.' But he answered me not, and it did seem to me that he were in deep communion with the Lord. I wouldn't be the one to interrupt him at that, so I passed on. I took a look at the pigs and the poultry penned up there. I looked round. He were still there . . . but a minute later when I did glance over my shoulder, he'd gone. I stared like. There was no sign of him. He couldn't have gone below in the time. Then I was struck all of a tremble . . . for something did tell me that he had gone overboard.

"Well, you do know the rest. I raised the alarm, but 'twas too late. No sign of him . . . and the ship travelling fast before a strong wind."

Humility Brown . . . lost! The news spread through the ship. A terrible and most shocking accident. There was sincere mourning among the Puritans for one whom many considered their leader. But there was none who mourned him so deeply as did his wife.

Her guilt lay heavily upon her.

She blamed herself. I sent him to his death as surely as if I pushed him over the side. There will never be happiness for me, since, when I stretch out to take it, he will be there to remind me of my sin. I cannot escape my guilt, because I wanted him out of the way. I believe I knew that he would do this thing if I offered him a temptation which he would be unable to resist.

But even the tragic loss of Humility Brown was forgotten when land was sighted. At last, before these sea-weary people lay the promised land. But Humility, like Moses, was denied the sight of the land for which he had longed.

For ever this sense of guilt will lie on my conscience! thought Tamar.

CHAPTER
SEVEN

To look on a strange land which might become home should he a wonderful experience. Tamar stood on deck with Richard and Bartle beside her, and gazed at the coastline which, as they grew nearer, became more and more distinct.

The *Liberty* was anchored now, and galleys and shallops were coming out to meet and greet her. The sailors were lowering the ship's own boats. A group of people was assembling on the shore, eager and excited, for the coming of friends from home was a great occasion indeed.

It was impossible not to experience a feeling of pride to be one of this band of adventurers; but it seemed to Tamar, as she stood there, that a shadowy figure was beside her — a thin man in wet garments and with a look of bewildered horror in his eyes.

She turned at once to look at Bartle. His eyes gleamed. He was the true adventurer, eager for new sights. From Bartle her eyes went to Richard, and she saw in his face the hope that he might play a useful part in this founding of a new community.

How wonderful it was to set foot on *terra firma* after all those months at sea, to be free from the stale smell from below decks which seemed for ever in the nostrils in spite of the fresh sea air! How pleasant to smell the air which had blown across meadow and forest!

Eagerly they were taken to the settlement, where the Elders of the Church and the Governor himself came to welcome them. The settlement consisted of one street which stretched for just over a thousand feet up the slope of a hill from the sandy beach. The houses were roughly made of hewn planks, but each had its garden reminding all the newcomers suddenly and poignantly of home. And even as they looked along that street—the result of much loving toil, hopes and hardship—they noticed the square enclosure in which cannons were mounted, so placed that they could, at a moment's notice, defend the street against attack from any direction. They had not done with danger; they knew that. There would be perils ashore to vie with those of the sea.

But now was the time for rejoicing. Friends from home were in the settlement, and although most of the newcomers were strangers to those who had already made their home in this spot, this was like a family reunion. Tamar herself remembered some of these men, for she had met them before the sailing of the *Mayflower*. Prominent among these were Captain Standish, Edward Winslow and Governor Bradford.

They asked after Humility, and she found she was too overcome by emotion to speak of him to them. Richard spoke for her.

"It was a terrible accident. A great shock to us all. And such a tragedy that it should have happened the night before land was sighted. For years he had thought and worked for this."

"Doubtless," said Governor Bradford, "it was the will of God."

And then, before food was prepared to welcome the newcomers, thanks must be given to God for their safe arrival.

It was an impressive scene — the ship's company and the settlers gathered there together on the beach at the bottom of Leyden Street, while the Elders gave thanks and all the population joined in the hymns of praise and glory to God.

After the service of thanksgiving, there was bustle and activity throughout the little township. The newcomers should see what Puritan hospitality meant. There was great delight when it was learned what the ship carried. Poultry! Pigs! Gold could not have pleased them more.

This was indeed a special occasion. Each housewife was busy in a little house, preparing her contribution to the feast of welcome. The newcomers were divided up among the households, and each woman vied with the others in providing a feast of feasts. No mere hasty pudding for the guests! No maize cakes or codfish! Nothing would suit the occasion but the great festivity dish of beans baked with pork and succotash.

There were so many wonderful things to be seen while the feast was in preparation. The children were running wild about the place, lifting handfuls of sand

and letting it trickle through their fingers, gazing with longing eyes towards the forest, aching to explore after months of confinement at sea. The settlers' children watched gravely, and some joined in; those who remembered home asked many questions.

The grown-ups talked; they could not stop talking; they talked of the first terrible winter, when more than half their number had died; they talked of the fire which had almost been a final disaster. Mr. Carver and Mr. Bradford, who had been sick in bed at the time, had all but lost their lives as well as their homes. Ah! That had been a terrible time — and all because of a spark that lighted the thatch of a cottage. But the Lord had looked after them; terrible tribulations had been theirs, but they had come through with His help and His grace.

Talk went on and on; and it was talk that raised laughter and tears — laughter for the tragedies which had brought sorrow at the time, but, in retrospect, could amuse; sorrow for the loss of so many who now lay buried in the New England soil. They told of the making of the plantation; of how they trapped fish in the shallow, rapid river which could be seen from where they stood, emptying itself into the sea; they told how they had discovered that the maize, which they needed so badly, would not grow in the sandy, stony soil until they had planted fish from the sea in the land; then did the maize grow in abundance.

Fish! The newcomers would soon realize that there never was such fish as that which abounded in the neighbourhood of Cape James. There was the

Cape itself, clearly to be seen on such a bright day as this. It was shaped like an arm crooked about a corner of the sea. They would see that the cod found in these parts were twice as large as those found elsewhere. What labour that saved in hooking and splitting! Oh, the Lord was looking after them. In the summer, besides the cod, came mullet and sturgeon. And what caviare and puttargo could be made from the roes! The savages said that the fish in these waters could be compared in numbers with the hairs on men's heads.

Fruit there was in plenty — mulberries, gooseberries, plums, strawberries, pumpkins and gourds; walnut and chestnut trees abounded in the forests; flax grew freely, and from it they were able to make the strongest of ropes and nets. Then there were beavers and otters, foxes and martens — and in the Old Country good money was paid for the skins of such animals.

It was indeed a "land flowing with milk and honey."

Oh, but those first months! Not then had the fruits of this land been discovered. Meat and meal had been sadly missed; there were too few clothes and bedding; no yarn for lamps; no oiled paper for the windows of the houses which must be built. The cruel cold had overtaken them, had found them unready; but their determination had been stronger than the harsh winds and bitter snows. They would never, they vowed, return to England or Holland; they had vowed to make this country their own, to build a new freedom in a new land; and this, with the help of God, they were doing.

The first settlers had discovered during their second winter that the first winter had been a mild one; then, in spite of the winds and snow they had had to endure, they knew that God was with them, for if they had been obliged to face a normal winter during their first months in the new land, not merely half of the new colony would have perished, but the whole of it.

There was much to tell, so much to listen to. They must tell of the great day of Thanksgiving when Governor Bradford had decided there should be a feast. It should be a sober feast—a solemn rejoicing, a means of showing gratitude to the Almighty for having brought them through great trials.

So Governor Bradford sent men into the forest to kill wild fowl, and there was rejoicing for three whole days.

The Puritans smiled in delighted reminiscence.

"My friends, what think you? Massasoit came to the feast. Massasoit was an Indian chief who had become our friend through the Grace of God and the diplomacy of our Governor and Captain Standish— and mayhap by the sight of our cannon. There was dancing and singing, and we were much put out, as you can guess, for this was a solemn feast, a tribute to Almighty God; and here in our midst were savages worshipping their own heathen gods . . . barbarians and pagans, showing us their dancing, their faces painted, their bodies all but naked. But we trust the Lord understood that they were our guests and that we must humour them. And their dancing and their nakedness was apart from the thankfulness which was in our hearts."

Now to the feast. The pork and beans and fowls cooked together tasted delicious. There was ale and gin to drink; and when they had eaten and drunk they got into little groups and talk broke out once more; and now most of this talk was of home — not the new home, but the home across the sea to which most of them had said farewell for ever.

Yes, it was a wonderful country to which they had come, but they thought of home continually. Here there was fish in abundance — lobsters, clams and oysters besides cod and mullet — but how often did they think of the rich red beef of England and good English ale! Nostalgia was like a disease; it attacked some more than others. Some had died, it was believed, of melancholy, because they missed the richly green fields of England.

Tamar, watching it all, was fired with enthusiasm. She wanted to live here among these brave men and women; she visualized a town which was not merely a street with its plantation and its little houses; she visualized a town — a great town where there was friendship for all, and no cruelty, no brutality. . . but freedom. Yes, freedom was the most important thing — freedom to live one's own life, to think one's own thoughts.

They went back to the *Liberty* to sleep, as there was not sufficient accommodation in the settlement.

Bartle talked to her when they were back on the ship.

"A noble venture that!" he said. "But not for us."

"Why not?"

"Pagans cannot make their homes with Puritans."

"Anyone can hope for freedom," she said. "Why should we not become Puritans?"

"You know that we never could be."

"They are a wonderful people. When I think of their arriving and seeing it, not as we see it now, but just a waste land, a sandy bank about which the water breaks . . . a gentle hill on which to build a town, and the forests in the distance in which the savages abound! What had they but their courage and a sea full of fish! I wish I had been one of them in the beginning."

"What has come over you?" he asked. "You change from one day to another. Have you forgotten that night when we thought the Spaniard was upon us? Then you promised that we should be together. You would leave your husband and come back with me. Now that he is gone, that surely makes everything easier for us. We need not consider him now."

"We have to consider him," she said dully.

"You talk in riddles."

"No. He is dead and I killed him."

"*You* . . . killed him!"

She blurted out an account of what had happened in the cabin on the night before Humility's death.

He was scornful. She was fanciful, he said.

"He killed himself. What nonsense is this! He killed himself because he lacked the courage to live."

"I killed him," she said stonily. "Almost in sight of the land he had longed for."

"You deceive yourself. As usual, your emotions cloud your vision. You think with the heart . . . not with the mind. How could you know that he would kill himself? Why did he kill himself? Because he lacked the courage to live. He brooded so continually on sin, that he saw it where it was not. Think no more of him. He was a weak man. If God decided he should not come to this land, then it was because he was unworthy. This is a land for brave men and women."

"I feel that there is a great weight about my neck. I killed him, and I must pay for my sin. I can find no happiness until I do. I knew that to-day, when I listened to what these people had to tell. If I stay here, if I try to do Humility's work, then I shall in some measure atone for my sin."

He turned on her angrily. "I do not know you. What of us? What of our life together . . . the life you promised me if we should escape the Spaniard to enjoy it? Why is it that when the road is clear for us you must build up these obstacles?"

"I am not young and foolish any more . . . not the woman to be excited by a lover."

He took her into his arms. "I will soon alter that!" he said grimly.

But she was determined. "Leave me alone for a while. I wish to think of this. I do not understand my feelings. Just now I can see nothing but his poor white face, his eyes so sorrowful, looking into mine. I can hear only my own voice saying cruel, brutal things to him; they cut into his heart like a knife; and they were the instruments that killed him."

Bartle turned from her in a passion. He was speechless with anger. He strode away from her.

She went back to her cabin and looked about her with fearful eyes, and it seemed to her that the spirit of Humility Brown was in that cabin. She lay sleepless, turning from one side to another in a vain effort to reach sleep.

It was dawn before she dozed; and then she dreamed that Humility was in the cabin, the water dripping from his sombre garments, while his hair hung dank about his death-pale face.

"Only by a life of piety," said the spirit of Humility, "can you atone for your sin."

*　　*　　*

Early next morning Richard came to her cabin.

"Do I disturb you, Tamar?"

"No."

"But you look tired. You have scarcely slept. I have slept little myself. Yesterday was a day I shall remember all my life."

"And I," she said.

"Tamar, you are going to be happy here."

She shook her head, but he did not notice; he seemed to be looking beyond her into a future which pleased him.

"When I saw the town they had made," he went on, as though speaking to himself, "I was filled with emotion. Their simple houses . . . small, bare and only just adequate. But think! They must first have

338

cut the trees before they could begin to build. Winslow was telling me that in those days they worked from sunrise to sunset, felling, sawing and carrying timber. He told me that, before the building could begin, many of the men fell sick, and some died. Those who were well enough worked when the weather would allow them. They worked with a will. I would I had been one of them. These men will be remembered as long as men are remembered. And what impresses me most is that on that first Sabbath day, although the need to get those houses built was great, greater still was their faith and their belief that the Sabbath day should be kept holy. There was no work on the first Sunday. I picture them; they had no meeting house — no house at all. I can see them giving thanks in the open air. Tamar, there is a greatness in these men which I have never seen before. Often I have thought I could worship the Carpenter's Son. It was not His own simple doctrines which I could not accept; it was the various complicated versions laid down by different Churches which I rejected one by one. But surely this simple life — this life of goodness and restraint — is the true life. The religion these men brought with them is the true religion."

"I feel you may be right," said Tamar.

"These first settlers were bolder than the Puritans we have known. The large majority of them spent years of exile in Holland. They did not wish merely to simplify the ritual of the existing Church, but to form a new one. That was why it was first of all necessary to fly the country; then to form a new community of their own."

"You wish to become one of them, Richard. I think that is what I wish. To work with them, to watch a great town grow here, a town where there is kindness instead of brutality, freedom to take the place of persecution. I wish to live here simply, as these people do. I *must* do that, because Humility did not live to do it."

Now Richard was watching her closely.

"I have been thinking of you . . . and Bartle," he said.

"What of us?"

"That you would now doubtless marry. He loves you and I believe you love him."

"I do not know," she said.

"You must be happy here, Tamar. It is necessary that you should be. You must make Bartle happy here. You need him, for I do not believe you can be happy without him. I think too that, although it is difficult for us to imagine him in this place, living the life of a Puritan, he may attempt it . . . for your sake. He could go back to England; he could resume the life which would naturally be his, the country squire, the lord of the manor. But, Tamar, you dare not go back. They would have taken you some time or other had you stayed. I always knew it. I was never at peace thinking of it. It might not have been for years . . . but do it they would. One day they would have hanged you. They would never have forgotten that you had the reputation of being a witch. That was why I agreed to come here. I knew you would never be safe at home."

"Yes," she said. "I felt that too. They looked at me slyly. They were awaiting their opportunity, waiting to find me defenceless. I often pictured them, coming to take me, as they came to the house that day, Simon Carter leading the way. And not myself only. There is poor Jane Swann. They would have had her. Perhaps even Mistress Alton and you, Richard. None of us was safe. And John Tyler and Annis, and Annis's children . . . they might have been taken for their religion."

"It is all religious persecution," said Richard vehemently. "You persist in believing yourself of the witch community because of an old religion whose rites and remedies have become known to you. It is all persecution. Religious persecution . . . from which we are escaping."

"Richard, I know I must stay. I must drive the Devil out of my soul."

Richard sighed. "So even now that you are a woman and a mother of children, you believe in black magic?"

"I know I am of the Devil," she said. "That is why I have murder on my soul." She went on before he could interrupt. "There is much that you do not know of me. I am full of wickedness. So is Bartle. That is why we cannot resist each other. He is brutal and cruel, barbarous and murderous. I am the same. Yes, I am. Let me explain; then you will understand. Bartle was my lover . . . years and years ago. I did not want him to be, but he forced that on me. Not as it almost was on that occasion when you saved me . . . but more subtly. And I—I know now—was secretly delighted that this should be so. I deceived myself into thinking that I hated him, but that was not so. Then I married Humility. I had no right to marry Humility. It was the Devil who persuaded me to do it. I see that now. If I had married Bartle, I should have had no influence over Humility. Bartle belonged to the Devil already and it was Humility's soul the Devil wanted."

"What are you saying, Tamar? You are hysterical."

"You think you are wise, Richard. So you are . . . wise in book-learning. But you know nothing of women like me. I saved Humility's life and I was proud of that; and it seemed to me that because I had saved it, that life belonged to me. I know now that that was the Devil whispering in my ear. I deceived myself into thinking that my soul was saved, so that my marriage should not seem incongruous. I see it all so clearly now—my cruelty, my barbarity. You know what happened. Then Bartle came home. Of course I wanted Bartle. We were of a kind. We quarrelled; we hated; and we loved each other madly. It was always like that. And coming over on the ship I knew that I wanted Bartle and I wanted my children . . . but I did not want Humility—so I killed him!"

"You are not talking sense, Tamar. John Tyler saw the end of Humility."

"John Tyler was there when he fell overboard. But why did he fall overboard? There was no reason for it. It was a calm morning. Why should he have fallen

342

overboard? He deliberately went over; he killed himself because I had seen to it that his life was impossible to live."

"I can see that you are working yourself into a passion of grief. It was no fault of yours that he went overboard. He loved you; you had given him children; you were accompanying him to the land he had always longed for. His dearest dreams were all about to be realized."

"I killed him, I tell you! I taunted him to his death! His prayers angered me, hurt my pride in myself. It was not for love of me that he had married me. He told me that continually. . . not for the love of my body but for the sake of the children we must have to populate the colony. I could not bear it, so I proved to him that he was as lustful as any man, that he deceived himself but he did not deceive me. Then I taunted him. He was, I told him, not only a sinner, but a hypocrite. The truth was too much for him. He believed he was going to eternal damnation. He was guilty of one of those seven deadly sins about which he was always preaching—Lust. All the years he had been practising lust—not as Bartle practised it, boasting, swaggering, showing himself to the world for what he was. No! He practised it under a cloak of piety. . . under cover of darkness. Those were the words I used to him. And so he went out and killed himself."

Richard took her by the shoulders and shook her gently. "Tamar, what are you saying? I am going to get you a glass of spirits. Then I am going to make you lie down. I am going to make you rest and, when you have recovered, I shall talk to you. You have let yourself become overwrought by this terrible tragedy. You have been over-excited by the last few days. When I have talked to you, you will see this more clearly. Humility's death was an accident. He would never have killed himself because of what you call a lustful act. You were his wife."

"He thought I was with child. I had lied to him . . . because I did not want him. He thought I was with child, I say . . . and still he . . ."

"You must be calm, Tamar, or you will be ill."

She took his hand; hers was quite cold.

"I am calm," she said, "and in my calmness I see myself a murderess. I sent him to his death, and all the work that was to have been done will be left undone. I can only be at peace if I take on that work. Richard . . . Father . . . try to understand me. Try to help me."

He put his lips against her forehead.

"I understand, my dearest child," he said. "I understand. I will help you. Together we will do his work."

*　　*　　*

The days passed rapidly. Stores were unloaded, pens set up for the pigs and poultry. There was timber to be felled, as many more houses would be needed. Then there was the perpetual hunt for food. If they had been content to eat the fish which abounded off their shores, they might have saved much time, for it was only necessary for a few small boats to go out for a day's fishing to bring back enough to feed the community. But they felt the need of flesh. Lobsters, oysters, clams and cod could not completely satisfy them; they must hunt the deer of the forest.

The children were made to work, fetching and carrying. Tamar watched Dick and Rowan running hither and thither with the younger members of Annis's large family and others. Even Lorea was given small tasks to perform.

"There is no idleness here," was the rule. "There is no privilege. Those who would live in houses must build them; those who would eat must work."

But the children were delighted with their new life. Everything was so strange and exciting; the changing colours of the sea, which was somehow different from that sea of Devon; the sandy bank on which the water broke violently; the ship lying there between the bank and the land, the ship which had meant adventure and exploration; the Cape which could easily be seen on clear days; the swiftly flowing river emptying itself into the sea; the Cheuyot Mountains in the distance; the town itself spreading on the hillside; the wild birds — geese, cranes, herons; and beyond, the forest. Dick's eyes were turned again and again towards the forest — the enchanted forest in which lurked red-skinned men. Dick was awake early every morning, was tired out every night. Dick was enchanted with the new life.

Richard had plans which had met with the approval of the Governor and those in charge of the settlement. Richard had brought carefully chosen books with him and proposed teaching the children. It was absolutely necessary that they should learn to read and write. They could not be allowed to grow up ignorant, or they would not be able to read the Bible and teach their children to do the same.

That, it was confessed, had been a matter of great anxiety to the leaders of the Pilgrims. There had been little time to think of education; they had been too busy trying to keep alive. Richard, finding that he could be useful in the new community, was in high delight. Tamar announced her desire to help him; and, Richard said, as there was now quite a large juvenile section of the population, he would need a helper, and who better than his own daughter, whom he himself had taught?

This suggestion was received with slightly less enthusiasm than the first. A certain James Milroy, a middle-aged widower, whose wife had died the previous winter, volunteered the suggestion that it might not be meet in the eyes of the Lord that a woman should teach male members of the community.

Richard challenged this view, declaring that he would need help and that it was for him to choose his helper; he chose his daughter. The matter was allowed to rest there, but, looking round at those stern faces, Tamar felt sudden anger rising within her. She must keep her lips tightly pressed together to stop the flow of words which afterwards she would wish she had not uttered, for even as she opened her mouth, she had seemed to see Humility standing among those men.

So instead of making angry retorts, she determined to show by her ability that a woman could do the work as well as any man, and that, providing she was a good and enthusiastic teacher, her sex could be of no moment.

Richard's house was to be the first of the new houses, as it was also to be the schoolhouse. While it was being built, a few Indians came to watch. They stood about, their faces painted vermilion to show they came in peace; they smiled and chattered together. They offered wampum and deerskins in exchange for saws and oiled paper. "*Mawchick chammay*!" they insisted. "Best of friends!" They laughed as they watched, for it seemed to them that the ways of the white men were strange and wonderful.

Annis and her family were split up between other families so that they might have a roof over their heads while they were waiting for a house of their own. Annis went about in a state of bliss.

"Why, mistress," she said to Tamar, "this is indeed a great land. I know now how feared I was, every time John went out, that they would have taken him for questioning. If you did but know how wonderful it is to have lost that fear. And they do think a lot of John here. He be so good with the land. The Governor, he did say to me: 'Your man is the kind we want here!' Yes, he did. And Christian and Restraint are fine workers too. And he said: 'And you, daughter, with your fine family. You are the sort of woman we want, a woman who knows her duty to God, a pure woman who has given us children.' Oh, mistress, I be so happy. This be the promised land."

Mistress Alton was living with another family until the time when Richard's house should be built; then she would become his housekeeper. In the house where Mistress Alton dwelt, James Milroy also lived; and Tamar had heard that James Milroy was looking for a wife.

"Who knows?" said Tamar to Richard. "Mistress Alton may find a husband in her new country!"

Bartle was giving Tamar cause for anxiety. He was even more apart from this community than she was. He was accepted as the Captain of the ship bringing stores and colonists. He never attended prayer meetings, and was not expected to. He had said that when the spring came he would take the *Liberty* back to England, report on the colony to London, and arrange either to bring or send the stores and cattle which New Plymouth needed.

But Bartle, of course, had no wish to become a part of this community, whereas Tamar was growing more and more certain that within it lay her salvation.

Bartle was angry. This, he declared, was yet another phase of her perversity — the perversity which had dogged them since their first meeting and ruined their lives. Would she never learn her lesson? It was always wait . . . wait . . . wait. Did she not know that her prevaricating had been responsible for all the misery they had endured?

"*Now* is the time!" cried Bartle. "Not to-morrow . . . or next year! Now! *Now!*"

348

"You must try to be understanding," she said. "You must help me."

"Humility Brown was in our way when I came home. He is no longer in our way. We are free . . . free to marry, and still you say, 'Wait!' We grow old, waiting. We are both past the first flush of our youth, and still you say, 'Wait!'"

"We are *not* free, Bartle. Humility is between us."

"He is dead!"

"He lives on to haunt me because I killed him."

"What nonsense! He killed himself. Or it was an accident. Yes! It was an accident."

"You cannot say it was an accident just because it makes a prettier story."

"I can and I will. He is dead; his life is done with; and ours are short. You try my patience as you ever did. You know what I am like when I get impatient. I refuse to wait. I refuse to waste my life."

Her eyes filled with tears. "Oh, Bartle, I beg of you . . ."

"It is no use begging of me! I ask you to marry me, to sail back with me to England in the spring. Come! That is the life for us. We will stay there."

"Richard says I shall never be safe in England. They know me for a witch. They will remember always."

"Do you think that any would dare hurt my wife?"

"I should never be safe in Devon where they know me."

"That is not why you will not go back. You would not be afraid of them!"

"I will not go back because I want to live here. I want to be of these people. I must live a life of sacrifice and restraint. I know it. It has been revealed to me. They have revealed it to me by their goodness."

"You will change your mind."

"I do not think so."

He caught her hand in a grip that hurt. "You are a fool, Tamar. You set yourself ideals which you cannot live up to. You think with your emotions. *You* can never live among Puritans. There is nothing of the Puritan in you. You belong to me as I do to you. I marvel at my patience. One of these days I will make you see how wrong you have been to waste our time. Indeed, I will not allow much more time to be wasted. Do not stand there looking sad and holy, or by God, I will take it upon myself to show you that there is nothing holy about you . . . and no need for sadness!" He turned away, but before he had gone a few paces he turned once more to face her. "Think not that I shall endure this state of affairs. You will see."

She was trembling. She remembered that smile so well, that flash of the intensely blue eyes. Her heart was beating fast, and she knew that she wanted him to come back, to repeat that he would wait no longer. But Humility seemed close then, Humility, with his white face and wet clinging garments — a sad, repentant ghost. "Pray," said the ghost of Humility, "pray for help to fight your lust."

She prayed as she turned and ran back to watch the builders at work on that house in which she would work with Richard for the good of the colony.

However, it seemed that even Bartle had a place in this community. He went off into the forest with the hunters. He was an expert shot, and there was meat in plenty whenever he was of the party.

"You are a mighty hunter, friend," he was told. Shrewd eyes smiled kindly on him. "Stay with us!" said those eyes. "There is work for you here; and in time God may see fit to save your soul from eternal damnation. He has given you the eyes of a hawk, the fleetness of an Indian, the strength of three men. There is work for you here."

But Bartle saw no permanent place for himself with them. It was merely that he could not resist the thrill of the hunt, and it gave him great pleasure to come back after a good day in the forest and see the eyes of the people glisten in anticipation as they gazed on the spoils.

One day Dick was missing, and Tamar was frantic with anxiety.

It was a bright winter's day with a keen frost in the air. She imagined her son lost in the forest, injured perhaps, unable to move, spending the night there . . . the cold night. It would kill him. The winters of this land were more rigorous than the winters of Devon. It was realized by many that the winters they had known at home had scarcely been winters at all. In Devonshire a whole winter could pass without a sight of snow; it was one of the most temperate spots in a temperate island. Now they were learning what a real winter could be, and it was harder to bear for those who came from Devonshire than for the men from colder East Anglia and Holland.

She must find her child, but she dared not let it be known that he was missing, for fear he had transgressed the rules; and if he had gone into the forest, he certainly had. They were right, of course, these men with their sternness. Children, they said, were born in sin and must be led away from it. This often meant harsh correction; and there were a good many beatings administered on the instructions of the Elders of the Church. But even if they were right, it must not happen to Dick, for he was a proud child, deeply conscious of his dignity. He was herself all over again, and he had learned to be like Bartle too. He would be resentful of public humiliation, since he thought himself a man already, worthy of a man's privileges.

If she found Bartle, he would help her to search for the boy and bring him back so that his misdemeanour might not be known.

She made her way down to the shore, determined to row out to the *Liberty*, find Bartle and ask his help. Her heart-beats quickened. She could imagine Bartle, cruel as ever, making conditions. "I will find the boy, and in payment for returning him to you and keeping his sins from the Puritans, I demand . . ."

Someone was calling her name and, turning, she saw coming towards her, James Milroy, that middle-aged widower who had objected to a woman's teaching boys.

"You are anxious on account of your son," he said. "I can tell you where he is."

His eyes studied her with disapproval and she put up her hand to tuck a straying curl under her cap.

"You know?" she cried. "He . . . is safe?"

"It would seem so. Sir Bartle has taken a party on a day's hunting in the forest and the boy is with them."

She was filled with relief, but James Milroy shook his head sternly.

"If you would care to take the advice of a friend who wishes you well, this is it. The boy should not be allowed to spend so much time with the Captain. That man is a sinner and he will lead the boy into temptation. His language offends the ears of all men of God. He has an evil reputation."

"I thank you, sir," she said, and her eyes flashed, "but the boy is mine and I think I know what is good for him."

"There I disagree, and so would the Elders. The boy should not have absented himself without permission. I insist that on his return the necessary correction shall be administered."

"You mean . . ."

"'He that spareth his rod hateth his son.' That boy is already spoiled. He needs a father."

"I assure you that I am the best judge of how a child of mine shall be brought up."

She turned and walked away, her head held high. Had she stayed another moment, she would have been unable to control her furious anger.

The hunting party returned at the end of that day with enough meat to provide the whole settlement with a good meal. Tamar saw them coming, saw Dick striding along beside Bartle; and she felt a pride rise up in her. Dick was almost a man.

James Milroy was there to watch the return of the party, and the very way in which his thin lips were pressed together told Tamar that he was going to demand the punishment of her son.

She saw the man approach the boy and lay his hand on his shoulder. She saw the boy's eyes flash as he moved closer to Bartle.

Then she heard Dick's voice, high-pitched and indignant. " 'Twas hunting! 'Twas finding food! That is a good thing to do."

Tamar's heart leaped, for Bartle now faced James Milroy, and Bartle, drawing himself up to his full height, was laughing in the face of the man, with that bold insolence which Tamar knew well.

There was a hush about them. Pleasure in the return of the hunters with good meat was lost, for here was a troublous note introduced into the harmony of the occasion.

"I took the boy with me," said Bartle. "If any has to answer for his going, then that is myself. What do you wish, sir — to challenge me? Come then, I am ready. Shall we fight with the sword or the fist? It matters not to me. Nor will it to you in less than a minute for, by God, I swear. . ."

But one of the Elders had approached them, had laid a hand on Bartle's arm.

"Sir Bartle, I beg of you, restrain yourself."

Bartle growled: "Let him leave the boy alone, then. Anyone who dares lay a hand on him answers to me."

"It is forbidden," said James Milroy, "that children should go into the forest without the consent of parents or the authorities."

"He came with his parent's consent," said Bartle.

"I know that to be an untruth."

"You dare insult me?"

But James Milroy, although he knew himself to be no match for the great blustering Captain, was not a coward. He would not have been of this community if he had not been a brave man. He fervently believed in the righteousness of what he was doing.

"It is you who insult the truth, Sir Bartle. His mother was anxious. She was looking for him. I met her and told her where he was."

Bartle's eyes narrowed. He would have laid his hands on the man, but the Elder said: "His mother is here; she will tell us of this matter. You were anxious, were you not, Mistress Brown? You had not given the child permission and it was for you to give it, as the child, alas, has no father to guide him."

Tamar glared angrily at the Puritan, James Milroy.

"The boy had my permission to go. He is allowed to hunt with Sir Bartle whenever he wishes."

James Milroy looked at her in startled horror. He would not have been surprised if the heavens had opened and Tamar had been struck dumb or even dead.

What is the use of my trying to be one of them? Tamar asked herself.

She was a pagan; she and Bartle were of a kind. What cared she if she must tell a lie to save her son pain and humiliation! And what cared Bartle?

*   *   *

Afterwards she was remorseful. She had been wrong. Better for Dick to have taken his beating than for her to have perjured her soul.

Moreover, she had given way to Bartle; she had sided with him and the old ways against the Puritans and the new.

"The idea," said Bartle, "of wanting to punish a boy because he goes off for a day's hunting! Leave him to me and I will make a man of him."

"He must learn to obey rules . . . the rules of the community in which he lives."

"He will learn what it is good for him to learn, with me as his teacher."

"I would have him grow up good and noble."

"As his father?" said Bartle. "A poor frail thing of a man who jumps into the sea because he is tempted to make love to his wife!"

"How dare you!"

"Now that is more like yourself. By God, I'd a thousand times rather see you stormy than pious."

She was about to blaze at him when she seemed to see the ghost of Humility standing beside him; and it was as though she saw Bartle through Humility's eyes — the Devil incarnate, there to tempt her.

She turned away, but she heard Bartle's laughter following her; and she guessed that plans were forming in his mind.

After that Dick hardly ever left Bartle's side. Dick worshipped Bartle. Once the boy looked at his mother critically and said "*You* used to be more like Sir Bartle, Mamma. Now you are becoming like these people."

"Dick," she asked earnestly, "don't you like living here with these people?"

"I like living here," he said significantly, "because I like hunting with Sir Bartle. One day. . .I shall go sailing with him. When he goes back to England, he's promised that I . . ."

The boy stopped. But she understood. Bartle was winning the boy from her.

She was tormented by the thought. She prayed constantly. She could not talk to Richard of this matter, for Richard wished her to marry Bartle. Richard had not believed in her first conversion; he did not believe in this one.

A few weeks after the arrival of the *Liberty* another ship called at New Plymouth, and aboard her were Dutch settlers from farther along the coast. Great hospitality was shown to the guests, for, as the Governor said, he and the entire colony were happy when people came as friends instead of enemies.

These Dutchmen expressed great admiration for the New Plymouth way of life; they were astonished that the Pilgrims had experienced so little trouble with the red-skinned men; the French and Dutch in other parts of this great continent had not found the natives so amenable.

Tamar knew then that this was due to the example of goodness and honour set by the men of New Plymouth. So pronounced and unswerving was this code that it was one which savages could see was desirable. These Englishmen were born colonizers, as was no other nation on Earth; they possessed a natural dignity and a way of straight-dealing which was apparent to all men, whatever their colour, whatever their creed. Brave they were; but so were other settlers who had left their homes for a new life in a strange land. But Tamar saw this quality, which they possessed in a larger degree than men of other nations, as a calm dignity, an ability to suppress feelings, whether of anger or joy, so that those who gave vent to such feelings must inevitably find themselves at a disadvantage when opposing such men; there was a slowness to anger in these men, but once righteous indignation was aroused, there was in them a determination of purpose, stubborn insistence on finishing what they had begun; and these qualities made of them men to respect and to fear. Among such men — and such men only — could she follow magnificent examples and work out her salvation.

Christmas was near and Tamar planned a celebration for the children. There should be, she promised them, dancing, games and feasting. The children went dancing down Leyden Street, all chattering about the Christmas feast.

Word came to Tamar that one of the Elders wished to speak to her, and she went along to his house.

"Sit down, dear sister," he said. "I must have speech with thee. I have heard of the feast you would give on Christ's birthday."

Tamar waited and, after a pause, he went on: "Our Lord Jesus, sister, was a Man of Sorrows, and it is not meet that the day of His birth should be celebrated with feasting and games. That day should be given to prayer."

"But . . ." she began.

He lifted his hand. "Hear me out, I pray you. I thought I would tell you first, before it is explained to the children that there cannot be this . . . this bacchanalia. You have, I fear — in your ignorance, I know, and not from wanton guilt — imbued them with the wrong ideas. Fear not, sister, we do not blame you. We merely wish to show you the folly of your ways."

"But it is simple fun for the children. It is no . . . bacchanalia. It is just a little pleasure . . . a little fun."

"Dear sister, you have brought old ideas with you from England. All that wickedness we left behind us. There is not room for it in the New World. Do not fret. We have seen you striving to become one of us and are pleased with your progress. We wish to help you, and that is why, in addition to explaining to you your mistake about Christ's birthday, I have asked you to come here."

She lifted her eyes to his face; she knew they were beginning to blaze. She wanted to run out of this room, which seemed suddenly oppressive. She noted the shelf which contained a few books, chief of which was a translation of the Bible done in Holland; she looked down at the rushes on the floor, and from the floor to the windows with their oiled paper; and she suddenly remembered with an almost intolerable nostalgia her bedroom in the house at Pennicomquick with the carpet on the floor and real glass in the window, and the bed with its rich curtains. She wanted to escape from this restricted, primitive life; she wanted to be free. Free? But it was to this land she had come in search of freedom.

She suppressed the thought. Humility seemed to be there, pointing an accusing finger at her. She waited as patiently as she could.

"You are a young woman still. You are a strong woman. You have bred children and could breed more. It is your duty to God and to your new country to have children to worship Him and cultivate your adopted land. You are too young to remain unmarried. Pray do not look startled. I have good news for you. There is one among us who is prepared to marry you, to guide you, and to be a father to those children you already have, while he will endeavour to give you more."

She felt her lips curl in uncontrollable scorn. "And who is this man?"

"James Milroy. A good man, a noble man, a man who has long dedicated his life to the service of God. He has watched you protectively since you have been here. He has felt you and your children to be in need of correction and guidance; and he feels that God has selected him for the task. He is willing—nay, anxious—to obey the will of the Lord."

"If he looks for a wife," she said, "there are others more worthy than I."

But the Elder did not notice the edge on her voice. "That may be. But our dear brother Milroy was never a man to shirk his duty when he sees it plain before him. He is therefore willing to take you to him as his wife."

"That is generous of him indeed. You may tell him this: When I marry, and if I marry, I shall choose my own husband."

"You make many mistakes, sister. Your life is full of mistakes. You have brought evil ideas with you from the Old World, and you cling to them. You have set yourself up to teach our boys. We like that not. A woman's duty is not to instruct men, and these boys will one day be men. Nay! We would see you as other women—at your spinning wheel, helping in the fields at harvest, and, above all, a wife to give us children. Yes, dear sister, we have accepted you. One of us offers to take care of your life, to guide you into the paths which will lead to your salvation and the glorification of God."

She was too dazed to speak. She could only think: James Milroy! That man!

And when she pictured him, the quiet, solemn-eyed man changed in her mind's eye to Humility Brown.

The voice went on: "You are of the weaker sex, dear sister; and it is easy to see that in the Old Country you have been spoiled. Your father continues to spoil you. We are pleased with him and the work he is doing for us, and we know that one day he will be completely with us. We shall rejoice on that day. But there is much he too has to learn. You have been unfortunate in your upbringing and we are sorry for you. You have been given beauty; and beauty, dear sister, is not always a gift from God. Or it may be that it is given by the Almighty as a special burden to be carried through a life. Women are frail creatures. We must never forget that they are not the equals of men. They must never forget that they are the weaker vessels. They must remain subservient to the good men who marry them. Never forget that it was Eve who listened to the temptation of the serpent. It was due to Eve that Adam, our forefather, was turned out of Eden. Adam was weak; but Eve was wicked; and all women are descendants of Eve as all men are of Adam. Women are more easily tempted to sin, being of weaker intellect than men, and therefore must obey their husbands in all things. Children are born in sin and must be sternly led to righteousness. It is a great task which falls upon us men."

"A great task doubtless!" she said.

"And you will allow me to send Master Milroy along to your father's house?"

She lowered her lids that he might not see the blaze of her eyes, and when she spoke her voice was scarcely audible, such an effort did she have to make to control

362

it. "I am too sinful for such a man," she said. "It will be well for such an Adam to find a more worthy Eve, someone who has not had to carry this heavy burden of beauty through her life."

"Your modesty is not unbecoming . . ." began the Elder.

But she said hastily as she turned to the door: "I will bid you good day."

She hurried to the beach and dragged the nearest boat to the water. Furiously she rowed out to the *Liberty*.

Scrambling aboard, she cried to one of the sailors: "Tell Sir Bartle I am here. I wish to see him . . . at once!"

She leaned over the bulwarks waiting, but she did not have to wait for long. He gave a mighty roar of laughter when he saw her. Unlike the Elder, he knew her rages when he saw them.

He took her hands. "This is a joy, to have you visit me." Then he pulled her towards him and kissed her firmly on the mouth.

She held him off. "I . . . I have just come from the Elder . . ." she said breathlessly.

"I do not think that Elder has pleased you greatly."

"Pleased me! I am infuriated!"

"That delights me. It is so long since I have seen you in a rage . . . much too long."

"I am sinful! I am a descendant of Eve, who is responsible for all the sin in the world. I have been handicapped by the burden of my beauty. And now . . . *now* . . . it pleases Brother Milroy . . . *dear*

Brother Milroy. . .to guide me into the paths of righteousness! He will look after my children and give me more. In short, he is prepared to marry me. . .for the sake of my soul, I am told, and so that I can supply more children for the colony!"

"Ha! Yet another Humility Brown! And what said you to this dazzling proposal?"

"I said I would choose my own husband."

"That was well spoken. And you told them, I believe, that you had chosen already."

"I did not."

"That," he said, "was remiss of you." He drew her to him once more and this time kissed her tenderly. "No matter, we will tell them together."

"I do not mean. . ." she began.

"But I do. The time has come, and you can no longer delay. They are right when they say such as you should not remain unmarried. Plague on them! They would marry you off to their Elders! And in your mood of these last weeks you'd have had another Humility Brown if I had not been here to stop you. Listen, sweetheart. You don't belong here. We don't belong here. We'll marry and sail away. Would we could go to-night! But that's impossible. We'll not tempt death when life looks good. But as soon as these gales cease. . .as soon as the sun begins to smile again. . ."

"Brother Milroy!" she cried. "That man! You can imagine how he would look after my children. Poor Dick! Poor Rowan! Poor little Lorea!"

"Think how delighted *they* will be when they know about us! It is their dearest wish that I should be their father."

"You have put a spell upon them."

"As I have on you . . . and as you have on me, Tamar."

"Was it magic you learned in foreign places?"

"I know not. I only know that I love them and they love me; and that I love their mother . . . as she loves me."

"If I married you . . . would you . . . could you give up all thought of returning to England? I mean, would you stay here? Of course you will sail back to get stores . . . and mayhap to adventure up the coast. That you should do, and I would go with you. What I mean is: Could you make this place your *home*?"

"Is that what you want?"

"I feel this place has something to show me. I think of Humility. Oh, do not be impatient. You say I did not kill him, but I know I sent him to his death. That hangs heavily on my conscience, and I should never be happy if I did not do what I feel I must do. And now I know that I want to stay here and try to lead a better life than I have so far lived."

He took her face in his hands and his blue eyes gleamed with great tenderness.

"Once I said I would go to hell for you. Well, if I would do that, surely I could endure a Puritan settlement."

"I will marry you, Bartle."

He held her tightly against him and his laugh was one of great joy and triumph.

"We'll get married," he said, "and we'll build a little house. We'll start it to-morrow. We'll live in a little Puritan house among Puritans. . .for as long as you want to. . .but I know that won't be for the rest of our lives. And one day you'll say, 'Let us sail away. There are other places in the world.' I would not take you back to England to live, though, for Richard is right. But mayhap we might sail into the Sound one day. . .just to see Devon again. . .that greenest of green grass, the coombs and hills, that rich red soil. . .But we should not stay, for I should be afraid of their witch-prickers and what they would do to you, since, if aught happened to you, what would be my life? What has it been without you ever since I met you?"

She tried to stem the great excitement which was creeping over her.

"So you want me, Bartle, not because it is good for a woman, a descendant of Eve, to have a husband to guide her; not so that you can give children to the colony. You want *me*. . .because I am myself. . . because you cannot be happy without me? That seems a good reason."

When he rowed her back to the shore they talked about the cottage they would build.

"It will be like a cottage on your estate at home," she reminded him.

"It'll be as no other place on Earth!" he answered.

Richard was delighted with the news. As for the two elder children, they were so enchanted that they must dance about the room; and Lorea could not keep still, so excited was she at the prospect of owning such a father.

It was unfortunate that the Elder, misunderstanding Tamar's meaning, should have sent James Milroy along to make an offer for her hand, and that he should have arrived just as Bartle and Tamar were making their announcement.

Tamar smiled pertly at the man, disliking him through no great fault of his own but because he reminded her of Humility.

Bartle's eyes, as they fell on the man, were full of malice.

"Here comes Master Milroy to have a word with you, Richard," he said.

"Pray, sit down," said Richard. "You must drink with us."

"I wish to speak to you in private," said James.

"Can it be," said Tamar, "that you have come to ask my father for my hand in marriage?"

The Puritan flushed.

"Ah ! I see that is so. I have been told of your desire to guide me, to save my soul, and to make my body fruitful. You are too late with your offer, sir. I have decided to marry Sir Bartle Cavill."

There was silence in the little room. Richard looked with dismay from the newly affianced couple to the Puritan. The latter, poor man, was very shocked, and the colour stayed in his face. Bartle and

Tamar looked completely mischievous. Ah! thought Richard. This then is the end of another phase in Tamar's life. She is no longer going to be a Puritan; she is now going to be herself.

Dick was so excited by the great news that he forgot the presence of the Puritan. "Sir Bartle, I shall call you Father from now on. I shan't wait."

"I shall call you Father too!" declared Rowan.

"Lorea too!" said Lorea.

And the children seized Bartle's hands, and danced round him as though he were a pole and they Maytime revellers.

James Milroy looked on the scene with horror.

He rose and said calmly: "I beg your pardon. I have made a mistake."

And as the door shut behind him, Bartle swept Tamar into his arms and kissed her hungrily, while the children applauded. But Richard looked on uneasily.

*   *   *

Their house was made ready for them. They had declared their desire to be married before the magistrate, and the simple Puritan ceremony was over.

Tamar no longer thought of being a Puritan; she only thought of being happy. This, she realized, was what she had been wanting all through the years. It did not matter now that it had come late; it was never too late. She had almost forgotten that a man named Humility Brown had ever existed.

They lay in their small room in their tiny cottage, and both of them thought of another room, with a curtained bed and a wide open window. But never had they known such happiness as this.

In the bitterly cold first weeks of their marriage they were snug in their little house. There was no need to think beyond the winter. They were happy now. In the spring the *Liberty* would return to England and Bartle would take Tamar with him, for they had agreed that never again would they be parted for long.

There were times when Bartle went off on a hunting expedition into the forest. Once he was away two days and a night. Those were the longest hours she had known since her marriage. But home he came safely, with meat for the settlement.

It was pleasant for Tamar to slip into Annis's cottage and sit by her fireside and see her contentment, enjoying contentment herself.

"Ah!" said Annis. "You be happy now. At last you be happy. . . happy as you never were before. Sir Bartle, he be the man for you; and 'tis right and proper that you should be Lady Cavill. I always knew he were the man for you, wild though he be, for you be wild too, mistress my lady."

"No," she said. "I *was* wild, Annis. I have changed. I want quiet happiness and peace now and for evermore."

Annis did not speak, but she knew that peace was not what Tamar would find with Sir Bartle. He wasn't the one for peace. Humility Brown was the one for that.

"Don't mention *his* name to me!" cried Tamar.

Annis trembled. She was always frightened by Tamar's way of reading her thoughts.

"He were a good man," said Annis, "and happy he'll be at this moment, I'll be ready to swear, to look out through the golden gates and see you happy."

"I said don't speak of him!" cried Tamar; and she got up and went home.

Then for a while it seemed that Humility Brown was in the cottage. She was happy, yes. But she had bought this happiness with the death of Humility Brown. He would always be there, she believed, to mock her at odd moments, ready to spoil her pleasure in the new life.

It was not a good life, she feared. It was gay and full of laughter; full of passion and quarrels too. Bartle was quickly jealous. He even accused her of smiling in too friendly a fashion at James Milroy, which infuriated her while it sent her into mocking laughter, so that he in his turn was infuriated. But such scenes ended in passionate embraces. She herself was jealous at times, accusing him of infidelities, remembering the reputation he had had in England and reminding him of it.

So after those first weeks of blissful contentment there came those sudden gusts of anger and passion; they were two violent natures let loose and enjoying their anger when they both knew that it would end in passionate reunion.

Not a tranquil life — a wild and exciting life, even here in a Puritan settlement, just as she had always known it would be with Bartle. Yet how had she ever lived without it?

Only when there was trouble with the Indians and Bartle went off with some ten men under Captain Standish with muskets and cutlasses — only then did she know the depth of her love for him, only then did she realize that she would rather die than lose him again as she had once before.

John Tyler was one of the men who went with Captain Standish, and that brought Annis even closer. During those eight days they were together constantly, exchanging confidences, telling each other of their love and the life they led with these men, while the children played noisily outside and only little Lorea sat on a stool listening to them.

Back came the men, victorious — only one of them, who had caught an arrow in his back, the worse for the expedition.

She clung to Bartle, and there were many days and nights when they were gentle with one another, all violence forgotten.

Then she fancied that Bartle was becoming resigned to this life of hunting and protecting the settlement from the native redskins. Why should he not? It was a man's life.

She was happy at the thought of their living in the little cottage until they went to their graves — she with her children about her, tending her garden, cooking maize cakes, perhaps learning to spin with the expert touch most women acquired.

She should have known such a life could not be for her, nor for Bartle. They were not of these people, and they were tolerated only because they were known to be birds of passage. Bartle had never pretended to be one of them. He was Captain of the ship which had brought them; he had built a house, it was true, but when he had gone it would still be a house, and houses were desperately needed in New Plymouth.

And then occurred an incident which shocked Tamar as she had not been shocked since the day she had found poor Jane Swann escaping from her tormentors.

It concerned Polly Eagel. Polly's husband was a quiet man, and Polly would never have thought of becoming a Puritan if she had not married him. Polly was flighty, fond of admiration; and James Milroy for one was deeply aware of sin such as Polly brought into the settlement. It was not the original Pilgrims, serious-minded, righteous, ready to die for their faith whom he felt needed supervision; they were as stalwart as ever. But newcomers had emigrated for a variety of reasons — for the love of adventure, to make a change because life was hard at home. The Captain and the crew of his ship were evil men. As for Tamar — and he thanked God nightly that he had been saved from the calamity of marrying her — she was a wanton creature. She had lured him on, he knew now, not because she wanted a good man to instruct and guide her, but that she might tempt him to lust. Much wickedness had come into Plymouth with the *Liberty*. It must be stamped out, and James

Milroy was going to do his duty and see that this was done.

He had been suspicious of Polly Eagel for some time. She was a pretty, fluffy-haired little woman, forever fingering her hair and letting it peep out from under her cap as if by accident. He had set a watch upon Polly Eagel and — glory be to God! — he had himself been led by divine guidance to discover her immorality with one of the sailors from the ship.

Now the sailors did not come under Puritan law. Their souls were their own, which meant that they were the Devil's. Eternal damnation was to be their lot in any case. But Polly Eagel was a member of the Puritan Church, and as such must suffer the necessary correction.

Annis came bursting into Tamar's cottage to tell her the news.

Annis was excited. This was like something that might have happened at home.

"Mistress, have 'ee heard? Have 'ee heard what Polly Eagel have been up to? Caught she were . . . by Master Milroy. Caught right in the act, so I did hear. Oh my lady, he has told the Elders, and Polly have been taken off. It seems that one thing she'll have to do is to confess her sin before us at the meeting house. Then she'll take her punishment. My dear life! The shame of it would wellnigh kill a woman! Not that Polly Eagel's the sort to die for such. She's a brazen piece and no mistake. It's poor Bill Eagel I'm sorry for."

On the day of Polly's confession, the meeting house was full of an expectant congregation. Tamar was there with Richard. Bartle never attended at the meeting house.

Tamar was struck by the gloating anticipation showing in the faces about her; she felt sickened by the scene. Perhaps that was because she was a sinner herself, and felt she was no better than Polly Eagel. Polly had committed adultery; Tamar was guilty of causing her husband's death; perhaps that was why she could feel no pleasure in watching a sinner brought to justice, as these righteous people could.

The Elder talked for a long time. In the front row of seats sat Polly Eagel; her face was white, her head downcast. She did not look the same gay girl who had come out from England, and whom Tamar had noticed during the voyage when she had heard that Bartle had once been interested in her. Now was Polly brought low. In the front row, near her, sat her accuser, James Milroy, his arms folded, his eyes lifted to the rafters of the hall as though he knew God to be up there, smiling down His approval on the acts of James Milroy.

The Elder preached of sin . . . sin that had crept like a fog into their midst, sin that must be crushed and defeated. Of all the great sins of the world, there were few to be compared with Adultery; and there was one among them who stood guilty of this sin. She had confessed and repented, and that was a matter for rejoicing; but God was a just God, and such sins could not in His name be allowed to go unpunished. It might be that through a life of devotion to duty this miserable sinner would come to salvation. This was for God and herself to decide. Her partner in sin was not here to stand beside her. His was a lost soul. But let no one imagine he would escape the wages of his sin. He would burn eternally in Hell, though he thought here on Earth to continue his evil life. Polly Eagel would now stand forth.

Polly stood up and turned to face the congregation.

She was scarlet and pale in turn, and she spoke so low that those at the back of the hall had to crane forward to hear her words.

She was a miserable sinner; she had defiled her marriage bed. She gave details of the place and occasion when her sin had taken place, as she had been told to do. Eyes glistened. Puritan hearts beat fast. Tamar watching, thought: it would be better if they might dance now and then, or see a play acted. Then they would not be so eager to take their entertainment from another's misery.

And suddenly, in an overwhelming pity for Polly Eagel, she hated them all, hated the Elder with his hands piously folded, hated James Milroy with his eyes turned piously upwards, hated all those who stood in judgment, with their sly eyes and their tight mouths. But almost at once she realized that she hated them because she should be standing there beside Polly Eagel, for she was a greater sinner than Polly.

Polly's confession was over, but that was preliminary to her punishment. A solemn procession went from the meeting place, led by the Elders and dignitaries of the settlement, Polly among them; other important members of the community followed, and after them came the congregation.

They went to that raised platform whose significance Tamar had not realized before. The post there was, of course, a whipping post. As for the gallows, she had accepted such an erection as a necessary part of any community; it was just that in such a one as this, it had seemed to have been put there merely as a warning. Gallows and whipping posts were a part of the Old Country; she had thought they had no place in the New.

Polly's hands were tied behind her back and she was forced on to a stool. Tamar saw the brazier, the hot irons; she heard Polly Eagel give one wild, protesting shriek before she fainted and fell back into the arms of one of the Elders.

It was some time before Polly appeared in public, for she had had to serve a month in the house of correction. Tamar had looked once into that poor mutilated face, and she could never bring herself to look again. Clearly she had seen branded on Polly's forehead the letter A; and the sight of the scorched and tortured flesh had enraged her.

She was weary and disillusioned. She was like a traveller who thought he had travelled far along a road that was beset with hardship, only to find that he had been walking round in a circle and had moved only a very short distance from the starting point.

*　　　*　　　*

The snows had disappeared and the harsh winds had softened. Spring was coming to New England.

Polly mingled with the people, the A standing out clearly on her forehead, her head downcast and all the natural joy drained out of her. Whenever Tamar saw her she averted her eyes. She felt as she did when she was with Jane Swann — poor Jane, who had become vague, hiding in quiet corners, not hearing when spoken to. She sat in her father's house, spinning. When other women sat at their spinning wheels the sound of their singing would mingle with the hum of the wheel. Jane was never heard singing.

It was perhaps easier to live a Puritan life in the cold of winter. But when the bluebirds and the robins were building in the forest and their songs filled the air, when the fruit trees were in blossom, the young men and maidens would look towards each other and think that life could not be all work and prayer, as their serious Elders seemed to believe it should be.

Two young people were whipped publicly for the sin of fornication. They had, they declared, every intention of marrying, but spring had taken them unaware. That was no excuse; so they were punished before they went through the simple marriage ceremony. They were told that their sin merited death, but since they were members of a new colony which needed children, they would be given a chance to regain salvation through a life of piety and devotion to God.

The Elders were deeply concerned at this time by what seemed to them a hideous menace. It was not fear of famine or hostile Indians that gave them their greatest anxiety; it was a certain Thomas Morton.

To the Puritans this man was the Devil in person. He was a swaggering fellow very proud of his scholarship, describing himself as "Of Clifford's Inne, Gent." He had come to New England a few years before with a Captain Wollaston and a company of men, their idea being to start a plantation. This they had set about doing not very far from Plymouth, at a spot which they had named Mount Wollaston. But Wollaston had grown tired of the hardship such a project had entailed and had sailed off to Virginia in the hope of finding an easier fortune. The same Morton—as the Puritans said—had, by some evil means, ousted those left in charge by Wollaston, and taken over command of the place himself. And the first thing he had done—and this in the eyes of New Plymouth was an indication of his character—was to rename the place "Merry Mount."

The state of affairs between New Plymouth and Merry Mount was far from cordial. Morton accused the Puritans of disregarding the laws of England by denying the marriage ceremony to the colonists and supplying some simple form of their own. The Puritans retaliated by accusing Morton of selling firearms and strong drink to the Indians and so endangering the lives of all the settlers in New England. The real cause of the trouble was that the people of New Plymouth were Separatist and those of Merry Mount, Episcopalian.

As the days grew warmer, Bartle made preparations for the journey back to England. All day the small boats were busy, transferring stores from land to the *Liberty*. Many turned away from the sight of the ship, for it made them think of home. Polly Eagel would shudder when she saw it, and touch the letter on her forehead. Annis took her youngest down to the beach to show her what was going on; but Annis was sad, seeing the ship's preparations, because her beloved mistress was sailing away on that ship. Tamar had said she would come back, but who could know what might happen to prevent her?

Yes, indeed, spring was a time of disquiet, for spring was to be enjoyed by youth and lovers. There were many marriages, and it was said that there should have been many a whipping to precede those marriages, if the watchful Puritans could but have found sufficient evidence.

Mistress Alton and Brother Milroy were friends together; they were of one mind, devoted to the Puritan cause, so eager to bring straying footsteps back to the path of righteousness.

It was Thomas Morton, the Episcopalian of Merry Mount, who now also took a part in the shaping of many lives.

The Elders were storming against him at the meeting place, but the young and the lively could not help it if their eyes turned towards Merry Mount; and they whispered together of the goings-on at the "Mount of Sin" as an Elder had called it.

For Thomas Morton was setting up a maypole on Merry Mount. At home they had danced round the maypole for many years, since it was an old English custom to make merry in the early days of May as a welcome to the spring, a thanksgiving for the burgeon of the year. The master of Merry Mount was a merry man, and there was drinking and carousing in his settlement.

He had set up an idol, thundered the Elders; yea, a calf of Horeb. He would realize he had made a woeful place indeed of his Merry Mount when he felt the vengeance of the Lord.

But Thomas Morton cared nothing for the Elders. He had come to the New World to make a fortune, trapping animals for their skins and trading with the old country; and doubtless he had found the Indians' desire for what they called "the firewater," and their keen delight in European firearms, very profitable. And now he had committed as great a sin in the eyes of the Elders of New Plymouth as any, so far, in setting up a maypole.

Excitement was high in New Plymouth. All the men from the ship had decided to pay their homage to the "Calf of Horeb." It would be like a bit of home, they said, to dance round a maypole.

All through the days before the first of May there were sounds of revelry on Merry Mount. There were shots from cannon to herald the frivolity, and the sound of drums came over the clear air. The maypole was a pine tree to which had been nailed a pair of buckshorns. It could be seen for miles.

In the morning Bartle took Tamar out to the *Liberty* to show her how far preparations for the return journey had gone.

"In a few weeks we shall sail for England!" he said, and excitement gleamed in his eyes.

But when she thought of England she must think also of terrible things; of her mother in the cottage, of the women she had seen at the town hall being searched by the prickers, of the seamen begging in the streets. She looked back at the land and thought how fair it was in the morning sunshine, with the faint mist rising from the meadows and the sparkling river losing itself in the sea, and the nearby forest and the distant mountains. The settlement itself was not exactly beautiful, but there was about it something which moved her more deeply than the beauties of nature. Those little houses represented bravery, courage, sacrifice. She wished her gaze would not stray to that spot where the platform would be with its whipping post and its gallows. She wished she could shut out of her mind the memory of Polly Eagel's scream as the hot iron touched her forehead. She wished she need not think of Polly, walking through the village street, her head downcast, all the saucy gaiety gone from her, branded for life.

But Polly had sinned, she reminded herself.

So have we all! came back the answer.

And then: But this is not cruelty such as I have seen at home. Nevertheless, it is cruelty.

She told Bartle of her thoughts, and he laughed and caught her to him.

"You want a land of your own," he said. "There will be no winter in such a land. It shall always be springtime, and there we shall be eternally young. Food grows on the trees and you and I stretch ourselves out on the grass and love and love and love . . ."

Then she laughed with him that she, the most imperfect of beings, should demand a perfect world.

Bartle said: "We will call at Merry Mount and dance round the maypole. It will bring memories of home; and when you see the merrymaking you will be as eager to slip away from these shores as I am."

She could not help being excited at the prospect of hearing merry laughter, of dancing at Bartle's side. She had missed these things; she had missed them too long.

She wanted to ask Annis to go with them, for Annis loved gaiety; she was on the point of suggesting it, but she refrained. It would not be good to tempt Annis; Annis was so happy in the new life; she was saved, and she would not have the same inclination towards frivolity that she had once had. Had she forgotten, wondered Tamar, those occasions when she had met John in the barn on her father's land? She made no reference to them when she had heard that the young people were to make public confession and suffer a whipping for doing what she and John had once done.

Bartle and Tamar took one of the boats and went along the coast to Merry Mount. It was late afternoon and all the settlers on Merry Mount had turned out to help in the preparations for the fun. Indians, naked

382

but for their belts of wampum, stood about watching: some with solemn faces, some smiling at the antics of the white men.

Thomas Morton welcomed Bartle and Tamar.

"Come, my friends, laugh and be merry with us. Life was meant to be enjoyed."

He knew Bartle as the Captain of the ship which was shortly to sail away, and he knew Tamar was his wife. So this was not such a victory as it would have been had he, with his maypole, been able to lure some of the Puritan young people over to his Mount. Still, all were welcome.

A pageant had been planned by Morton; there was a special song compiled for the occasion in which every man took part: there were old dances which had been danced in England as long as any could remember.

Dusk came, and with it the festivity was at its height. Flares were lighted. Indians crept in with their women and danced their native dances. In the light from the flares, the painted faces of the Indians glowed, their bodies gleamed — some naked, some adorned with deerskins; their heads and faces oiled; their straight black hair cut in the style of their tribe; the paint on their faces, red and vermilion, to show all who looked their way that they came in peace and not in war. About their necks were beads of *wampompeag* to match the belts about their loins.

It was a strange, fantastic sight, with the lights from the flares shining alike on the faces of white men and red men.

Morton had provided a good deal of drink, and the Indians cried out in joy at the prospect of indulging in some of the white man's "fire-water." To them this magic water, which burned the throat and intoxicated the mind so that those who took it seemed filled with great joy, was the most wonderful thing the white men had brought with them.

The Indians sprawled on the ground near the maypole, clapping their hands in time with the songs, ecstatic smiles on their faces, delighted to be present at this feast of the white men. The maypole they imagined to be a god of the white men as were Kitan the good god and Hobbamocco the evil god of their own. They were ready to pay homage to this strange god while never swerving in their devotion to their own, for gods were gods and must be treated with respect, to whatever men they belonged.

The song of the day was sung again and again:

"Nectar is the thing assigned,
By the Deity's own mind,
To cure the heart opprest with grief,
And of good liquors is the chief."

Voices were raised in the chorus:

"Then drink and be merry, merry,
merry, boys. . . ."

Both Bartle and Tamar were caught up in the excitement all about them. They danced with the rest, round and round the maypole. In the light from the flares Tamar saw some of the young people from New Plymouth, furtive yet determined. They had risked a terrible punishment in order to dance round a maypole.

And then, among the milling crowd of sweating men and women and painted Indians, Tamar caught sight of James Milroy. His eyes glared at her as he watched her and Bartle, dancing with their arms about each other.

She laughed with a wonderful sense of freedom. It had occurred to her that James Milroy desired her even as had Humility Brown; and the knowledge had come to her that she would be able to forget the death of her first husband for long periods at a time during the years to come. These men who had seemed so saintly were hardly different from their fellow men whom they despised. Such thoughts brought relief with them and she asked herself slyly: Does Brother Milroy come to watch the merrymaking or to spy? And in any case, whatever he comes for, he comes for his own pleasure, as do the rest. Where is the difference then between one and another of us?

She was sick of the hot smell of bodies, and the fumes of gammedes and Jupiter were in her head. That liquor had been potent.

"Come," she said to Bartle. "Let us seek the cool of the forest. I am hot and tired, and weary of the noise and singing. I have had enough and would rest."

He was nothing loth, and they went together into the forest, where he laid his cloak on the grass that they might lie down together.

It was peaceful in the forest, lying there among the trees; there was no sound but the call of a bird, the murmur of insects, a rustle in the undergrowth that might have been made by musk-rat or beaver. Now and then they heard the sound of human voices whispering, and they knew that they were not the only lovers to steal away from the merrymaking for the sake of the peace of the forest.

Through the darkness came the sound of fresh outbursts of revelry.

"Give to the melancholy man
A cup or two of it now and then;
This physic will soon revive his blood
And make him of a merrier mood.
Then drink and be merry, merry, merry,
       boys..."

Tamar thought that the Elders had spoken aptly when they had compared the revellers of Merry Mount with the Children of Israel dancing round the golden calf. But people must sometimes laugh and be merry. Life should not be all drabness surely; and if the Lord of Merry Mount worshipped drink and riches as the Puritans said he did, had not the Puritans set up their own golden calf of pride, bigotry and intolerance?

Where had these thoughts come from so suddenly? She did not know; and Bartle was close to her, and they were alone — or almost alone — in the forest.

*　　*　　*

May Day brought a climax. Life became furtive and sly after that. There were more punishments in the weeks following that May Day than there had been since the *Liberty* had arrived. Confessions were made in the meeting place and it was clear to Tamar — who felt that everything about her was becoming gradually clearer — that these stern-faced Puritans and their hardmouthed wives were going to the meeting place with more alacrity than they had before. Some of those who had sinned gave details of their sins; they received their whippings and were married.

Tamar had been seen at the revelries, but she had been there with her husband, and Sir Bartle was not of the community, although Tamar was considered to be. Her marriage was deplored, and she was looked upon with suspicion, but she was in the charge of her husband and no punishment was suggested for her to endure.

It was discovered that two people among them were Quakers, and these two were tied to a cart's tail and whipped out of New Plymouth. They were warned that if they came back they would be hanged.

There were great crowds to witness the whipping of the Quakers.

And then Mistress Alton began to recall the iniquities of Annis's past life, and she spoke of these — as she felt it her duty to do — to Brother

Milroy, with the result that John and Annis Tyler were summoned before the Elders.

Tamar was in the meeting place, and Richard was with her when Annis and John made their confession.

Richard had tried to persuade Tamar not to go, for he saw in her eyes something which alarmed him. He knew that since the death of Humility she had been trying to become a good Puritan, and he knew also that this was because of some twisted notion that by doing so she could expiate her sin. She had, by long and arduous practice, suppressed something which was essentially herself; but that which had taken months to cover up, could leap out without a moment's warning.

Richard kept close to her. He knew that she was very concerned, because her affection for Annis went deep.

Annis had changed since the accusation had been made against her. She had become like an old woman; the flaming colour in her cheeks was tinged with purple and her eyes showed her bewilderment. She had tried so hard to win respect; she had been so ready to love the new land and the new way of life; and now to hear that her old sin was remembered against her, brought her such shame that she could not hold up her head. She had neither slept nor eaten since the terrible accusation had been made.

Young Dick was with Tamar and Richard as they made their way to the meeting house; but as they were about to enter, Richard said to Tamar: "Go on,

Tamar. I'll be with you in a moment. And Dick...here a moment, please."

Tamar, who could think of nothing but Annis at this time, hardly noticed what was said and went on into the meeting house.

When she had gone, Richard said to Dick: "Your father is on the *Liberty*. Go out to him and tell him that he must come at once. It's very important, I feel, that he should be here. Tell him I have sent you to fetch him and that he must come at once. If we should be in the meeting house he should go to the whipping post and wait for us there. Tell him he must be here for your mother's sake. He must be at hand when Annis is punished, in case he is needed. Tell him I am afraid...afraid for Tamar."

Dick ran off, thrilled by what seemed an important mission.

Richard went into the meeting house.

"Where is Dick?" asked Tamar.

"I sent him away. It is not good for him to witness such spectacles."

She nodded. She had caught sight of the bowed back of Annis, and tears had started to her eyes.

She listened to the droning voice of the Elder. Sin, sin, sin...! she thought. They think of nothing but sin! They are obsessed with sin, so that they see it all around them.

"This is a long-ago sin, but sin does not grow less with the years. It lies across the soul like an ugly mark on a clean garment. It is necessary to dip that garment in the blood of the Lamb if it should be whiter than the snow. Repentance is not enough. Repentance there must be, but expiation also. . .Brothers and sisters, among us of late, sin has been rampant. Since our wicked neighbour of the Mount of Woe set up a golden calf and worshipped it, there has been evil even here among us!"

Tamar was clenching and unclenching her hands. Richard took the hand nearest his and pressed it.

"Calm," he whispered. "Be calm, my darling."

"Richard. . .not Annis. I *love* Annis. She is like a sister to me. She is my friend. . ."

"We live in an imperfect world," he said.

Angry glances were directed towards them. Whispering in the meeting house was a sin as deserving of punishment as any other sin. But now they were forgotten, for Annis and John Tyler had stood up and were about to confess their sin.

Tamar heard Annis's voice as though it were coming to her over the years.

"We was young. . .and we was sinful. . .and we did meet in the barn. . .and because we did know no better, there was great sin between us. . ."

Tamar seemed to be reliving the past, seeing herself in Pennicomquick, mixing a potion, muttering a charm, listening to Annis's confidences as they lay on their straw pallets together.

Not Annis! This could not happen to Annis. She wanted to shout: "Do not be ashamed, Annis. It is they who should be ashamed. You are a good woman, however you sinned in your youth. You and John were happy. You loved this land. You asked for nothing but to work here and be happy and good . . ." But her lips were dry, her mouth parched and her voice lost to her.

Annis was going on: " 'Twas no fault of John's. He had no say in it. The sin was mine, so I hope you'll not punish him. It was a charm I got from a witch. So John had no say in it. There was a child . . . my first, my Christian. I named him Christian so's he could be better than his mother were, and so he is. 'Twere no fault of John's that our boy were born out of wedlock. He were took off to prison for going to the meeting house, and so we couldn't be married . . . and our child were born . . ."

The Elder spoke. It was true, as in so many cases, that the woman was at fault. He did not doubt that. She had, on her own admission, consorted with witches in the hope of leading a man to damnation. For that she should have her strokes increased. But the man could not go without punishment. The godly are free from any spells that might be made from witchcraft, since the Devil sows his seed in fertile ground.

As they left the meeting house for the platform, Tamar tried to call out to Annis, but no words would come. She saw Annis walking into the bright, hard light of day and she felt that her heart was breaking, for she had not known until now how she had loved this friend of her childhood, girlhood and maturity. Words crowded into her mind: "Take me! Whip me! I gave her the charm." And then: "Whip me if you dare! Judge me . . . judge us both . . . if you dare!"

Annis's back was bare for the lash. A garment had been discreetly laid across her breast with a string to tie it about her neck and keep it secure. She was tied to the whipping post, and she did not look like Annis. Her plump face sagged and there was a hideous purple colour in her cheeks and on her lips — a dark and ugly colour.

Tamar would have run forward, but Richard was holding her firmly by the hand.

"Let us go," he said. "You do not want to see this."

He was looking anxiously about him to see if Bartle had come.

"I will stay!" she said. "I *will* stay. I must be near her. I cannot run away because I dare not look."

She turned to him with blazing hatred in her eyes.

"Do you know what I would do if I had the strength of ten men?" she demanded. She did not wait for him to answer: "I would leap up there. I would tie the Elders and Brother Milroy to that post. I would use the whip on *them*!" Her voice broke and tears ran down her cheeks. "Annis!" she whispered. "But what has *Annis* done? What did she ever do. . .but want to live and be happy?"

The whip whistled in the air. It seemed to be poised above Annis's bare back for a long time before it fell.

A weal leaped up on the tender flesh. There was a heartrending cry as Annis slumped at the post.

The whip came down again, but this time there was no cry.

Tamar wrenched herself free.

"I must go to her! I *must* go to her. What am I doing standing by. . .while they do that to her?"

She had pushed her way through the crowds before Richard could stop her; she was mounting the platform. The man with the whip was standing back a little, staring at Annis's body, for he had noticed something strange about her inert figure, her purple face, her lips which hung open and her staring eyes. Annis was curiously still.

Tamar knelt beside her.

"Annis," she murmured. "Dearest Annis, speak to me. It is your own Tamar. What have these murderous brutes done to you? Annis. . .look at me. . .speak. . .speak. I command you, Annis! Don't dare disobey me. It is I. . .Tamar." She was sobbing because she knew what those about her had yet to learn. She did not need to put her hand on Annis's heart to know that it had stopped. They had killed Annis; they had piled such shame and ignominy upon her that they had broken her heart.

Out of her grief grew a mad and uncontrollable rage. She snatched the whip from the hand of the man who had used it; she lifted it and would have struck him had not someone seized her and taken it from her.

She cried out: "You have murdered Annis. You have killed my friend. I hate you. I wish I had never seen your smug faces. You are cruel. . .evil and wicked. I hate you. I hate you. I hope you will all rot in hell as you deserve to do. . .you. . .and you. . . and you. . ."

One of the Elders knelt down by Annis and untied the ropes which bound her to the post. There was a deep silence everywhere as he laid Annis gently down, and looked into her face.

"I fear she is dead," he said slowly.

"Dead! Dead!" cried Tamar. "And you killed her."

Richard was standing beside her on the platform. "Come away, Tamar. Come away."

But she would not move. She stared at the dead body of Annis while memories, bitter, poignant and sweet, crowded in on her.

What right had these people to stand in judgment on dear sweet Annis?

Words fell from her lips. Her eyes flashed and her hair fell about her face. Many watching began to pray, for they were sure that the woman who stood before them was a witch.

She shouted: "You murdered her. . . all of you. Do you think I am deceived by you? Do you think I have not seen Brother Milroy's sly eyes upon me? You men have desires as other men have! Oh, but you are so pure, are you not? We must have children for the colony. . . not a woman's body to caress and give you pleasure. I hate you. I loathe you. You sin equally with the men of Merry Mount; but they sin merrily, and I could be happier with merry sinners than with brutal murdering ones. Freedom! What freedom is there here? Look at Polly Eagel! Have none of you ever sinned. . . in thought perhaps, since you would lack the courage to sin in deed? Freedom! You

394

speak of freedom to worship God. Yes! Freedom to worship Him as you would have us worship Him! We are offered that at home in England. What of the Quakers you whipped out of Plymouth? What had they done but worshipped God in a way different from your own?"

Brother Milroy had caught her by the arm; another helped him to hold her.

Mistress Alton, her voice high-pitched with excitement, shouted from the crowd: "She is a witch. The Devil forced her on her mother. We knew her for a witch in the old country."

"So it is you!" shouted Tamar. "You...you wicked old woman. You...who killed Annis with your cruelty. You wanted James Milroy for yourself, did you not? But his lustful eyes were turned on me. The Devil gave me my beauty, they say; and they would enjoy it...ah, only for the sake of the *colony*! You sent the pricker after me when we were in Pennicomquick. Do you think that I did not know that? I despised you. Till now I did not know that you were worth hating."

"Witchcraft!" screamed Mistress Alton. "Witchcraft! She is a witch. She it was who gave Annis Tyler the charm which led John Tyler to sin with her. She is a witch on her own confession. Hang her quickly...before she casts her spells upon us. Look for the mark. Strip her, find it...and then...prick it! You will find that she is a witch. To the gallows! To the gallows! Lose no time, for she is evil. She is the Devil's own."

"Witch! Witch!" It grew in volume as thunder rolls. Tamar saw the gleaming eyes, the cruel mouths, and she thought: They have not had such excitement since they landed here. What is the beating of Annis, the branding of Polly, compared with the hanging of a witch?

Richard was trying to speak; he was holding up his hand and his eyes were full of agony. Dear Richard! To avoid this he had left his native land, and now it had caught up with them, as it seemed it must.

"Listen to me!" Richard was shouting. But his voice was lost in the cry of angry voices chanting: "A witch! A witch! To the gallows with the witch. The Devil's own. The Devil's own daughter. To the gallows! To the gallows!"

Tamar felt the breath of those who would seize her; her gown was torn. The more brutal among the crowd were surging on to the platform, and she felt she had seen these faces before. Puritans were no different from others.

But now someone was forcing his way to her. An arm was about her. One of the men who had pulled at her bodice was sent hurtling off the platform.

She was aware of the glitter of blue eyes and the flash of a sword; she felt weak with sudden emotion.

In the last few seconds she had forgotten Bartle.

CHAPTER
EIGHT

The *Liberty* had rounded Cape James and was sailing down towards Chesapeake Bay.

With her sailed all those who wished to leave the settlement; the Swanns and their family; John Tyler and his, for they could not bear to stay with people who had killed Annis; there was Tom Eagel with his wife Polly; and there were some of the young couples who had danced at Merry Mount and been brought to shame through the prying eyes of Brother Milroy. There was Richard, with Tamar and her children.

The sun was sinking in a sky of blood-red which was staining the waters; soon the *Liberty* would be shut in by darkness.

Tamar came on deck and stood beside Bartle. He put an arm about her and held her tightly against him. He laughed then; for he was not displeased to feel his ship beneath him.

And she laughed with him, sharing in his mood of exultation. For the second time in her life she had narrowly missed the gallows. She would never forget that moment when Bartle had stood beside her on the platform, his sword flashing in the sunlight with a promise of death to any who dared lay a hand upon her. And those people had fallen back, afraid, until the Elders, who did not love violence, had commanded order. Richard had spoken then and told them that he and his daughter were going to leave New Plymouth, and that they would never return. The *Liberty* was theirs; they had brought provisions with them, and they would take away as much as they had brought. Then they would go in peace.

"We came here to escape violence and intolerance," Richard had said. "We thought we had made that escape, but we find we were wrong. The small Church is as intolerant as its bigger sister. We have but escaped from one to another of the same kind. We shall sail forth in the *Liberty*. We shall try to find a place for ourselves somewhere in this great country. The way may be long; our path may be set with dangers; but liberty will be the reward, and liberty must be fought for and won by bitter fighting, great hardship; it may be constant hardship; that we cannot say, for having fought and won we may have to continue fighting to retain this precious gift. Only those who are ready to fight the fight should come with us."

There were some, it seemed, who were ready.

Bartle gripped Tamar's hand as they watched the sun begin to dip into the sea; they watched until the pink stain on the waters turned to a dark green.

"Whither are we going?" asked Bartle. "Whither will this pox-ridden bucket carry us?"

"She will carry us whither we should go," answered Tamar. "Somewhere in this vast land we will find freedom, for in our thoughts we have already made it the land of freedom."

The water was changing colour once more; away to the east it was now an inky black.

Bartle mused: "She's a frail thing, this *Liberty*, to face wind and rain, pirates and savages."

"We are in danger," said Tamar. "We all know that. From hour to hour, minute to minute, we are in danger. But what we seek is worth facing all the dangers the world can offer us."

They were both silent while the darkness came down upon them and wrapped itself about them so that they could no longer see the heaving water.

But the *Liberty* went steadily on.

THE END

The publishers hope that this large print book has brought you pleasurable reading. Each title is designed to make the text as easy to read as possible.

For further information on backlist or forthcoming titles please write or telephone:

In the British Isles and its territories, customers should contact:

ISIS Publishing Ltd
7 Centremead
Osney Mead
Oxford OX2 0ES
England
Telephone: (01865) 250 333 Fax: (01865) 790 358

In Australia and New Zealand, customers should contact:

Bolinda Publishing Pty Ltd
17 Mohr Street
Tullamarine Victoria 3043
Australia
Telephone: (03) 9338 0666 Fax: (03) 9335 1903
Toll Free Telephone: 1800 335 364
Toll Free Fax: 1800 671 4111

In New Zealand:

Toll Free Telephone: 0800 44 5788
Toll Free Fax: 0800 44 5789